HEARTSBLOOD

HEARTS-BLOOD

A NOVEL

PAUL MARTTIN

A SEYMOUR LAWRENCE BOOK
DELACORTE PRESS / NEW YORK

This book
is for
SHARON

HEARTSBLOOD

INTRODUCTION

Three floors above Kraft's office, a patient's heart, beating at regular intervals, hesitated and nearly stopped. The patient had suffered a heart attack seven days before, and had he been cared for at home, or by a physician less capable than Matthew Kraft, a certain heart drug might not have been given. At this instant on the seventh day, conduction gone awry, the nerves supplying the heart would have begun transmitting irregularly, paused, and ceased sending impulses to allow it to beat.

Since the patient was under the care of Dr. Kraft, he felt only a momentary sensation of fullness, and then the effect of the drug caused a normal heart rhythm to be resumed. The patient's heart beat on in regular fashion. Neither he nor anyone else knew that his life had been saved.

Dr. Matthew Kraft, professor of medicine and chief of cardiology at the Eastern Massachusetts Medical Center, belched loudly. He quickly reread the two notes his secretary had put on his desk while he was at grand medical rounds and lunch. The first note said that Andrew Essai, one of Kraft's young instructors, had asked repeatedly whether Dr. Kraft had really sent his galley proofs back to the journal, *Science*. Kraft probed for a piece of hamburger stuck in his teeth and threw the note away; he'd have to talk to that Essai. The other note held his interest. It said simply, "Head of Bolliston Society called, wanted a résumé of your academic career. Will call back at two."

Kraft patted his stomach reflectively. Were they going to ask him to give the annual discourse on the art of medicine again next year? If so, why the hell did they need a *curriculum vitae* from him. He had given the lecture twice and they never asked for a résumé. Why would they want that now? Kraft did not crumple this note, but left it on his desk. He stood up to his full height, six foot three, and stretched. It was nearly two o'clock, and Lee would be driving him to the combined conference at the Metropolitan Hospital in a couple of hours. Matthew Kraft lit a cigarette, strode across the hall and into the laboratory.

"Essai." His shout carried to every corner of the five or six small laboratories.

"Yes, sir." A chair squeaked and the thin instructor emerged from his lab, holding a pipette full of fluid in one hand.

Kraft motioned to him. "Come into my office," he said loudly.

Andrew Essai glanced at the full pipette. "Yes, sir, right

3

away," he said softly after a moment, and he set down the pipette on top of the centrifuge, with a rubber stopper against each end.

Kraft preceded the instructor across the hall and into his office. An instant before Essai would have been ready for the question, Kraft asked, "Essai, what's all this crap about my sending galley proofs in to *Science*?"

Essai shifted his weight and looked up quickly. "I'm sorry, Dr. Kraft, I didn't want your secretary to get involved with it."

"With what?" Kraft demanded.

"Well," Essai began, "*Science* said after they got the galley proofs my paper would appear in four weeks. It's been six weeks today. I just thought I'd check," he said lamely.

"It's our paper, isn't it, Essai?"

"Yes, sir, it is."

Kraft ground out the cigarette. "Well, goddammit, then don't say 'my paper.' It's our work."

Essai furrowed his brow. "I did all the work," he thought, "yet he gets his name on it since it's his department. I don't think he even understands the paper."

But what he finally said was: "Yes, it was ours."

"All right. What the hell are you hesitating for? I sent the galley proofs back, but I had some second thoughts about the wording, so they didn't go back until a month ago."

Essai looked upset. "What wording, Dr. Kraft?"

Kraft lit another cigarette. "Sit down, Essai. I didn't make any revisions as it turned out. But between you and me, the writing was lousy. Don't they teach people how to write English in medical school or college?"

"It took two weeks, and you didn't change anything?" Essai asked quizzically.

"Damn right. What the hell's your hurry? No one's going to scoop you. You know," his voice dropped to a conversational level, "you young guys are in an awful hurry to publish these days. Don't be so impatient."

Essai looked at the floor. Of course it wasn't important to Kraft—he had his position, his stature in the field. How odd to hear Matthew Kraft extol the virtues of restraint and reflection. No more impetuous man existed, he thought.

"What's the matter, Essai, you act as if you don't believe me."

"I do, Dr. Kraft. But this is my first real research paper. The other two were clinical, case reports with some special studies. I'm anxious to see how this one is received. I don't think I can make a career in academic medicine writing up case reports. I guess that's why I'm so impatient," he ended apologetically.

Matthew Kraft inhaled an immense volume of cigarette smoke and blew it across the polished desk at the instructor. His voice was scornful. "Doc, let me tell you a few things. There's nothing wrong with clinical research. Especially these days, when you supposedly bright guys bury yourselves in the lab and never want to come out. You think you can make a name for yourself with pure laboratory work. Well, that's crap. You're still a doctor, caring for patients. And listen to me; there are new diseases to be discovered at the bedside, new signs, new methods of diagnosis, new ways to treat people. Or do you think there is nothing new to be learned from patients?"

Essai shook his head. "There is a lot to be learned at the bedside. But can you establish a reputation for yourself without doing laboratory work?"

"Lab work. Lab work." Kraft hissed. "I did lab work; I wrote a paper on the work of the heart, and I go into the laboratory every day. Anybody can push out some papers from a laboratory, and talk glibly at conferences about 'clinical application of the basic research.'" He paused. "But take that 'lab rat' and put him in the clinical situation, at the bedside of a sick patient, and he'll fall apart, he'll run back to the safety of the lab. Never forget that being a doctor is a clinical trust. The patients don't give a damn how much you know about centrifuges and antibodies—they want you to take care of them. When's the last time you took care of a patient, Essai?"

"A long time," Essai admitted.

Kraft squashed the cigarette and lit another. "I know, you're too busy in the lab, setting up the next experiment, writing the next research paper. Well, doc, I've got a bit of a reputation myself in the field of cardiology," Kraft paused to inhale, and the words came out on a stream of smoke, "and I made it by caring for patients the best way I could."

Essai was on the verge of saying that that had been the generation just past, when clinical brilliance was enough. But Kraft had hesitated to let him add a word of praise. "I know," he said slowly.

Kraft jabbed the air. "If you know, bright young man, then don't criticize me for holding on to your paper for two weeks. Use the two weeks to read some cardiograms, listen to murmurs, listen to patients as they give symptoms. Do it twenty hours a day and after a while they'll know who you are without reading a tiny little *Science* article."

Kraft was ready to continue, and Essai sat framing a hurt reply, but Kraft's secretary buzzed to say that Dr. Manson of the Bolliston Society was calling back. "All right," he barked, "I'll take it now." Kraft waved Essai away, saying quickly, "Don't be in such a rush to publish, Essai. Examine a few patients once in a while."

Essai walked out of the office and past Miss Graf, Dr. Kraft's all-knowing secretary. Safely into the hall, he thought over what he had been told. "Sure, Dr. Kraft. 'Examine a few patients, be in charge of a busy ward, and put in twenty-hour days as the years and all the rest of life passes you by.' I hear you. Only don't sit on my *Science* paper." It occurred to him that part of his anxiety about the paper appearing in *Science* reflected his desire to establish himself quickly with some research papers, and then make some quiet inquiries about openings in departments elsewhere. He had been with Dr. Kraft for three years, and the returns were scanter and scanter, especially weighed against the frustration of being one of the "young men" in Dr. Kraft's department. "A thirty-two-year-old 'young man,' " he thought ruefully.

Matthew Kraft, on the other hand, was wondering about something different. He listened intently to the English-accented voice at the other end of the line. "Dr. Kraft, Dr. Manson here."

"Yes?" Manson was the president of the Bolliston Society, and the world's leading kidney specialist.

"Dr. Kraft, I wanted to check on a few points. I'll explain why in a moment. Your textbook on physical diagnosis in heart disease is now in its third edition, I understand."

"Yes."

"You wrote several chapters in the last two editions of Harrison's and Cecil and Loeb's textbooks of medicine, and have edited the *Yearbook of Cardiology* for the last six years. Now, Dr. Kraft, we have searched the literature and find you the author of about a hundred and sixty papers, either as senior or contributing author. Is that figure approximately correct?"

"Now it isn't, Dr. Manson. I can give you the whole list, but the number is closer to two hundred and ten. Probably thirty or forty appeared in journals published abroad, such as the *Acta Medica Scandinavica*." Kraft paused. What the hell was Manson getting at? The annual discourse?

"Well, Dr. Kraft, we'd like to get as complete a list as we can. Now you have also lectured to classes for fifteen years at three medical schools in Boston, and have sat on a number of advisory committees, state and national. We can send you our summary, and see if the list is complete."

"That's fine," said Kraft, running a hand through his gray hair. "But why so much interest in my work? Has it something to do with the annual discourse on the art of medicine? I've given the talk twice, and you didn't ask me all these questions."

The British voice was unruffled, calm. "Well, you'll probably be hearing from us about that matter very shortly. No, this is something else. The American Academy for the Advancement of Science contacted us last month."

"Yes. The A.A.A.S. I'm a member." What the hell was he getting at?

8

Manson hesitated. "They asked us to review your career. If things proceed properly, we will recommend your name, and it will be one of the five submitted from this country to Stockholm."

"Stockholm?" Matthew Kraft's voice wavered for the first time in a decade.

"Yes. The Nobel Prize committee, you know."

A hundred thoughts rushed to the edge of his mind, but he pushed them aside and made his voice businesslike, matter of fact. "Thank you, Dr. Manson. That's quite an honor, even to be considered. Please send me the lists, and I'll make the résumé as complete as I can."

"Fine. Thank you, Dr. Kraft. We'll be in touch."

Matthew Kraft cradled the phone gently, another departure from his usual manner. He lit a cigarette, keeping his hand steady. He took a puff and sat back. For a few moments he allowed himself free rein to imagine himself as the Nobel Laureate, the trip for the acceptance, even the flood of congratulatory telegrams. Then he sniffed disgustedly. In the last few years the Nobel Prize in Medicine had been won by men who were M.D.s but never left the lab. Last year it had been for the synthesis of insulin, the year before for research on the pathways of the nervous system. "And I wrote one paper on the work of the heart, plus some small things from the lab," he thought resignedly. "I'm a clinician, involved in clinical cardiology." He stood up and went to the window. "They'll never give the prize to a clinician again. Nowadays you've got to make a reputation as a research biochemist to win a Nobel Prize." Angry, he stomped out of the office, and crushed his cigarette in the ashtray on Miss Graf's desk.

She looked up concernedly at him. She thought for sure the call from the Bolliston Society would make him happy. Had it been bad news?

"I'll be in the clinic, seeing a patient," he said quickly. "Tell Lee to be ready to drive me over to the Metropolitan at a quarter to four."

"Yes, Dr. Kraft." She watched him leave. How could anyone speak to the great physician in a way to make him angry? A man of his stature. All the doctors who spoke slightingly of him behind his back called him when they became ill. Would he never get the respect and love he deserved? Joan Graf hurriedly finished typing the letter she had started, then went into Dr. Kraft's office to empty his ashtray and dust the windowsills. He had forgotten to take his stethoscope to the clinic—she touched it lovingly, then picked it up and ran down the hospital corridor after him.

Chester Cornelius licked the stud of the blue leather chair with spitless tongue as he pushed it along. His cheek and shoulder pressed familiarly into its cool back, and he slid to the left every few steps to peer around the row of studs and check on the corridor ahead. At the door of the Finch Conference Room he paused, straightening up. He opened both doors, then wiped the chair with his own graying handkerchief. Grunting, he flipped the heavy chair expertly onto one leg, rotated it, and backed into the dim room. With loving care he set it into place a few inches from the long, waxed table, and brought the right side out a little so Dr. Kraft could sit down without having to move it himself. Cornelius dusted the table in front of the chair, though it was already spotless, and he checked to see that the maximum number of straight hickory chairs were spaced appropriately around the table. Dr. Kraft's chair took the space of two of the others.

It was ten to four. Chester Cornelius quickly erased the blackboard and moved the X-ray viewbox so Dr. Kraft would be able to see it without turning. Finally, Cornelius polished an ashtray he had gotten from the interns' lounge, and set it in front of the blue chair. With a nervous look at the closed door, he sat down abruptly and ran his arms along the cool leather. "Matthew Kraft," he announced to the empty room, "your chair is ready for you." As always, his tongue scraped teeth on the "th" of "Matthew," and he realized giddily that in a few minutes he would greet the great doctor, go to pick up his pay, and after a short walk would feel the first draft of Miller's hit the back of his throat.

He heard steps and scrambled out of the chair, wiping it yet again. The intern and resident rushed in, talking about the order of the cases for the cardiology conference. Within a few minutes all the hard chairs were filled with medical students, house staff, and all the cardiology staff from the Metropolitan: George Winston, the chief, several research fellows, and the intern on the service, who was being told by the resident to present the X-ray diagnosis case first.

Chester Cornelius walked into the hall and set the door ajar, glared as a tardy medical student scurried past him, and then set the door ajar once more. At two minutes after four, the door on the Blossom Street entrance opened, held wide open by Dr. Lee, and Matthew Kraft swept down the hall. Cornelius licked his dry lips as the huge man with the short gray hair strode toward him.

"Good afternoon, Dr. Kraft. Got your chair all ready for you, sir." Cornelius nearly bowed as he opened the door to the Finch Room.

"Thank you, Chester." The iron voice boomed out the phrase for the thousandth time, and Dr. Kraft entered the room full of doctors. The door swung back against the small Korean doctor, who would now wait patiently until he heard voices and then slip quietly into the back of the room.

But Chester Cornelius did not even see the Korean doctor. He was already hurrying to his locker with the thought of the paycheck and the bottle of Miller's and the leathery thirst. Later on tonight he would say slurringly to his wife, "Dr. Kraft looked to be in fine spirits today," and he would speak with the authority of wide experience as a judge of men.

"The first case is a quick one, sir, an X-ray diagnosis," the intern said nervously, sliding a chest X-ray into the viewbox. He switched on the viewbox light and waited for the word to go ahead.

Kraft did not say anything. His silence served to draw attention to himself, for the intern was looking at him. As always at the conferences, tension crept into the room.

"Go ahead." The quiet voice was that of George Winston, passive, reassuring his intern to begin. Though he was the chief of cardiology at the Metropolitan, Winston became chief functionary at these sessions, guiding the discussions, patching the lacerating wounds Dr. Kraft inflicted weekly at his visits here, doing his best to reduce the tension. It was as though he were urging the whole assembly not to fear Dr. Kraft, the great doctor from across town.

The intern began to present the case in the classic fashion: first the history of the patient, with principal attention to the present illness, then the past history and review of symptoms referable to various organ systems, then the physical exam, laboratory findings, and finally, the X-rays. Most cases could be presented in eight or ten minutes, but the intern had been urged to make it short, so he began by omitting the chief complaint of the patient.

"This case is a forty-two-year-old man who presented with high blood pressure of recent onset."

"Stop!" The word hit like an exploding shell. The intern gulped and played with the edge of the X-ray film. Every eye was on Matthew Kraft, who stared at the intern with unconcealed disgust. George Winston began to say something, but Kraft interrupted him. "When you present a case," he said to the pale intern, "it is customary to begin with the complaint of the patient. Please do so when you begin again. Secondly, do not start with the words 'this case.' The word 'this' indicates that the patient is in the room, which he is not; and the phrase 'this case' suggests to me that you have already de-humanized him. He is not a case, but a patient, hopefully still alive after your care. Please start again." Kraft had lowered his head as he spoke, but now he raised it and sat back, staring at the X-ray.

"The patient is a forty-two-year-old white man who presented himself in the medical clinic with a chief complaint of 'cold feet.'" The intern hesitated as thin laughter trickled out from the back of the room, but it barely reached the edge of the glowing table.

Matthew Kraft permitted himself a small smile. "As cold as your feet?" He waited until the real laughter reached a peak and fell. Then Kraft put his hands on the sides of the blue leather chair. "Thank you for presenting so succinctly. You may sit down. The rest of you might stop laughing and realize that the diagnosis has just been given to you."

Tension flowed back in. Did the one sentence and the X-ray allow Dr. Kraft to make the diagnosis? The doctors stared at Kraft, then at the X-ray. Kraft looked expectantly around the table and toward the back of the room. He could see three of the men in his own department; a fourth, Jam Wah Lee, sat too far in back and too low in the seat. But he knew no clinical medicine in any case. Of the others, Harvey Lerner, the cardiogram reader for Kraft, looked bewildered, and Ed Pruden jerked his head quickly, like a nervous rabbit. Only Andrew Essai looked intently at the X-ray.

"The diagnosis is obvious," said Kraft. "Pruden, what is it?"

Ed Pruden coughed. "Well, the heart seems large on X-ray. Uh—"

"Lerner, tell them."

Harvey Lerner said, "I have a few questions to ask, if I may."

Kraft shook his head negatively. "Dr. Lee, are you back there? Can the chemist give us the answer?"

"No, sir," the Oriental voice said quaveringly.

"George," said Kraft softly, "how long was the patient in your hospital before the diagnosis was reached?"

"Oh, four or five days." George Winston smiled the pitiful smile of a man publicly being shown a truth until then his own private error.

"During which no surgical consultant was called, of course," snapped Kraft.

The audience listened even more closely, if that were possible. How could this be a surgical case?

Matthew Kraft stood up. Winston's smile became larger and emptier. "Tell me this, George. Did you see the X-ray the first day?"

"Yes," admitted Winston.

"Looked at but didn't see," corrected Kraft. He took two steps to the viewing box. "The diagnosis is obvious from the history and this X-ray. The patient has a kinked aorta; a coarctation. He has cold feet because the blood flow to his legs is decreased. The X-ray shows the characteristic notching of the ribs." One forefinger pointed at the ribs on the film, and every eye followed from his body to his arm to the finger pointing at the X-ray, where the slight but obvious notching of the ribs could be seen. "You students. Do you see this?" Kraft's tone became mocking. "The rest of you no doubt see this easily."

Two students stood up, and one of them took a step, but they both sat down abruptly, realizing that they should wait for Dr. Kraft to give them permission to rise. The whole roomful of people was still, as still as the pictures of former chiefs of medicine at the Metropolitan whose faces stared from gold frames on the walls with uncommenting intelligence.

Essai stood up, saying, "I can't see the notching from here," and he walked quickly toward the viewbox. At his third step, Kraft said quickly, "Well, come up and look," and at once several students and doctors rushed up to see the notching. Essai looked at the X-ray, shook his head in assent, and walked back to his seat. A sound, like the monitor on a cardiac pacer, beeped high in Kraft's mind, but it stopped and did not recur.

All the time that the group examined the X-ray, Kraft sat in his blue chair, thinking about Essai and how he had asked about his *Science* paper, how he had stood and broken the spell just now. When the room quieted down, Kraft said, "Perhaps Dr. Essai can explain why this man did not seek medical attention until the age of forty-two, though his aorta had been kinked since birth."

Essai looked up sharply. "Perhaps because you were not called to see him earlier," he shot back.

The mental beeper went off again, four or five times. Matthew Kraft gripped the leather arms of the chair. "Impertinence is always a substitute for knowledge," he said flatly after a long moment. "For some of the inexperienced men, as well as the students, it's worth pointing out that symptoms of heart disease often escape detection because the patient involuntarily restricts his activities. I'm sure this patient experienced shortness of breath with exercise, and so avoided strenuous activity without realizing it."

Kraft glared at Essai, then released his grip on the chair and went on anecdotally. "This is especially true in angina pectoris," he said. "I remember a well-known symphony conductor referred to me with angina, who denied having had chest pain until a few weeks previously. As you know, I believe that angina pectoris is not of sudden onset unless it first occurs with a heart attack. But the patient denied chest pain on effort. Then I think it was Pruden—wasn't it you, Ed?"

"Yes," said Pruden, answering with his syllable of assent at just this point in the "conductor story." The story was told to a different group of interns and residents each time.

"Pruden mentioned that the conductor was well known for his stage mannerisms, especially the propulsive waving of arms on the podium. It seems for the year or so prior to my seeing him, the critics had noticed that he had become less exuberant while conducting, and thought he was a better conductor because of it. When I questioned him intensively, he finally related the symptom of heaviness in both collarbones during moments of particularly exciting music, which he attributed to muscle strain or emotion. Of course this was the first occurrence of angina, which he avoided by literally exercising less, without realizing it. The exercise restriction helped keep the critics at bay as well, it seems; an unexpected benefit of illness," Kraft concluded.

The laughter around the room, easy and brief, sufficed for applause. Winston used the moment of levity to ask about how the patient with coarctation should be managed. Then two other patients were presented in detail. At five thirty, Dr. Kraft asked, "That it?", rose (as did the others, a second after he did), pushed hard against the back of the leather chair, and left the room through the door held open by a smiling Dr. Winston.

Jam Wah Lee hurried from the back of the room to catch up with Dr. Kraft and drive him back to his hospital for evening rounds. Of the thirty people remaining, each sought out his own level, but the conversations were all about Kraft. The conductor with angina pectoris was mentioned several times, and Krellenstein, a pudgy and nail-bitten student, waved his arms energetically and shouted, "My collarbones feel heavy." Lerner, at the other end of the table, said sharply, "Grow up. This is a hospital conference room." The medical students silently picked up books and coats and walked into the hall, where the voice of Krellenstein was heard again, softly at first.

Essai put on his coat and paused near the knot of interns and residents at the X-ray viewbox, looking yet again at the X-ray of the man with the coarctation. They commiserated with the luckless intern who had presented the case, and each one mentioned a time when he had been singled out for Dr. Kraft's special teaching methods. The resident going off duty for the evening was telling the "on" resident about his cases. Essai remembered times three years before, when he was chief resident in cardiology and had stood in the midst of a group just like this after each conference. Now he was an instructor, away from the patients and safe in the lab. He bit his lip, remembering that he had to go back and check some protein determinations he had left unread in his lab. He wanted to get a ride back, but Pruden and Lerner were busy talking with George Winston at the far end of the polished table. Essai took a last look at the faces of the former chiefs set in the gold frames on the wall. Leaving, he wondered, "Could they have diagnosed a coarctation after one sentence?"

A janitor came in to remove the blue chair a few minutes

after six, though he did it without ritual, and he excused himself as he pushed it past the three doctors standing together in the gloomily lit room. Ed Pruden was still discussing the case of the coarctation with Lerner and Winston, as though the story were a ballad transmitted and polished in the retelling.

"What I can't understand," Pruden exclaimed, "is the speed with which he made the diagnosis and used it as a teaching case. Tell me, Harvey, have you ever seen a coarctation in this age group?"

Harvey Lerner laughed. "You forget, Ed, I'm just an old cardiogram reader. When the boys send down the cardiograms to be read, they don't give me much clinical history. I could never make the right diagnosis with sketchy information."

"Aha," said Pruden triumphantly. "But if you were Matthew Kraft you could do it by looking at his X-ray. Of the thousands of cases he sees, he remembers each one. He never forgets a patient, or an X-ray. What a genius!"

Winston said quietly, "I'll bet he's forgotten one or two."

Pruden ignored him. "It just occurred to me that we should tape these sessions, and then pick illustrative cases in clinical cardiology. In a year we'd have over a hundred, each one discussed by Dr. Kraft."

"And your breathless editorial comments," added Lerner. He paused. "Actually, it's a good idea. We could describe the cardiogram in each case—"

"Your descriptions, of course," Pruden said.

Lerner assumed his rabbinical posture. "If Dr. Kraft asked me to contribute, I would be glad to add what I could."

Winston nodded in assent. "I like the idea. We could use it for teaching students and house staff, and circulate it around the hospital. But nothing formal."

"What do you mean 'nothing formal,'" said Pruden indignantly. "Think how popular such a collection of cases would be. Of course they could be published. We might even include transcripts of his comments so the reader can see how Dr. Kraft arrives at the diagnosis."

"No," said Winston.

They both looked at him. Ed Pruden spoke first. "Why do you say 'no' like that? This would be a chance to see how Dr. Kraft employs his skill—no, it's more than that—it's his particular genius; when he applies that genius to helping us solve our problems, we should be grateful to him. Not only grateful, but we should celebrate that genius, that Socratic insight. A book of the kind I'm thinking of would be a kind of tribute to the man, a document of the clinical insight one sees only once or twice in a whole generation of physicians."

He stopped, not so much because Lerner and Winston weren't listening—they were observing him with unusual concentration—but because his voice had risen and was echoing shrilly off the picture-lined walls of the conference room.

George Winston folded his arms in front of him. "Ed, it's no good, and I'll tell you why. Take the case of the coarctation. Do you think we presented it to show how clever we are at arriving at diagnoses?"

"I don't see what you're driving at," said Pruden warily.

"I see what he's driving at," said Lerner, "and I must say I agree with you, George."

Pruden was about to report Kraft's genius to the group yet again but George Winston silenced him with an uncharacteristically raised hand. "Wait, Ed. We presented the case to give Dr. Kraft the chance to make the diagnosis, and to use it as a teaching case for the students. We also presented it so the rest of you at Eastern Mass. Medical can hear about our interesting cases. Now I'm the chief of cardiology here at the Metropolitan, and I don't like being instructed, but I'm willing to be lumped with the students, house staff, and junior department men for Dr. Kraft's didactic purposes." Winston paused, and pulled on his gloves. "Dr. Kraft can instruct me, and be graceless in the process, but I'm not willing to see these exercises preserved in print, because if they are, we will pick and choose our cases for the published book, not the conference, and the conference will suffer. I'm sorry, Ed, but as far as I'm concerned, that ends it."

"Amen," said Lerner.

Pruden looked at Lerner as though the benediction had been a curse. "I never expected that kind of assent from you, Harvey."

Lerner tried to think of the proper response, but Winston looked at his watch and excused himself to both of them. "Ed," he said, "I thought your idea was good, but I can't go along with it. Excuse me, gentlemen, my wife is waiting for me. I'll see you next week." Winston suddenly extended his ungloved hand; a handshake was somehow in order.

Pruden looked, but Harvey Lerner shook hands. "Good night, George."

When he had left, the two men edged closer together, as though the gloomy room were a cave in which they had been trapped.

"That Winston," stated Pruden angrily, "that Winston is a frightened man cowed in the shadow of a great man."

"Kraft?"

"Of course."

Lerner shrugged. "I think Winston is a very nice man, and between us, a good doctor."

"Not compared with our chief," said Pruden doggedly.

Lerner nodded, but said nothing.

Kraft and Lee were stuck in traffic. To Lee it made no difference. Wedged into the lock step of rush-hour traffic, transporting his superior from the Metropolitan back to his own hospital, listening **2** more for the shifts in his speech than for what he said; it was all part of the flux of time. Without knowing it, Lee capitalized on the white man's hesitation to intrude on the alleged inscrutability of the yellow. Lee loved biochemistry, and he used the driving time to think about enzymes. Over the years he had developed a theory of how enzymes catalyzed reactions, employing the concept of chance arrangement—how light coming from different angles could vary shadows cast by objects. His two favorite subjects for thought were enzymes and shadow formation, and most of the events of the real world passed through his mind unaltered.

During the five thousand days he had driven his superior from place to place, they had occasionally discussed medical research, or less commonly, personalities in the lab. After all, Jam Wah Lee was senior research associate, and he had written many papers with Dr. Kraft on little projects. Very rarely they talked about events, such as the fall of Syngman Rhee, or the qualifications of a Presidential candidate. Finally, though Lee would not admit it, he used waiting periods (when Dr. Kraft went somewhere and he stayed in the car) to think about Dr. Kraft. He understood hardly anything about him, except that he lacked control at every level. But today was an ordinary day, and Jam Wah Lee thought about an article in the last issue of the *Journal of Biological Chemistry* concerned with a new method for assaying enzyme activity in rabbit liver.

Dr. Kraft, in contrast, shifted his weight from one buttock

to the other, irritably crossed his left leg over his right, and waited for the policeman at Charles and Boylston to wave them on. Angrily he looked at his watch. It was six ten, and he wanted to see his patients at the hospital and get home to eat and prepare tomorrow's cardiology rounds.

"Jesus Christ, will you look at that cop?"

"What?" Lee blinked as though just awakened.

"Can't you hear? That stupid cop is asleep up there at the corner." Kraft moved his left hand over and hit the horn three or four times. "C'mon, you bastard, stop making things worse and let us through."

Lee shrank back against the seat. Their horn-blowing had started ten cars doing the same thing, and Kraft watched smugly as the traffic cop moved a few steps toward the line of cars and then stopped, not knowing which of the insolent drivers to reprimand. Finally they began moving.

"It seems to have had some effect," said Lee, soothingly.

"You're damn right it does, Lee. Cops only move fast when they run to get paid off. One's worse than the next. What if an ambulance were trying to get through? It would sit here while all the women put on makeup in the mirror. Christ, they raise the property tax every year and haven't built a new road in a decade."

Jam Wah Lee listened to the flow and timbre of the speech, not the words, and correctly decided that he need make no further response. At Tremont Street the traffic moved more easily, and they arrived at the Eastern Massachusetts Medical Center ten minutes later. In the doctors' parking lot, Kraft hurriedly opened his door. "Wait here, Jam Wah; it shouldn't be more than fifteen minutes."

"I'll be here," Lee said. The door slammed with characteristic force. Jam Wah Lee rested his head on the back of the seat. Was X-ray diffraction really the ultimate method for determining the purity of enzymes? He fixed his eye on the gray wall of the research building and squinted slightly as though trying to read the answer in the twilit evening.

"Look, Connie, I've got to go," protested Schachter.

"Go if you want to."

Steve Schachter looked at his chief resident and shook his head. "You know I can't. Maybe I will anyway. Tell Kraft I had to leave early."

Martin O'Connell grinned. "Fine, Steve, I'll tell him my assistant resident was called away by his girlfriend, and so had to miss the evening walk with the chief to see his patients. I'll say you couldn't bear to see her overcook the roast beef."

"All right, all right." Schachter looked hopefully at the elevator. "Doesn't Kraft have any home life?"

"Sure," said O'Connell. "Tomorrow is his cardiology conference, just like every Friday. So tonight Kraft will barricade himself in his study at home, and prepare a talk."

"Can't he do it by now without preparing? And why won't he let anyone else talk at that conference?"

O'Connell glanced around and turned toward Schachter. "Steve, he never lets anyone else do anything. Someone once said he's like a temperamental symphony conductor. To me, a better analogy is to a puppet show."

"No kidding," said Schachter. "Do you really think he—"

The elevator door opened and Kraft stepped out, stethoscope around his neck. One hand motioned to them. "Let's go, it's late."

They said, "Yes, sir" in unison.

As they walked to the south end, Dr. Kraft asked, "Did the Correlia girl have any more trouble?"

O'Connell nudged Schachter. "No, sir," said the assistant resident. "We tried to reassure her that she'll get this fast heart rate once in a while, but she's sure it means she has serious heart disease."

O'Connell led the way in, pausing slightly at the door to face Dr. Kraft, whose stethoscope brushed his arm as he passed. Inside, the Negro girl sat up as she heard Dr. Kraft's voice.

She smiled warmly. "Good evening, Dr. Kraft."

Dr. Kraft smiled. He looked quickly at her neck veins, which rose and fell at a rate of seventy beats or so a minute. "I see your heart rate is perfectly normal, Iris."

She laughed and showed her teeth. "How can you tell every time what my heart is like just by looking at me?"

"I watch the pulses in your neck. Now let me listen." He motioned to Schachter to shut the door, and the patient raised her hospital gown. Kraft warmed the head of the stethoscope with his hand, and first felt her apex beat with the palm of his right hand flat under her breast, then listened for a minute or so. He listened longer than he usually did, and O'Connell felt his own pulse rise as he thought, "He hears a murmur, and I didn't listen to her this afternoon." Then he figured that Dr. Kraft was probably using the extra seconds to think of how to talk to her and reassure her.

The gray, crew-cut head turned suddenly. "O'Connell, did you hear a murmur today?"

"No, sir."

"Schachter, she's yours, isn't she? Did you?"

Schachter looked quickly at O'Connell. "No, sir, sounded normal to me."

Iris Correlia looked wide-eyed and scared. Dr. Kraft turned back to her and, for the first time, felt her pulse at the wrist. "Neither did I, Iris. Your heart is perfectly normal."

She sighed. "Oh, Dr. Kraft, you scared me by asking that question."

"I know I did, Iris, and I'm sorry. But in a way, I was conducting a little experiment. You see," he went on, "you have a normal heart, but when you were frightened for a few seconds by what I said, your pulse suddenly went way up, and when I said, 'Your heart is normal' it dropped to seventy again."

"But you say it is normal?" She could have been a child asking her father about sounds in the night.

"Yes, it is, Iris. The only unusual thing about you is that when you are excited, your heart rate doubles suddenly and then drops just as fast to normal, instead of rising a little, as most hearts do."

"But you say that's not dangerous?"

Dr. Kraft's voice was lulling. "Not in the least. Some doctors who are unfamiliar with this problem might scare you by looking surprised when they hear or feel such a fast pulse."

She nodded in assent. "That's right, that's just what happened when I went to the clinic the first time."

"You have a normal heart, Iris."

The smile filled the room. "Now I believe I do."

Dr. Kraft stood up. "Do you want to go home in the morning?"

"Could I?"

"Of course. You can do whatever you like when you leave, no restriction on your activities at all. Dr. Schachter, the resident, will see you in the morning before you go." He began to walk out and motioned again to the two residents, the command to fall into line behind him.

"Thank you, Dr. Kraft." Her melodious voice carried out into the hall through the door he had opened a second before she said it.

"That's quite all right, Iris," he said over his shoulder.

Schachter was about to say something to Dr. Kraft, some phrase of congratulation or praise. No wonder his patients loved him. But Kraft held up the motioning hand in a gesture that made them remain quiet and listen. From the next room, the cardiac monitor sounded an unvarying series of couplets.

They stood in the hall listening to the abnormal beep—beep. Finally Kraft motioned for O'Connell to give the follow-up on the patient.

"Mr. Krachik," he said. "Well, he was free of chest pain today, but we aren't sure what to do with his medicine."

Kraft interrupted him. "You're the chief resident, O'Connell. Let your assistant give me the information. Are his heart enzymes still high?"

O'Connell looked at Schachter. "Yes, sir," said Schachter. "They're just as high as when he came in with his coronary."

Kraft sneered. "Look, doc, a man does not come in with 'a coronary.' He comes in with a myocardial infarction, or at least, with a coronary thrombosis. The lay term 'heart attack' is vastly preferable to the word 'coronary,' an anatomic term of no significance. Now begin again. How is Mr. Krachik?"

"When he came in with his myo-car-dial in-farction (Schachter stressed every syllable exaggeratedly until he saw Matthew Kraft's shoulders hunch and his head lower, and then he went hurriedly on), he had enzymes of over two hundred. They started down but with his arrhythmia yesterday—the coupled beats—he went back up."

Kraft stamped his foot. "'He went back up?' Or did his enzymes rise again? Perhaps he went up to heaven under your care."

"Sorry, sir, his enzymes rose again yesterday."

Kraft raised his head from a lowered, charging position and went into the room.

"Mr. Krachik, how are you feeling this evening?"

"Fine doctor." The voice seemed to come from the machines surrounding his bed, not from the pale man who lay with his arms folded. The cardiac monitor was attached to his chest by a perforated band of rubber stretched around him, keeping the six greased electrodes in place. Mr. Krachik had had the habit of lying with his hands folded across his chest, but now with the electrodes there he rested his hands across his face with the thumbs in front of each ear. Sometimes when he realized that the monitor's *beep—beep, beep—beep, beep—beep* transmitted a rhythm of his own heart which was abnormal and very dangerous, instead of the regular *beep, beep, beep* he had heard the first four days in the hospital, he would press his thumbs tight over his ears to keep out the sound. But the absence of any sound except the trembling of his thumbs frightened him even more, as though he would make his heart stop by not hearing the *beep—beep*.

Had he been an eloquent or emotional man, he would have explained this to the doctors. But he was a recently retired shoemaker who wanted to live only to see the Czech countryside before he died, and at times he thought all the machines and noises were part of a plot to frighten him to death.

The two young doctors stood back at a distance as the older man with the warmed stethoscope turned off the machine and listened to the patient's heart. Mr. Krachik felt safest with this doctor, Dr. Kraft, because his eyes did not change when he heard something bad, as did the eyes of the two young doctors, and the first feeling to come out of the eyes each morning and evening was a smiling reassurance.

"Turn toward me just a little, Mr. Krachik."

"Of course, doctor." As he turned toward his left, one of the electrodes came loose and Mr. Krachik knocked Kraft's arm away. He pawed wildly to keep the electrodes close to his chest, lest he die. Kraft sat back suddenly, startled by the unexpected movement. The two residents moved together to feel Mr. Krachik's pulse, which beat in coupled rhythm as before, and O'Connell saw the loose electrode. He was unsure which of the two older men to reassure first.

"Dr. Kraft, he felt the electrode come loose and went to reach it. Mr. Krachik, everything is all right."

Kraft felt the man's pulse himself, and smiled. "Mr. Krachik, this cardiac monitor upsets you, doesn't it?"

Mr. Krachik wanted to say that the bother of its presence was much less than the fear of death in its absence. He shook his head vaguely and said, "Whatever you want, Dr. Kraft."

"Well then, it's rather important that we continue to have a way to follow the rhythm of your heart. So we'll keep it on. Otherwise you are coming along all right, except you must continue to lie quietly." Kraft smiled at the patient.

"I will do that, doctor."

The three doctors went outside and O'Connell closed the door. "I think he is very frightened; maybe he's developed psychotic thinking."

"You mean he worries about dying as a result of his heart attack? That certainly is unusual, Martin," Kraft went on, sarcastically. "I suppose you would be dancing with nurses in your room."

O'Connell said nothing. He was sure enough of his point to risk this kind of deprecation.

"Well?"

"I'm not at all sure about it," said the chief resident, "but this is the third time I've seen the intense concern in patients when an electrode slips off or the nurse changes the straps. In the last two cases the patients both told me they began to feel that their hearts were beating in response to the beeping coming through the electrode."

"You mean they were being paced," corrected Kraft.

"They thought that, but we explained to them that they weren't on a pacemaker which electrically stimulated their hearts, but a monitor that recorded what they themselves were doing. But they continued to believe that the machine was giving impulses to their hearts. The last patient, Mrs. Halter, went so far as to say that her wristwatch was signaling the monitor to make her heart beat and if her watch stopped she would die."

"Well, she was obviously a psychoneurotic," said Kraft, dismissingly.

"You don't hold much with psychiatric explanations of things, do you, Dr. Kraft." Schachter, impatient with their slow pace and the "coronary" reprimand of a few minutes before, blurted this out.

Kraft lowered his head slightly. "Yes, I do, Steve. I think for example that if you had been properly punished in your youth at the first sign of insolence and sloppy thinking, you would have grown up a lot sooner, especially in terms of developing the appropriate attitude toward your superior." Schachter involuntarily took a step back. Matthew Kraft shifted his gaze to O'Connell. "And you, O'Connell, if you want to go in and explain to Mr. Krachik that he is critically ill because he has psychiatric disease involving his coronary arteries, you have my permission to do so. Of course, I wouldn't change the diagnosis on the medicine sheet if I were you. The nurses will see it and refer you to the headshrinkers. Not that several people around here couldn't use it!"

The two residents looked at Dr. Kraft and did not say anything. The man with the furious eyes held them immobile for a few more seconds, then walked between them into 603, where Mrs. Swanson was finishing her supper.

"Good evening, Dr. Kraft. Dr. O'Connell said I might be able to go home tomorrow if my clotting time comes back all right."

"Did you tell her that, Martin?" The sawtooth of tension rose with his voice.

"Well, you said we just had to straighten out her coumadin dosage and she could go then."

Matthew Kraft shouted. "Let's get it straight! I don't want to have to keep reminding you. I'll decide when my patients go home, and I'll tell them when they are to go."

Mrs. Swanson put her hand up to her mouth. "Oh dear, I'm afraid I said the wrong thing."

Kraft felt her pulse. "It's not you, Mrs. Swanson. Sometimes my residents think they run the service. I'll see how you are tomorrow, and then we'll talk about your going." Dr. Kraft dropped her wrist as though it were hot, and charged out.

They went on to the first of the four-bed rooms without saying a word. In all, they saw the next twenty-two patients in the time it had taken to see the first three. Steve Schachter said little and let O'Connell do the talking. After all, he had been chief resident since the previous July and knew how to handle the boss; Schachter only had a two-month rotation, thank God, which was coming to an end tomorrow.

Schachter admired Kraft in spite of himself. While talking to a patient he used every second to his advantage, feeling the pulse, gauging neck veins, palpating the chest, squeezing a calf for tenderness and in a few minutes he assessed things exactly, and the patients felt reassured that their doctor had seen them and examined them.

It was seven o'clock when they finished. They walked back to the nurses' desk, Dr. Kraft thinking over what patient to discuss at his conference on Friday morning. "What have we got for tomorrow, O'Connell?"

"Well, the patient who fooled us the longest was Everett Mann, you know, the one who finally turned out to have pulmonary clots."

Dr. Kraft paused. "Didn't he come to us labeled 'heart attack,' and then the house staff thought he might have a collapsed lung?"

"That's right." O'Connell wanted to look at his watch, but stopped himself.

"Maybe I could talk about the problem of diagnosing chest pain. I haven't done that for a long time."

"Fine, sir."

"I'll see you tomorrow at rounds." Dr. Kraft turned suddenly on Schachter, who was glancing at his watch. "Dr. Freud, is your hour with us up already, or are you checking your heart rhythm."

Schachter dropped his hand. He had not been out of the hospital for thirty-seven hours and did not want to say anything that would keep him from getting out on his night off.

"By the way, Schachter," inquired Kraft, "where is your intern?"

"Dr. Maltern's wife is about to deliver, and he wanted to leave early."

"I want the house staff to be here when I see my patients," said Kraft to Martin O'Connell. "If they want to take off early they can ask me for permission. Let's not let things get any looser up here. Maltern's wife can deliver a baby without his help. In fact, if he misses my rounds up here again, this hospital can do without him altogether."

O'Connell nodded. "Yes, sir."

Dr. Kraft stalked off. Schachter looked at O'Connell. "Chief resident, how do you take all this?"

"With plenty of Maalox," said O'Connell wearily.

"I'm so impressed with your behavior in the face of irrationality," said Schachter, "that I'm going to give you the chance to eat some well-done roast beef tonight. Want to stand in for me?"

O'Connell grinned. "I like it rare too. Besides, I'm married and you no doubt have some after-supper exercise with the cook, right?"

"After a day and a half on duty here I couldn't perform for the Virgin herself."

"A good thing," said O'Connell. "Just make sure Maltern has the case ready for tomorrow."

"OK, Connie. So long." Schachter tossed his reflex hammer high in the air and caught it while walking away.

Dr. Kraft walked down three flights of stairs and unlocked the lab door. His lab was the first on the right, the only one with a window, and closest to the centrifuge, refrigerator, and balances. His technician had gone home at five, as they all did—exactly eight hours in the service of science and then home—but she did careful work, and at least left the place in decent shape. The day's experiment was summarized on the sheet of lined paper, which by long custom Kraft reviewed at the end of the day.

The sacrificed rabbit's heart had been perfectly normal. This animal, and eighty-three before it, had been fed a diet constructed to deplete the heart muscle of contracting substances. The hearts should be abnormal, weak, flabby. They were not. Kraft clenched his teeth for a moment, wrote a big 84TH EXP.-NEGATIVE on the top of the page and put it into a blue notebook. He turned back to the last five experiments, then ten, then thirty. Negative. Negative. Negative. Negative. He dropped the notebook heavily on the floor. They did not award Nobel Prizes for negative results. He took a look around the other labs, in a hurry now to go back to the car, to get out of here.

Down the hall, in one of the smallest labs, the door was open and Andrew Essai sat pipetting a row of tubes. At the sound of steps he looked out and seeing Dr. Kraft, he took the pipette out of his mouth and rested his finger on the last tube handled so as not to lose count.

Kraft brightened. "Working late, Andy?" It was a pleasure to see a man in the lab at seven.

"I've got to get this protein done, and check my standard curve. It'll be just a few more minutes."

"Getting anywhere?"

Essai smiled. "I think so. I'm getting some positive results."

A wave of jealous anger washed over Kraft and subsided again. He saw Essai look at his face strangely. "Oh." Kraft said the single word quietly and turned to go. For an instant, in turning, he thought he heard the mental ping or beep he had heard at the Metropolitan conference, though he couldn't recall the circumstances. At the same time, he visualized the moment thirty years ago when he sat in the laboratory one night and Lippschitz came by to say sardonically, "Kraft, I thought you were like the rest, afraid to work after dark."

"Remember, Essai, what my old boss Lippschitz used to say, 'The best research is done after sundown and on weekends, when the little people have gone home.'"

Essai fingered the tube of bluish fluid. "He certainly was a great one for aphorisms, wasn't he?"

Kraft glared at him. "Sonny, there was great truth in what he said."

"Yes, sir."

Kraft charged out, ripping open a new pack of cigarettes. The aphorism was his, not Lippschitz'. That punk Essai. Pruden, Lerner, Lee: they were meek jackasses. But Essai. He and his positive results. Kraft remembered his eighty-four negative rabbits. Essai, that independent bastard, had results. What a cocky son-of-a-bitch he was.

Preoccupied with Essai, he was nearly to the elevator before he remembered that he needed some reprints and notes from his file here to read tonight for the talk in the morning. Angry anew, now at himself for forgetting the talk, he went back to his office at a trot, fumbled for a moment with the lock on the outer door, then opened it and the second smaller door that led to his reprint room. In his sanctuary he felt better at once.

He had written for reprints faithfully over the last twenty-five years, and though his secretaries had made out the postcards for the articles he checked in *Current Contents* each week, he insisted on filing them each day himself. "And goddamnit," he thought grimmly, "I wrote away for reprints myself the first ten years." Safely in his private place, he pulled down a large lever to the right of a metal cabinet, and three shelves of manila folders clicked into place. As though selecting an appropriate wine, or a good cigar, he pulled out folders and lovingly flipped through them. He selected four folders, labeled "Anatomy," "Muscle Diseases," "Shock," and "Pneumothorax," and from them picked out thirty or forty articles. These were for background, not really related to heart disease, but they contained hundreds of facts which, sieved and weighed, would highlight the points he wanted to make.

Out of the "Pneumothorax" file he took the article, "Collapsed Lung Simulating Heart Attack." Rapidly he read it over again, recalling the neat clinical point that the pain of one condition could mimic the other. He smiled. That article had appeared in 1952, and he had read it the week it appeared. The same week he embarrassed the dean of the medical school during grand medical rounds by suggesting that the patient just presented with "unusual coronary pain" most likely had a collapsed lung. The dean had been discussing the case as one of a heart attack in a young man. Matthew Kraft licked his lips, remembering that his own diagnosis had been proved correct when the chest X-rays were reexamined.

He collected the articles he wanted, then put up the three shelves and swung down six more. One shelf contained his own articles and previous lecture notes. Quickly he went through it, selecting twenty references and a few old notes. Then he pulled out the bulky files on "Angina Pectoris" and "Blood Clots; Lung and Coronary Arteries." The "Angina" file was subdivided into three, each weighing nearly ten pounds. With the other selected reprints on top, he carried all four files into his office, breathing heavily with the sudden effort.

Flipping through the older reprints took but a moment; he knew that literature by heart. But the newer papers, or those describing new techniques, took longer to sift. These papers were hard to read, hard to remember, and the snappy young men schooled in biochemistry always referred to the most recent work. It occurred to Kraft that he collected more articles each week than he could read, even if he did nothing else.

Shaking his head, he went through all the files, and finally he was satisfied. Of the hundred articles he had picked, he would glance through about ninety, read ten, and then at midnight, his wife in bed, he would eat a couple of sandwiches and go back upstairs to begin assembling his talk for the next morning. The prospect exhilarated him.

He lit a cigarette, inhaled deeply, and slowly let the smoke out, picking up the heavy files again. He stood for a long moment, contemplating their weight (heavier each year), the printed collation of the best minds in medicine and cardiology. And his own contribution, he thought, was at least as great as the best of them.

Standing there, holding the heavy papers, a stray thought occurred to him. Until a few years ago he had written in a big, loose-leaf notebook each night before going to sleep, writing down things he had read, seen and heard in patients, noticed on X-rays and cardiograms. Many nights he had fallen asleep with the pressing warmth of the notebook on his chest. Now he had a hint of the same sensation, as though one of the files in his hands had been propped on his chest. He looked down. Nothing was against it, though his arms ached slightly from holding the heavy files. The left arm ached more than the right, probably because he was right-handed. The easy comfortable pressure persisted, then intensified a little. Was his shirt too tight?

He took a deep breath, but the pressure was still there. Suddenly he noticed he was sweating. The pressure was no longer comfortable, but insistent, disturbing. Two thoughts collided in his mind. The first, chillingly certain, was that he was having a heart attack; the second, that the mass of papers should be set down. "No, no," he said aloud, but later he was unsure whether the "No" had been against the fact of the heart attack, or the fear of dropping the weight of all his collected data.

"Hold on," he thought vaguely. Again he did not know how he meant it. Slowly he bent and set down the files, but grasped one paper at random and clenched it in his sweaty fist. The other hand, now free, came to his pulse. Strong, steady, but there—a premature beat, a compensatory pause—then regular. Ten heartbeats marched regularly—then another "skipped beat." Matthew Kraft leaned forward slightly, palpating his pulse, and tried to keep from panicking. But each thought unnerved him anew. He could have been lecturing to medical students. Mortality during the twenty-four hours following the first heart attack is no more than fifteen percent. But if the patient is thirty pounds overweight, the risk doubles. If he smokes two packs of cigarettes a day, it increases again. If the onset is with exertion, even lifting and holding a weight, the chance of a large infarct of the heart increases.

"I could drop dead now," he thought. "The premature beats are another bad sign." He made himself slide away from the thoughts, and try to decide what to do. He had not moved in nearly a minute, afraid to do anything. Schachter and O'Connell might still be up on the floor, but it was several steps to the phone, and walking was out of the question. It was after seven; Lee in the car would never hear a shout, no one was here this late.

"Essai!" He thought it and shouted it at once. The door was closed, and Kraft looked at the glass, praying to see Essai's face. "Essai." Dragged out, the last syllable became an ancient wail for help. Kraft felt the sweat and the painful pressure and thought he was going to die.

Essai heard his name shouted and stood up, startled, watching the one milliliter pipette roll to the edge of the lab bench and break skittering on the floor. At the second shout, a scream of fear and pain, he ran to Dr. Kraft's office. Through the glass he saw an aging man with gray hair, pale, feeling for his pulse. Essai forgot that the man was a professor of medicine, the country's leading cardiologist, his mercurial and egotistical boss. He opened the door, providentially unlocked, and went to help the patient.

"Thank God, Essai. I'm having an infarct."

"Do you have pain?"

The word was forced out with a grunt. "No. But pressure. Sweaty. Premature beats."

Essai felt automatically for his right-hand pocket, but there was no use for a stethoscope in the lab, and Essai could not remember at that moment where his was. Kraft's stethoscope was in the pocket of his white coat, draped over the chair. Essai took it. "Sit down, please."

Like any patient who is convinced he is all right as long as he remains motionless, Kraft shook his head. "No. No chair."

Essai looked around the office. Partly hidden by a folding screen was Dr. Kraft's examining table. Quickly he pulled it out, and pulled up the foot rest. "Lie down."

"I—"

"Lie down, please."

Assisted, Kraft lay down. At once the pressure diminished somewhat. He lay quietly and watched the young man unbutton his shirt and listen. Kraft felt the premature beat, the classic "fish-flopping" sensation, and watched the young doctor's eyes change for a moment as he heard it. "I'll have to teach him not to do that," he thought. But he felt better, being cared for by a physician, even Essai.

He watched Essai go to the phone and dial an in-hospital number, and a minute later Dr. O'Connell was there, and then an Irish nurse walked in, with syringe in hand, and efficiently gave him a stinging injection in the arm. Essai stood over him, very much in control.

"It's morphine, a sixth. They're getting a room ready for you upstairs. We'll put you on the monitor, just as a precaution, of course." Essai hesitated. "Shall we call George Winston?"

At any other time Matthew Kraft would have said, "Winston, that tool?" but now he realized that as chief of cardiology at the Metropolitan General, Winston was the logical choice. Essai's hesitation was obviously explained: if each doctor as patient had a slightly better man for a physician, who took care of the best one? Kraft nodded, already cottony from the morphine. "OK. Make the call to Winston. But Essai, you keep an eye on me too. Don't go running off to some theatre."

Essai smiled wanly. O'Connell was staring at him. How characteristic that Kraft's first compliment in years be followed by a paternal interdiction. "I'll be here," said Essai. "By the way, should we contact your wife?"

Kraft had forgotten about her altogether. "Of course," he said quietly.

"Fine. Now we'll get a portable chest X-ray as soon as we get you to your room, to make sure there's no—nothing else."

Kraft smiled dreamily. "I taught you that. No evidence for pulmonary clot or collapsed lung, but rule it out with an X-ray." The morphine made him langourous; even with the pallor and sweating, he was as relaxed as they had ever seen him. "You're all right, Essai. Just stay away from the concert hall."

The tension on 6 North, the cardiology service floor, rose perceptibly each time Matthew Kraft strode onto it. This time he was wheeled onto it, and the result was an apparent confusion and disorder which comprise first-class medical care. Essai had been plunged involuntarily into clinical medicine again, and after the moment's hesitation outside Kraft's office, he acted as though he had never left it. He gave Martin O'Connell, the chief resident, a list of duties relegated to an intern in any other situation: "Private room, move someone out if necessary. Room with an oxygen outlet close to the nurses' station. Have them bring down a cardiogram machine. Get the chief of anesthesia and the 'crash cart.' I'll call

Winston." By a stroke of fortune, Schachter, the assistant resident, had not yet gone home, and O'Connell canceled his night off and the roast beef dinner with his first phrase: "Steve, stick around. Dr. Kraft's in with a coronary. Get the 'crash cart' outside the door of six-twelve." Schachter smiled his disbelief only for a second, and when he saw the tension in O'Connell's face, his smile stopped and he ran quickly down the hall.

Essai called George Winston at home. He came at once, arriving just as the nurses finished making up the bed, Kraft lying next to it on the cart, with monitor leads on his chest. He was dozing, and for a frozen instant Winston thought he was dead. Then he heard the regular beeping, and Essai, seeing his face, said, "It's the morphine."

Winston, Essai, O'Connell and Schachter lifted him off the cart onto the bed, and Schachter looked at the three other physicians and whispered, "A million dollars in talent, lifting two million."

Dr. Kraft opened an eye and said quietly, "A humorous Dr. Freud, no less." Schachter almost let go from surprise. Then Kraft smiled. "It's OK. I'm glad you're all here."

Kraft closed his eyes again. He felt himself set onto the bed, heard Essai tell the nurse to take the monitor to the far corner of the room and turn the beeper down, and realized that the sound of the beeper did unnerve him. Not an hour ago he had been reassuring Mr. Krachik about the monitor, and he sensed that O'Connell and Schachter had been right after all. He remembered his criticism of their comments. He thought of apologizing, but instead opened his eyes. George Winston was studying his cardiogram, the others politely looking over his shoulder.

"I'll tell you," Kraft said to them conversationally. "My cardiogram shows normal rhythm with occasional premature ventricular contractions, and the earliest signs of an anterior wall myocardial infarct. No Q waves yet."

Winston actually gasped. "Matthew—Dr. Kraft, you shouldn't look at your own tracing."

"I didn't. But I felt the premature beats. The location has to be anterior, with the symptoms I had. If it were inferior, I'd have had belching or 'ulcer pain' or some intestinal complaint. There's nothing to it. Look up my article on anatomic locations of coronary ischemia, it's in *Cardiology* in 1952 or 1953. Essai, did you call my wife?"

"What?" Essai had been listening to the professor, not the patient.

"My wife. Oh, and tell Lee to go home. He's still waiting in the parking lot. Tell him a clinical problem has arisen, and I have to stay. Hah," he snorted, "if it's not biochemistry, he's not interested."

The X-ray technician arrived with the portable apparatus for the chest film, and gave everyone a respite. Essai went out to call Mrs. Kraft. Three years in the department, he had never met her. Halfway through dialing, he realized he did not know how to tell her.

"Dr. Kraft's residence." Soft, reserved voice.

"Mrs. Kraft?"

"Yes?"

Essai cleared his throat. "Mrs. Kraft, this is Dr. Essai, Andrew Essai, calling from the Medical Center. I'm an instructor in your husband's department."

"Is he all right?" How fast she had caught his tone.

"Well, he had some chest pain in his office, and we've put him to bed here in the hospital."

"Heart attack?"

"Well—"

Her voice was trembling, but insistent. "Is he in any danger right now?"

Essai wiped his forehead. "We don't think so, but it might be good for you to come down here."

"Tell him I'm leaving now."

"Wait, Mrs. Kraft. Please drive slowly. He's doing fine, and the pain's gone." Essai hurried to reassure her; he knew with what disregard anguished relatives drove to a hospital.

She was calm. "Thank you, Dr. Essai. I'll be careful."

"Six North. I'll wait here to meet you."

"Thank you." She hung up and Essai looked at the phone. What kind of person married Dr. Kraft?

He went down to X-ray and waited till the chest film came through, looked at it carefully, made sure there was no collapsed lung or wedged-shaped infarct of the lung. Then he sent the technician home. Waiting for the elevator to go to 6 North, he remembered that Judy would be at the apartment, checking the time angrily and selecting her choice of weapons. Well, he thought ruefully, she would probably have till midnight to get herself ready. He knew he could not leave until the patient was stable, till the period of possible shock or life-threatening rhythm disturbance was over.

The chief of anesthesia sat in a straight-back chair outside the room, fiddling with the endotracheal tube and waiting almost nonchalantly. Essai saw him and felt relieved. If the damaged heart stopped, or began to fibrillate in rapid, ineffective quivers, any of them could beat on the chest, electrically shock the heart to help restore normal rhythm. But they needed an airway, a tube into the trachea at once, lest in the rigors of the disturbed rhythm the patient choke, or his tongue fall back, or a seizure cause his breathing to cease. So Dr. Malatesta sat quietly holding the tube, pretending not to listen to the cardiac monitor just inside the door, though any long pause or series of rapid beats would propel him into the room.

"Dr. Malatesta, it looks all right now. He had just a few premature beats. It looks like a pretty mild infarct."

Malatesta nodded at Essai. "I'll stay out here for a couple of hours." He still had on his blue scrub suit from the day's surgical cases on which he assisted, but he would stay all night if necessary. He patted his pocket and felt the plastic container of green digitalis pills. Kraft's name was on the prescription; he had cared for Malatesta's rheumatic heart disease for ten years.

Winston stood inside the door watching the monitor. He circled his thumb and forefinger, smiling, telling Essai that the rhythm was normal. Kraft heard the step, however, and awoke. "Ruth?"

"No, it's me, Essai."

Kraft scratched the gray hairs on his chest. Again, as in his office, Essai was mildly shocked at seeing them. Kraft was his boss, the master clinician, not a patient.

"Listen, Essai, I've been thinking about my conference rounds tomorrow."

"The conference? We'll call it off, of course," he said easily.

Kraft roared. "Like hell you will! It's mine; I decide what we do with it." He glared at Essai.

Four syncopated beeps sounded. Essai and Winston each took a step, and Essai saw a scrub-suited leg come around the corner.

The rhythm reverted to normal. Malatesta did not come into the room. Essai reached for Kraft's pulse anyway, unwilling to believe the auditory evidence. Kraft looked pale, but said, "It's all right. Two sets of coupled beats are nothing. But if it's six or eight, get some lidocaine in here and make sure that bastard Malatesta is around."

"Yes, sir."

Kraft sniffed. "Now, where were we?"

Essai was afraid to say the words "your talk at rounds tomorrow"; he was losing his confidence.

George Winston stepped up, easy and calm. "Matthew, it's time to get some rest."

Kraft waved him off. "In a minute. I remember now—I'm deciding about rounds."

Winston said, "If I could be of any help—"

Kraft stared at him, then smiled. "Yes, my wife will be here soon. Could you wait outside and kind of prepare her?"

It was not the answer Winston had expected. "Of course," he said quietly, and walked outside.

Kraft watched Essai, waiting for Winston's footsteps to fade. Then he motioned Essai over. "Listen," he whispered urgently. Essai had never heard him whisper, and straightened up. Kraft took his arm and spoke low, rushed. "Listen. Winston belongs over at the Metropolitan General, not here. He's chief there, and professor, but I know he'd love to get this department. Well it's my department, Essai, and my rounds. Don't let him get near those conference rounds tomorrow."

"I—"

"Shut up and listen." Kraft held on to him and stared into Essai's eyes. Essai thought his soul was being looked for, though in retrospect, it was Kraft's being shown.

"No one else has given those cardiac conferences in eighteen years, and I'd rather have my lab technician talk than let an outsider take it all away. Essai, you have Miss Graf get you the tape of my Bolliston lecture of the year before last. It's on the production of heart sounds and murmurs. You announce that I've been hospitalized with chest discomfort. Don't say 'pain,' and say, 'a mild heart attack has not been ruled out, but seems unlikely.' Say it just like that. Then play the tape. It goes for about an hour. Then you and Lerner and Pruden answer any questions about my talk. That's how I want it, Essai. If by next Friday I can't give my own rounds," he hesitated, blinked twice, and nodded, "then we will see. All right, Essai? I'm counting on you."

"Yes, sir."

Kraft took a deep breath. "Make sure I get morphine every four hours. I still have some pain. And don't send Malatesta home before midnight." Kraft winced and furrowed his brow. "Have the nurse come in. Is morphine every three hours too often?"

Suddenly Essai's eyes filled with tears. He turned his head and walked out, saying quickly, "I'll get it now."

Essai stood at the nurses' desk, watching Winston talk to Mrs. Kraft. She had come off the elevator as the nurse left Dr. Kraft's room, and after five or ten minutes alone with her husband, she was introduced to George Winston. Essai could hear him, sympathetic and careful, a good physician.

"—If he does all right tonight, we can expect a smooth course, though it'll be six or eight weeks before he's back to normal."

"In the hospital?" She seemed horrified.

"No, no. Three weeks or four here, and then rest at home." Winston motioned to Essai. "Dr. Essai will be in close touch as well." Tactfully he said, "You have met Dr. Essai before?"

"No, I don't believe so. How long have you been in my husband's department?"

"Three years, Mrs. Kraft." He shook the dry hand, and looked at the oval face, gray-streaked hair.

She smiled. "Goodness, we should have met by this time. Well, my husband asked me to thank you for being here, for offering to take care of him. He has confidence in both of you as physicians," she concluded.

The mild professor and the instructor stared at each other for a moment. They both knew that Matthew Kraft was incapable of such a gracious statement. For his part, Essai was doubly astonished, bracketed as an equal with the chief at the Metropolitan, George Winston.

She saw their look. "And I know that both of you will respond to his needs." An iron edge weighted her voice.

Winston nodded his head shyly. "Of course we will, Mrs. Kraft."

"Dr. Essai," she said, "my husband is sleeping. Is there somewhere nearby I could sit, an empty room or something?"

Essai went to the desk, and came back shaking his head. "I'm sorry, but all the rooms are full. The only possible place is in the treatment room, across from the nurses' station." He pointed to a dark door diagonally across the hall.

"That's fine."

Essai got the key and opened the door. The only chair was the chair in which vital capacity measurements were done. It was a huge, cracked, white enamel chair. Essai saw her start when she saw it.

"I'll get you another chair out of one of the rooms," he said quickly. "That one is for patients to sit in when their capacity to breathe is measured."

"No, this enamel chair is fine." She pointed to the metal kymograph. "Don't you cover that with carbon paper and then the needle traces a record of the patient's breathing?"

"Yes," said Essai, surprised. "Are you in the medical field yourself?"

She smiled at him. "No, not really. But I was once in a medical experiment and sat in such a chair."

"Well, Mrs. Kraft, you can stay here all night if you want. I'll be here for several hours yet."

"Fine," she said. Essai left, and she sat down in the enamel chair. She looked out the window, expecting to see an incendiary sunset, but it was already dark.

For the next few hours as Ruth Kraft sat and remembered the life they had shared, her husband lay in the drugged and thus fearless darkness, permitting the morphine to move him freely from one association to the next. On waking after short periods of sleep, first came the awareness of the strap on his chest, the monitor, Essai thin and bent in the chair at the window, Malatesta outside, and Ruth somewhere close by. All were meant to give him reassurance and none did. They were symbols of scientific order or emotional concern, and Kraft felt that his fate for the next few days rested elsewhere.

Nor did the next point touched mean much, the quick mental recitation of his past life. Even with morphine, he viewed his *curriculum vitae* as something akin to a particularly good growth stock, full of rises, expansions, and increases. Then the reciting mind turned from victories to a catalogue of factors inciting his heart attack, and he could easily imagine a blackboard with the reasons listed. Half a million cigarettes, heavy meals, nights in the study, the exhilarating tensions of one clinical crisis after another, the lack of exercise, rest, vacations. He saw them in chalky clarity.

"A new heart," he thought easily. "New heart, new start." He meant to smile at his silly rhyme, but drifted to sleep instead. Dreamily he saw the chalked indictments on the left-hand side of the board, and a shimmering, developing, embryonic heart on the right. Like a student he watched the demonstration film, one chamber to two, development of septum primum and secundum, thickening heart walls, elongation of pink, patent coronary arteries.

"New heart." He was awake again. Essai stirred in the chair. Had he whispered it or said it aloud? Kraft sighed against the chest strap and washed the board clean. He read the few key words on prognosis for him: Initial Recovery; Risk of Recurrent Angina; Recurrent Infarct; Constant Danger of Sudden Death. "Wait," he said to the lengthening list, "I can change the way I live." He had said it often in lectures. "After a heart attack a man can live a very long time if he changes the way he does things."

Kraft blinked, wide awake, and tried to make the blackboard disappear, but the words wrote themselves: "If the country's outstanding cardiologist changes the way he does things, he will not long remain so." God, it was true, true, new. "I need a new heart." How? Ream out his clogged coronary arteries? Impossible. Transplant? He smiled to himself, but he was already trying to recall what he knew about Barnard's cases, Shumway's. He had always dismissed reports of new surgical techniques with the phrase, "more stethoscopes, not scalpels." Even surgeons who replaced hearts were written off as glamour boys.

He looked over at Essai, dozing. Young man, perfect heart. Malatesta outside, bad rheumatic heart. Wife Ruth, fluttering, feminine, flowing, flowery . . . again he fell asleep. After the next injection of morphine, his waking dreams converged again. Every vital organ in him was normal, and his brain remarkable. Scour the literature, find the surgeon, take the chance, and be a new man, or better and more truly, the same man with a new heart. Kraft sighed, felt more than heard the regular monitor, and eased into the coddling warmth of sleep.

By the age of twenty-five, Ruth Sherman had learned how to balance an extraordinary intelligence with primary feeling responses, and possibly because the balance was reflected as loving kindness and grace, she was the most sought-after woman in Cleveland, Ohio. Women with more glamour hated her, and intellectual companions secretly regarded her as simpleminded, since they invariably misread her naturalness and simplicity. The eligible young men of Cleveland loved her and pursued her, from the library at Flora Stone Mather through Polish restaurants on the West Side to the perfumed corridors of Severance Hall at intermission. As a group they were thinkers and discussers, and the intellectual women could never understand how her phrase, "I liked the music," sufficed for concert-going dates who could spend hours dissecting the performance, and usually did. Glamorous women snickered at her long straight hair, the absence of makeup, the disinterest in all but the simplest clothes, yet she moved easily in a world of beauty, their private domain but her real home. Ruth Sherman felt about marriage as she did about life—it was to be taken with an informed celebration of feeling, or not at all. In a period of four years, however, she deflected offers of marriage from several men, and she began to wonder if the celebration were to be private forever.

Had she met Matthew Kraft, the research cardiologist, at a party, she would have smiled pleasantly after a few moments of friendly conversation, excused herself politely, and moved on. Scientists were as calibrated as their tools, and she avoided them completely. How ironic, then, that their first meeting started as no more than a scientific experiment.

A friend of hers, Althea Carr, was a medical student at

44

Western Reserve, at a time when women rarely began in medicine and never finished in it. Althea had volunteered to have her arterial blood studied just before and after breathing varying amounts of oxygen, and the tall husky doctor with black hair drew her blood expertly at five-minute intervals, made sure she felt well after the experiment was concluded, and handing her the fifty-dollar check, asked her to send other female volunteers to his laboratory. Althea met Ruth Sherman two nights later at a Budapest String Quartet concert. Both of them introduced their dates, and Althea burst out that she was treating her fiancé to the concert, courtesy of Dr. Kraft.

"You mean courtesy of your own blood," her date broke in.

"It was nothing," said Althea. "Ruth, you should volunteer for his study. He has the black science eyes, asking you how you feel in little asides. What he really watches is the color of the blood. It's really an experience, and besides," she concluded, "it's fifty dollars honestly earned."

"Selling your body again, eh girl?" Her date intoned the words ghoulishly and they all laughed.

"I'd like to try it," said Ruth. "It's not dangerous, is it?"

"No, just three needle sticks and breathing fast for about fifteen minutes."

Althea's date motioned to Harold Enright, a young lawyer fortunate to see Ruth for an evening. "Hal," he said, "only women are paid fifty dollars for breathing fast for short periods of time."

Harold smirked and pressed Ruth's arm. "I would gladly pay," he said.

During the Mozart that followed intermission, Ruth decided to let Harold squeeze arms elsewhere, and she began to think of volunteering, not because she needed the money—though it would help—but to be part of a scientific study. She called the medical school the next day, Friday, and three hours later, with the September sun shrugging off the day, she sat quietly in a plain enamel chair listening to the doctor. He was tall, about six three, husky as an athlete, with surprisingly thin hands that moved with unwasted precision. As he talked, he set up the rows of tubes and checked the equipment.

"Miss Sherman," he said evenly, "this experiment is not dangerous for you, and I am paying you simply because most people do not freely give blood samples to doctors, nor do they enjoy the sense of breathlessness at the end of the breathing experiment. I want you to understand that the high price is not related to any danger to the volunteer."

"I understand." She watched him, fascinated. He was the ultimate scientist.

"When I hold up one finger," he explained, "you are to breathe deeply and rapidly until I put it down. You may feel light-headed, but only for a moment. I will draw the blood after one minute, during which you breathe in time to my hand hitting the table. Then we will repeat the same thing three times after you breathe from the mouthpiece in front of you. The cardiogram will record your heartbeat throughout. If while breathing from the mouthpiece you feel dizzy, raise your right hand. Then you can stop and rest and we'll try it again."

"Fine."

"Now let me check the cardiogram straps." When he was near her, tightening the bands on wrists and ankles, she was aware of his immensity, his compulsion. He seemed absolutely sure of himself, but only at the expense of depersonalization; she half expected to see him plug his finger into the wall.

"Could I ask a question, Dr. Kraft?"

"Yes?"

"Would you rather work with male or female volunteers, that is, do men cooperate better with instructions?" She added the last clause from embarrassment, though the question was meant to break up the man, if only momentarily, into his separate dehumanized parts and, perhaps, the one or two fragments of humanity. She expected him to blush, or draw back, since he was holding her left ankle as he applied some lubricant under the strap. Instead he went on, without a hint of pause.

"For significant data, I need twenty studies with men and twenty with women. Most of the men were medical students; you are the eighteenth woman."

"Oh. I have never been referred to as 'the eighteenth woman.'"

The sun ignited the southwestern clouds and set. Dr. Kraft turned on the light, checked his tubes, and held up a finger.

Ruth Sherman obediently breathed fast and hard, thinking "deep" "deep" "deep" with each breath in and out. She became momentarily dizzy and Dr. Kraft, watching her intently, shouted, "Slow down a bit," and as she did, the dizziness passed. As the minute was up he said, "Follow me," and his hand slammed—slammed—in slow, perfect cadence, and she followed him, nearly ecstatic at his imperative command. It was as though the hand were rising and falling of its own, and her lungs were wired to it, expanding as contact was made. She felt her heart pounding with excitement, not effort, and tried to calm herself, aware of the cardiograph needle jerking, and fearful that her desire—for now it was desire— would be visible to any casual reader of the printed strip.

"Stop." The hand stopped and she did, and Dr. Kraft set another stopwatch going, wound a tourniquet tight around her arm, and drove the needle into her right brachial artery. She did not watch the spurting red column in the syringe but rather his face, and while the brief pain lasted she bit the edge of her lip and stared at his intense face. He said, "Since you have been hyperventilating, you may not feel the need to breathe at all during the rest periods. Please hold your breath until I take the needle out. Then you can do what you want till the next phase of the experiment starts." His voice was level and even, and his total preoccupation excited her even more. I am his captive; he is in fact taking my breath away; he is sucking my blood. The needle came out, Dr. Kraft took a step to his right and quickly scanned the running cardiogram strip. "He sees my heart, he will know my soul," she thought, and seeing his thin hands slide along the paper, she felt herself fondled, exposed, aroused. She clenched the cool white enamel arm rests and let go.

"Are you all right, Miss Sherman? Your heart rate is rather fast."

She smiled. "Fine. Tell me what to do next."

"All right. Another fifteen seconds and you breathe in the oxygen through that mouthpiece. Start when I tell you." He checked one watch, stopped it, and commanded her, "Breathe." She put the soft rubber mouthpiece into her mouth and breathed as deeply as she could. He came toward her and she heard his voice from a distance, as though she were awakening: "I'm going to put this rubber clamp on your nose so you continue to mouth-breathe." She nodded, slightly dizzy again. "Easy," he said calmly. He stepped to the kymograph, the slowly rotating drum fitted with carbon paper on which a needle connected to the tubing wrote a record of her respiration. After a few seconds, it seemed to her, he said, "Now follow my hand again, and breathe only when it hits the table. Start." The autonomous hand slammed rhythmically and she sucked in the air with measured ecstasy. "Stop." The hand stopped again, disappointingly, and she sat without breathing, waiting for the needle plunge. He took the nasal clamp off, and unwrapped a new syringe and needle. When he leaned over and it came in, she shuddered and he looked quickly at her. "Are you all right?"

His scientist's eyes showed professional concern, and the realization that his only interest in her was as the eighteenth female donor of breath and blood gave her the freedom to respond as she wanted to. "Dr. Kraft," she murmured, "I have never felt better."

He looked over again, grunted, walked to the cardiogram and held her heart in his hands once more. "Now we will start the second of three runs, this time with slightly less oxygen. By the way, you can take a breath if you want."

"What?"

"You haven't breathed for a minute. It's perfectly normal,

of course," he explained. "After hyperventilating you could sit without the urge to take a breath for five minutes or so. Now get comfortable and when I say so, fix the nasal clamp and breathe into the mouthpiece."

"Get comfortable" he had said. She moved her legs slightly and was astonished to feel a slippery wetness inside her thighs. She blushed for the first time in her life. Dr. Kraft stared at her, and as he started to ask again, "Are you all right?" she shook her head in assent and said, "I feel fine, doctor, honestly." During the next period of breathing and slamming ecstasy, she felt more than thought: I want to have an affair with him. No emotion on his part, no marriage on mine. But I want this machine to make me submit. The thought made her heart rate rise again, and glancing sideways at the cardiogram strip, now touching the floor and arcing hugely, she saw the inverted Vs of her heartbeat run closer together. "Stop thinking," she told herself, and she succeeded in making herself as utterly personless as the chair, the rotating black drum, the man with black hair.

Somewhere, far away, a door opened and closed and the intimacy she had sensed so acutely began to break up, even before she heard the other man's voice. When it came, rigid, narrow and Germanically accented, the fine mist of responsiveness and desire was swept away, and she found herself sitting in a hard enamel chair breathing in time to a doctor's command.

"Dr. Kraft, what is going on here?"

"Excuse me, sir, just a moment. Now, miss, stop breathing *NOW*." The hand stopped and she watched him ready the syringe. He fumbled for a moment with the needle. The tourniquet was too tight, and her right arm felt quite painful. Finally Dr. Kraft took off the tourniquet, and said to her in a low voice, "Once more, Miss Sherman, and we're all done."

"Dr. Kraft, are you deaf? Please turn toward me."

"Just one moment, please, Dr. Lippschitz, until I cap this needle."

A medium-sized man with a face the color of dirty sand

came into Ruth's view, and a hand reached across her to click off the kymograph. The sleeve and starched cuff nearly touched her face on the way back. "Excuse me, miss." Whether the excuse was for what had just happened or what was about to come, Ruth Kraft, neé Sherman, never decided. Matthew Kraft took a single step toward the kymograph, but Dr. Lippschitz barred his way. "Please, just a few more minutes and I will have finished the experiment." There was a note of urgency in Dr. Kraft's voice, almost a warning. "Wait here, Miss Sherman, we'll resume in a moment."

"You will not resume." Each word rose half a note, and the older doctor actually clenched his fist for emphasis. The scene was satiric, farcical, but Dr. Kraft was undergoing a strange transformation, and Ruth sensed that no matter how ridiculous the two of them looked—Dr. Kraft knotting his black eyebrows and scowling; the older man Prussian, dictatorial and seemingly frightened—they were engaged in a scene of confrontation whose genesis spanned months or years, and they were implacable adversaries.

"Dr. Lippschitz, if I get one more blood sample on this volunteer, the study will be over, and with two more—"

"This study is over. There will be no more volunteers." The German voice was final, unyielding.

Dr. Kraft looked at Ruth, but focused on a point past her. Whether he was hesitating or planning his tactics was for the moment unclear.

"Matthew, I have received no sign that you hear me."

Dr. Kraft made a kind of shrugging motion with his shoulders and casually turned off the cardiogram. Ruth instinctively put a hand to her breast to see if her heart was still beating. Dr. Kraft observed her and smiled absently. He had his back to the other man. "I think we should discuss this, Dr. Lippschitz, perhaps in your office," Kraft said evenly.

"Look at me when you speak to me," snapped Lippschitz.

Before her eyes, Ruth saw her lover's face hood over, the shoulders hunch up. His head lowered inch by inch and his features became distorted by terrifying anger. Had Dr. Kraft donned a mask he would not have appeared more strange to her.

He wheeled. "Dr. Lippschitz, you have no right to ruin my study and interfere with my research. I tried to discuss the matter with you when you cut off my funds for volunteers after the twentieth one. I explained that no journal would accept a paper based on such a small group. When you refused I paid the volunteers myself, and I do the work after the regular day ends. You must permit me to continue, or explain your arbitrary and ruthless decision, that is, if you understand the reason yourself." Dr. Kraft finished breathlessly, as though being allowed to finish was an unexpected surprise.

"Is that all, *scheisskerl?*"

"What?"

Dr. Lippschitz bowed to Ruth Sherman, sitting motionless. "My dear lady, excuse me for using that word in your presence." Ruth Sherman would have laughed out loud at the incredible parody of graciousness and breeding the German doctor displayed, except for the look on his face.

"Dr. Lippschitz, you must explain your actions."

Dr. Lippschitz was still inclined forward, bowing to her, with pursed lips suggesting a benediction. As he straightened, his lips opened and widened in a travesty of a smile, and the off-color face turned to Dr. Kraft. "Dr. Kraft," he began softly, "you are my employee. I pay you, provide laboratory space for you, assign patients to you on whom you practice—and I mean 'practice'—your scanty medical skill, and as you know I am directly responsible for the research you carry out. Ahh, ahh," he raised a forefinger as the young man prepared to speak, "I repeat, in case you were unable to grasp what I said, that you are an employee and I can hire you, give you new duties at different pay," he hesitated, "or fire you, dismiss you, and see to it that you never again receive a position in hospital medicine." His voice was much higher and louder. "So think over what you say, lest you cut your throat with your own tongue."

"I do not mean to insult you, sir."

Oh no, thought Ruth, the threat has got to him.

Lippschitz literally smacked his lips. "That's better. Now perhaps you will pay the volunteer fee to this young lady, who has been sitting patiently, and I must say obtaining a view of the younger men at the Cleveland City Hospital that is quite distorted, though the example she has seen is a—ah—shall we say, an unrepresentative one." Herman Lippschitz paused and inclined his head toward her again. "Then, Matthew, perhaps you can frame your questions to me in a somewhat more acceptable fashion."

Ruth stared at Dr. Kraft who was still hunched a little. None of the three of them knew what he would do. Then he said, "As I mentioned before, sir, I do not mean to insult you."

"Quite so."

"There is one point, though, where you could help me understand something." Kraft's voice was low, docile, harmless.

"Yes? I'll try to make you understand. What is it?"

The voice became quieter. "Why do you undermine my research?"

Herman Lippschitz hesitated a second. Then he laughed. "Hah, hah, hah; Matthew Kraft, I believe you're acting a bit paranoid. Yes, I believe you are. Here you are in a well-equipped laboratory, quite nearly better than mine, well-lit, well-heated, with an abundance of glassware, electricity, and the privilege of pursuing cardiac research under one of the best men in the Middle West, perhaps even the country. That is quite sufficient, it would seem." Here Lippschitz paused, as though to drink some water. "But, as you well know, my dear Kraft, I am also a consulting editor for the *American Heart Journal* and *Circulation Abstracts*, and if you remember correctly, I suggested that if the results of our work on the heart and oxygen saturation are worthwhile, then I would do what I could to place a nice abstract in *Circulation Abstracts*. So," he made a gesture to Ruth Sherman as though she were a debate judge, "it seems that not only have you no reason to act in such an improper and ungentlemanly manner as to insult your superior with the phrase 'undermine research,' but in fact I would think it right for you to offer apology and thanks, apology for your ill-considered remark, and thanks for the opportunity I have given you."

During these remarks, Kraft's face showed a range of emotion from anger to bemused attention and Ruth was struck with the absolute awareness and feeling that she loved Matthew Kraft. As a scientist, plunging and controlled, he could have been a thrilling lover for her, but he was also a man of feeling and responsiveness, as she now saw, and through the terrible anger and hostility that shortly filled the room, her love for him covered and warmed her.

The bemused, bent man scratched his head. "Do you wish my apology and thanks now, sir?"

Lippschitz closed his eyes for a moment and extended his right hand, benignly.

"First," said Dr. Kraft, "I would like to thank you. In these last five years you have taught me a great deal of internal medicine and especially cardiology, and though my natural inclinations are not toward clinical medicine, I feel adequately prepared to see sick patients, when the occasion arises. I also thank you for keeping my clinical duties to a minimum, since you know I am particularly drawn to laboratory research, and my efforts in this area, small as they are, would be much less if I did not have ample time to do research."

"Continue, Matthew." Lippschitz' smile nearly shut his eyes.

"I must also offer you an apology, if I may make a prefatory remark first."

"Of course, Matthew, I am a reasonable man."

Kraft stood up straight. "Until recently, my research was primarily pathologic research on the conduction paths of impulses through the heart. Without your help I could not have done the dissections." He spoke as though from a text.

"Here I must interrupt you, Matthew, to say that my skill

in this area is directly due to my years of training at the Krankenhaus in Munich under the late Professor von Koppenhagen, perhaps the greatest of the pathologic anatomists."

"Yes, sir." Kraft cleared his throat, and there was silence for five or six heartbeats. "In the last year I have begun to study not the pathology of dead hearts but the work of living hearts. You provided me with the special equipment to do this work, and it is proceeding quite well. You suggested I study twenty volunteers and write an abstract for *Circulation Abstracts*. As you know, I had strong feelings about studying an additional twenty volunteers to expand the scope of the paper and submitting the article to the *American Heart Journal* or to *Medicine*. Now I owe you the apology. Until a few moments ago, when you were talking, I did not realize an important fact, and I apologize for not realizing it."

"Yes?" Lippschitz nodded expectantly.

"I apologize for overlooking your blindness."

"What? *Was?*"

"Your blindness, sir. I am truly sorry."

"But Matthew, what is this? You are making a little joke."

"No, sir."

Lippschitz sensed it coming, but his curiosity was too great. "Well, explain yourself."

"I will, but let me finish, Dr. Lippschitz."

"Go on. Let us go into your office." They edged to the office like wary jousters, without a word to Ruth Sherman, who sat motionless in the enamel chair. They closed the door, but the building was silent and as Kraft's voice grew louder it seemed he was addressing a crowd from an alcove.

"My research produced unexpectedly good results, proving that the cardiac output rises to keep pace with increased oxygen needs, and does so within a very few beats. Further, as you know, I have shown that decreasing oxygen in mild degree does not significantly alter the work of the heart. These two points, if well documented, would be a real contribution to a basic understanding of cardiac mechanisms. In short, it is an original contribution, not the journeyman work of a clerk. You are blind, sir, in both eyes as it were: in one, because you fail to see that research today is increasingly directed at analysis of mechanism, not description of end results; and you are blind secondly, and more importantly, because you would suppress research in your laboratory that strikes out in new directions. In fact, you are trying to do that to me. You cannot bury me in *Circulation Abstracts,* and if you block me when I apply to other journals, I—I, I will go to the trustees of the medical school and explain what you have done."

Lippschitz's voice was high, screeching. "*Gott in Himmel,* listen to this crazy man. I know what you want, Kraft. You want to be recognized as a great new research genius today, and as the outstanding assistant professor tomorrow, and head of a department of cardiology next week. You tell me that you are the vanguard of the 'new wave' and I should recognize that. Hah! You said before you had done the research of a clerk. I can tell you why, Kraft. You *are* a clerk. You walk through the wards in a daze, as though the sick patients frightened you. I see you seek out the safety of the laboratory, where sick people make no demands, where families of sick patients will not find you and beg you to do more to heal the patient. I told you to spend the days on the wards and work in the laboratory at other times for a good reason, and not the one you say. It was to make you adequate to call yourself a doctor."

"I don't believe that." Kraft's voice was tremulous. "What you say may be true; that I prefer the laboratory to the wards."

"Of course it is true," cried Lippschitz.

Silence. Then Kraft bellowed, "But that's not the issue. The issue is this: are you afraid to see my research accepted as something new, and would you use your influence to keep me from seeking my own level in research medicine?"

"After this outburst, Kraft?"

"No, goddamnit, no. Before this. At the point when you said twenty volunteers were enough. Why did you stop me then?"

"I did not stop you. As your superior I oversee your research, and you are wasting time and money on an effort that at best can be of only mild interest." Lippschitz was trying to dismiss it.

"Dr. Lippschitz, will you let me submit my work to the *American Heart Journal* and see what happens?"

"Of course not."

"Why not?" Kraft barked it out.

"Because, my impudent young friend, I am not an instructor as you are, unconcerned with reputation and ready to publish a preliminary study as though it were a book in the Bible. I am Herman Lippschitz, a man who was invited to join the editorial boards of two respected journals, to whom fifty or more young men write each year asking for a position in the laboratory or on the wards. Patients come to me from all over Ohio and occasionally from much farther away, and I chair meetings of the national heart conferences and examine candidates for eligibility to call themselves cardiologists."

The voice became triumphant as Lippschitz made his point. "Can you imagine for a moment that I would endanger my reputation, or that of my laboratory, by allowing the impetuous work of a nearly unbalanced young instructor to be challenged by the readers of such a paper? They would laugh at *me* for being so foolish as to allow your paper, with my name on it, I might add, to be submitted to one of the bigger journals. Kraft, you are a naïve young man, and I am surprised at you."

"I know of your influence, Dr. Lippschitz, and I came here originally because of your reputation in the field. But I find myself bound to do things as *you* want, at a time when I have ideas of my own. The research on the work of the heart is good. I will submit it myself, if you do not advance it for me." He was defiant.

"You will not." The German accent added force to the words.

"I will."

"Kraft. I am not a vengeful man. I urge you to avoid a step that will ruin your career. I think the research shows promise, and in a few years may have matured into something really good."

"A few years?"

"As I said, you cannot be an assistant professor tomorrow. Now we will submit your work as an abstract, and I will guide you along a slightly altered path, and perhaps in a year or so you will have a fine paper for the *Pathologic Reviews.*"

"No, no, no!" Kraft shouted.

Lippschitz' German flooded out. *"Sei still.* Be quiet; you have exhausted my patience. If you submit an article over my head I will see to it that you never again hold a position in research medicine in this country. I can do it. And incidentally, your usefulness here will come to an abrupt halt."

"Is that all, sir?"

"That is all. Oh no, just one more bit of advice—one you may not want to hear, but which I know is the truth. No matter how hard you work, no matter how diligently you study, even if you should abjure research for the bedside, your ultimate goal will not be reached. Listen to me, Kraft . . ." Ruth Sherman strained to hear the voice of the old doctor, but the last comment was whispered and she could not hear it. It must have been the phrase, "You are doomed to mediocrity," for Matthew mentioned it that night, and he sometimes doodled the phrase, or parts of it, in succeeding years. She would find it scribbled on scraps of paper in his study on nights after long days when he still had work to do, and said, "I think I'm too tired to work tonight." Invariably he stayed up late and did the work, and in the morning she found the crumpled scraps. Without knowing it, Lippschitz had given him the motto that spurred him to extraordinary achievements in the years that followed.

Kraft had gone with Lippschitz into his office an aroused but unself-conscious and confident scientist; he came out a struggling doctor. Lippschitz swept by the two of them, pausing only to glance at the half-completed kymograph reading with infinite contempt. He left, slamming the laboratory door so that the enamel chair vibrated, and the two people remaining in the room moved to one another as though to ward off the still inanimateness around them. Ruth did not know what to say to the man in the starched laboratory coat who stood with his hands in his pockets. He looked scared and empty, but not empty as though something had been drained; rather some strong substance inside him had been chemically neutralized, or burned off. The struggle was entirely silent, and as though badly set gears were straining to move equally against one another, there was a deceptive sense of no motion. Kraft had set his shocked eyes on a middle point between himself and the woman and his hands-in-pocket stance seemed uncharacteristic and stiff—he was as fixed in position as his equipment. Ruth waited for the natural response that had always been hers, and when it did not come to her, she prayed for it, to help this man whom she loved return to life, no matter what that return meant to her.

She stood up, and without taking a step, touched his arm with her hand. "Let's get something to eat, Dr. Kraft."

He looked at her as though she had just come into the room. "What do you want?" he asked blankly.

"I have been here the whole time, Dr. Kraft. I heard everything. I think we should leave the laboratory and get something to eat."

"All right." He turned as though to begin cleaning up, but made the faintest shrugging motion and kept his hands inside his pockets. "Get the jacket out of my office," he mumbled. Ruth went quickly into the small office. Chemical charts and carefully plotted curves with legends filled the walls; a formless wool jacket hung over the back of the chair. She brought it out, and they walked to the door of the lab. He said, "Excuse me," in a polite voice and turned out the light. In the darkness she heard his hands move to unbutton the lab coat, and it fell crackling to the floor. Then he reached toward her and she felt his smooth fingers brush her cheek. "Excuse me," he said again, and he moved his hand down to hers, took the jacket from her hand and put it on. They walked down the inky hall, and she brushed against him continuously, hoping that he knew where steps were and would not kill both of them out of plan or omission. "Is there a light?" she asked, whispering.

"Yes. Wait here." He lit a match and she saw that they were two steps from a flight of stairs leading down. The match went out. Ruth said loudly, "Matthew Kraft, find the light switch."

"Certainly," he said, and a moment later the hall was flooded with light from ill-covered bulbs set every forty feet or so along the ceiling.

"Is there an elevator?"

"Of course," he said, surprised. "What are we doing taking the stairs? The elevator is the other way."

She smiled with relief. "Let's hurry," she said. "I'm getting hungry."

Safely down, they left the research buildings and passed into the hazy nostalgic air of late September. She led the way, past the old buildings of the clinical wing and the ugly administrative hulk. They walked on, toward downtown Cleveland, without touching or talking, like the oldest of friends. After they had walked two miles, Ruth recognized the buildings of the West Side and the smell of Middle-European cooking. She had no idea what to do with the man at her side who obviously let her manage for both of them, but his dependence made her strong. That there was the slightest connection between the slamming, moistening scientist's hand of two hours ago and that of the manchild accompanying her now was truly unbelievable. A few blocks ahead was the corner of Euclid and Fortieth, and if she were not mistaken, the Lischuk Café was only a block or so along Euclid.

"Dr. Kraft, how would you like some Hungarian cooking? Nothing fancy, but good. They probably have roast duck, very crispy, with noodle pudding. How does that sound?"

"Fine, that's fine. Are you from Cleveland, knowing your way around the city like this?" He sounded like a tourist.

"Yes, I was born here. Were you?"

"Yes." She saw the big man shake his head. "No, no, what am I saying? I was born in Hartford, Connecticut. Now it's been rezoned and they call it West Hartford, but the streets look just as dirty when I see them now as before."

"Oh? I was never in Hartford. Excuse me, I think we turn right here to get to Lischuk's." They went on, talking animatedly about Hartford, the fine fall weather, the advantages of duck over goose, and the difficulties inherent in living in a large city. One could see they were a well-matched couple; he perhaps an inch too tall for her, rather big-boned, and she a bit too concerned about his reactions to the mildest statements. But they were engrossed in each other's presence, and the dining couples in Lischuk's looked at the smiling man and woman with envy as they entered.

An hour later, Kraft finished his third helping of noodle pudding and gazed over his napkin at the slim woman watching him. He cleared his throat. "My name is Matthew Kraft," he said. "And yours . . ."

"Ruth Sherman. I work for the *Plain Dealer*. I went to Flora Stone Mather, that's at Reserve, and then started as kind of a social-news gatherer for the *Plain Dealer*. Now I've moved up, or at least to a different level, where I look over ads and stories and make suggestions to help them along. It's hard to explain, but they think I can tell what people from twenty-five to forty expect to read or see pictured as fashion or vacation sites. So really, all I do is look at an ad and say, 'The shoes should be open-toed,' or 'It might be better for the train traveler to be reading *Life* than the *Post.*'"

"Do they pay you for that?" he asked, amazed.

Her oval face creased, and the warm laugh welled out. "Of course. They pay me quite well, actually, and praise my services, though they can hardly describe my job—they just say I'm an editorial assistant."

"In charge of ambience."

She frowned, but kept the laugh. "That sounds sinister."

"No, not at all." Kraft hurried to correct the impression. "Ambience implies the general environment, the factors that make up a scene. Obviously, not many people can spot false notes. It's quite a skill."

"I guess so. I love music of all kinds, now that you mention notes. I spend as much time at Severence Hall as I do at the paper. Sports are out, unless you count long walks."

"Well," began Kraft, "I can't say I spend more time at concerts than I do in the laboratory. I'm a doctor you know, at the Cleveland City."

"I know," she said, suddenly grave.

"What's wrong, Ruth?" His expression was quizzical for only a moment, then he scowled frighteningly, and finally, the rapids traversed, he shook his head slowly. "Listen to me. Jesus, you must think I'm insane."

She reached quickly and took his hand. Her dark eyes were soft. "I think you're pretty special."

The phrase, her softness, let him out of the box, and he started recalling how it was. " 'I'm a doctor at the City,' I said. Oh Ruth, you should know; your arm is probably still sore from all the needle sticks and blood drawing. Please forgive me, Ruth, for forgetting your name. I was so involved in the work, just a few hours ago, and then the scene with Lippschitz and—"

"Yes?"

"And I guess I forgot that you were there and heard it all. You were so cooperative a volunteer, you know, many people aren't, especially women, when the needle is jammed in and they have to follow my commands to breathe."

Remembering, she was jealous that others had done what she had. But then she sensed, truly felt that other women could not have experienced what she had known that afternoon. For the second time that day she blushed. "I could not have responded the way I did," she said cryptically, "had you not been so detached and efficient. Though I must say I like you just as well over roast duck."

"That's good. I mean it." He squeezed her hand. "Because you'll never see me in the lab like that again."

"Was it me?" she asked, alarmed.

"No," he replied absently. The squeezing pressure tightened and relaxed in consonance with his words. "I'm finished with Lippschitz. He taught me most of what I know, but the idea of returning to work in the lab he lights and heats and equips and runs is simply nauseating to me. And I was right, I know I was, realizing that he sees me as a threat and won't admit it. Or as I said it to him, he is blind to his own attitudes. He told me I was doomed to mediocrity. I can't go back to the lab. And he is just the kind of Prussian who will keep his word about blackening my name everywhere in research if I submit the paper where I want to. I don't know, Ruth; I'm not sure what to do now."

She said nothing, but regarded him with full eyes and listened. When the restaurant closed a half hour later they went out and walked endlessly, hand in hand, and he described his attitude toward research and Lippschitz, the disparity between his growing confidence in the lab and Lippschitz' carping, his feelings of clinical inadequacy and fear of sick patients, his increasing frustration in a profession that seemed to have a niche for everyone but himself.

She was so much in love with him that she did not believe it. That whole evening, until he kissed her under the front porch light as the gray dawn tilted the night, she tried to put her feelings for him into a palpable shape or form that might be removed, examined from a safe distance, and if judged sound, be reinserted, like a key into a lock. But it was precisely her ability to feel instead of think about how she felt that made her unique, and in any case, Matthew Kraft's physical presence and overpowering hold on her made thoughtful introspection impossible. She felt so loving toward him, so concerned for his needs, that she never questioned what had happened. Since she loved him, she could never pity him, and as the chorus of clucking tongues grew to a crescendo in the hospital and outside of it, Matthew Kraft turned to the truest thing he had ever experienced, her love for him, and grew to love it, and then her.

Three weeks later, Kraft took his first vacation in five years, and went to Martha's Vineyard off the Massachusetts coast, ostensibly to think things over in the late New England fall. Each day brought a spectacular blue sky, subtle changes in the October leaves, and an increasing sense of desolation, as though when Kraft stepped off the steamer in Vineyard Haven, the Islanders shipped the last tourists out and retreated into their homes. On his fourth day he walked the nine miles to Edgartown and wired Cleveland, and on the sixth day the steamer docked under the finest sun of all to discharge a single passenger, running from the deck with long hair flying to fall headlong into the arms of the burly man standing at the customs shed. "Why did I wait four days?" he asked her. She put her arms around him and left the ground to kiss him on the lips. "Be thankful it wasn't five," she murmured.

A startled justice of the peace married them that afternoon, the latest in the season he had ever been called, he said. The wedding supper was held in his home, with music provided by the justice's twelve-year-old grandson furiously pedaling a player piano with both hands tight on the seat. The justice took the opportunity to ask the doctor about his wife's chest pains, and after a consultation in the patient's room, with appropriate formality, a cheerful report was issued by the young cardiologist, and a number of glasses of hard cider were consumed to toast the health and happiness of the whole party. The justice's wife rallied sufficiently to join in the last few toasts, and slipped away, returning with a hamper of sandwiches and canned goods, which she presented to the newlyweds as they left for the Edgartown Inn. Matthew and Ruth Kraft were not seen on the street again for a day and a half, and the Islanders commented approvingly that the marriage seemed to be off to an auspicious start.

On New Year's Eve and early New Year's Day, 1942, seven inches of snow fell on most parts of northeastern Ohio, and the trip through Akron, Canton, Genoa (on Route 30), and Massillon took twice as long as Matthew Kraft had figured. But the sun came out just before noon, the roads became slushy, and clumps of wet snow fell heavily from telephone poles and trees overhanging the road. The '38 Ford had little trouble in the slush, yet he drove the last six miles from Massillon to the Magnolia State Hospital at a hesitant pace. He turned off State Highway 21 onto a plowed two-lane road, and the holiday sun reflected dazzlingly off the snow-covered fields and trees.

Kraft shifted into second gear and moved slowly at about twenty miles an hour. He reached over and touched his wife's coat sleeve. "How does it look to you, Ruth?"

"Beautiful, Matt. It feels as though we're driving into the center of a huge lit bowl."

"Hmm. If the directions in the letter are as right, we should see a sign and turn off to the left." He unrolled the window. "Oh, the air smells fresh out here."

"It's wonderful," she said. She watched the speedometer between fifteen and twenty, and shifted her legs away from the heater.

"There it is, up there," her husband said quickly. They drove slowly toward the sign:

MAGNOLIA STATE HOSPITAL

Under it, partially covered with snow:

P. HEINRICHS, SUPT.

Just past the sign the main road curved off to the right, and as though the scene could only now be viewed, they stopped at the fork, and Kraft got out of the car to see where they were.

His breath frosted the air as he surveyed the area. To the right, starting about a hundred yards down the plowed road, the first of several buildings, about the size of large college dormitories, could be seen. He could see three such buildings, and the smoke from the chimneys of two more. The gently sloping, snow-covered fields fell smoothly away toward the west, except for one stubbly with winter wheat under the snow. Five miles away, the smokestacks of the Republic Steel plant in Massillon were holiday-still.

The fork off to the left inclined slightly, and a small cottage sat white and silent on the left-hand side of the road. Smoke rose from the chimney of another building further ahead, but the house was not visible. The sun and snow had rendered everything mute, and Kraft stamped his wet feet in the slush to hear something besides his own breathing. Then he came back to the car. The familiar rusty whine of the starter kicked them back into life. "Ruth, this is it."

She leaned over and kissed his cold face. "I like it," she said happily.

They drove in first gear off to the left, and passed the silent cottage, then came past an open area about two hundred feet wide. Snow fell off two huge oak trees as they passed. A plain brick house under the smoking chimney came into view ahead of them. Near the plowed driveway was a wooden sign under the mailbox—DR. P. HEINRICHS, SUPT. Kraft pulled into the driveway. He rubbed his eyes with both hands. "Wait here," he said to his wife. Then, quickly, he got out of the car and walked up the shoveled front walk.

Before he reached the front door, it opened and a short man holding a pipe and wearing a sweater took a step out, extended his hand and smiled. "I'm Paul Heinrichs, and you must be Dr. Kraft," Ruth heard him say. Her husband shook his hand, and the two men went inside the house. Ruth Kraft picked up Matt's gloves from the seat where he had left them, and held them in her two hands, looking down the clean, sunlit snowfields to her right.

In the living room Kraft sat stiffly and tried not to stare at the face of the man who offered him a cigarette. It was the open face of a sailor, or an outdoor man, full of freckles and creases. But the eyes held Kraft. They were intensely blue, and one could look away from them only with an effort. Dr. Heinrichs filled his pipe and looked at Kraft. "To tell the truth," he began, "I was surprised to get your letter. We started running the ad in November, and when the war started we were sure that there'd be no response to it, what with the doctors getting commissions. You heading for the service soon?"

Matthew Kraft hastened to explain. "No, I'm not. When I was a second-year medical student I had bloody diarrhea for several months, and I finally saw Dr. Jansen in Chicago. He said I had ulcerative colitis, and advised me to watch my diet and see him every six months. After that I had only one more episode, just after my internship started. When I wrote the army, in November, after I was married, I would have volunteered for the medical corps, but they contacted Dr. Jansen and finally said they wouldn't take me."

"I see." Kraft felt the blue eyes boring into him. "Well, I'll tell you a bit about me. I'm fifty-eight, been here eight years, and a widower for ten. No kids. I knew something about hospital administration, and I had run a psychiatric ward in Detroit. The state offers me a pension, and they finally gave me the funds to get a man to help out." He paused. "That means, a man to do a hell of a lot of work. Are you the man, Dr. Kraft?"

"I hope so, sir," Matthew Kraft answered fervently.

"Paul. It's Matthew Kraft, isn't it?"

"Yes."

"Matthew, we run a census here of about four thousand patients. Half of 'em have been here fifteen years and will probably die here, mostly schizophrenics. Neurotic patients with money go to private clinics, but the poor ones, or depressed ones with uncaring families, get sent here. They form about a quarter of the population, and we try to get them out when we can. Then we've got an observation ward, where criminals are sent for us to decide if the state can try them as sane people. A handful of alcoholics and drugs addicts, not many psychopaths. The last thousand of them are old people with cerebral arteriosclerosis, you know, just past the edge a bit and liable to forget to eat, or noisy at night, or confused. They've got all kinds of diseases, some curable, occasionally infectious. We have about four hundred deaths a year."

"Four hundred?"

"Mostly the older arteriosclerotics with heart disease. One or two suicides a month, who get past all of us, nurses and doctors. All we've got to sedate patients with is Luminal. In the winter, some diphtheria and a lot of pneumonia. Oh, I forgot heart disease; about half the deaths get autopsied at the Massillon City Hospital, and a large part of the group show changes of high blood pressure or coronary artery disease."

"I see. Do you send sick patients into Massillon, too?"

"Nope. Just dead ones. The city fathers, or city children I should say, don't want our 'crazies' to contaminate their clean wards. So we have a small building here with about forty beds, and two wonderful nurses. That's where we keep the sickest ones."

"How many other doctors are here?"

Paul Henrichs sucked on his pipe. "Well, I've got two doctors with me, both psychiatrists. One's a drinker, but pretty good, the other one is Romanian and maybe psychotic himself, but he does his work."

"That's it?"

"That's it, Matthew. A man from Ohio State is working with insulin shock therapy, and he spends a month here from time to time. We've got X-ray equipment and a technician, who also does the blood work, but no one to read the X-rays. The state gave us five cardiogram machines last year, four more than we needed, and the Massillon Ladies Club gave us a sixth one last Christmas, and we train the nurses to take the cardiograms, but we kid ourselves about being able to read them. As long as I've started I'll give you all of it. If you come on with us, you'll run the forty-bed ward, of course. Then the nurses, God bless 'em, pick out the other patients who look sick, or whose heart disease is kicking up, and they have a list of patients to be seen. We've got fifteen buildings with patients in them, and probably five or ten people who need to see a medical doctor in each one. When surgical problems arise, we've got a man in Massillon and one in Canton we call, and sometimes they come out and transfer the patient to the hospital, but not all the time. I know it sounds frightening, but that's it. Each year we discharge some patients home, and since I got here, we've had more discharges than deaths. If that's a sign of progress." Paul Heinrichs chuckled wryly.

"It sounds fine," said Kraft. "How about the pay?"

"Yes, the pay. The ad in the *Journal* said 'salary open.' That word 'open' was not my idea. The pay is forty-eight hundred, plus the rent-free cottage down the road. I guess you passed it?"

"Yes."

"You get your food, too, or you can go shopping in Massillon. Actually, the pay is forty-four to forty-eight hundred, depending on qualifications. We never figured on an application from someone like you." Paul Heinrichs stopped and the blue eyes bore in.

Kraft averted his eyes. "I want to learn some clinical medicine, and have a chance to see a lot of sick patients. I did some research before." His eyes came back up. "I'd like the job, Dr. Heinrichs."

"Paul. Well, you're our man, Matthew. Why don't you go and ask your wife in and we'll have some cake and coffee. By the way, how old are you?"

"Thirty-two."

"Wouldn't play tennis by any chance?"

"No, I don't. Sorry."

Heinrichs laughed, and stood up. "Don't worry, it's not a condition of employment. Last summer I played with a schizophrenic patient, and I never knew where he was going to put the ball." They both laughed, and Matthew Kraft went to the front door and opened it. From the car, Ruth Kraft heard her husband laughing. "Ruth, come in," he called. As she stepped into the snow, exultant, it occurred to her that she had never heard his laugh before.

They lived in the cottage on the grounds of the Magnolia State Hospital for five years. For the first eight months or so, Kraft did not leave the grounds. Each morning at seven thirty he saw the patients in the sick ward, and then went from building to building examining those patients who the nurses thought needed his assistance. At one or two Ruth had lunch ready for him, and half an hour later he went back to the sick ward. He saw new patients, if he had decided to transfer them from the regular wards, and in a makeshift office near the nurses' desk he read journals and charts, and made notes of what he read. At five he looked at the X-rays and called instructions to each building, ordering digitalis for patients whose enlarged hearts confirmed his impression of heart failure, the new sulfa drugs for patients with pneumonia on chest X-ray, and salt restriction if chest fluid was present. At six he read the cardiograms with Friedberg's and Tice's textbook propped up on the table in front of him. He left his home number with the nurse in the sick ward, and after supper, if there were no calls, he wrote what he had seen and learned in a huge loose-leaf notebook, two or three pages each day. He usually fell asleep with the notebook or a journal lying on his chest.

By June he had observed seventy elderly schizophrenics with heart disease, noting that they fell into two groups; the ones with relatively mild mental illness could suspend the mental illness, as it were, and give a clear account of symptoms of chest pain, whereas the second group developed bizarre new symptoms of mental illness which turned out to be angina pectoris as the symptoms were explored. No less than six paranoid schizophrenics who attempted suicide were discovered to have angina; and each recalled later that another patient or a nurse or some imaginary person "was squeezing my chest," or "was trying to press the life out of me." When nitroglycerin was given to the patients after exercise and onset of the squeezing, the symptoms went away, though the schizophrenia did not.

Matthew Kraft and his wife visited Paul Heinrichs on Sunday nights—or he walked over for supper—and they talked about chest pain in schizophrenics. By the end of the summer they had written a paper, entitled "Angina Pectoris in Schizophrenics: A Diagnostic Challenge," on the one hundred patients they had now seen.

Ruth remembered July fourth of that summer, when the three of them sat in wooden lawn chairs behind the cottage, listening to the crickets, the sporadic bangs of firecrackers set off by patients and visitors, and occasionally the groan or scream of a patient. Heinrichs had smoked his pipe and talked about stars, and how the July sky was the best summer sky. Matthew sipped a beer and looked up as Paul talked.

"I never looked at stars before," said Matthew. "In Cleveland the steel smoke is between you and the sky."

"Same way in Detroit," commented Paul. "Only there it's the smoke from the Ford plant."

"I see a lot more here."

Paul looked over. "Enough to write up a paper on the angina?"

Matthew was still. "Maybe," he said at last.

"What do you think, Ruth? Your husband is hesitating."

"It's up to him. He usually hesitates for a good reason."

"What's the reason, Matthew?" The smoke from his pipe rose slowly, blotting out stars for a moment and then relighting them. Paul Heinrichs puffed and Ruth Kraft waited, but Matthew looked into the sky as though he were too involved with observing the heavens to reply. Finally Paul knocked the ashes out of his pipe on the edge of the chair. "Ruth," he asked, "have you got another beer?"

"Of course," she replied. She stood up quickly and went into the cottage.

"Now I'll take a little guess, Matthew. You're afraid that the paper will be read by a fellow up in Cleveland, and once he knows you're here, he'll end it all for you."

Matthew's head jerked down and around. "How did you know that?"

Paul shrugged in the dark. "That's unimportant. I'll tell you what I think. Since it's a clinical paper, he won't care one way or the other, and he certainly won't do anything. Besides which, you work for the state now, and so do I. I hired you here, and if they ever brought pressure on you they'd have to deal with me."

"How do you mean?" Matthew's voice was wary.

"C'mon, Matt. You've made this place a hospital, not a charnel house. It's obvious even to the state. Should anyone ever make you pack your bags before you wanted to go, you could give me a ride to the train station on your way."

"Is that the truth?" Matthew Kraft was afraid to believe it.

"It is, Matthew. If you go, I go, and since I'm planning to stay for awhile, you might as well. How about writing up that paper?" Paul Heinrichs' tone was still breezy, jaunty. He might have been suggesting a trip downtown.

Matthew Kraft took a swallow of beer. "OK," he said, "but you're senior author."

Paul's laughter rang out in the warm evening, as Ruth Kraft opened the screen door. "What is it?" she asked.

"Come out here," called Paul. "Your husband thinks I should be senior author." He laughed again. "Matt, you did all the heart exams and read the cardiograms. It's your paper."

Matt grinned. "Ruth, listen to Paul. He's just pulled two clever tricks on me."

"What were they, dear?" God, he was relaxed with Paul Heinrichs.

"He has me ready to write the paper, and be senior author, and worst of all, he has me nearly believing it's the right thing to do." Kraft chuckled pleasurably.

She walked over and put her hand on his shoulder. "He has me believing it too."

The paper was ready in September and Kraft sent it in to the *Ohio State Journal of Medicine*, where it was published as a lead article two months later. During those two months Kraft continued to add to his notebook, and he stopped propping up Friedberg's and Tice's textbook when he read the cardiograms. In November he clinically diagnosed a rupturing aneurysm in an elderly man, and though the surgeon in Massillon did not believe him at first, he listened when Dr. Kraft described the bruit, flank pain, and falling blood pressure. The surgeon came out and saw the patient, but at that time only occasional patients were operated on, and the old man died the next day. The case was discussed at the Massillon City Hospital medical rounds, however, and Dr. Kraft was invited to make a few remarks. From that time, he was asked to come to rounds in Massillon every week, and by Christmas, when his paper had appeared, he was given limited admitting privileges in the hospital.

Within a year, two general practitioners and an internist in the area had asked him to come practice with them, but Kraft declined. He continued to examine over fifty patients a day, read as many X-rays each evening, and kept up with fifteen clinical journals, though it was 1943 before he could bring himself to subscribe to the *American Heart Journal*. Another winter came, and another spring, and that summer Kraft made one bad error, diagnosing his wife's nausea and vomiting as gallbladder disease. It was Paul Heinrichs who correctly diagnosed the condition, only two months after Ruth herself knew she was pregnant. The day of his son's birth, Kraft was lecturing for the first time at the Mercy Hospital in Canton, and he had Paul Heinrichs check the maternity ward of the same hospital every few minutes. Paul returned to his seat at the back of the lecture hall each time with hand raised to show that there was time. Kraft finished five minutes ahead of schedule, cut the questions short, and went to the labor wing as his wife was being wheeled through, pale face wreathed in birth pain. He made the orderly stop, and kissed her. "I'm so happy, Ruth, that you waited till my lecture was over."

"Matthew, Matthew." She smiled wonderingly. "Only my

husband could say that." Paul caught up to them and stayed a few steps away until she went into the delivery room; then he talked with Matthew for the next half hour while Matthew smoked six cigarettes and repeated, "It's time, it's time, why don't they come out?" On his seventh cigarette they let him go in and see his wife and son, and the big man stood there in his surgical scrub suit. "He's much too small, what's the matter?"

The obstetrician smiled. "They say you're an excellent cardiologist, Dr. Kraft, but you don't know a damn thing about babies."

Kraft kissed his wife. "Dear, does he look all right to you?"

"He's fine, Matt. How was your talk?" She was flushed and jubilant.

"Fine," he said. "I'm proud of you, Ruth."

That evening he was back on the grounds of the hospital, and stayed up late catching up on the cardiograms and X-rays. To shake off the sensation of being alone in the cottage, without Ruth for the first time, he began to write an expanded version of his cryptic notes on physical diagnosis. When Ruth and Mark returned, he had outlined his plans for an article stressing certain points in physical diagnosis in heart disease, points he felt were understressed in standard texts. Before the article was published, first as a series in *Circulation* and later as a monograph, his son Mark was able to carry a book to his father. In the intervening three years, Kraft published articles on the saline test for the diagnosis of heart disease (Paul Heinrichs puckishly suggested refrigerated beer as the standard solution), bloody pulmonary clots presenting as tumor on chest X-rays, unusual cardiogram abnormalities after heart attacks, and the preliminary note on disappearance of chest pain and angina following the use of digitalis.

The year the war ended, Kraft was invited to speak in Akron at the Summit County Medical Society, and he was named consulting cardiologist at the Mercy Hospital in Canton. Two doctors returning to the States after the war wrote him and asked if positions were open in "his department," and with

Ruth's help he composed a reply that Paul Heinrichs found hilarious. Especially the phrase, "the patient population is composed of psychotic persons, and most physicians are un-nerved themselves at the thought of caring for four thousand of them."

Finally, and in a way most significant, Kraft decided to publish his paper, "The Work of the Heart: I. Oxygen Need." Again, it was Paul Heinrichs who urged him to publish it, but he could not prevail on Kraft to submit it to the *American Heart Journal*. The asterisk after his name, when it went in to the *Annals of Internal Medicine*, gave his affiliations as, "Formerly, instructor, Cleveland City Hospital: current address, Magnolia, Ohio." "If you mention the State Hospital, they'll wonder if you're a patient," commented Heinrichs lightly.

The *Annals* accepted it within weeks, and when the article was published, no less than eighty requests for reprints arrived at the small cottage on the State Hospital grounds. During the first few weeks after publication, Kraft lived as though suspended, admitting to Paul Heinrichs, "I'm afraid Lippschitz will not let this rest, and the worst thing is, I don't know how he'll get at me." Paul Heinrichs said nothing but spent more time with the Krafts, and the end of suspense came from an unusual source. Deeman Alford, Kraft's technician for a year at the Cleveland City, had gone to medical school and was an intern at the same hospital when he wrote for a reprint. Included on the postcard was the following: "Dr. Lippschitz saw the article and boasts it's really his work; says you stole his idea. Mentioned 'But now they say he is a clinician—the patients will hang him soon enough.' Only he believes that, Dr. Kraft."

The news that Herman Lippschitz had apparently contented himself with verbal attacks gave Kraft intense relief, and as though the last restriction had been lifted, he began to publish clinical articles in journals that he had avoided before. Paul Heinrichs noticed the change in the tall man, and he said one evening in 1946, "Your time here will soon be up, I think."

Kraft paled. "Have you got someone else, Paul?"

"Don't be silly," Heinrichs snapped. "This job is yours as long as you want it. But soon mail of another kind will arrive, as it usually does to men like you. Well, we've had you for four years."

Kraft smiled, and reached for the stack of clinical charts on patients with atypical angina. He and Paul went through each one, and they later published the report on fifty cases, entitled "Atypical Angina," in the *Journal of the American Medical Association*. An editorial appeared in the same issue of the *Journal* entitled, "Bedside Research—Its Continuing Value." When Kraft saw it, sitting in his small office in back of the ward, he doubted it had anything to do with him, and when he read it, astonished, he left his work early for the first time since the birth of his son, and walked the familiar road from the ward to the cottage as preoccupied and remote as any patient on the grounds.

This is what he read:

> With the end of the war, reports of research projects lying dormant for four years or more are now being propelled into print at an astounding rate. With more and more money available for scientific equipment, technicians, and laboratory animals, it is possible to discern some new trends in medical research. The bulk of papers submitted for publication stress laboratory investigation, and authors often decry or barely accept the "clinical investigations" of previous workers, as though the usefulness of bedside observations by keen and incisive clinicians were of little interest except to the patient involved. That the need and value of bedside research persists is elegantly demonstrated by the article in this issue of the *Journal* by Drs. Kraft and Heinrichs. Without recourse to laboratory methods more sophisticated than the six lead cardiogram, and armed only with stethoscopes and penetrating history-taking ability, they have unearthed a number of unusual presenting complaints in angina pectoris, and amply

demonstrate their thesis that the commonest disease in the heart can present with protean symptoms, which the astute clinician must keep in mind.

This valuable addition to the medical literature comes not from a well-financed, high-powered university center, with grant support or new techniques of coronary angiography or vectorcardiography. Rather, the article is the product of the clinical efforts of two clinicians relying on the tools at hand, and the results show how sufficient these tools are. With the trend toward increasingly specialized research of questionable value to the practicing physician, it is gratifying to note the art of medicine and medical research practiced for the benefit of patients, and in this case, the readers of the *Journal*. In a real sense, Drs. Kraft and Heinrichs point the way, and the path is easier as a result of their efforts.

When he showed it to Ruth, flushed and stammering, she read it, smiled, and kissed him meltingly. The whole scene was odd to Kraft. He was unused to being home during the afternoon with the sun pouring into the living room; a riptide of passion flooded through him, and above all he felt and transmitted to Ruth the weird floating sense of elation. Mark was playing in the kitchen, and Ruth Kraft called out breathlessly, "We'll be in the other room, Mark," as they led each other tumbling into the afternoon bed.

At three, and again at four, Kraft said, "Dear, I've got to go back," and each time she heard in his voice the strange note, almost a plea, that compelled her to keep him with her, and away from the hospital. And so she would kiss him again, and say, "I'll call and say something came up," and they laughed like newlyweds at the pun. In the kitchen, playing with unaccustomed freedom, Mark seriously rolled small balls of pie dough from one wall to the other, and wondered if it were a holiday. To Matthew Kraft, his father, it was more than a holiday, and as the elation dissolved all the compulsion and reserve that had encased him for four years, he felt the fantastically strange sensation of joy. Ruth Kraft reveled voluptuously in the miraculous warmth, and she was later to recall that this afternoon and the Friday afternoon in Cleveland were the happiest moments of her life with him.

It was nearly six before Kraft thought to call Paul Heinrichs and tell him about the article and editorial. At first Paul did not believe it, and after he did, they watched him from their front yard, hard with late winter freeze, as he walked with the inappropriate gait of an old man feeling like a very young one. Ruth rescued the pie dough from Mark, and after apple pie and coffee that night, Paul Heinrichs brought up a subject for the first and only time. In typical fashion, Ruth remembered, he started at the edge, hesitated there, and then bored in.

"You know, Matthew," Paul began, staring at his pipe, "sometimes I wonder if I didn't work here as kind of a voluntary commitment."

"Commitment to what?"

"Committed. As though I committed myself here, to the mental hospital. After all, I was depressed after my wife died, felt useless and washed up. I guess I thought about it because of the editorial in the *J.A.M.A.*, which kind of shows how healthy we are now, compared with before." The blue eyes saw Kraft's head start to shake negatively. "Why do I say we?" Paul went on. "Just a figure of speech, now that I'm speaking from the throne. Or did I mean it? Did you commit yourself here in the same sense, Matt?"

Ruth held her breath. Matthew lit a cigarette, and said nothing for a moment. "I guess I don't follow you, Paul," he said quietly.

The doctor moved out again. "I don't know, Matt—put it down to the reflex speculation of a psychiatrist." Kraft began to sit back a fraction, and drew on the cigarette. As his shoulders touched the back of the couch, Paul commented, "But it seems to me when you came here that New Year's Day you were asking me to admit you."

Kraft snapped up. "That's a lie," he blurted out. "You had an ad in the *New England Journal*. I wanted to learn some clinical medicine. What is this crap about 'commiting my-self'? Was I acting crazy, was I paranoid? You saw me then, Ruth, do you believe this crap Paul is saying?"

"I'm not sure he means it that way, Matt."

Kraft ground the cigarette out violently, as though it were the glowing fuse on a bomb. "For chrissake, Paul, what's the matter. Don't you like my work here? You ought to, you've got your name on a hell of a lot of papers I happened to write."

"Matthew." Ruth's voice was shocked.

Paul sighed, long and easy. Kraft looked at the calm man and became even angrier. "Don't give me that professional sigh, Paul. I'm not one of your patients. At least not yet."

The older man's face was set. "That's right, Matt, you aren't."

"Damn right," said Kraft, standing and lighting another cigarette. He looked at his wife uncertainly, and she stood at once and put her arm around him. "Paul," she said, "I think we better continue this some other time."

"Fine," answered Paul Heinrichs, standing abruptly. For a moment they looked like people posing unwillingly at a party. "Unless Matt wants to keep going on it," Paul said quietly.

"Hell no, you started it. All this crap about being committed. You know, Paul, sometimes when you talk like that, like you just did, you sound a little unbalanced. You know, crazy." Kraft stopped, and the silence was fearful.

Paul stiffened for an instant, then pocketed his pipe. "You may be right, Matt. Sometimes I say some crazy things."

Matthew Kraft looked at the wall and avoided the probing blue eyes.

Heinrichs bowed an inch, as though unsure whether to shake the big man's hand. Ruth thought of Herman Lipp-schitz bowing. "Night, Ruth, thanks for the dinner. Swell pie."

"Thank you, Paul," she said formally. Paul left, and Kraft turned quickly to his textbook notes. "Got to get busy on this damn thing," he announced. "Wasted the whole afternoon. I don't want to get behind on it."

"All right, Matthew," she said. She did the dishes slowly,

happy for the work, and looked into the living room only twice. Her husband was sitting at the desk with a thoughtful look on his face, but he did not write anything down. Mark began crying an hour later, and she rocked him back and forth and prayed that her husband would talk to her about what his thoughts were, but he never said anything.

The sense of being detached from her husband's feelings arrived that night and became her constant companion thereafter.

Three weeks later, Kraft received a letter from D. K. Silby, chief of cardiology of Eastern Massachusetts Medical Center, congratulating him on his *J.A.M.A.* article, and wondering if Kraft could stop in to see him when he was next in Boston. Another such letter came from a man in Chicago, but here a familiar message was spelled out: "We would like to talk over the projected makeup of our cardiology department, especially as regards the clinical end of things, where we could use a strong pair of hands, first helping and later possibly leading." Kraft had not risen to the bait because, as he said shortly to his wife, "That bastard Holman in Chicago is no better than Lippschitz. He wants me to be his boy for a few years. No thanks." In the spring of 1947, Matthew Kraft took the train from Cleveland, saw D. K. Silby at the Massachusetts Medical Center, and they moved to Boston five months later, Ruth pregnant with Susan. Kraft hardly looked at the cottage as they drove away, and he later said that he had notified Paul Heinrichs of their departure only a month before they were to leave. "That should have given him enough time," he had stated flatly.

At first they lived in the South End, and Matthew walked to work, and only in 1949 did they move, first to Brookline and then Lexington, with Jam Wah Lee, the Korean instructor, driving Kraft to and from work. Kraft's entrance into the Eastern Massachusetts Medical Center could not have been more spectacular. The young men in the department thought D. K. Silby was insane to hire as assistant professor a clinical hick straight out of a mental hospital job in Ohio, but his first week there, Kraft diagnosed a case no one else had been able to figure out, and he was proven right at surgery. The first Saturday at rounds, when the associate chief, Mokodean, was discussing aneurysms, it was Kraft who asked the first question: "Dr. Mokodean, how could you fail to mention scleroderma as a predisposing factor; you yourself reported a case of such an entity in the *Archives of Internal Medicine* in 1938!" Kraft told Ruth about it that evening with relish, and he was satisfied that the laughter and congratulatory pats on the back were sufficient evidence that the men in the department respected his ability. She had thought to ask him if they seemed really friendly to him, but hesitated, and then asked instead if he would have any hospital night duty. As she was to find out, he spent every other night there until 1950 when he was named chief of cardiology, and his Friday morning rounds and Sunday cardiogram sessions became institutions in the medical world of Boston.

Kraft's being named chief of cardiology had come only after a prolonged struggle between D. K. Silby, retiring from the post, and Robert Mokodean, who hungered after it. Mokodean had worked conscientiously and well for eleven years as associate chief to Silby, and until Dr. Kraft suddenly arrived in the department, his ascension to chief in due time was a foregone conclusion. Mokodean enlisted the aid of Ellsworth Harrison, chief of medicine at the Eastern Massachusetts Medical Center, when it became clear that the retiring Dr. Silby had not made up his mind. Harrison thus dutifully pointed out to Silby that Kraft was still primarily a clinician without significant research publications after two years in Boston. Moreover, he said, cardiology was increasingly the domain of the laboratory research man. D. K. Silby showed Harrison the editorial in the 1947 *J.A.M.A.*, and said, "Kraft is in the beginning of the 'log' phase of his career. Till now he has been lagging in a sense, not so much from laziness or circumstance, but because his potential energy has gathered to a great height, and the water is only now starting to spill over the dam.

Harry, this institution can reap the rewards of his work even as he does, and the volume of the work will dumbfound all of us."

Harrison read through the editorial. "Is he this good, Dave?"

D. K. Silby sat forward. "He is the best doctor I ever saw or heard of."

Harrison raised his eyebrows. "For a man slow to praise, Dave, you just crawled out on a limb."

"Nope. Kraft has got it, and whatever moves him to work is a force that is amazing to watch. I don't know where it comes from, but he hasn't let up in the two years he's been here, and I doubt if he will."

"And Mokodean?" Harrison stressed each syllable of the name.

Silby twisted the earpiece of his stethoscope. "He would be a valuable associate of Kraft's," he replied finally.

Those ten minutes decided it. Mokodean spent hours talking to Ellsworth Harrison, not aware that the decision had already come down against him. The news of the battle spread with the academic winds to the rest of the country, and Mokodean received a short note from Herman Lippschitz in Cleveland, now retired. That note gave him new hope, but when he showed it to Ellsworth Harrison the same afternoon, Harrison glanced at it and said, "Dr. Mokodean, this letter is for us and not other people. In fact it is not even for you. You have forced me to act before I wanted to; Kraft is our man. I'm sorry." Mokodean wrote an incoherent letter of resignation to Harrison the next day, and by the end of the week he had left Boston for Los Angeles. The announcement of Dr. Matthew Kraft's appointment as chief of cardiology and professor of medicine was made in time for the Sunday papers.

Only Matthew was unsurprised by his appointment. He knew he was better than Mokodean, younger and tougher than Silby, and he had convinced himself that Paul Heinrichs was talking nonsense when he had suggested that Matthew doubted his own competence. Doubts and sentiment weakened a man. It was that simple, Kraft knew.

That Sunday eighteen years before, Ruth Kraft reflected, was the end of the beginning. It was as though the announcement had galvanized Matthew Kraft into action, his pace to that moment no more than a leisurely warm-up. The phone rang in the Brookline house all day as people read the papers, and she told all the callers that the doctor was at the hospital and was not expected back before evening. The small pile of congratulatory telegrams remained unopened for several days, and the first year as chief, Kraft worked exhausting eighteen-hour days as though he were being paid in salt. Her music room became his den, then his study, then the extension of his office. The years were best remembered by glancing at Dr. Kraft's *curriculum vitae*. When Mark was seven, in 1951, the first edition of *Clinical Diagnosis of Heart Disease* was published; and in 1952, when Susan contracted pneumonia and her father spent four mornings in a row away from his office and at her side, he also wrote eleven papers, four of which were the product of the new cardiac fellows, two more from Jam Wah Lee. The saline test to detect obscure heart disease was published in 1953, with no less than forty cases, all of them studied personally by the author. It became known in every medical school in the world as "Kraft's test" for heart disease. In 1954, Dr. Kraft chaired the clinical cardiology sessions in Atlantic City, edited the *Yearbook of Cardiology*, and guided two associates and three fellows through more than a dozen research projects. Also in this year, though not recorded in the *curriculum vitae*, he began to work anew in the laboratory. But with so much time devoted to consultations, teaching, administration of the department, supervision of research fellows, reading and writing papers, he had to turn over the bulk of the work to laboratory technicians, most of whom resigned after a few months with him. He cut his graying hair in a crew-cut style, to lengthen the time between haircuts; sitting passively seemed to him an intolerable waste of time. Honors came to him, and his work enveloped him.

In time, their son Mark went to Mt. Hermon, and later to Yale, his father urging him in their occasional talks not to go into medicine unless, "You are willing to regard it as a kind of priesthood." It was Matthew Kraft's most introspective remark to his son, and one Mark never forgot. When he dropped out of the pre-medical program at Yale to major in psychology, Kraft traveled to New Haven, forbidding Ruth to come along, and he returned the next night, shockingly tired. "He wants to be a psychologist. He wants to help shrink heads. Can you imagine that, Ruth? He wouldn't listen to me." Mark's vacations thereafter were spent in Florida, or with friends elsewhere, and his father acted as though Mark were a patient lost to follow-up.

Through all this time, Ruth's tragedy was the loss of her responsiveness to a husband and the subtle replacement of feeling by calcifying ritual. At first she fought the loss, then mourned it, and finally stopped thinking about it. She began to attend concerts on Friday afternoons, became proficient on the recorder, and developed a reading skill in Spanish, and later, German. They moved to Lexington in 1960 and she spent time in the garden, made some furniture, and became an accomplished French cook. Once she helped collaborate on a biography of famous graduates of Northwest Territory schools, but Matthew became irritated seeing her at a writing desk with source books and files of university clippings, and she gave it up after six months.

She awoke, knowing she was alone. It was dark, the middle of the night, and again, for the thousandth time in their marriage, she stifled the urge to cry out, "Matt, come to bed. It's late." He would answer, "Pretty soon," from his study, as he did on the rare occasions when the isolation of her life flooded her and made her call. Especially tonight she dare not call, since Thursday night before his cardiac conference, or cardiac rounds. However he called it, she knew it was his ninety minutes speaking in a lecture hall with medical students and doctors gathered to hear him alone, to be witness to his virtuoso performance. That it was accomplished by a nearly religious devotion to work each Thursday night was known only to her. She listened for the familiar rustle of papers, a grunted oath, monographs dropped solidly on the floor. She heard nothing. Her back ached—the soft bed—

She clutched the enamel arm rests and knew where she was. This night they had all been inconvenienced while he lay sleeping. She climbed stiffly out of the chair, groped for the light switch, and rubbed her face. She stepped warily into the hall.

The night nurse reading a chart at the desk was startled to see her.

"Oh, you scared me. You're Mrs. Kraft."

"Yes. How is my husband?"

"Fine, he's fine. I checked him ten minutes ago." She pointed vaguely at the chart, and Ruth Kraft saw with a flash of anger that his name was on the side; this anonymous nurse was reading all the details of his illness. She was about to say something, then did not. The nurse was also caring for him, she reminded herself.

Outside the room a doctor slept in an easy chair. It was not the Italian anesthetist in a blue surgical shirt and pants, but this man slept with the ugly tube balanced on his lap in the same way. She tiptoed around him. Inside the room she heard a regular beeping sound and knew it recorded the beating of her husband's heart. Its regularity was comforting to her.

Matt was asleep, open-mouthed, uncharacteristically snoring. "It must be the sedation," she thought to herself. She watched him a long time. For the first time in many years she felt limitless love for him. She bent and kissed him, as softly as she could. Then she took his hand.

He stirred and half awoke. "What is it?"

"It's me, Matt. Ruth."

"What?" In the dim night light and the glow from the monitor she saw his hand try to scratch away the monitor strap, fail, scratch again, and awake. "What? Where—"

"It's all right, Matt. You're in the hospital."

His black eyes dilated with recognition. "Oh yes, I'm a patient." He patted her hand. "Have you slept, dear?"

She nodded, full of feeling. He was concerned for her. The angry thought cut through her tenderness: "Must he have a heart attack to become concerned about the woman who loves him?" Then she throttled it, smiled at him, and said, "I'll be outside."

In back of her she heard a rustling. "What is it? Has he arrested?" The voice was loud. Frightened, she saw the thin young man rise up, stethoscope in hand, and switch on a harsh overhead light.

Kraft understood the interruption before she did. "Relax, Essai, my wife came in to see how I was doing."

She turned toward him, furious at his intrusion. The young man held the stethoscope in one hand, and scratched his head. "Oh. Sorry."

Matt fell asleep again after a while, and she went out to find Essai splashing cold water on his face in the utility room.

"I'm sorry, Dr. Essai, but I thought my husband and I were alone."

He looked like a little boy. "Oh. OK. Just wanted to make sure he didn't—hadn't—"

She shook her head. "I know," she said professionally. "The risk in the early stages is abnormal rhythm of the heart, often fatal. I should apologize. You're sleeping in his room to help him."

"Right." He smiled, then frowned. "But asleep I'm not of much help."

"Tell me, what are his chances. Really?"

Essai was waking up; he looked at the tired woman talking to him. "Pretty good," he said honestly. "He's over the worst part. Of course, for a man who works hundred-hour weeks, full recovery is a long way away."

In the darkness of the end of the night, she felt bold and conspiratorial. "Are you married, Dr. Essai?"

He grinned. "Not exactly. Share bed and board. But I shared neither tonight. She'll think I stayed at the hospital all night out of spite. Or vindictiveness. That's how her mind works, I'm afraid."

She caught his feeling. "Get out then."

Essai looked at her. "Easier said than done."

She smiled. "Easily done. Leave, or throw her out."

"Sure."

"It's true. If you're a good doctor, and have a sensitivity for other things, you can ill-afford that kind of woman."

Essai formed the word "Right!" but suddenly realized that he was talking to the wife of Matthew Kraft. Fully awake, he tried to remember if he had said anything terrible. He had the feeling that they shared something aside from Kraft. "Well," he said at last, "your husband is coming along well."

She nodded, seeing he had closed up. "Thank you for staying with him. I notice Dr. Winston and Dr. Malatesta are gone."

Essai looked alarmedly around her shoulder. "No, Dr. Firat is here. He's the chief resident in anesthesia. Malatesta probably 'split the night' with him. And George Winston will be back in the morning."

"Good." She looked at her watch. A quarter to six. "Do you think I could go home and freshen up?"

"Sure." Again the familiar response, Essai thought. "Yes, I think he'll do well, Mrs. Kraft."

"All right. I'll go home for an hour or so. You must bring the lady over some evening for supper."

"Supper? At your house?"

"Certainly. Matthew will have a number of days at home." Now it was her turn to be confidential. "Thank God. Even if it has to be by way of illness. I want a husband, not a professor." She blushed, and covered her mouth.

He was nodding. "I know." They were sleepy, early-morning friends. "Your husband needs you and counts on you more than he admits."

There was a long silence. "Sorry," he said.

She touched his hand. Again he became aware of the unexpected feeling. Was it concupiscence? "I believe the lady who has you is rather lucky," she said.

"You are a very gracious person."

She turned. "If he asks for me, tell him I've gone home to change."

The first light of day struggled against the fluorescent night. "I will," he said formally.

She waited for the elevator and he went busily to the nurses' desk. He needed to check some blood pressure readings on the patient, and wanted to stop thinking about the doctor's wife.

Matthew Kraft felt fingers on his chest. He awoke to sunlight and the smile of Carolyn Reiss, head nurse on 6 North.

4

"Morning, Dr. Kraft. Strap too tight?" Except for the momentary hesitation of "Dr." she treated him like any other patient.

"No, fine, Carolyn. Surprised to see me this morning?"

She shrugged. "Now, turn on your right side and I'll rub your back."

"Like hell you will," he spouted. "I'll not be treated like an infant, goddammit. I'm a sick adult, not a sick child." He felt hopelessly frustrated. Every Friday morning at this time he looked over his notes for the talk. Now, without a change in any aspect of his life, the department, his ability to think and read, he had been struck down. A collection of fibrin and red cells probably no bigger than a kernel of rice had lodged in one of his coronary arteries, and as a result he had to lie quietly with a greasy strap across his chest and miss his own conference.

Miss Reiss stood watching him with her arms across her chest. Kraft looked up. "Don't gloat, goddammit. I've got to lie here while you're up, doing things. Christ, I knew I should have stopped smoking. Or lost some weight."

She sat down on the edge of his bed. He was about to reprimand her. He felt strongly that the bed was the patient's, and no doctor or nurse should ever violate the patient's privacy in this way. But she spoke first. "Dr. Kraft, I'm going to tell you something. You're a patient here, with a heart attack, and I'm going to help take care of you. Now you hired me personally six years ago to be head nurse on your floor. Right?"

"So?"

88

"The thing that worried you was that your so-called prestige patients would get poor care because they thought they were immune to disease and death. Remember? You told me that a corporation president or senior Senator would do himself harm if he were not treated like every other patient."

"Certainly," said Kraft. "If they thought they were privileged, they'd be insulted by someone asking how their bowels were."

Miss Reiss wagged a finger at him. "All right, then. Our present coronary patient is forty pounds overweight, and because of the monitor has to lie quiet for at least forty-eight hours. Isn't he a setup to develop a bedsore on his backside, and won't the complications of such a sore immensely compound the problem of his care?"

"Of course," Kraft agreed, still thinking of the mythical patient. "It could become infected, make the patient restless, cause fever with accompanying fast heart rate—"

"Well, you do very well with the theoretical patient," she said. "Now turn to your right side, Dr. Kraft. You're the patient."

Kraft looked up at her. She was smiling and determined. He sniffed exaggeratedly and slowly began to turn to his right. "Help me turn," he murmured, very much like a small boy.

As she massaged his back, buttocks, and shoulders expertly, she gave him instructions, rapidly enumerating the ways he should handle himself. He listened. "Now a whole stream of people are going to want to visit you, and every one will tire you more, especially those with whom you have always been the master, the superior. Some of them will say they visit you as a friend, for your benefit, but it's really so they can stand over you and think 'He's weaker, right now, than I am.' "

She felt his muscles tense, and hurried on. "So I would advise you to have no visitors, except for the men in your department and your wife, at least for five days or so. Dr. Lerner and the rest will want to help too, and they'll hover around you. You have to face it: for the next couple of months, let them help you, or else the service will start to deteriorate.

Take this morning—your private patients expect to see you. You have to delegate responsibility to your men, not for good, but so that you can gather it again later on."

"I don't trust any of them," Kraft admitted gloomily.

She nearly slapped instead of massaged. "Be realistic," she instructed him. As she talked, she knew that only by concentrating on the flabby haunches of this aging man could she talk in so bold a manner to Matthew Kraft, and the thoughts came to her: This is why I made him turn.

"You've got to be realistic. If you are a good teacher, these subordinates of yours can take responsibility. They have to. And you recognize, of course, that for a while you cannot run everything as usual, not if you want to recover completely."

Her subject was silent, listening. She poured some more massage cream out of the plastic bottle and looked momentarily at the ceiling. "Just another minute. Sorry if this is cold." She kneaded it in. "And if you want to know the truth, I think you have to look for a man, in or out of your department, to start help carrying the load with you."

His hand curled and caught her wrist, squeezing hard. "No! I can't take that. Don't say that. It's mine, my department!"

"Let go."

He let go and turned partially. "I appreciate what you say, Carolyn. But don't go too far," he warned.

"OK," she said lightly. "Now let me turn you back over and adjust these straps." She knew she would be massaging his back tomorrow and the next day. If the seed of the idea grew in him, it could be lifesaving. That he had accepted the seed was clear to her as he turned back. He was thinking about it, and smiled absentmindedly at her.

Kraft had called a meeting for noon, and told Miss Graf, ashen when she saw him as a patient and obedient when he told her what to do, to get Lerner, Pruden, and Essai to his room. When Winston came in to check the patient, Kraft begged to have the monitor removed while he talked to his men. "Just for an hour, George," he said. "I have to be strong." Winston was set to say no, but then he comprehended the plea and acquiesced.

At noon, when the three men came in, Matthew Kraft was sitting propped up, busily reading *Circulation*. He had on a pajama top, there was not an instrument in the room, and he looked like a prosperous physician in the hospital for an annual checkup. One hard look at Essai sufficed to keep the latter from expressing his astonishment that the cardiac monitor was gone.

"Thank you for stopping by, gentlemen," Kraft began in an authoritative voice. "George Winston thinks it may be a mild infarct, though nothing is settled. I'm getting heparin, just in case. How did the conference go?"

"Fine, sir," said Pruden quickly. "The recorded talk was magnificent, as your talks always are."

"Thank you," said Kraft dryly. "Did you arrive in time to hear all of it?"

Pruden began to answer, but Kraft interrupted. "Were the fellows there?"

"I saw Nichols," offered Lerner. "I didn't see Calia."

Essai nodded. "He was there."

"I hope so," said Kraft. "I want each of you to take it upon himself to see that things stay right. I want the technicians to stay till five, and no stretched-out lunch hours. I have asked Miss Graf to contact any two of you about telephone consultations that come in. Do this well; remember that a doctor is calling in for help, and it means that he is honest enough to realize he needs help. Don't patronize him."

Harvey Lerner took a small pad of paper out of his white coat and began to take notes. "Harvey," Kraft sneered, "if you have to write it down, forget it."

Lerner guiltily put away the pad. "Sorry," he said.

"Now," Kraft continued, "Sunday morning is the cardiogram reading session. I want that kept up. Lately the interns have been missing, and I know there's grumbling about the session being on Sunday. But I want it that way. Forty-hour-a-week doctors should go into another field," he said warningly. "Lerner, have you got some good cardiograms for the session?"

"Yes."

"All right. Come up here after it's over, and tell me who was there. Now let's see, anything else."

Essai nearly raised his hand. "Yes," he said. "Saturday is specialty conference, and cardiology is slated for tomorrow."

Kraft patted the bed impatiently. "Goddamnit, I could talk about the differential diagnosis of chest pain. Well, put it off until some later date." He stopped for a moment. "No, wait. We had originally decided to discuss Mr. Mann this morning at the conference, as an example of the difficulties of making the diagnosis in a man with chest pain."

"Right," said Essai.

"You were going to discuss it, sir," said Pruden.

Kraft showed his teeth in an expression simulating a smile. "So I was. Mr. Mann had every possible condition considered, from collapsed lung to blood clot in the lung, but the diagnosis was not made till I saw him on Thursday."

"Right," said Pruden quickly. "We were all over the lot till you straightened us out."

Essai was thinking that Kraft should have seen Mr. Mann on the first day and not the sixth, but he had had too much to do, private consultations and administration and research to take care of, and so the "service" patient had not been seen by the chief for nearly a week. But he said nothing.

"Essai, you look troubled." Kraft remembered the beeping yesterday when Essai had spoken up; the same look was on his face now. Jesus, that had been only yesterday; now his whole life had changed.

Essai started to say something, but Kraft pushed on, trying to set them all on edge, and so fight off the feeling of impotence that grew in him. "The conference will go on tomorrow as scheduled. I want each of you to talk for twenty minutes on the approach to the patient with chest pain of unknown cause.

Have the patient's case presented for the first five minutes or so."

Pruden protested. "But Dr. Kraft, the conference is tomorrow—that's not much time to prepare a talk."

"Pruden," Kraft stared at him, "you've been in the department for five years. If you can't talk for twenty minutes about the approach to the patient with chest pain, you better stand aside and let the men do it." Pruden's eyebrows went up. "Don't look at me as though I'm making a radical suggestion. If you don't want to talk tomorrow, fine. The other two can take thirty minutes each. You, Pruden, can see my private patients here on the floor instead and report to me on how they're doing, how I should handle them."

A vague grunt emanated from the pale man. "Ahh, well—"

Kraft turned the knife. "My third suggestion is that you call one of your poker-playing doctor friends and set up a private practice somewhere. That is, if the rigors of academic medicine are too great. You haven't been pulling your weight for years, and now you'll pull it or get out. I hear you praise me with every breath." Kraft now took a deep one. "Well, Pruden, I pay you fourteen thousand a year, and made you assistant professor, and if I want a lackey to praise me, I can hire a high-school dropout at a third of that salary."

Pruden gulped audibly. "I'll speak tomorrow for twenty minutes if that's what you want, sir."

"Good. Now, Essai, you go around today to see my patients with the house staff, O'Connell, Schachter and the intern. Then report back to me. Harvey, you and Ed go down to keep an eye on the lab and the office. Come up at six tonight and give me a list of the calls. The journal meeting will be held tomorrow as usual."

He dismissed them and returned to reading *Circulation;* Essai went to find the intern and residents, and Pruden began to say something to Harvey Lerner, but Miss Graf stepped off the elevator and motioned to them. "There's a Dr. Johnson on the phone from Hartford, for Dr. Kraft. He wants some advice about a patient with intractable heart failure." For a moment, neither of them moved. "This way," she said, pointing to the stairs. Reluctantly, they followed her.

Joan Graf had never met Ruth Kraft until the time of Matthew Kraft's heart attack, but then, neither had Lerner, Pruden or Essai. Finding a warm, intelligent woman had pleasantly suprised Essai, but Miss Graf had labored for her beloved boss fully believing that Mrs. Kraft, whoever she was, had to be an insensitive person who misunderstood him. Each day for eleven years Miss Graf compulsively carried out every duty he gave her, answered every call, kept records of the time men showed up for work, who said what, where dissension existed. For all this she expected no reward save that Dr. Kraft would continue to let her serve him. Occasionally she dreamed they were lovers.

He had entrusted her to go into Scallard Hall early Saturday morning and set up the tape recorder in the locked drawer under the lectern. Mr. Mann was presented, and the three physicians discussed the approach to the patient with chest pain. She came in after the conference, unlocked the drawer and carried the tape recorder to Kraft's room. She knocked and went in, and was introduced to Mrs. Kraft, sitting quietly near the window. Joan Graf tried to hide the machine from Ruth; it was something between Dr. Kraft and herself, not intended for other people.

Kraft glanced at the tape recorder as she entered, and after introducing the two women, he asked Ruth to get him a morning paper.

"Of course," she said. "Nice to meet you, Miss Graf." She walked out, biting her lip. Her husband read journals, books, patients' charts, releases on new drugs, manuscripts submitted to journals—but he did not read newspapers. She wondered about Matthew's secretary.

"You didn't run out of tape?"

Miss Graf shook her head briskly. "No. I set it on the low

speed. The fidelity is probably poor, but at that speed a spool runs for three hours."

"Good girl." He watched her rewind to the start, and listened for a moment to make sure the sounds were not garbled. Then he switched off the machine.

"Thank you, Joan."

She nodded, but her heart swelled. How she loved him.

His voice dropped a bit. "How are they doing, without me?"

"It varies," she said simply. "Should I go on?"

Kraft nodded.

"Essai is the best," she said. "But once in a while he stops, as though thinking over whether he likes what he's doing. He gave advice to Dr. Hammell from Albany, and did very well, but then when he set down the phone he said, 'Just another opinion, made law by emanating from Dr. Kraft's department at the Mass. Medical Center.'"

"Goddamnit, that Essai is too brainy for his own good. He doubts everything. How about the rest?"

"Dr. Lerner is trying very hard, but he talks everything over afterward with the others. On a difficult cardiogram he even called Dr. Constant at the Metropolitan." Miss Graf stopped as she saw Kraft's face. "Sorry, Dr. Kraft."

"No, no, if that's how it is I want to hear it. He doesn't trust himself. And Pruden?"

"Frightened by it. He broke things in the lab all day yesterday, and shouted at one of the fellows for leaving the centrifuge on, when he himself had done it."

"And the fellows?"

"I don't know," she said. "They wonder what's going to happen to their program. One of them, Nichols, said he didn't know with whom to talk about his research, now that you were up here and Essai had started in with patients again."

Kraft looked surprised. "Really? He looks to me as the head of research as well as the clinical end?"

"Yes."

"Well, well. Old Kraft can still help out the young Ph.D.s

with questions. Why doesn't he go to the Korean biochemist?"

Miss Graf shrugged. "The fellows rarely ask him about things. I guess he's off in his own world and they can't really talk to him."

Kraft confided in her. "So they look to me for research advice. Well, do you know what Manson from the Bolliston Society wanted when he called me? I may be one of five Americans nominated for the Nobel Prize in medicine."

"No." She was unbelieving. "No."

He grinned. "There's a chance. Even though I'm an old clinician and not a fancy biochemist."

"Oh, Dr. Kraft, I'm so happy for you." Tears filled her eyes. Kraft stared at her, surprised. "Please excuse me for this," she said.

"OK. Take it easy. I'm going to listen to this tape." He smiled, then suddenly said, "Do me a big favor. And keep it secret. Go over to the library and look up "Heart Surgery" and "Heart Transplants" in the *Index Medicus*. Most of it is dog stuff, in the surgical literature. Bring me a copy of every article written in the last five years. But tell no one."

"Of course," she said, standing. "Is the Nobel thing a secret as well?"

Kraft had a vision of himself with a new heart. In Stockholm for the prize with a new heart. "Well," he said, "kind of a secret."

Miss Graf left the room and went to the elevator to go down and over to the library. She looked like a woman in love. Ruth Kraft passed her with a newspaper, and looked at her oddly. "Is everything all right?" Ruth asked.

"Yes, yes. He's to be nominated for the Nobel Prize. Isn't that an honor, even to be nominated?"

"What?"

Miss Graf nodded. "Yes. He got the call two days ago."

The elevator door opened and so averted a scene. Ruth watched the secretary disappear behind the door. Ruth had been sent "to buy a paper," the secretary smiled a lover's smile, and her husband told Miss Graf about his nomination for the Nobel Prize, something Ruth had known nothing about.

She began to walk long-leggedly to the door of the room, but slowed at once. He was thirty-six hours past a heart attack, she thought. There could be no issues now.

Pruden's excited voice greeted her, muffled on the tape, as she knocked and came into the room. Matthew turned it off quickly. "Thanks for the paper," he said.

"All right, Matthew. You know, I would be happier having Mark and Susan here."

"You called them, didn't you?"

"Yes, Mark was worried, wanted to come right up, but I told him you would rather he not come unless you were sicker."

"Probably wants to hire a good lawyer for his share of my estate. Keep him away." Matthew Kraft closed his eyes. "I'm tired. You should go home and get some rest too."

But I want my children here, she thought desperately. "I think I'll do that. I'll be back tonight."

"Good-bye, dear." He kissed her quickly and she went out. Not ten seconds later she again heard the recorded voice of Ed Pruden.

Kraft listened to the tape several times. It was obvious that Pruden had taken notes from some of Kraft's own lectures in the past, and mouthed the words without real understanding or emphasis, with the result that they sounded hollow. The restlessness of the audience in the background confirmed it— he was talking to himself, and not even with his own words.

Kraft took a piece of bond paper from under his pillow. The names of the three men were on it: Lerner, Pruden, Essai. He crossed out Pruden's name. Then he listened to Lerner's talk. Lerner had tried hard, making references in every other sentence to a research paper, trying to say something in a short time, and suffering from a lack of organization. Also, Kraft noted grimly, he had misinterpreted a paper on lung clots, and left the audience with the false impression that enzyme determinations were not helpful in differentiating between heart attack and lung clots. Kraft knew that paper by heart. He had written it five years before.

Perhaps Lerner had read too many papers for so short a talk and became confused, but Kraft shook his head again and again as he heard Lerner repeating the error. He also realized that Pruden and Essai, both in the audience, let the error pass. Kraft scratched his itchy chest. "I would have flattened him in an instant," he thought ruefully. Lerner was a capable cardiogram reader, he concluded at last, but not a man of the caliber Kraft was looking for.

That left Essai. He spoke good English, and most important, he was the one of the three who stressed the concept that the physician needed no more than the history and physical exam to travel most of the way toward a diagnosis when confronted by a patient with chest pain. Essai was weak when discussing the literature, and never mentioned collapsed lung in the differential diagnosis of chest pain, but Kraft stopped and re-played the tape twice at the place where the instructor had said, "Most doctors think of 'chest pain' in terms of the patient with a 'routine coronary,' or 'a routine pulmonary clot.' It's worth emphasizing that the only thing routine about chest pain is the interest of many physicians assessing it. The best physician thinks in complex ways about his patients, even if the final diagnosis seems most pedestrian."

Kraft liked that. Essai should have documented his points better, been more dramatic. But he thought in concepts. Kraft circled his name. Even in doing so, he became depressed. Essai had the desire, often expressed, to make more of his life than a great career in research medicine. He read *The New York Times* instead of a medical journal as he ate his lunch, Kraft remembered. He did as little as possible in the clinical area and contented himself with careful but unin-spired laboratory research. Rather than see some patients, he spent his free time away from the hospital, and everyone in the department asked him about a play or a concert before they got tickets, knowing he kept up with cultural events in Boston. If only he possessed the priest's devotion to his calling—

Miss Reiss came in. "How's everything, Dr. Kraft?"

"Well, I don't know," he said wearily to the nurse. "By the way, you didn't give me my backrub today."

"I know. Busy at the desk. I'll be in tomorrow and do it in the morning."

And the next day, Sunday, he again lay on his right as she massaged his back. The monitor strap was off, and Kraft had spent a pain-free night. On his side, feeling the skilled hands, Kraft started talking.

"I can't decide what to do, Carolyn. I'm fifty-nine, and I know I'll be back to work. But the whole department depends on my being there, my working actively to keep everyone going right. I couldn't give that up to an outsider, could I?"

"I don't know. How about the men in your department?"

Kraft grunted. "Essai's the best of a poor lot. He'd need a lot of work."

"Why a poor lot?" she asked mildly.

"Who the hell knows." He gestured with his free left arm. "They're afraid to work, to give themselves up to medicine. They act as though without a leader they're powerless to act on their own."

"Were the men under you always like that?" she asked.

She turned him back over. He looked into her open face. "No. But the independent ones I dumped. Smythe went to Chicago, Kirsch into practice. Cooper was a fool, but aggressive as hell, and now he's chief of cardiology in San Francisco."

"Would you consider bringing one of them back."

He glared at her. "Not on your life. Once they leave me, the bastards, they're on their own." He dropped off into a moody silence. "If they leave, they're out," he said finally.

"I see."

Kraft struck the starched sheet irritably. "Christ. Stuck with Essai. Some night they'd be looking for him—with a sick patient there, and he would be at Symphony Hall." Then he brightened. "But I'm coming along fine; and in a few weeks all this talk about successors and new men taking over will sound like claptrap."

That afternoon, however, he had recurrent chest pain, though the repeat cardiogram showed no change, and he was given morphine. As the morphine took hold, he again felt the langourous release, and the rigor of fear ebbed away. For a few minutes, he let his mind wander, peacefully, and he faced the truth in its truest form—he lost his illusion—and so disillusioned, he thought about his situation. As Miss Reiss took the monitor strap off for good the next morning, he told her what he had seen, and then swore her to secrecy.

"You were right," he said to her. "I've got to be realistic. Even if I recover fully, and I damn well expect to, I cannot go on forever. I certainly can't let the department become just another cardiology service, and the thought of an outside man taking all this over seems worse than just letting it slide."

"Yes?"

Kraft made a sweeping gesture with both hands, and then folded them in his lap. He spoke quietly. "Carolyn, it's a hackneyed thought, but new to me. I'm a self-made man. And medicine is my whole life."

She said nothing.

He furrowed his brow, trying to express it. "Can you imagine how I feel about medicine? When I was growing up, it seemed astonishing that some people, by virtue of training and skill, were permitted to care for the sick. And earn a living doing it. And then"—he paused—"and then to find out that by being dedicated to this kind of exalted work, one could become famous, and build a reputation, and gain academic honors— well, it was a miraculous revelation to me."

"I see."

He made a fist. "So when you suggested the other day that I had to look for and train a successor, it seemed you were saying that this golden thing I have is to be given up, voluntarily no less." His voice rose to the old resonance. "Well, I'm just not going to do that, I thought. No, I'm not."

Then he lay back and smiled. "But the truth I saw is that I'm going to. Again it's hackneyed, but I want what I've done to grow, not disappear with me."

The nurse said quietly, "It's a hard thing to face."

"Right." Kraft's voice shook. "To be reminded of one's mortality is not easy to take."

For a few minutes they said nothing, and she straightened up the room, not usually a head nurse's duty. As she was about to leave, Kraft said, "And I know who it is, the man I'm going to train. But this is between you and me."

"Of course," she said. "Who?"

He almost whispered it. "The concert-goer. Essai."

But the next day Miss Graf arrived with a manila folder full of articles. Kraft discovered, read, and reread the series of articles by Fermanian and his surgical group at Columbia on heart transplants in dogs. His technique was better than Barnard's, he thought. Better than Cooley's. Studying the papers minutely (he had only heard of them before), he glimpsed his own salvation. That glimpse became the most private thing he owned, and he began to plan his approach to make it reality for him.

Essai checked on his rabbits in the animal room, turned out the light, and walked back to his lab. It had been only a week since Matthew Kraft's heart attack, but Essai felt as though he had been racing at the quickened tempo for a month. Lerner had admitted to the same thing, though Pruden rushed back and forth in the lab, exhorting everyone on "to greater effort," as though he were leading cheers. Miss Graf sat at her desk and somehow found out everything, which she kept to herself and later precisely reported to Dr. Kraft.

Essai yawned. *Science* usually arrived on Thursday, today, and he wondered if his article would appear. He came back to the lab door, and stopped a second yawn halfway. On his door was a note from Miss Graf: "Dr. Kraft wants to see you before you go."

He looked at his watch. Six thirty. He'd better call Judy before he saw Dr. Kraft. Wearily he dialed the phone number of his bachelor apartment.

"Hello."

How her voice managed to tinge the most commonly used word in the world with both sexual awareness and melancholy was something Essai had never understood. "Hi, Judy, it's me."

"Are you still at the hospital?"

"Just leaving, honey. I have to see Dr. Kraft for a minute. Have you eaten?"

"Of course not, I was waiting for you. Could you stop off and pick up some dessert?" The faintest reproach sharpened her voice and dissipated the melancholy.

"Sure. Sorry it's so late."

"Andy, will you be coming by Charles Street?"

"Yeah, what can I get you?"

"Not 'you,' Andy, 'us.'"

Andy looked at the ceiling of the lab. "Dear, what can I get us?"

"Well, just near Mt. Vernon Street there's a new little shop. I stopped there the other day. They have the most delightful soups and desserts, and cheeses. Could you ask them for a can of gazpacho soup, and get something for dessert?"

"Gazpacho soup? What the hell is that?"

She became instructive. "It's a kind of tomato soup; you add water and a bit of lemon juice and it's marvelous cold soup. I didn't have time to make it from scratch. Don't be hesitant, they'll known what you're asking for. Gaz-pa-cho soup."

"Thanks, I got it." He twirled the phone cord irritably; she had done everything but spell it out.

"Also," she continued, "we're out of Scotch, in case you want any tonight."

He remembered something. "Hey, listen, honey, did you notice if the new issue of *Science* came today?"

"I didn't pick up the mail. I guess it's down there. You know the mail is never for me here."

"OK, Judy, I'll be home in half an hour or so."

"I love you, Andy." The melancholy was back.

"Me too, honey. I'll see you."

He put back the phone and left the dark lab with slow step. "Don't get depressed," he thought to himself. "The article may be in the new issue of *Science,* and tomorrow all over the country doctors and scientists will be reading your article. Also, you are a physician, an instructor in medicine in Dr. Kraft's department, relatively free in the harness, and you are heading home to a comfortable apartment on Berkeley Street currently shared by a loving, if truculent, woman of the world. Faithfully taking Enovid," he added hopefully.

At the elevator, he pressed the button, went up to 6 North, and wondered what Dr. Kraft wanted. Quickly he thought over the possibilities. Either he was to be chastised for not working enough, neglecting his lab work now that he had taken on clinical duties, or not giving Pruden and Lerner, both slightly his senior, the deference and respect they deserved.

Essai knocked, though the door of 612 was half open.

"It's me," he announced.

"It is I. Come in anyway."

Essai looked at his knuckles for a moment and throttled the angry resentment that rose in him. Then he walked in. "Did you want to see me, Dr. Kraft?"

He looked toward the bed, to the left, but Kraft's voice came from the far corner. "Over here. Turn on the light, please."

Essai did so, and saw Dr. Kraft sitting in the deep lounge chair with his feet up and some journals in his lap. Essai ventured a comment. "Oh, I thought you didn't agree with the cardiac chair program."

Kraft nodded. "I don't," he said briskly. "I know Levine says it's as good or better for the patient than bed rest. But I can't talk over serious things lying in bed. Bring the straight chair over here."

"Oh, God," thought Essai. "Like the child to be punished, I have to bring the chair over." Morosely, he picked it up and carried it to where Kraft sat.

"Close the door," said Kraft. He watched the young man's lips tighten. When he had returned, he motioned for him to sit down. After a few moments, as Essai's face showed that he expected anything but good news, Kraft opened his closed hand.

Essai looked down and saw a key, like the kind he himself had for his lab and the door of the cardiogram room. "What is it?" he asked.

Kraft peered at him. "It's the key to my reprint file room," he said. Essai looked confused. "You may have access to it."

"But—but why?"

"Essai, I want you to give the talk at cardiac conference tomorrow."

"Me?" His voice was that of a boy's.

"Yes." Kraft watched him. "What subject do you want to discuss?"

"Well, I don't know. That is—I—"

Kraft flipped the key to Essai. The confused young doctor half-reached for it, watched it clatter to the floor, and after hesitating only a moment, reached and picked it up. He looked at Kraft. "Do you have any suggestions?" he asked.

"Yes. Talk about pericarditis. We have that patient—"

"O'Brien?" Essai volunteered.

"Right. O'Brien. He has typical pericarditis. You'll find a hundred or so papers in that file." Kraft scratched his head. "It's up to date, at least to last week. Of course, when you get to preparing your remarks on diagnostic tests, it's worth going into some detail about my saline test."

Essai shook his head. "Are your own papers in there as well?"

"Yes, I presented the experimental results at several conferences in the last few years, and took notes about some of the experiences of others. You'll find that on buff sheets attached to my original papers."

Essai nodded. "Uhh," he began, "uhh, this is for tomorrow, right?"

Kraft moved close to Essai, until the gray crew-cut head was inches away. "Yes, tomorrow. I've done it that way for fifteen years. Tape the talk if you want, and refer to it when you give the talk again."

Essai felt the key in his hand. He could think of nothing to say.

"Oh, by the way," Kraft added smoothly, "I want you here about seven fifteen tomorrow."

"Morning?"

"Yes, doc. Give the talk to me first, and I'll make a few comments, and then you'll be ready for the conference. Always give the talk first, if only to a wall." Kraft waved him away. "Better go and start working on it. Stop here in the morning."

Essai stood up. "Thank you," he said.

"Seven fifteen, goddamnit," Kraft bellowed. Hearing the voice at its old pitch, Essai nodded, replaced the chair, and left.

A few minutes later, with a heavy manila folder under his arm, Essai left the hospital. Hundreds of thoughts swirled about him, but he decided that it was best to regard this as what it seemed to be: he was to substitute for the chief, temporarily indisposed. Next week it would probably be Lerner or Pruden. He shook his head to scatter the thoughts, and looked around him.

On the street, a short walk from Massachusetts Avenue, he came suddenly into the Boston evening, which unrolled like a long strip of moving pictures as he walked a block on Massachusetts Avenue and up Washington Street. The traffic was a hopeless tangle, as usual at seven thirty, and girls sat close to the young men who raced their car engines and waited for the Massachusetts Avenue light. In the next block and for six blocks on Washington Street, the bulk of the pedestrians were weaving drunks, men and women, stopping only to unscrew the top of a pint of Three Monks burgundy or Gallo muscatel and suck avidly, as though through a nipple. They stopped and drank, Essai had long ago decided, only to prevent spilling any. He walked quickly, faster than the choked traffic, refusing the beaten request for dimes from alcoholic men, for shoeshines from Negro boys, already old, and from two women outside the Cozy Bar at the corner of Broadway, one of whom leaned exhaustedly against the thick plate glass. "Hey, mister, want to buy a lady a drink?"

"Sorry, miss." What if the Negro boys asked for drinks and the women carried shoeshine kits slung over their shoulders? Essai looked down at his scuffed shoes. He'd probably get a shine from the prettiest of them.

Past Broadway Street he smilingly declined the offer of the lolling Gypsy inside the door, "Tell your fortune? Plenty of luck." Two doors up, a naked bulb haphazardly illuminated a sign that read AVEROF, and Essai stepped inside the tiny Greek restaurant. Helena saw him and came toward him, smiling. "Hello, doctor, here for supper?"

"No thanks, Helena, just wondered if you could sell me two pieces of baklava?"

"Sure, sure. You don't want supper? I have egg-lemon soup tonight."

His mouth watered at the thought of the golden soup with rice, and in fact, at the prospect of a quiet, solitary meal in the humid restaurant with the smell of lamb in everything. He sighed. "No thanks, just some baklava for dessert at home."

"You married now, doctor, eating at home?" The question was open, anticipatory.

"No, Helena." The finality of the phrase sent her hurrying back to the kitchen, and she came out a few moments later with a small bag.

"Here is the baklava. That's forty cents. Come in for supper sometime." She was forty, and nearly illiterate, but her name and manner, her whole way of conducting her affairs, in fact, suggested to Essai a beauty and graceful pride peculiar to Greek women.

He walked outside into the cold air, swinging the paper bag and manila folder in time to his steps, and stopped at the light, opening the bag to smell the honey and nuts and fragrant dough. A weaving sailor and his girl passed him as he stood, saying loudly, "Go shit in a bag, buddy." The girl giggled as they went on.

"Thanks," Essai shouted back, his face flushed. He moved quickly toward the Common, past the bars and littered alleys. Outside the Saxon Theater a line of fifty or seventy-five couples waited in the cold to get in to see the eight o'clock showing of *The Sound of Music*. The men were conservatively dressed, nearly all hatless, and the women wore the fashionless coats and shoes that passed for style in Boston. One dumpy female had a run at least six inches long in her right nylon, Essai noted scientifically. She would probably love *The Sound of Music*. He played his little game, deciding from the rear what the front would look like, and what kind of face her escort would have. Eastern Europe Jewish with thick dark hair and too-red lipstick, he thought; husband nervous and thin, hypertensive. He came abreast of them in the slowly moving line and looked back.

"Andy. Andy Essai, how are you?"

"Oh, hello, Harvey. Good evening, Mrs. Lerner." The embarrassment at knowing the couple he had just dissected, coupled with his natural feelings about Harvey Lerner (civility barely covering contempt), and the cold wind stinging his cheek—all combined to make him a forlorn and almost pitiful figure.

"Just wending your way home from the shop, Andy?"

The young instructor scratched his head as though he weren't sure. He hid the folder as best he could. Then he smiled lopsidedly. "Yes, I am. It's funny, Judy told me to pick something up on the way home and I don't remember what it was. Now what should I do? Call her?"

"How long have you two been married, Dr. Essai?" Rebecca Lerner asked politely.

"Rebecca," barked Harvey Lerner.

"What?" muttered Essai blankly.

The cardiogram reader took over. "I think what Rebecca is suggesting, Andy, is that it depends how long you have known the lady in question. If for a short time, you can call and coyly admit you forgot, and add you can't wait to see her. If for a long time, well—"

"Say little and bring her some candy or take her to the movies," said Mrs. Lerner.

"Rebecca, wait a moment," Harvey Lerner reproached her. "That's not why I'm taking you to this film tonight, though Lord knows I could pick a better one."

Rebecca Lerner nodded several times and explained to Essai, "You see, Dr. Essai, the other reason to take her to the movies, your wife—ah, I mean the lady, that is—is to relieve her of the boredom she endures looking after the children."

Lerner was perturbed. "Dear," he protested, "that's quite unfair. Until recently you went to the concert every Friday with Mrs. Kraft, until she gave up her subscription, and a babysitter sat with the children all afternoon. Now admit it."

Essai began to edge away. "Well, excuse me, folks, nice running into you but"—he gestured vaguely to the line of couples, now slowly beginning to uncoil past the box office—"I've got to get home."

"Oh my," said Rebecca Lerner, putting a chubby ungloved hand to her lips, "of course, you wouldn't have children either, that is—you and the lady—but . . ."

"Dear, please. Good night, Andy. See you at cardiology conference in the morning." Lerner smiled with the look of a man straining at stool.

"Good night, Mrs. Lerner. Harvey." His last image as he turned to continue walking was of a couple staring emptily at each other.

The wind at the corner of Boylston and Tremont Streets blew his long brown hair in all directions, and Essai haphazardly put a hand to his head, as though keeping a cap on, and tried to sort things out. Lerner was not a bad person, but he used his superciliousness as protection against a dumpy wife who never said the right thing. The strain of the last week showed as well. He was probably escaping his work and his wife at the movies. It was news that she and Mrs. Kraft had gone to the symphony together in the past, because Essai could not imagine Ruth Kraft with any real interests other than supporting her husband, "keeping the house nice" for him, or at best, using herself to shield his rough edges from others in social settings. But if she did insist on the symphony, was it to spend Friday afternoons with other women of prominence in Symphony Hall, the music merely an obbligato to a social event? It certainly would be unusual to invite Mrs. Lerner along, if one's reason for going was to be seen in fashionable company.

The light changed. Essai clutched at the folder and the brown bag containing the baklava, and ran across past the Boylston subway station and through the cold Common. Running, swinging the bag gently, he put behind him the Lerners, Krafts, tinseled films, and in fact, the city. Shapes of dark,

end-winter trees passed him on either side as he ran, and
he felt like a schoolboy hurrying home to supper, and then,
abruptly slowly down, like a young lover hoping for a letter.
From run to trot to walk he slowed, finally stopping at the
edge of the treeless, now grassless ground covering the underground garage. Above him, as in a slightly tilted bowl, the
stars and moon burned silently, and Essai stared at the huge
feathery iris about the moon. "A ring around the moon," he
murmured. "The scientists explain it's merely a concentric
layer of ice crystals," he continued. "Augurs nothing more,
perhaps some snow within twenty-four hours. But for me,
for me . . ." his voice dropped and became silent, but as he
began walking his mind continued the phrase ". . . for me,
today is the day *Science* arrives, and could it be that my
article appears today? And tonight I prepare a talk on pericarditis." As he came to Arlington and Beacon, past the fine
buildings with dead blue windows, he kept up the litany,
and as he came within sight of his apartment on the near
side of Berkeley Street, his whole manner became one of
intense yet detached commitment. He could have been a
gambler sweating out the last hole card. "C'mon, you're going
to be there. Don't play with me, just be there when I open
the journal, and let the cold print keep me warm." Almost
against his will he walked more quickly and pulled open the
outside door of the apartment building. The air was smoth-
eringly warm. In the dim light no mail showed on the small
table. Without thinking, not yet ready to give it up, he unlocked the inside door with a cold key and looked sideways
to the right of the door, where the magazines occasionally
were set on the floor.

He saw his name in type, but it was the wrapper to the
New Yorker, empty. Judy must have taken it up. With his
foot, he shoved the brown folder aside. Under it was *Science*,
a photograph of crystals on the cover. He picked it up and
flipped two pages to the contents page. It was not in the
Articles section. It was not in the Issues section. "Contents
continued overleaf." At the top of the next page he read:

Reports

P. 626—Antinuclear antibody in rheumatic fever: An im-
munochem. study—Essai, A. G., Reinsborough, J., and Kraft,
M., Dept of Cardiology, E. Mass. Medical Center, Boston.

Essai leaned against the wall and casually turned to page
626. He felt as though everything were happening in slow
motion. There was the picture of rabbit muscle with flecks
of fluorescence where the human serum and dye had been
applied. The reproduction was good; he had first seen that
picture twenty months before. Of eighty serum samples, none
had given so positive a result as the second one, the one
photographed and reproduced. The curves, the tables, the
honed phrases—it was at once foreign and familiar, like seeing
a photograph of yourself in someone else's album.

Essai went back outside and buzzed his apartment, heard
the door click, and went up the stairs, sixty of them, two at
a time, giddy and exultant as if he were leading a group of
exhausted sprinters effortlessly to the wire. At the top, Judy
had opened the door an inch, and Essai pushed it open, uncertain how to tell her so she could share it with him.

He hit her rump gently with the manila folder and the
issue of *Science*. "Hi, honey, how are you?"

One braceleted arm flashed back and nearly grasped the
journal. Essai involuntarily jerked it away. "Please, Andy, not
when I'm over the stove like this."

"OK." He was in no hurry, equable and easy, triumph calm-
ing him. He appraised the woman fixing his supper. She wore
her wheat-colored hair in an anachronistic ponytail, and it
brushed her shoulders as she worked. Her frame was big and
strong, with long legs that directed the watcher's eyes up,
to disappear tantalizingly under the blue skirt that curved
and sloped toward and away, promising a dizzying ride. Her
broad shoulders and arms would have been masculine had
not every gesture been informed with feminine grace. Her
face as she finally turned to him was flushed, open and intel-

ligent, and her full breasts thrust against the soft blue sweater; only the gray eyes showed reserve.

"Hi, Andy, do you have the soup?"

Essai looked at the brown bag, still in his right hand. "Forgot it," he answered, opening the bag. "But smell this dessert, baklava, made in her own kitchen by the Greek lady. Here, smell."

Judy Lemonning took a step and glanced into the bag, then sniffed quickly. "Don't smell anything, but then I've got all the damn cooking smells in me." She sniffed again, and smiled, then kissed him. Essai felt his geniality pushed aside by passion. He grasped her breast with his right hand, still holding the bag, and kissed her and tried to open her mouth.

She backed away. "Not in the kitchen, honey. I didn't just move in yesterday. Now could you do me a favor and go out and get me the gazpacho?" Essai held up the copy of *Science* in his left hand, and set down the paper bag. He wanted a free hand for emphasis. "Honey, forget the soup with the Spanish name. I have in my left hand a copy of this week's issue of *Science*."

She held up a warning hand. "Andy, I had planned on the soup. Now do you want me to get it?"

His eyebrows went up, but he was still full of good humor. "Lemonning," he began good-naturedly, "forget the soup. A.G.E., young tonight, urges you to listen. What he would have you do is sit by candlelight with the meal and the baklava, and read aloud about fluorescent antibodies against the hearts of rabbits." The lopsided grin doubled the lines in his face. "Here. Page six twenty-six."

Judy took the journal and turned to page 626, read the title, shook her head, then saw the name of the man whose quarters she had shared for seven months. She looked up smiling, eyes and all, and moved against him and opened his mouth with hers, and her hand went down to touch him as they sagged against the refrigerator.

"Lie down, baby," he whispered.

"My skirt, the floor." She began to shake her head. But her

other hand moved to the back of his neck, and they touched and tasted each other.

In retrospect, to Essai at any rate, it was at this moment that his future course with her was decided. What was not apparent to him until even later was that his own course in medicine was irrevocably altered as well. For at this moment the smell of an electric train came first to her and then to Essai, and as she pulled away and swore, "God, the garlic rolls, they're burning," the telephone rang.

"Forget the rolls," he commanded her, but the hands on him had slipped away, and Judy angrily opened the oven door to a puff of acrid smoke. The phone kept ringing.

In two strides he grabbed the phone. "Dr. Essai," he announced tensely.

"Matthew Kraft, Essai. Started on the talk yet?"

"No, no, sir, I haven't had supper yet."

"Oh. Well, did you get the folder of reprints on pericarditis?"

Essai looked over at the fat pile of reprints. Lemonning stood watching him, hands on hips.

"Yes, I got them all right."

"Well, listen, there's a paper of Hazlitt's in there from Baltimore, critical of my saline test. Before you start making notes, I want to warn you about stressing that crap that Hazlitt calls a 'critique.' His charges are stupid; he's jealous that he didn't come up with the test before I did."

"Yes, sir."

Kraft's tone softened. "Now, of course," he said easily, "I'd mention Hazlitt's paper. Don't give the impression that you're sliding over it because it's critical. But let them know tomorrow what you think of it—unsupported speculations about risks of the test that simply aren't risks at all. Take it from me."

"Yes, sir." Essai's face felt a bit sweaty.

"Fine. Fine. By the way, Essai, if you want the advice of a man who's prepared a few more talks than you"—the chuckle here was a mirthless grunt—"I'd suggest working for three hours or so, then eating lightly, then working hard to pull it together. It's something like preparing for an athletic event.

You train yourself, condition yourself, and the work shows in the end result. Believe me. You're sure you got the whole reprint file?"

"Yes, I do. Thank you for your advice, Dr. Kraft."

"Oh, think nothing of it. I'll see you tomorrow morning." Slam.

Essai looked at the phone. He felt Lemonning examining him.

"Well? You must have caught hell; you're sweating with fear."

"Judy, I am not sweating with fear. It was Matthew Kraft though, giving me handy tips on preparing my talk, and exhorting me to do my best for the greater glory of Kraft and the Medical Center. Oh, and maybe cardiology."

"What talk?"

"I forgot," he said. "I guess I was all worked up about the *Science* article. Kraft asked me to give rounds tomorrow, and talk about pericarditis."

She looked at the burnt rolls in her gloved hand. Her eyebrows came up before the eyes. "Doctor," she asked icily, "what are 'rounds'? What is 'pericarditis'? And if you have to prepare a talk for tomorrow, what do I do with the tickets to the Juilliard?"

"Oh no! The Juilliard tonight? I thought it was tomorrow." He looked at his watch. "It's too late anyway; the concert starts in half an hour."

"Fine." She crushed the rolls slightly, rustling like paper. "Now define the words 'rounds' and 'pericarditis,' if you would."

"All right, Miss Designer," he said hotly. "'Rounds' originally meant the trip around the ward from patient to patient. Medical jargon being what it is, rounds later came to mean the discussion of a patient's case, whether at his bedside or in a lecture hall. Cardiac rounds are held every Friday, and a patient is briefly shown, his history presented, and then after he is wheeled out, the discussion of his case begins." Essai took a breath. "Dr. Kraft has discussed all the cases since I've been there, each Friday. As you know, he had a heart attack a week ago. He asked me to give the discussion, or discuss 'at rounds' tomorrow in the lecture hall.

" 'Pericarditis' is inflammation of the wall of the pericardium, the sac lining the heart. We have a patient with that condition in the hospital. Dr. Kraft gave me his reprint file and notes on pericarditis," Essai motioned to the folder, "and tonight I will work for several hours preparing the talk. I'm sure that Lerner and Pruden will actively start hating me as soon as I say the first word."

She thought of congratulating him when she heard that Kraft had picked him, sensing more accurately than he what the implications were. But with the word "hating" she felt the jealous flash as though she herself were Pruden or Lerner. His *Science* paper, his selection as discussant tomorrow—she hated his success, and so said what came first to her mind.

"Wonderful, Andy, just wonderful. Before this, you were a young doctor who couldn't make up his mind about me. Now you're a dedicated physician who has been spared the need to make such a decision."

"What are you talking about?" he asked irritatedly.

She changed the emphasis slightly. "Since you came home you have spent most of the time on the telephone, finding out that you can't spend any time with me tonight. You showed me an incomprehensible *Science* article I'm supposed to gush about, you forgot the soup I asked you to get, and all you can think about is getting me down on the kitchen floor. While the rolls were burning and the whole dinner went to hell. And not a word from you about how my day went today, which I can assure you was not so good." She finished by dropping the last of the burnt rolls into a bag. "Boy, I could use a drink."

"Me too," said Essai morosely.

"You remembered the Scotch, didn't you?"

"Forgot."

Judy ran a hand along her ponytail. "Well, please do me a

big favor, and go out and get the Scotch. Forget about the soup, I'm not hungry. And dump these rolls in the incinerator too," she added.

Essai put on his jacket and she handed him the bag as he opened the door. He peered in and sniffed at the black rolls. Then he put his hand in and took them out. "Hey," he said, "that baklava's still in here."

"What?" Judy walked to the easy chair with the *New Yorker*.

His voice was edgy. "I said that the baklava was still in here, and I was on the verge of throwing out the whole bag."

"Screw the baklava."

"What?"

She stood up, legs apart, and looked steadily at Andrew Essai. "I said, 'Screw the baklava.' Would you like a translation into medical jargon?"

Essai picked out a burnt roll and tossed it to her, underhand. Then he fished in the bag again and took out one of the pieces of baklava. He bit into it, and talked with his mouth full. "Excuse me, Lemonning, for talking with my mouth full, but I didn't grow up in Far Hills. Now when I come back I hope to find you in a different frame of mind, since this is a day of rejoicing for me." He took another bite. "In fact," he mumbled, "I strongly urge you to be in a different frame of mind; and with some food on the table and your charcoal sketches off it."

Quickly he opened the door and closed it behind him. Two steps later he heard a thud, a sharp one, against the door. His eyes narrowed and he reached into the bag and withdrew one of the burnt rolls. "Slightly smaller than a baseball," he thought, "and lighter than a snowball." He turned and wound up but did not throw the roll against his side of the door. Rather he dropped it through the landing, three flights, heard the satisfying *thwock* at the bottom, but did not look, and took out the second piece of baklava, part of which he put into his jacket pocket and part of which he ate, walking slowly down the stairs.

They ate half the meal in silence. Essai had ruined his appetite with the pastry and the arguing. Occasionally he looked at the ominously large folder on the couch. He was "breaking training" by eating before he worked, Kraft would have said. The tensions of Judy's silence and Kraft's call pressed on him; he took a deep breath and cut methodically into the breaded pork chop. Judy Lemonning had eaten almost nothing, but now she took a bite, chewed carefully, and then looked up brightly.

"I tried to read your article while you were out."

"You did? Did you understand it?"

She shook her head. "I tried to figure out the caption under the picture of the heart muscle, but couldn't even get that part." Her hand moved toward his, but didn't touch it. "I really want to congratulate you, though, on having it published."

Essai smiled. "Thank you. The first praiseworthy phrase for my research. It really means something to me." He leaned over and softly kissed her.

Judy pushed her chair back. "That's fine," she commented. "But what did Dr. Kraft think?"

Essai became reflective and stared at his fork. "Well," he said, after a moment, "frankly I'm not sure he'd understand just how the detection method works."

"But his name is on the paper."

"Judy, you don't understand—"

"I'm trying to," she said sharply.

"Sorry, honey. Dr. Kraft is the professor, and boss, and nominally in charge of all research done in his labs. So he has his name on all papers that come out of the lab. In fact, he can exercise a kind of pocket veto over anything he doesn't like, or worse, any person he doesn't like. It's just another way of his letting you know that he is the boss. Usually the threat is implied: 'Do it the way I like or I won't let it go,' and no paper goes out without his OK."

"What if he doesn't like a paper for reasons that turn out not to be sound?" she asked.

Essai shrugged. "He's got you, Judy. It goes even deeper than that. Part of his research funds come from drug companies, as do the research funds for most labs, and it happens that Waring Company gives him over six thousand a year, which they say can be used to investigate new drugs. Well, he accepted an inquiry from them to use their new nitroglycerin preparation on his patients, and about forty patients got the drug. I doubt if he wants the word spread, but one of the fellows last year, Mike Weinberg, spent a lot of hours collecting information about the patients. Weinberg and Ed Pruden went over the data and compared the patients as a group to another group equal in every way, age, sex, and so on, except that the latter group got the standard nitroglycerin preparation."

"They were the control group, right?"

"Right, the control group. Well, what Weinberg and Ed Pruden found was that the group getting the Waring drug not only had less relief from chest pain, but there were six documented heart attacks in that group, and only two in the control group. They finally wrote it up as a paper, though Pruden was very uneasy about it. That all took place a year ago, and Dr. Kraft still has the paper in his drawer with several others."

Judy lit a cigarette. "Wait a minute, Andy. From what you say, he's suppressing information about a dangerous drug. How can he get away with it?"

He raised a cautioning finger. "Hold on, baby. I know that Weinberg brought it up on several occasions, and once even good loyal Ed Pruden mentioned the paper, and Dr. Kraft said either that he was still reading, or that he was trying to decide if the two groups, the experimental and control groups, were really similar."

"Meanwhile he got his six thousand from that drug company this year, right?" Judy puffed on her cigarette reflectively, listening to his answer.

"Yup. He uses a hell of a lot of rabbits in his own research, and he doesn't get his own research funds from the hospital or the government. So you figure out where he gets his research money."

"But I thought you said Dr. Kraft was a great clinical bedside doctor. Why does he do research? And if he approves every study and doesn't understand your research with the rabbit heart, why did he let you submit your paper?"

"Well," commented Essai, "he let my paper go out because it wasn't tied up with drugs, and I explained the method to him on a couple of occasions. In fact, I presented the abstract in Philadelphia last year, and a few research cardiologists asked when the paper was coming out. His stature is elevated every time another paper comes out."

"Fine, but what about his own research?"

Essai stood up and went to the cupboard rack above the refrigerator to get a drink. On his way he noticed a few black crumbs on the carpet near the door. "Thud, thud," he thought. Because he saw the crumbs and heard the noise in his mind again, he decided not to ask her if she wanted a Scotch. He looked at the manila folder. He sighed, forgot about the Scotch for himself, and poured a glass of ginger ale.

"What about his own research?" she repeated.

He walked back. "I don't know about that, Judy." The ginger ale tasted too sweet and he set it down. After a pause, he said, "My own view is that Matthew Kraft is trying to ride two horses. One of them, skill at bedside medicine, is hard for many doctors to ride. For him it's easy. Or he makes it seem easy. He's unquestionably the best clinician in Boston and maybe the country."

"Really, Andy?" Excellence fascinated her.

"Yes, really. If the Nobel Prize were given for outstanding clinical knowledge and teaching, he would win it."

"Isn't it?"

"No," he stated simply. "The best scientists win it. And that is the other horse—scientific inquiry, or lab research, call it what you will. When I talk about academic medicine all the time, what I mean is a man who is not primarily a practitioner, practicing the art, but someone who spends his energy investigating diseases so others can practice their art more scientifically." Again he paused. "You know—" he began.

"What?"

Essai furrowed his brow. "I can't figure out where Matthew Kraft fits in. He did research at one time, I know, and he wrote a paper called 'The Work of the Heart.' But it was published in a clinical journal, *The Annals,* not a research journal. And before the subtitle was the numeral 'I,' as though there were to be others. But he never published 'II' or 'III.'"

"Maybe he tired of that work," she suggested.

He shook his head. "No, not Kraft. He was starting a series of research experiments that would have been classic papers on the work of the heart. But he stopped. Some people say he had a run-in with his boss, and left Cleveland, and went to a state hospital in Ohio. That's where he learned his clinical medicine. And he learned it better than anyone else."

"But he still does research?"

"Yes, he does. Maybe he thinks he can't be a real professor, an 'academic physician,' unless he does. But his lab techniques are only fair, and his ideas aren't workable in a research sense. He gives ideas to men like Lee, the Korean, and they publish little research vignettes. But nothing solid."

"Maybe he's doing it to win the Nobel Prize."

Essai looked at her. "Maybe. He's already professor, he has a national reputation. But it's not enough, Judy. Even if he had the Nobel Prize he would keep trying to do research." Essai stood up and walked a few steps. "You know," he began, turning, "maybe he thinks his skill at teaching and at the bedside is so easy, or easily maintained, that it can't be good. That it's a trick of nature, like holding one's breath for two minutes without training, or running well." Essai gestured at the manila folder. "Take the 'pericarditis talk.' He could give a great talk without preparing anything. Yet he does prepare, as though he were giving it for the first time. He teaches well, he is better at the bedside than anyone else.

"But he insists on spending hours each day thinking up research projects. Each day he talks about experimental heart disease in rabbits. How it's 'key work' if only he can train his technician properly, get the first positive result. So his technician sacrifices a rabbit a day, and reports a negative study every evening to him."

"I'm going to report all you people to the S.P.C.A., killing those rabbits."

Essai smiled. Judy did not smile back. "What is it, Judy?"

"Maybe I'll just report you to the S.P.C.H., cruelty to humans. Why didn't you ask me if I wanted a drink? Should I offer you a dollar for it? Or is it the usual bar Scotch? Seventy cents should do, then. Wait, I'll go and get my purse."

"Oh, Jesus Christ," retorted Essai, angrily. "Sit down and I'll get you a drink. I didn't like the idea of you throwing rolls at my head, that's all."

Her curiosity and interest in Dr. Kraft expired. "I didn't throw a roll at you."

"C'mon, Judy. I heard a thud just after I closed the door, and I still see crumbs down there. So if you feel like lying, at least become a better housekeeper."

She was only a few feet away from him, and she took a step and actually swung her open hand at his face, but he batted her arm down and she followed through, knocking his full glass onto the carpet. Essai stared at the big triangular wet spot and the ice cubes melting quietly on the rectangles of the carpet. "Judy," he said at last, "clean it up."

"No." Her face was congealed and hard, but in waving her head back and forth the lovely ponytail swished, softening her look and making her seem younger. "You do it."

"Judy—"

"Listen, Andy, can't we ever talk about what I do? About my plans and feelings and ideas?" Tears started down, mastered the slight incline at the fine cheekbones, then dripped steadily to her sweater and the floor.

The floor was getting its share to drink, thought Essai inappropriately. "OK," he said grimly. "Start talking, but clean off the floor. I'll get you a Scotch."

She got a sponge and wiped ineffectually at the stain, but picked up the ice cubes and carried them to the sink. She passed him and suddenly bent to put her face into the small of his back. Essai felt her wet and warm, and half-turned to touch her hair.

"Sorry, Lemonning."

She sniffed, nodded several times, and blew her nose. "I don't like being like this, but some days it doesn't go very well. It's just too bad your big day had to be a bad one for me."

"What big day?"

She gestured at the journal, still on the couch. "Oh, your paper," she whimpered. "And you give the talk tomorrow."

"That's right." He had forgotten he had the talk to get ready.

"Well," said Judy in a new voice, falsely cheerful, "I saw Hans Lieds today."

"And?" Essai was thinking about the work ahead of him tonight; he had to start on it now. Get away from this neurotic broad, he thought selfishly.

"And he thanked me for showing them my portfolio, but said they 'Didn't have just the right slot to use any of your designs just now, Miss Lemonning.'" Mimicking the phrase her voice became high and strained. "That queer bastard."

"Easy, baby."

She glared at him. "Well, he is, he and his 'associates,' all looking *me* up and down, with my portfolio in the corner."

"How about the coffee house design? Didn't they like that?"

She shrugged. "Of course they like it. They liked everything I had to show them. It's the worst kind of reception; the bland expressions of interest, the lack of straightforward criticism, and all the time I could tell they were invoking the old prejudice against the woman designer, the young person." She stopped and looked over Essai's shoulder, with a face so baleful and malevolent that he instinctively turned to see if anyone were there. "And the whole hour these gay little clowns in turtleneck sweaters or ascots would come through the office and point at my coffee house design or the outdoor patio sketch and say to one another, 'Oh, look at that simply wonderful use of restricted space,' and 'She's got a marvelous sense of the way things ought to be, you know.'" Judy lapsed into tense silence.

"You wouldn't want to take a job in a big design place, just helping plug the holes there while you waited for your chance?" Andy suggested. Her gray eyes regarded him with ice; his name was no doubt being added to the list of the day's enemies. "I guess it's toughest outside New York," he ended lamely.

She sat forward a little in the red cloth chair and dropped her chin onto a wide palm. "Keep going," she said quietly. "I'm tougher than you think."

"What did I say now, honey?"

She got up and retrieved the issue of *Science* from the couch, then sat down and began prattling away in a frightening monologue. "Oh, Dr. Easy, is that it? oh pardon me, of course we here at the Northern Medical Center are pleased to have the chance to assess your work, and articles like this—thin and fragmentary though they are—do show promise. Yes, you've got quite a nice series of preliminary reports here, but short on the controls and just a trace shy on clean, steel-trap thinking, the kind we here at Northern simply demand from even our junior men. Now mind you, Dr. Esia, we think this work shows considerable promise in the research area, and wonder if you wouldn't benefit even more from a few years of—well, shall we say seasoning—yes, just a few years of the rigorous, first-rate clinical research we feel you're capable of, done perhaps in a bigger center, say in Chicago, a center where you could share ideas with physicians of a trace more—uh—more mature research instinct, as it were. To be brutally frank, Dr. Essey, even the best research man can do with a few years of plugging up the holes, helping busier hands guide the rough edges, all the time learning his skill, making contacts, getting the feel of research medicine from the inside.

"What's that, Dr. Assay? You feel you've done your apprenticeship? These papers here show it? Well, as I began to say just a moment ago, we'd certainly like to hear more from you when your work takes on a bit more substance, a trifle more thoroughgoing critical insight, say in a few years, or maybe ten or forty or a hundred?" Her voice rose to a shriek, and she raged up out of the chair and hurled the now-crumpled journal at the pale man sitting on the far end of the couch. Then she sniffed, looked at her large hands with the tapered fingers, and began sobbing and talking again. She went on for about ten minutes, and only the restraint of the physician in the presence of a hysterical patient kept Essai from beating her into silence with his fists. It also occurred to him that since the odd meeting with Dr. Kraft in his room tonight, much of what she said lost its validity. He forced himself to listen to her, if only to assess the patient's complaint.

What she was telling the doctor in wobbling fashion was that by living with him she had sacrificed everything and gained nothing, feeding his ego from her own soul as it were, stripped of independence, forced to submit to the life of a passive housewife, without the salve of marriage and certainly without the balm of love. She had no life of her own, she said, and by becoming subservient to him—at first to please him and later to keep him—she had lost the ability to conduct her affairs in a creative fashion.

Essai felt sad, not angry at all, listening to the anguished torrent of words. He stopped listening again and watched her. The gesticulating hands moved independently of the rest of her, directing a hundred dismissing gestures at him, and the red face shifted incessantly, as though trying to escape from her cold and alien eyes. She appeared to be tearing herself apart, but when he tuned in, it was he who was being excoriated.

"So it's obvious," he heard, "that I underestimated entirely your ability to be a bastard. You want me to be responsive to your needs, only at the expense of my own feelings, and one needs no more proof than to see how you flaunt your puny success in my face at the very time I am being rebuffed. Well, do me a favor, Andy. Take your Scotch and your science and all those bound volumes of medical facts, and go away and leave me alone." She stopped, more from breathlessness than anything else.

"Hey, Lemonning, shut up for a minute," he said quietly. She appeared surprised to see him able to speak. The ripe-wheat ponytail curled over her shoulder and breast, giving her a coquettish look. She looked down at it and angrily flung it back.

"You really want to get at me, don't you, Judy?"

She looked around for a cigarette, then picked up her drink instead. "What are you talking about," she hissed.

He folded his hands judiciously. "Lemonjuice, I've know you for a long time. I was at Amherst when you were at Vassar, and I used to arrive by bus, the grimy biology major riding for hours to be with his debutante honey."

"Stop talking nonsense," she commanded. But she was quieting down, remembering.

"For the next few years," he went on, "you were at Cooper Union and I was in New Haven struggling through Yale Medical School. When I got a weekend off and came down, tired as hell and ready for soft, loving Judith, you were gaily announcing our plans for the weekend: quiet expensive restaurants, Off-Broadway plays, and the inevitable trips to Far Hills to show me the ultimate goal I should seek."

"We'd never let you in Far Hills," she muttered.

He raised a hand, and his voice rose with it. "Quiet. Then you went to Paris, originally with Janice Land, only to return a year later with a fashion photographer. As you remember, this absence dovetailed nicely with my internship in St. Louis, a job and town wholly unsuited for the Renaissance Woman." She started to speak but he stood up. "Just another minute, Citrus. Then the fashion photographer went gay on you, and the jobs were tough to get, and you insulted Emily Maloney the second week there, and Roger Halford got you into his apartment by asking you to show him your sketches—an unusual twist."

"Keep it up, you bastard." She actually bared her teeth.

"I plan to. The string was run out, and you were on West Twenty-Second Street, ready to become a part-time model, since Daddy's checks were more and more unpredictable. Suddenly I sent news that I had taken a job with Matthew Kraft in Boston, first as chief resident, then as instructor in his department. Boston, that's not St. Louis, hot and midwestern. No, sir. So you came up to stay a weekend, full of recipes for soup and Sauce Arturo, and a few items of clothing. The rest, I found out a month later, had been neatly packed and sent back to the little old truck farm out near Morristown. You moved in." Here Essai looked at her quizzically, then roared out as though the thoughts were passing through him and someone else was using the megaphone. "You moved in, you calculating bitch, and grabbed onto me as hard as you could. You said before I made you an instrument of my will. That's a joke, Squeeze. You thought you could become the wife of a rising young physician with a concentrated effort, but what you really wanted was to bind me to you, so I couldn't escape. The *Science* article, the talk tomorrow are the first signs to you that I'm not bound to you; I'm still rising on my own, and Hans Lieds today put you down just a bit more. Soon you won't be good enough for me. Isn't that a joke on the Vassar bitch? The pale student doesn't need the debutante after all. Tomorrow he's standing in for Matthew Kraft himself." He ended on a note of wonderment, as though he had just realized it as he said it.

She stood up, drawn and beautiful. "Excuse me, I want to use the bathroom."

Flustered, he bowed and pointed the way. "Of course, miss; it's the first door on the right."

He filled another glass a third full of Scotch, trying not to hear the crying in the bathroom. Then things settled down, and he was reassured by the domestic sounds: Judy blowing her nose, the toilet flushing; water running in the sink. He picked up the journal from the floor and counted the articles under the list of contents. Forty-two articles this week alone. He was author of one of two thousand papers in a year in one of a hundred journals, and his four-page article, the distillate of eighteen months in the lab, seemed suddenly as puny as she intimated it was. He shuddered, hunching his shoulders together to stop it, and drank the Scotch in three hot swallows. He did not want to stand in for Kraft tomorrow, attempt to emulate him, or be a loving son to him. Or to Lemonning either. He wanted to be at the string quartet concert, alone.

He started pacing around the small living room, wondering at how subtle shifts in feelings could bring him to question the meaning of his work the very day his first article appeared in print. For the last time he glanced at the *Science* article, ripped out the few pages, stuffed them in his back pocket, and nearly ran to the window, shoving it up to let in the fresh air. Friday-night couples were walking close, against the wind, and the light on the John Hancock Building glowed blue, predicting fair weather. Essai leaned out the window on both palms, looking for the ring around the moon.

A hand closed firmly on his ankle and for an instant, thinking he was being pushed out, Essai kicked back hard against something yielding, heard an "oof," and scrambled back inside. Judy was crouched over, her right hand on the arm of the chair, the left pressed against her groin. As Andrew stood up and looked at her, she sat back onto the couch.

"I thought you were falling out," she grunted.

"Oh, honey, I'm sorry. I felt the hand and got scared I guess. Did I get you in the belly?"

"A little lower than that, thank you."

He noticed that she had on fresh makeup and a different sweater. The tiniest needle of guilt pricked at him, making him thoughtful and vulnerable. Had he meant to kick her away, lashing out at her from self-generated frustration?

"Have you got a light, Andy?" She was serious as hell, and her eyes told him nothing.

"Sure, honey, here."

She bent, throwing away the words, "Were you planning on going out tonight?"

"What? Me going out? What time is it?" He squinted at the

tiny clock on the top of the bookcase, one she had given him years before. "Jesus, it's almost ten o'clock. I have to start reading papers for the talk."

She inhaled deeply and blew out the smoke, more tense than reflective. "I must have hurt her with that kick," he thought.

"Maybe you'd better go out for a while, Andy."

"Why?" For an instant he thought someone was behind him, perhaps coming through the window with the cold air, but he held himself from turning and looked instead at her. "What is it?"

"Well," she said, matter-of-factly, "I don't think I mentioned it to you over the phone when you called from work, but there was one bright spot at Hans Lieds' today."

"Yes?"

"One of the associate designers, Frantz Dewalt, seemed to like my portfolio, and he was a good deal more sincere than the rest of them."

"He wasn't a homosexual?"

She shot him a look. "I'm afraid I can't categorize people as well as you, doctor."

Essai took a step away from her. "Keep going."

"After my hour there with the rest of them, Frantz saw that I looked a little green, or at least crestfallen, and as it was about lunchtime—"

"I think I've heard this tune before," Essai said flatly.

"As it was about lunchtime," she continued scornfully, "and since he possesses more gallantry than you will ever know, he asked me if I wouldn't join him for some lunch."

"Wait a minute, Judy. If you felt all that disappointed and empty, why didn't you call me at the hospital?"

"At the hospital!" she hooted. "I'm sure you would have left your precious work on rabbits to come home and be with me. More likely, you would have suggested I come into the emergency room to obtain a mild sedative. Humanity cries for help, and science offers prescriptions for insomnia!"

"Lay off it," he warned. "Well, what happened to Dewalt? I'll tell you. He took you to a quiet though not intimate French restaurant but one, fortunately, where cocktails are served. Right?"

Her face took on the hate-hurt look of an hour before, and he felt lustful and angry again, knowing that he would have to glue the pieces together with sex to keep them from breaking any smaller, and chastising himself for wanting to.

"Right, right, doctor. And I had a small glass of pernod on ice, and he had one."

The mending lust rose and died, like an exhausted candle, and he caught her anger. "And you shed tears quietly, without whimpering."

"It wasn't a stage play, you bastard."

"Well, if it wasn't a stage play," he raged, "tell me how the real-life drama was played out."

She stood up, almost taller than he, calm eyes ready to observe his reaction. "He's coming over a few minutes after ten."

"Here?" He could have been asking an elevator man if he had the right floor.

"Here," she announced. "He wants to go over my portfolio."

"Your portfolio? I'll bet." Essai felt nauseated, as though he had been the one kicked in the stomach.

"I was impressed with him," she went on, "and he certainly improved my spirits. He has a really wonderful mind, like a steel trap, and he wants to go over my work critically. I think he can help me."

Essai exploded. "Will you cut out this 'steel trap' shit? Of course he'll look at your stupid portfolio, but mainly he wants your steel trap, the one between your legs that clutches and rips it off and turns out the victims bleeding afterward."

"You're a joke," she said shortly. God, but she was calm now.

"And you," he blazed, "are an emasculating whore."

She puffed at her cigarette. He grabbed it from her hand, and for a moment held on to it and seemed to expand, as though it were transporting some foreign substance into him. But he finally gave it back, not even crushed. "Fine," he said.

"You can talk to him here, and go through the dreary artist bit here, but go back with him to his place for the main event."

She said nothing.

"Or to put it another way, don't come back here afterward. If you're here when I come back I'll throw you out the window. And if you *do* it with him here . . ." His voice trailed off. The pork chops and baklava rumbled uncertainly in his stomach.

"He'll be here any minute," she said in a low voice. They looked like a pair of marathon dancers.

"OK." He got his navy-surplus pea jacket out of the closet and jammed his arms into it. In the bathroom he combed his hair without looking at his face. With the jacket zipped up and the collar against his neck, he felt the carotid pulse at over a hundred. He stepped back into the living room, eyes down, and picked up the manila folder. Kraft's textbook also went under his arm. To get it, he put his hand an inch from hers as it touched the table. She touched his hand. Mounds of tears were gathered in her gray eyes for the descent, and through his own blurred vision he had never seen her more beautiful.

"So long, Lemonning," he whispered.

She nodded. "You're coming back?"

He felt the folder and the book, and looked sharply at the woman about to betray him. "I'm going to the lab to get this talk ready."

"The talk should be between us, Andy." She stood and took a step toward him.

"No," he said loudly. "Have him help you move your stuff out. Go there if you want. I'll have many talks to prepare in this apartment."

"Stay. I'll call him." She could not believe he was actually saying good-bye like this.

"No." He nearly ran to the door, and slammed it. Three stairs down he heard her shout: "Study hard, doctor!" A dozen retorts occurred to him, but he gripped Kraft's textbook and kept on going.

The talk on pericarditis was finished at four thirty in the morning, and when Essai looked around the silent lab, all the equipment seemed changed. The centrifuges, refrigerators, even the tubes of cardiogram paste had acquired a foreign cast. Nothing was important to him now except for the sheets of notes he had made and the formed lecture that turned and rolled pulsing in his mind. He walked to his apartment through the cold streets of Boston, and only at the last minute did he dial his own number, praying that the disruptive female was gone. He let it ring twenty times or more, then hung up gratefully, trotted the last dark blocks, and once inside, set the alarm and fell heavily on the bed.

He dreamed hundreds of fragments; that he overslept his talk, that Kraft interrupted him and hit him in the chest repeatedly, saying "These are my rounds, impudent son," that Lerner and Pruden kept others out of the hall and he had no one to speak to, and finally, just before he awoke, that Lemonning took his notes away and scrawled on the Scallard Hall blackboard: "No Lecture Today."

Awakening, he thought he was late, but it was not yet six. He showered, changed his shirt, and over several cups of coffee read his lecture notes again. He thought Judy would have left a letter for him, but he decided to look around later. In some ways it was like nights before exams in medical school when one kept every other stimulus away, fearing the casual voice or newspaper headline that might pull the plug and cause all the rammed-in information to run out uselessly.

Kraft was awake when Essai knocked cautiously at his door an hour later. As though Kraft too wanted no distractions, he nodded a greeting and said, "Start talking, Essai."

George Winston sat at the nurses' desk, writing a note in Dr. Kraft's chart when Essai stepped off the elevator shortly after noon. Winston stood up and smiled. "They say you gave quite a talk this morning, Andy. Congratulations."

Essai looked at him, surprised. "Thank you."

"But our prize patient (Winston tapped the chart) is doing well. His enzymes are normal, the cardiogram is stable. He'll be back at work in three or four weeks."

Essai grinned lopsidedly. "That's fine with me. Then I can use the bed to be treated for exhaustion."

"Essai!" The shout carried to them.

"The man himself," said Winston quietly. "Andy, come over to our rounds at the Metropolitan next Thursday, and we'll give you a couple of tough cases to figure out."

"Oh, no." Essai blushed. "That's still Dr. Kraft's baby."

Winston shook his head. "He just asked me to invite you. Better rest up for it, doctor."

Going down the hall, Essai felt curiously depressed. Maybe he was too tired to appreciate Winston's invitation to be presented cases for discussion at the Metropolitan. But the real reason dropped in: he felt like a passive tool in Kraft's hands. Kraft should have told him, or better, asked him, before talking it over with Winston as though his acceptance were of no importance.

At the door he heard his own muffled voice lecturing. He knocked. At once a tape recorder snapped off.

"Come in, Essai."

Kraft was sitting in a chair. A journal half-hid the tape recorder.

"I didn't know you were taping it, Dr. Kraft." A dull cinder of resentment began to glow.

"Forget that, Essai. You should listen. It was all right, but you got rushed at the end and glossed over several points. And you say 'uh-uh-uh' every other word." Kraft watched him. He allowed himself a small smile. "But it was good. I just remembered that next month I've been asked to speak in

Providence. I ought to be on my feet then, but maybe you could give the talk and I might make a few comments afterward."

"You mean pericarditis again?"

"Sure. You can play this tape back, read your notes. Then check the latest journals to get a current reference or two. It's much easier the second time."

Essai felt the ache in his neck. "I hope so," he said wearily.

"It will be. You'll see."

Kraft was right. The week before Christmas, Essai drove the Oldsmobile to Providence, and Kraft sat next to him, talking about how good it was to be back on his feet. At the Rhode Island General, Essai was introduced by Kraft, and at the end of his talk he heard the spattering of applause for the first time. Kraft made some points again during the discussion, and stressed his own saline test, but he carefully kept it Essai's show. On the way back, he asked how Essai liked his new life.

"It's different, Dr. Kraft. I'm starting to get the feel of it, but I'm glad you're around again." Essai paused.

"What don't you like about it, Andy? Tell me."

"Well, Dr. Kraft, Pruden is not very happy about things. Harvey Lerner is easier on me, but Pruden digs all the time. Maybe if he had an occasional talk to give—"

"No, he won't goddammit." Kraft had become instantly angry.

"Oh, well—"

Kraft hit the glove compartment with the flat of his hand. Then he opened it, took out a pack of cigarettes, and lit one. He offered one to Essai, who declined. "Don't say anything, but I've got to have a cigarette once in a while. Winston says I can't." Kraft inhaled slowly. "Well, when you upset me, I've got to."

"Why? Why not Pruden for a lecture now and then?"

Essai was interrupted again. Lacking Lee's Oriental calm,

he engaged his boss. Kraft glared at him briefly. Then he began talking softly, but with the rush of words the authoritative edge returned. "No, Essai, not Pruden. Pruden is a nice man, and he helps teach medical students, he helps Lerner when the cardiograms pile up, and he sees a few patients for me in the clinic. He is a helper, a functionary. Lerner knows a little more, but he buries himself inside that cardiogram room and never comes out. I don't want to turn these things over to men who will do their duty like clerks. Between you and me, Essai, I would rather not turn the duties over at all."

"I see."

The curtain of smoke slid off the window at Essai. "Do you, doc? Do you know that I first spoke in Providence to an audience of eleven? Yes, eleven doctors. Today you had ninety. I got them there, or my name did, and you stepped in. Keep it in mind, buddy. The first talk I gave on my own was in Massillon, Ohio, twenty-five years ago, and they billed me as 'the crazyhouse doctor.' No one smoothed the way for me."

Essai clutched the wheel. "Well, if you don't want me to give any more talks, that's OK."

"Jesus Christ, Essai, don't get paranoid on me." During Kraft's hospital stay he had lost thirty pounds, and to Essai it seemed strangely as though a slim ghost of his boss were talking to him from the other seat. "Here I give you a chance to give talks, be the 'professor' at the Metropolitan conferences, and you get like this. Boy, I don't understand you."

"Yes, sir." Essai clenched his teeth. He wouldn't say anything else. They had another twenty miles to drive anyway, and he wanted only the solitude of his apartment and a long drink.

Kraft was chuckling. "Now I get it. Now I get it."

Essai said nothing. In the back of his mind he sensed that he had gained an indefinable advantage over Kraft. He had been the man picked; Kraft was supporting him. Kraft had just dismissed Lerner and Pruden, and Lee was out. If Kraft wanted to stay in his department he had no place to go for a man to help with the load. So Essai stayed rebelliously quiet.

"I get it," Kraft grinned. "OK, Essai. What's your rank? Your academic rank, I mean."

"Instructor. Dr. Kraft." He added the name after a tiny pause. No use pushing the advantage.

"Salary?"

"Nine thousand." He felt he was being interviewed.

"Fine," Kraft said quickly. He lit another cigarette. "The department of medicine meets next week. I'll put your name up for assistant professor. At twelve thousand. Effective the first of January. Consider it done."

"Thank you. I'm very surprised." Essai meant it. Kraft was notorious for giving low salaries and slow promotions.

They were nearly at the hospital when Kraft said, "OK, professor. You make attending rounds in January. On my floor. You do the intern and resident teaching, go around each day—you know, as I did. Of course, I'd like to follow the sick patients with you."

Essai laughed. "I'll need a lot of help from you, Dr. Kraft."

Kraft nudged his shoulder. "Of course. You be my legs for that month. We'll see how it goes. By the way, what plans do you have tonight?"

"None. Oh, a quiet evening at home."

"Well," Kraft laughed easily, "now that you're an assistant professor in the five-figure salary range, you might spend some evenings reading about new areas in cardiology, to cement your own new area, if you get me."

Kraft was this jovial only when the guillotine was well sharpened, Essai knew. Whose neck was on the block? "What areas, for example?"

"Oh, take the field of heart transplants, for example. Essai, do you know how much stuff is appearing in the surgical journals on transplants?"

Surgical journals? "Well," Essai began tentatively, "I don't keep up so much—"

"What? Don't keep up? This is the new wave in cardiology, professor." Kraft's tone was still mocking, but light, too light even for a man convalescing from a heart attack. "Great stuff," Kraft continued. "At Columbia there's a fellow, Armin Fermanian, who turns out paper after paper on things like transplant rejection, even anti-lymphocyte serum. He's kept dog transplant recipients alive for nearly a year. Others get headlines for their human transplants, but how many of those patients are still alive? Fermanian will wait till he's really ready; but then I'd wager anything he takes the lead in this field. And for a surgeon, he writes beautiful papers. I read one yesterday, in *Current Surgical Research*. You ought to keep up with that, Essai."

They were in the hospital parking lot, but Kraft seemed in no hurry to dismiss his driver. Essai shrugged. "I don't understand your interest in this, frankly, Dr. Kraft."

"Why." It shot at him.

Essai smiled nervously. "Well, you're quite critical of surgeons. Especially heart surgeons. So I always took the view you had. Any work from a surgical lab has to be read especially critically, and real advancements in human heart transplants are years away."

"When did I say that?"

Essai looked over at him. God, not ten minutes ago he had been promoted, an hour ago applauded in Providence, and now he was back in the defensive crouch. "I don't know," he muttered quietly at last.

"Now look, Andy, don't get upset. You did very nicely tonight, and I think the salary raise is justified." Kraft lit another cigarette. "But as you rise in academic medicine, people fire hard questions at you. Including questions on the prospects of transplant work. Don't you agree?"

"Yes."

"Now in the past," Kraft continued, "I've been hard on the surgeons, and I still think most of them are unfeeling butchers. But I've had time recently to read more, and I advise you for your own good to keep up with the surgical literature in heart disease." Kraft made an expanding motion. "Then you are really an assistant professor in cardiology, in all of it."

Essai sighed. "So I guess I spend the evening reading the

new stuff about heart transplants. I don't have many reprints on that."

Kraft nudged him. "I'm your library. I've got folders full on transplants."

"OK. But my first love is still rheumatic fever."

"Good, Essai. Pick out one of my folders, and read it over slowly. Maybe then the rheumatic fever file. You were hesitating down there in Rhode Island when they asked you about cortisone in rheumatic fever, by the way."

"I know. All right, I'll take a transplant file too."

Essai trudged home with three folders as it turned out, but spent most of the night trying to assess what his new relationship with Kraft was to be. Well, there was only so much he could demand, Essai decided.

Sleep eluded him that night.

Andrew Essai had subscribed to the Boston Celebrity series beginning in September, and the Juilliard String Quartet concert in November was the first event he missed. During the next three months, he missed the Philadelphia Orchestra and the Rostropovich concert, among others. He also stopped picking up *The New York Times* on the way to work. Lemonning sent him cryptic postcards from a Cambridge address, one saying, "Late at night I call, and get no answer. Who is she?" When Essai saw that one he laughed. "She" was "it," the slow progressive increase in responsibilities and position that kept him in the hospital late most nights, out of town every other week, and even, after the first of the year, at a "working dinner" at the Krafts.

Essai could not believe how Kraft worked. Mrs. Kraft would prepare a magnificent meal, which Kraft wolfed down, talking continuously about medicine. Essai and Ruth Kraft drank the wine, Matthew Kraft pausing between bites to say, "Easy on the wine, Essai, we've got work to do." After supper they went upstairs to the study, and for three or four hours they talked about a single subject in cardiology. Or rather, Kraft talked. He said he had to apologize for falling behind the recent literature, but he had promised his wife to spend three nights a week "downstairs," and so did not keep up as he had done before.

Kraft did not have to make excuses. Essai came to understand that his overwhelming ego was a function of what he knew. Not about wines, music, painting—but about what mattered. He had learned more cardiology and probably more medicine than anyone else. His knowledge of the literature was fantastic, and his approach to a subject, the way in which he studied it, was remarkable to observe. If a new technique appeared, he struggled to learn it, and he incorporated the new facts into the ideas he already held, especially the transplant research.

Each time the evenings were over, Essai drove home convinced that he would never know enough to call himself a real doctor, and committed anew to try to help Matthew Kraft keep his department the way he wanted it. In January and February, he gave talks on chest pain, rheumatic heart disease, congenital heart disease, and finally, after two supper sessions with Kraft, a talk on 'The Approach to the Heart Patient.' They traveled to New Hampshire, New York, Connecticut, and in February, to Los Angeles. Essai wrote the first draft of an editorial on new drugs ultimately appearing in the *New England Journal of Medicine* (Kraft changed every phrase to the better and, though unsigned, it was his) and Essai reviewed articles submitted to the journals *Cardiology* and *Circulation*. Though Kraft returned to full duties in the department, it was Essai who screened the outside calls about possible admissions, and he spoke at cardiac conference at least twice a month. Pruden stopped talking to him, and Lerner began to show him the deference reserved for a superior.

Only his laboratory research suffered. Essai came into the lab the last Friday in March, after a hurried snack in the cafeteria. It looked strange to him. He had not handled a pipette in nearly three months. His notebook was dusty, and the lab smelled of disuse. On impulse, Essai sat down at his bench and looked through his last few experiments, done the end of November. He was tired—tired after a twelve-hour day spent talking at cardiac conferences, making teaching rounds on the sixth floor, seeing two patients in clinic, and finally, at six, looking over the residents' shoulders as they cared for a man with a massive heart attack and complete heart block. Kraft had stayed as well, then left at seven saying to the resident, "O'Connell, Essai will stay for another hour or so."

So he had. The patient, Mr. Budick, was doing well. Essai called Dr. Kraft at home, gave him a follow-up on the patient, and wondered what to read at home that night. When he left the Eastern Massachusetts Medical Center, he felt uneasy in the cold March air, as though he should still be in the hospital, rechecking the man with heart block, giving the residents advice and managing the case.

But after a moment outside, he took a breath and spoke to himself. "It's not a priesthood for me yet. I should take a night off." On impulse, he went to Averof and ate egg-lemon soup and talked with Helena about Athens. The Greek music and heavy baklava took him away from the hospital in spirit as well as fact, and he left a little before nine, satisfied and happy, with a piece of baklava wrapped in waxed paper in his pocket.

Essai walked up Broadway, past the drunks, the giggling couples. He wondered where Lemonning was, whether she had sufficiently (or further) emasculated the designer in Cambridge. Remembering her wheat-colored hair, mouth-opening embrace, he shook his head wonderingly. He had had no woman close to him since the evening with her in November. For the first time he understood how Matthew Kraft could live month after month and be unaware of the passionate woman who was his wife.

He looked at the laughing girls who passed him with their dates. Again he shook his head. Glancing up, he saw the moon, ringed with a halo, as though it were going to snow. But it was March, late for snowstorms. Essai took a left on Boylston Street and walked across Park Square to the entrance of Peretti's tobacco shop. The warm lighted windows let good taste and gentility flow into the street. Essai pressed his face against the two big windows and gazed at the forty kinds of cigarettes, pipe tobaccos of every conceivable mix and tapered cigars, set in elegant patterns. Inside one could observe two salesmen, dressed in gray coats, waist-length. One was lighting his pipe, the other whisking a few flakes of pipe tobacco off the brass scales. They were what one would have expected; honest, deferential men, ready to offer a word of advice about a particular brand, though gently, without insulting the intelligence of the customer. Peretti's Prufrocks, thought Essai. The cheerful, orderly shop made him feel colder, more isolated, hostile. He yanked up his pea jacket zipper and walked in.

"Good evening, sir, could I help you?"

"Yes, thanks, my usual will be fine." Andrew Essai stared straight at him.

The man, holding a pipe in his square hand, looked blankly at the other salesman, who shrugged. He smiled at Essai. "And that, sir—"

"That, my man, is the brand I have been using for fourteen years. Have you by some egregious error forgotten?"

"Well, ah, it seems that it has slipped my mind. Yes, sir, now if you could give me your name perhaps I could look it up in our records, that is, if you've ever ordered my mail—"

"I have not." Essai pulled on the drawstrings of his jacket. "Oh, never mind, give me something like the British blend. Not all that stringy, fast-burning stuff either—something with a little burley."

Reprieved, the pleasant man in gray reached for a yellow tin. "Perhaps this, sir, our mixture number one twenty-five, slow-burning but very popular with European travelers."

"I'm in Boston, buddy. I live here. I work here. Have you got a Boston workingman's blend?"

"Well, now," the man was trying to decide if he was being put on. "Ah, Fred, do you think you could help this gentleman?"

The other man, peering through the scales as at a slightly

tawdry show, straightened up. "Fine, sir, what can I do for you."

Essai slouched. "Pack 'a Red Man chewin' tobacco."

"What?"

"Red Man. Plug cut. Quarter size."

Fred looked at the other salesman who was twisting the stem of his pipe. "Have we got any chewing tobacco?"

"I don't know; I'll check."

"Forget it," said Essai. "I'll get it at the bus station. Hear they got a better selection over there anyhow. Better tell old man Peretti to shape up this place." He wheeled and walked out.

Outside, he wondered where to go, then shrugged and turned to his left into the Trailways bus station three doors down. Behind the newstand an old man crouched over a copy of the *Morning Telegraph*. Essai waited till he looked up from the Lincoln Downs entries. "Got any Red Man?"

"I guess so. Wait a minute. Don't get much call for it."

"I'll wait." Essai held up his hands and looked at the palms; not a callous.

The man came back with the package. "Little dusty," he said. "Like I said, not many calls for chewin' tobacco."

Essai put down a fifty-cent piece, took the package and started for the door. "Hey, wait," the man called, "it's only twenty cents." Essai waved him off and went out. He took out a plug and set it high in his right cheek with his right thumb, chewed a few times tentatively, and spat a thin stream of saliva into the street. He went past Peretti's, where the two men again stood quietly, waiting to serve. Essai pushed open the door and held up the red and white package, turning his distorted face slightly to the left. "This is it, gents; Red Man— better tell old man Peretti to get on the ball." He thought about spitting on the window glass, but instead raced across Park Square, against the light.

At the opposite corner, he almost bowled over Ruth Kraft, waiting for the light.

"Andrew Essai, is that you?"

"Yes." What could he do with the plug of tobacco? To hell with it. He chewed once or twice. "I don't usually chew this stuff. What are you doing here?"

"I'm going to get some pipe tobacco in Peretti's," she said.

"Pipe tobacco? I've only seen your husband smoke cigarettes. Is he trying to switch to a pipe?"

Her eyes widened and she stammered, "Ah—yes, yes, I thought he should try it. All that smoking can't be good for him after the heart attack."

"That's right."

She smiled. "Come with me to Peretti's and help me pick some out."

Essai recalled the gray clerks. He pointed to his frayed jacket, then to his lumpy cheek. "No, I'm not—"

She laughed girlishly and took his arm. "Come on with me, shy one, it won't take a minute."

Fred and his cohort gave the insolent young man a mean look, but the lady on his arm was certainly respectable. She had a good effect on him too; before he had been insulting, now he deftly suggested some good blends and seemed quite accommodating. When they left, Fred said, "Could that lady be keeping him?"

The other man whisked imaginary tobacco off the scale. "Since they let the hippies onto the Common," he said mildly, "nothing I see around here surprises me any more."

Meanwhile, the young doctor and the professor's wife, walked toward the garage through the park. They were no longer arm in arm, but she walked close to him. She had on some wonderful perfume. "Let me drop you off somewhere, Andy."

"No," he said, "I'm just taking a walk. My apartment is near here."

She looked at him, saw how innocently he meant it, and smiled. "I'll bet you have a whole rackful of good wine there."

"No, no. I like it, but I don't know much about wine."

"You enjoy it when you have dinner at our house. I think it's nice to know and like nice things."

"If you have the time," he said.

They walked down the steps to her car on the first underground ramp. "Don't say that, Andy. Make the time. I'd hate to see your vocation change you."

He nodded, uneasily. They were in the car, and he associated it with Kraft, shoptalk, challenges and tension. Not perfume and softness. Suddenly he remembered Esther Rudnick's perfume. "Every older woman wants it," she had said, her hair over the leather seat, "especially from a beautiful man like you."

"Look," Andy said, his hand on the door handle. "My apartment is nearby." He blushed. Jesus, exactly what he didn't want to say. "I mean, I can walk from here."

"Fine," she said.

He looked at her oval face and breathed in the perfume. "Good night," he said.

"Good night." A trace wistful. Andy got out and walked quickly up the ramp. At the corner he moved closer to a tree, nearly hidden from the ramp. The Oldsmobile drove up out of it slowly, and down Beacon Street. Essai sniffed his jacket sleeve, wanting the perfume smell. He looked up to see her turn left on Arlington.

"She's coming around the block," he thought. "Don't do it. Don't let her see you." A minute later the car came by where he stood, and Essai felt the sweat under the jacket collar, but he did not move an inch. The Olds slowed, hesitated, then picked up speed and went down Charles Street toward Storrow Drive. "To the Drive and away," he thought. He should have stopped her when she drove by. What a perfumed exhilarating mess that would have been.

He rubbed his hands together, trying to remember how they felt when calloused. After his sophomore year at Amherst he had gotten a job as a laborer at Starret Housing, and when they saw his soft hands and heard he went to college, pre-med no less, they rode him all summer, and called him "shoveling doc." His boss was Harry Myers, who delighted in expressions like, "Another day, another dollar," or "Well, that's the worst of it done," and Harry Myers set aside ten percent of his wages for the church. After his junior year, Essai worked for Rudnick Builders, and he spent the week before he started twirling a spade handle two hours a day. He came on the job Monday with a package of Red Man chewing tobacco in his back pocket and callouses on his hands, and it turned out to be the best summer he ever spent. Never had life been so simple, so full of joy. He dug footers for new houses and raked cool wet cement down the shallow pits, sweating in the Maryland sun and making himself thirsty. When he walked into Estelle's with Sell and Jackson at three, he would ease his shoulders against the sweaty chambray shirt, wipe his brow with his sleeve, put the plug of tobacco in the Cliquot Club ashtray, and swallow the first draft beer with shuddering delight.

Esther Rudnick had liked it too, Essai remembered, thinking he was a college dropout and trying to find himself, and when he got her in the sweaty back seat of her '55 Lincoln, she said, "My bronzed God, Oh my bronzed God," over and over, while he inhaled the weird leather smell and grit his teeth to drive the shovel in better than old Rudnick himself.

Essai went into the Public Garden and walked along the empty pond bed. He spat again and again, trying to hit a rock about ten feet out, but gave it up and spat out the plug after he swallowed a little and remembered how sick one could get chewing after a long layoff. Things had last been as clean and unique as the leather and draft beer about ten years ago. Kids eight years old in 1955 would be working as laborers for $3.25 an hour this summer, hoping to show off the muscles in some beer joint to an older woman, maybe someone like Judy Lemonning. The flash of Lemonning and the no-man from the design place came to him. Had the two of them acted it out in his apartment? Essai picked up a few rocks and threw them out toward the island in the center of the empty pond, hitting the island two out of four. Then he sat down on the park bench and looked up at the moon. Even since he had last looked, the ring had diffused into a thick haze, and few stars poked through the high overcast. Essai stood up and looked over toward the east, where the smoke from the Edison stacks plumed out. It was his own wind vane, and the smoke pollution laws had not yet gotten to public utilities. The smoke poured into a column heading straight up, with the slightest lean to the southwest at the top. There was probably a northeast wind of one or two miles an hour, Essai thought, and with the ring and the haze, the temperature rising a little, maybe they were in for a March snowstorm. He hoped so; it would fill up the desolate pond bottom with snow and snarl up traffic heading determinedly to useless destinations. In any case, he concluded thoughtfully, they wouldn't call off ward rounds the next day. Only his heart attack had ever kept Kraft away from the hospital in the three years Essai had been there, and now Kraft was fully recovered.

Essai wanted a drink, anything to clear away the tobacco taste, but he didn't want it enough to leave the Garden, still all his. It was quite a garden in March, devoid of plants or flowers. But it was not a bad night. Essai shifted his weight and heard the slight crackle. He wondered what he had put into his back pocket; and just as he reached back to touch it he remembered it was the *Science* article. He had first put it there months ago the night he left Lemmoning, and he carried it around, like a diabetic with a card. He didn't touch it but brought his hand back and stuffed it into the small pocket of the pea jacket. He began to hum, then sang a tune he had thought up that same summer of 1955 when he learned briefly how to play a guitar:

> When I was a young man, courtin' I went,
> Ballin' all of the girls I saw,
> And as I grew older I came to see,
> I needed one woman, one woman, one woman,
> One woman, one woman, for me, I
> Needed one woman for me.

He sang it through, mournfully, surprised he remembered how it went. He got to the line "Who stroked my brow after terrible dreams" when he saw a man come walking up over the short suspension bridge spanning the empty pond. For a moment he did not believe what he saw, but it was Alf Saunders after all, two years later, walking carefully with a coffee cup and saucer in his right hand. Essai stood up, then sat down again and waited till Alf got over the bridge. Then he yelled out, "Hey Alf, it's me. Andy." The gaunt man stopped and said, "Hi, Andy," in a conversational tone, though he was about twenty feet away, and continued walking in the general direction of Park Square.

"Hey, Alf, come over here."

"OK. Here I come, ready or not." He casually slipped down the dead winter grass.

"How's it going, Alf?"

"Bad, Andy. Spilled half the cup when you yelled at me."

"Sorry."

Alf sat down gingerly. "It's OK," he said, looking at his cup. "Most of it's in the saucer anyway. You like drinking coffee out of saucers?"

Essai laughed. "Same old Alf. I haven't seen you around in a long time."

Alf grimaced and showed all of his teeth. "I've been around, Andy. It's you who haven't been making the scene."

"Still hang around at the Nines?"

Alf crossed one leg over the other and sucked up the coffee from the saucer, making a face. "No, to tell you the truth, Andy, I haven't. Me and Jim had kind of a bad scene in there one night last year."

"You did?"

"Well, Jim made it bad. You know, I needed a little green to keep myself in greens—ha-ha-ha, you know the old green bombers you'd never write me a prescription for."

"I remember."

"Well," Alf continued, "my friendly pharmacist down on Mass. Avenue was beginning to tire of my inventive excuses, and demanded a few bills. So, one night, I took myself over to brother Jim's pad, high atop Memorial Drive in Cambridge, and letting myself in with a key I cleverly discovered taped to the side of the mailbox, I decided to take a bit of the strain off the bulging bookshelves. He didn't need all those books. I'm tellin' you, Andy, his brain was rotting within from all that reading he was doing to stay a Harvard instructor, you know? Well, I took a few literary items to a very pecuniary Jewman down at Scollay Square, and got a few greens, for greens you know?"

"What did Jim say when he found out?"

"Andy, he was not happy." Alf shook his head deliberately several times. "He came into the Nines where I was brushing coffee grains in Margot's hair, and said, 'Where are they?' I said, 'No, you don't. Margot gets all these grains for her hair; you want grains, get your own coffee.'" Here Alf erupted into a loud, mirthless laugh. "Well, Jim stands straight as our mother taught him and says, dropping the Cambridge accent, 'Alfred, where are my books?' and I stood and put my hand over my eyes visor-fashion, you know, and said, very cool, 'Books many miles by pack mule. White man not reach till next full moon.' It was a scene, Andy. Margot starts giggling and the bar quiets down and Jim says, teary-like, 'What did you do with my books?' and I said, 'Jim, those books are turning' your squash into creamy apple butter and I believe I have done you a service, and struck a bargain in the process, by turning those compilations of musty lies into pharmaceutical miracles.' Then I take the few remaining capsules from my bare pockets and hold them up. Then, Andy (here he put a hand on Andy's knee and looked at him very seriously), my older brother struck me in the face. Twice. Though I am a strong man, and a hairy man, as you know, I deem it improper to strike back, and so I settle quietly to the sawdust floor, wolfing down the last of the greens as I went. Old Margot blew the bit with shrieks of 'He's hurt, someone get a doctor, he's hurt,' and neither you, Andy, nor any other doctor was on call just at that moment in the bar, and Jim gave me a terrible kick in the ribs and then old Pat Margionne who is an ex-Ranger and 'runs a clean bar' came over and threw all of us out into the street, and said never to come back."

"Did he ever get his books back?"

"Alas, Andrew, he did, and to the best of my knowledge, they are again in his high pad in the sky, where he listens to Indian music and screws Radcliffe undergraduates when not preparing classes for the Harvard men."

Essai smiled at his friend. "What kind of work are you doing, Alf?"

Alf looked around quickly. "Andrew, while I wait for someone to pick up my jazz copy book, a painstaking crib of the best five hundred jazz tunes of the last twenty years from records and sheet music, for the price of a thousand dollars for the master or twenty dollars for copies, I am reduced to working as a draftsman."

"Really? Full-time?"

"Alas, it is so. The friendly German U-boat captain, masquerading as a psychiatrist at the Mass. Mental Health, told me with real passion that he would not see me any more unless I got a job."

"How long have you been seeing him?" Andrew Essai hoped he didn't sound too clinical.

"Six months. I walked in there one day when I thought I saw a sign that said Pharmacy pointing in that direction, and there was a girl who looked like Margot sitting at the receptionist's desk. She looks at my pellucid earlobes and intones the phrase, 'This is the walk-in mental clinic. May I help you?' Without thinking, looking at her ivory throat, I say, 'My love, mental disease on the hoof takes a new dimension with me. Could you lead this lathered horse to the pharmacy?' Well, that's how it started."

"Is he helping you out?"

Alf fixed Essai as though if he stared without moving he might disintegrate him with a look. Then he sat up, looked away, and said, "Of course, my boy. I spill much less coffee than before."

"How many green bombers are you on?"

"Nary a one, Doc Andrew. Well, at night just one or two with warm milk to set my upcoming dreams aright."

Essai felt the eyes staring into his again, and became objective and uncomfortable. "You asked for it," he thought, "you called him over." Then, just as suddenly, his mood swung back into Alf's crazy groove. "Have a chew of Red Man, Alf." He brought out the nearly full pack.

Alf stood up, "No thanks, I'm off the hard stuff. Margot once said never to use tobacco in any form as it stained the teeth, and as I love her, I do as she says."

"Well, OK, Alf. Where are you heading now?"

Alf swiveled quickly and pointed in the general direction of the Edison smokestack. "That way. Met a woman who wants to do a death mask of my face. Pays in copies."

As he talked on, Essai watched his face in the gloom; skin stretched so tight over the bones that the grimacing smiles seemed involuntary efforts to relieve presure. Two immense dark bags circled the eyes as though to target them. Andy wondered when Alf had last eaten. He reached into his coat pocket and felt the piece of baklava, but decided after a moment not to offer it; for some reason he thought Alf would be furious at the implications.

" 'Under that phony tinsel is real tinsel,' " Alf was saying, "and when I told her *that* she suppressed a smile and reached for me."

"Hey Alf, you want to get a drink?"

"No, man, I drink in the beauty of the night, and that suffices."

Essai stood up. "Alf, I guess I'll—"

"Hey listen Andy, I have to go. Death awaits, masked as a lady. Say," his voice dropped and he came close, grimacing, "you wouldn't like to write out a small green prescription in return for death mask rights, would you? Use the mask for death rites; makes men weep and women turn on."

"Sorry, Alf."

Alf shot out a hand and Essai ducked, but it turned into a harmless wave good-bye. "See you, Andy. If you see Margot tell her Alf has a sackful of coffee grains at home."

"OK, Alf." He watched the man lope off, stopping every few

strides to toss the cup into the air, and catch it each time as he started to walk again. Essai turned away from him, but kept looking back to watch and see if he dropped the cup, and after Alf had disappeared he kept listening but he heard nothing, save the faint street noises. He sat down on the same park bench and played with the top of the tobacco package, but the eerie moonlight made him edgy—was it possible Alf had not been there at all?

Essai got up and walked out of the Public Garden. He was trying to remember the one time he saw Alf with Margot, and after a moment it came back to him. He and Alf had been sitting in the Nines, six months after Alf had left von Eckland and abandoned a career in architecture. Alf drank coffee and took pills, and talked about Margot, the girl he had just met who would fix everything up. His back was toward the door, and suddenly he had tensed and said, "Here she comes," without turning around. Essai had looked and seen a tall girl dressed in black with black stockings and heels, long black hair and a black fur coat. She was carrying a blue Pan Am bag out of which a kitten's black head poked fearfully. Alf was jittery, but stood up and turned to face her. When he saw her costume he said, "Margot, did you ever hear about the moth that flew in ever-decreasing circles about a candle light?" Margot wheeled and walked out and Alf had sat down, exclaiming, "How did she know it was to be an insult? I just made it up." Like most things he said, it sounded fresh from him but none of it was new. Essai hoped the psychiatrist knew what he was doing, treating Alf as an out-patient.

It was still early, not yet eleven. Essai walked down Beacon toward Berkeley, but stopped at Arlington, not wanting to go back to the apartment yet. It had become a monastic retreat for him. He doubled back to Charles Street and down to Cambridge, quickly past the Nines, then up Cambridge and Anderson Street and down Mt. Vernon Street to Louisburg Square. He was circling the Nines and he knew it. It was the only place he could go, unless he wanted to go down Washington Street into some hopeless bar. He and Alf were both walking the streets tonight, he thought ruefully. Same diagnosis?

The Nines, as always, looked from the outside like a funeral parlor on the verge of bankruptcy. Outside the narrow door Pat Margionne had stationed himself with a flashlight to check IDs, and at first glance it was hard to tell whether he was letting people in, or, with his bulk, keeping them in. Andy walked up and said, "Hi, Pat, how they treating you?"

"Well, doc, haven't seen you around in months. Woman keeping you tied up?" By blocking the door he made one talk till he decided to stop.

"Nope, just been busy."

"Seen that crazy guy or his brother, you know, the architect?"

"Nope, Pat, haven't seen 'em."

"I heard he left town. Just as good if you ask me."

Left town? It had been Alf in the garden, hadn't it? Andy licked the inside of his mouth and spat the tobacco. He wanted a drink.

"Full up, Pat?"

At once Pat stood aside. "No, no, go right on in. Busy, Friday night."

"Still packing them in."

"I run a clean place, Andy." The man would have been laughable except that he continually flexed his biceps under his shirt as he talked. Essai had to brush against him slightly to get past, scraping his other shoulder hard against the brick, and as they touched Pat said, "Some nice head in there tonight, buddy." Essai nodded and pushed in.

The uncirculated smoky air collided with him, and he winced. As he made out people, he saw many of the faces he knew from last year and the year before that. Except for a few college couples, the crowd was aged twenty-five to forty, all drinking beer, their conversations pitted against music from the jukebox—the tunes never changed. Patti Paige was singing "Cross Over the Bridge," as she had for twelve years—in progressively scratchier tones. On the right were eight booths, filled with smoking men and women, content to talk just under the music, so it was unclear whether anyone was being heard. The bar was filled too, and in the back, shrouded, Charley Squires slept on a stool with a dustmop in one red fist.

Only the gritty familiarity made Andy stay. He got Schlitz without a glass (the bartenders all looked syphilitic and Essai had never drunk out of glasses here), and he edged to the side next to a booth, smoke-squinting eyes looking it over. He remembered Bill Treet's remark, drinking beer with Andy, on his nights off from the psychiatric residency at the General: "I'm going to stop coming in, Andy, there's more acute disease in here than on our ward."

It was true, of course, that most of the regulars were forlorn fugitives from the outside world, some probably hallucinating, some psychopathic, most just lost. Each year the place got busier, less well-ventilated, the beer more expensive and the music scratchier. But Andy realized that the place itself was here, as a kind of refuge, and barring a scene such as Alf and Jim had put on, it was open to all. "Even to me," he thought quickly. He finished the cold beer and got another. Twenty minutes later he got a third, slouching slightly, and Patti Paige sounded better to him. After that one he went to the men's room—no soap, no hot water, no towels. The walls were no longer painted red; rather they were so densely marked with obscenities that they resembled an undecipherable palimpsest. But the ceiling remained untouched except for the black crayon saying that had never been written over—"In the beginning there was Roger."

Essai made his way back to the bar, holding the empty third bottle. He ordered another one, and went back to his observer's post. On impulse he set down the bottle on the edge of a booth table and put a plug of Red Man in his mouth. Intermittently, he spat carefully into the empty bottle in his left hand and took a drink from the Schlitz in his right. He knew that when he took a gulp from the wrong bottle, it would be time to stop and go home. The breakfast dishes would be on the table from this morning, a half-read journal article near the coffee cup. At least Lemonning had kept the place cleaned up. And that swishing ponytail when she wanted to excite him. Anger twisted through the pleasant feeling of drinking, and he spat inaccurately at Judy Lemonning and the no-man designer. A moderate trickle of tobacco juice ran down the side of the bottle through the label and spread onto the back of his left hand.

A white handkerchief passed into his view and wiped off his hand, then went up the bottle and wiped that. The hand that held the handkerchief was a woman's hand, Essai sensed with relief, and he smelled a perfume he recognized.

He turned and said, "Do you do that often?"

She looked straight at him. "Do I look like I do?"

"No." Essai smiled at her. "Why me?"

She turned away shyly and Essai took the chance to appraise her—short, fine blond hair halfway to her shoulders, small up-tilted breasts in a soft blue sweater, sandals on small feet, and thin fine ankles. And then, having gone from hair to breast and down, knowing she was now watching, he came back to her face: light indeterminate eyes in a real smile, nose short and funny, wide-open smiling mouth with even teeth.

She smiled at him, thin and flushed, thinking, "Why him? A sad-eyed watcher of life who knows his bag but is half in it. The geniality and sadness all mixed up. I'd like to kiss the sadness out."

Essai had seen her smile freeze as she thought. She had the look doctors gave complicated patients. Melancholy rinsed him, and he turned from her and looked straight ahead. He had a mouthful of tobacco juice, and resignedly spat it out on the floor.

"If you miss too often, they won't give you a nickel for the full bottle and you'll have to settle for two cents on the empty." The voice was soft and close to his ear. Andy did not look, but said, "I know that perfume. It's by Avon, isn't it? They don't sell that perfume any more."

"Nearness," the voice said.

Essai continued to look straight ahead. "I'm not nuts," he said, "but I don't think a real voice has spoken to me in a couple of hours. If you are real, kiss my left ear."

There was nothing and Essai thought he had gone too far, or worse, he thought, starting to turn and look, that this healing woman would not take the case.

"Don't turn," the voice commanded. "If you do, I'll miss your ear."

He waited. A sensation of something, then the perfume, then the sound of lips parting, and he felt warm lips on his left ear. She took the beer bottle filled with tobacco juice out of his hand, and said, "Now you have a free hand, if that isn't too symbolic a phrase."

Essai put his arm around her and felt a solid woman, slipless since the sliding quality was absent, and took in the pervasive softness. She started to say something, but Patti Paige roared out again at the same moment. He said, "What?" and bent over to hear, to get his ear at her lips again. She kissed his ear again. "That's all you get," she murmured. "Two kisses for half a bottle of tobacco juice."

"We'll have to talk about it. Now, what were you going to say, I mean before that, when the music started?" Andy was talking louder than he wanted to.

"Nothing. I was licking my lips. Or about to."

His arm moved her toward him an inch. A tiny frown appeared. She said, "This place is full of observant people. Very clinical types."

Essai looked up, and indeed two or three men were watching fixedly, as though they had paid admission. He wanted to leave, but not without her. He said that to her, straight as he could, though he knew his voice was full of passion, and he didn't want her to go with him for that. At least not only for that.

"Fine," he heard her say. "But we've got to get your bottle out of here. I mean the one I've got, not yours. Drink your beer."

He nodded, exultant. The bottle he held was nearly full,

and he put his head back and drank half of it. "Here," he said.

She took the bottle and drank out of it. He watched her put the bottle up to her lips, and the tongue crept out just as she touched the glass edge. Then she gave it back and he finished it. "Don't worry," he said, and they turned and went the few steps to the door. They opened it into the unyielding back of Pat Margionne, and for a second Essai thought it was a dream, where one could never get out and away. Then Pat took a step and the girl scurried through. Andy followed her closely, hiding her for the most part, and the bottle she held close to her sweater. He held out his empty bottle and said quickly, "Night, Pat. Ooops, forgot to leave this off."

Pat took it. "OK, Doc." He glanced quickly at the girl. "Come back again," he said. The girl smiled and took Essai's hand and they went quickly along Charles Street and down Pinckney, nearly running. She giggled and held up the bottle, then in a gesture that set him ablaze, licked the top of the bottle half full of his tobacco juice. He stopped her at the alley just before Brimmer. She held on to the bottle as he said, "Now come here," and reached for her under the coat and kissed her. The incredibly soft lips parted after a moment, and she flitted her tongue about randomly. He felt her heart pound against his pea jacket, and she broke off the kiss and took a step back. He felt himself being looked at, the way he had appraised her, and except for the embarrassing bulge just below the bottom of his jacket, he did not mind. She saw it and passed it, and went down and then came up again.

"Hi," said Essai.

"Hi. Is that 'doc' a nickname?"

"What 'doc'?"

"The 'doc' that old latent Pat back there said 'so long' with."

"Yup. Nickname. Name's Nick. Nick Fompanolla."

She frowned. "Back in the shell, eh, my friend?"

"I don't know what you mean." He flushed.

"I'm not being mean," she replied sharply. "Name's Mary Meany. I take in wash on Monday, Wednesdays and Fridays. The rest of the time I do other things."

"*Ach so,* und vot other things, miss. Please speak into the mike, there."

She looked at the beer bottle in her hand that he was pointing at. "Can't talk into this, Mike," she blared with a country accent, "somebody licked the damn top and the thing doesn't work. Funny, did just a minute ago."

He was losing it. "Sorry," he said. "I'm a doctor. Andrew Essai. Andrew G. Essai, as a matter of fact. A.G.E. That's why I never carry a briefcase."

The smile came back. "Let's walk for a while, Andy. My name is Angela Lynne."

"Angela Lynne what?"

She laughed. "Last name is Lynne, middle name is Turner. My mother's maiden name."

"Hey," Essai exclaimed. "Is Lynne with an 'E'?"

"Yes."

"Well, my middle name is George. So we each have six, six and five letters in our three names."

"Really," she exclaimed, mocking just a little. "We must get on to horoscopes."

"No," insisted Essai. "That's good. You're good, as a matter of fact. All day, all year, it's been frustrating, not really a bad life but just different than I wanted. You know?"

She nodded. "Like walking half the distance to a line and never getting there."

"Right. Just like that. And then, just now in the Nines, expecting nothing, I meet you and go over the line, in one big step." He reached into his pocket. "Here. Have some baklava. I knew I was saving it for something."

She took it and bit into it. He watched her teeth sink in and suddenly he remembered reading about the primary process of thinking in schizophrenics, and he thought of Alf: the characteristic representation by analogy, the simplification of syntax and omission of explanatory words; condensed, involuted epigrams and puns that were funny only if one did not realize that the speaker thought in the same ways all the time. Watching the girl bite into the baklava he felt certain that primary process action also occurred, as when she had licked the bottleful of tobacco juice, or even kissed his ear. He sensed that events would proceed in just this way, without the need to modify, explain, or circumscribe acts. The strangest awareness he had ever experienced came over him, and in a soft voice he said, "Angela, come here."

They were in front of the Church of the Advent, and she began to move toward him, then stopped and said, "Follow me," and ran down Mt. Vernon Street past Embankment Road, stopping momentarily and then darting through traffic on Storrow Drive to the grassy plain in front of the Hatch Shell on the edge of the Charles River, where she slipped off her coat, putting it next to an old tree, and put her arms out: "I've got no coat on. Keep me warm." Breathless, he enfolded her and they knelt and lay on the coat, moved by the same unspoken instinct.

It was, he sensed, like hammered metal which is beaten into an ever wider and thinner edge, until the mind longs to stop it lest it shatter, yet at the farthest tolerable limits of breadth and thinness it widens and thins on and on, taking on a new shape, and with it, a new definition of the space it supplants. He plunged, bucked, and felt her small hands digging into him. They narrowed and widened the space between them until their locked forms became the expanding, beaten metal. He did not know anything; whether her eyes and mouth were open or closed, silent or shouting, warm or cold. He was out of his skin, finally for the first time freed from thought and doubt and rationalization, and he gave himself up willingly to the giddiness of boundless sensation.

Their passion ebbed bit by bit, and the trip back was marked by short bursts of overflowing feeling in their own way even more satisfying than the sustained passion, since by contrast the receding waves reminded them where they had been. Andrew Essai opened his eyes and looked at Angela's, tightly shut, where single tear tracts glinted laterally from either side. She opened her eyes, and smiled, and closed them again. "The way down is nice too," she whispered. Essai smiled and pushed once, then again, like good-bye kisses at the door. Each time her exhausted flanks pushed back, voluptuously weak. Only slowly did Essai begin to notice the surroundings again—with a somewhat incredulous shock. The cold air laced him from hips to knees, and under his still-zipped jacket the sweat trickled down his shirt and arms. He heard an airplane overhead. "My God!" he exclaimed, "we're in public."

"So we are." She too was returning. Andrew began to stand up, but she said urgently, "Pull your pants up first." He did so dazedly, and she straightened her sweater, crumpled up to but not over her bra. Then they both stood up and looked around, coming back fully, but with measured caution, as though emerging hesitatingly from a wrecked car. Andy helped her on with her coat, and glanced quickly at the dark field to his left, grateful that a police car or crowd of spectators were absent. They moved slowly away from the pressed ground, and walked close to the shell. Andy whistled a few notes, tentatively.

"Tonight the Hatch Shell was witness to a great event," he began in mock-reportorial tones.

"Don't talk it. I mean, don't talk about it."

"Why not?" he said irritatedly, almost angry.

She took his arm. "Sorry," she said, "but to me it's better unassessed, unanalyzed."

He felt her warm arm and her presence, and knew she was right. They went up to Charles Circle. He walked slowly, with no idea where to go.

"Are you mad, Andy?"

"No. You were right though. Thinking about it is fine, but talking about it isn't."

She went up on tiptoe to kiss his cheek. "C'mon, I'll make us some coffee."

"Fine." Relief poured in and mixed with the luxurious emptiness. With the single phrase they started walking away from Berkeley Street, and he was spared explanation about why his apartment, like an extension of the hospital, was the wrong place to go. He felt immensely grateful to her. He wondered where her true instincts arose, then stopped thinking about it and was happy to walk along with her.

"Should I get some Scotch, Angela?"

"If you want to. Not for me though."

"You don't drink."

"Sometimes," she replied, squeezing his arm. "Not now."

The liquor store was closed; it was half past eleven. "If you want something, I've got some brandy, I think," she said quietly.

"OK. I see what you mean about not wanting liquor. Why dull anything?"

"Precisely," she said.

They took the Hill slowly, and were nearly at the State House when she stopped him. "Here we are, just on the corner of Joy," she hesitated, "Joy Street, that is."

"Up here?"

Her arm restrained him. "I could explain it now, but you'll see soon enough."

"Don't tell me you have roommates?" he asked incredulously.

"No." She laughed. "Let's go."

Inside she rang and a female voice answered. "It's me, Mrs. Lynne," she announced into the metal grid. As the door buzzed, the word "Mrs." roared home and Andy instinctively took a step back, faced with the possibility of confronting an incensed husband.

Angela pushed the door open and turned back. "There's no husband up there, so don't worry." She bit her lip, watching him to see if he would run.

"OK. But slow, my calves feel like knots."

"I'll have to rub out the knots," she said suggestively. "C'mon, it's on the third floor."

He stood there an instant longer, then moved up. On the third floor a door opened and a young girl looked into the gloomy hall. "Hello, Mrs. Lynne."

"Hello, Sally. Did she give you any trouble?"

"No."

Andy was edging directly behind Angela, as though to hide himself.

"This is Mr. Essai. He's a friend of mine."

"Hello." The schoolgirl's eyes were big.

"Hello."

Essai walked into the furnished living room, depressingly small except for one window that faced west, down the Hill and out over the Charles River into Cambridge. He went to the window at once and looked interestingly at traffic moving along Memorial Drive, while in back of him, the young woman, with whom he had just lain out there on the ground, paid the schoolgirl some money and said good-bye.

"Good-bye, Mr. Essai," the schoolgirl said.

Essai turned halfway. Would she remember his name? "Good-bye." As the door closed he finished turning. Angela was smiling. "Boy, do you look guilty. Well, you wanted to come here instead of go there. To your place. Am I right?"

"Right," he admitted.

"OK. The rest is coming right up." She walked through a narrow hallway and said a few words to someone, and in a minute a sleepy-looking blond girl of three or four came down the hallway from a room on the left, rubbing her eyes. Behind her, Angela looked at her and at him. "That's Mr. Essai, a friend of mine, Alix."

Alix looked at him sleepily, uncertainty. "Hello, Mr. Easy."

"Hi. Is that your whole name, Alix?"

The girl nodded "yes" quickly, then "no."

"What is it?"

She looked up at her mother. "Alexandra," said Angela.

"Wow," commented Andy to the girl, "that name is bigger than you are."

The girl nodded "yes" very slowly. "I know," she said.

"Me, I've got a short first name. Andy." He looked quickly at Angela. "Oh, no," he burst out, "all our names start with 'A.'"

Angela laughed. "There you go again, Andy, with the letters

and names. I wish I had an owl handy, to look at the entrails."

Essai wrinkled his brow. "What?"

Alix mimicked him exactly. "What, Mommy? Why do you want an owl?"

Her mother picked her up and kissed her. "To help me write a story about Oscar the Owl, which I'll tell you about tomorrow."

"Now, Mommy."

"No, I told you a story before I went out. "We'll save this one for tomorrow. Now say good night to Mr. Essai, love."

The girl looked down from her triumphant perch. "Do you know any stories?"

"Tomorrow," her mother said firmly.

"Good night, Easy Andy." They all laughed.

"Good night, Bright Eyes."

Alix looked at her mother. "Are my eyes bright, Mommy?"

She was kissed. "A little," Angela said, "but more sleepy." She went back down the hall, and Essai turned to the window, momentarily contemplating a leap. You can't just stuff a hole with lovejuice and not get the return, he thought gloomily. Those kissing lips in the Nines turn out to belong to a married mother. I guess married. "The action of primary process," he said sardonically to himself. "Boy, did I call that one wrong."

Not only had he called it wrong but he now realized he missed the Scotch. He opened the window a few inches and knelt, to see more clearly the black plain fronting the Hatch Shell, partly hidden, as though writhing figures might be observed from even this height.

"Don't jump, Andy, the door is right here if you want."

"I wasn't about to," he said, waiting till his composure returned. He wondered if she were reading his mind.

"Fine," she said. "Are you going or staying?"

He touched the zipper on his jacket. "Do you want me to go, Angela?"

"No." He waited for the qualifying phrase, the explanation, but she said the one word and stood quietly, a little away from the door.

"OK," he announced. "Cover your eyes, because I'm going to remove my jacket." She didn't smile, but watched him, and took his jacket and left it on the edge of the couch. For some reason, seeing it there made him feel better than if she had hung it up in a closet somewhere. In case he had to run. She continued to look at him.

"Can I use your bathroom?"

"Sure," she said. "Just there on the left." He started to tramp out. "Quiet," she warned, "Alix is asleep."

He lightened up and went into the bathroom. He urinated, washed his hands with some fine-smelling soap and, with the water running, looked into her medicine cabinet. Nothing more sinister than a bottle of baby aspirin. Had he expected needles or syringes?

She was busy with the coffeepot when he came out, and for an instant, he was astonished not to see Judy there. But Angela was a half a foot shorter, thinner, and somehow more self-contained.

Angela smiled at him when he came in. She bent down with the plug. "Self-perking coffeepot," she said, "but it's a long reach to the plug."

"Here. I'll do it." Their hands met, and they knelt together, as though readying themselves for prayer, or a sprint. He touched the fine blond hair tentatively. "I'm sorry," he said finally. "I guess I'm acting a bit caged."

She kissed him: straight, formal, passionless. She had turned on the radio, and the music and the first smell of coffee quieted him. He sat with his back against the side of the chair, and they both watched the steam as she talked.

"If I said my husband was doing consecutive twenty-year sentences for armed robbery and assault with intent to kill, you'd be out the door." She said it like the first sentence of a story.

"Is he?" Essai looked at his jacket.

"Wait. I'll get there. I went to the Bradley School of Social Work, and in the third of the four years, I had to spend six weeks at a psychiatric service of a state hospital. Learning psychiatric social work." She looked over at Essai, resting his chin in his cupped hand. "I don't think I'll go on."

"Please, I'm listening."

She stood up. "I know. You must get that look when you ask a patient questions. You don't really listen, except for the things that help you make a diagnosis."

"That's unfair, Angela."

She hesitated, then went on. She got two cups, talking, but still hedging her words. "I was in social work for a while, and I know about that kind of listening, because I did the same thing with cases. I felt just like you do; everyone's got a story, and the final common pathway is usually disappointment, unfulfillment, or some other long word meaning 'sad.' Right?"

"I guess so." Her insight frightened him; he briefly mourned his lack of it.

"It's so. If you wanted, you could tell me the same kind of story, even though you are entirely successful, a doctor, and handsome at that. You could tell me a story too, couldn't you?"

Essai nodded. "I could."

"Well," she stated quietly, "you were so goddamn suspicious when you saw my daughter and all, that you kind of made me tell it. I don't mind really." She filled the cups. "Cream?"

"Do you have any of that brandy, Angela?" He felt rotten, and angry at himself.

"I think so." As she went out into the kitchen, Essai stood up and sat down in the chair, properly. She came back in. "At any rate, I was an idealistic social worker, or student, and a pretty good one. While working at the state hospital, I met a man, Sam Lynne, who had committed himself for heroin withdrawal. He said at the time it was marijuana, and I believed him." She sat down in a chair opposite Andrew Essai and handed him the bottle of brandy. He poured a little into his coffee.

"Sam Lynne was like a small boy who wanted to be loved," she continued. "When an addict is off the stuff, and even when he isn't, he has such an air of helplessness about him, though he's tough around the edges, that one is drawn to him.

Or at least I was. He used to tell me I was the kind of person who could help him, give him self-esteem. For me, he said, he'd get a job, since he would have someone to work for. I went on to another course away from the hospital, and a few weeks later he was discharged, and started seeing me." She started at the handle of the coffee cup. "He was kind and loving, Andy, and he showed me poetry he had written in the hospital. I loved him. Three months later we got married, and I got pregnant with the speed of light, and then worked for a while since I knew I'd deliver before the school year ended, and the administrators of the school, liberal people all, thought the wife of a past drug-addict was not quite their kind of student.

"Then he got back on drugs. It was like a crazy chess game, where you can sense the moves. My friends had warned me before I got married that addicts always went back to drugs, that I'd find myself working to support his habit. That's how it was. But it had been so easy for me, when I loved him, to go to school and work ten or twelve hours a day and keep the apartment nice for him and love him, all with hardly any effort."

Tears spilled over. "Suddenly I was using all my energy trying to feel I really loved him, and I still had to work and he had gotten demanding. As only a small boy can," she added.

"OK, Angela," said Essai.

She put up a hand. "Wait," she said sniffling. "It's almost done." He gave her a handkerchief and she blew her nose, then sat up. 'He tried a couple of jobs but they were suspicious of him and as they got suspicious and watched him, he became more fearful and started again; at first, cough syrup. In a month he was back on heroin. I was seven months pregnant, and I told him I had to save my last few paychecks for the baby. He left, and a few weeks later held up a tavern and shot someone. The bar owner recovered, and Sam is in prison for good."

"Parole?" asked Essai weakly.

"Hmmh. Two twenty-year consecutive sentences, not concurrent. And he's hardly the model prisoner."

"Then what?"

She shrugged. "After Alix was born I went to a psychiarist and asked him how to expunge the guilt I felt. I figured it was my telling Sam I had no more money for his habit that led him to commit the crime."

"You were too hard on yourself."

"That's what he said. He said, 'How many more paychecks did you have to give? Five? Eight? What would he have done for money while you were in the hospital.' It took a lot of hours before I believed it."

Essai frowned. "Why don't you change your name back, to your maiden name, I mean."

"With a baby? No, I couldn't give her up. I guess I had given up one child—Sam—and I couldn't give up the other."

"So what do you do?"

A small smile came out. "I write children's books. That's the silver lining part of the story. At first when Sam was in prison I wrote him long letters, and he asked me to tell him a lot of stories. He's like a kid, I told you. Well, that's what he wanted, children's stories. A friend of mine saw a few of the letters and told me to submit the stuff, and I laughed at her, but finally I did."

"Like Oscar the Owl."

"Right," she smiled. "How's the coffee?"

Essai drank it, hot and astringent with the brandy. Then he sat back. She was appraising him. "What is it, Angela?"

"Still planning to go?"

"Nope."

"Good." She sighed, as though she had just passed an exam. "Excuse me," she said, and stretched, hands up and grasping for the ceiling. At the top she stopped, and brought her arms down fast. "One more thing."

"What's that," asked Essai.

"Jesus," she exclaimed, "all I do with you is explain myself." Her hands were in fists. Essai reached over, touched her breast, then curled his hand around her neck and brought her near to kiss her. "Not quite all," he said after a moment.

She sat on his lap and counted his gray hairs. "We met under rather odd circumstances tonight, you and me, that is."

"Hmmm."

"Hmmm yourself. 'Ex-wife of drug addict kisses ear of stranger in bar, then has sex with him in public. Police alerted.'"

"Stop it." Their roles were reversed. Now he was trying to avoid the conventional response.

"I get a sitter every Friday night," Angela explained. "Sometimes I have dates, and sometimes I go to movies. I'm a rabid moviegoer. Tonight I went to the movies with a girlfriend, and she said I should go into the Nines with her while she looked for her boyfriend. She was talking to him while I was waiting at the door."

"And you saw me."

"Right. A little kid watching the action, sad-eyed. But you knew your bag."

He pulled his head away from her breast. "I what?"

"Sorry," she said. "You looked like you knew what you were doing, what you were about. Most of the people there had no idea what was really happening to them. But you did. And besides, you had that sad watching look that makes you very sexy, or rather, makes women want to get close to you."

"Not mother me? I knew one girl like that."

"I don't mother anybody except my daughter," Angela said determinedly. "Besides," she added, "you're a man, not a son."

Essai put his hand on the inside of her leg, above her knee. The stretched wool of the skirt goaded him. "And you, Angela, are a real woman."

She unbuttoned just the top button of his blue shirt. "I've never seen eighty percent of you, Andy."

He reached under the sweater. "I could say the same thing. Does your daughter sleep in the only bedroom?"

"Wait till I unbutton your shirt."

He put his hand on her head and drew her to him. "With your teeth, baby."

"The way up this time is going to be nice and slow," she said. "Sip a little coffee, darling."

"I will. Keep working on those buttons."

"Sip that coffee," she murmured into his shirt. "You won't last two more buttons."

Andy held the cup and watched the coffee shake. "Not even one, Angela."

"Remind me," she said through clenched teeth. "I've got some knots to rub out."

"Start now," he said breathlessly, leaning back.

Somewhere he heard a toilet flush. The sound was strangely soothing to him, as were the occasional cries in the street, car horns, even a rattling beer can. He was stretched out on the rumpled sheets, with one half-covering him, infinitely heavy it seemed. The bed was hard as a slab, but the pervading sense was one of softness. With a great effort Essai looked at his watch in the glow from the blue nightlight. One thirty. He took off his watch, lay back, and heard her bare feet pad on the carpet. She moved softly, as thought not to wake him.

"Angela," he whispered.

"Here I am, darling." She slipped into bed next to him, and he turned and brought her close and kissed her. He moved his free hand over the smooth shoulder, under the arm, over the breast, and caught the uptilted nipple between his fingers. His hand moved away, came back, moved across to the other one, sympathetically hardening, then down across the flat belly and past the silken hair to the soft leg. Her hand started at his face, closing his eyes, and then hesitated at his mouth, stroking the corners, till he licked the hand and it dropped soundlessly down. They caressed each other long after they had to, tipping each other over the edge and past it.

He groaned and began to lift himself over her, but she said,

"Don't move," and went with her tongue where she had with her hand, over his trembling eyes, at the corners of his mouth, nibbling. After a time he kissed her shoulders and hands, and she rubbed his lips with her fingers. He drew back, and they did not touch for a moment, then came shuddering together, and he felt himself pulled down into her. He imagined he was back digging footers on the construction job, only this time straight down, and the further he dug, the more the sunny sky gave way to moist darkness. He longed to descend until the last sliver of blue was gone, and dug furiously on. He felt his ears covered, by earth or hands he could not have said, and eyes closed, deaf to all sound, mouth locked to hers, he was aware only of the smell and enveloping touch of the earth.

Then he inched back a bit, and knew where he was, and tried to burrow all the way in again, but the sky widened and he came to himself and the hands left his ears (they were hands after all) and he was back breathing deeply in the arms of the soft woman who lay humming or moaning beneath him.

"Are you all right? Angela, did I hurt you?"

Her eyes opened. "Hurt? You took me to a place I never knew."

"Me too," he said softly.

They rolled apart. Essai felt the lead of sleep creeping up his limbs. "I'm falling asleep. Wake me in a while. Or will you sleep?"

Her voice came from far away. "I'll wake you," she said.

The little girl was crying, insistent, and Essai dreamed he called to the neighbors to ask them to make their daughter stop crying. The bed lifted imperceptibly and he awoke long enough to realize that Angela was out of bed. A hall light went on, and he turned away from it, falling into sleep. He thought he heard talking between a mother and child, then awoke and listened to Angela and her daughter.

"Alix, it's the middle of the night, and I'm very tired. Now if you need anything, just call and I'll come in."

"But I want to come in your bed, Mommy."

"You can't do that, sweets. Now, Mommy will be in her room and you in yours, and you call me if you need anything. Good night."

He heard her start to close the door, hesitate, then close it tight. She called out "Good night," again, and the faint reply came back. Andy got out of bed and looked through two slats of the venetian blinds. It was not snowing yet. He wondered if the wind was still from the northeast. Angela came in.

"What's wrong," she whispered.

"Just seeing if the snow has started."

"Snow? I didn't hear anything about snow."

Essai gestured, dismissing his credentials as a weatherman. The hall light was still on, and as Angela stood near the bed, backlit, he could make out the breasts and pyramid of the legs through the pale nightgown. Again he began to stir. "Listen, would you think I was crazy if I used your phone to call the weather number? To see about the snow, you know. Or to hear about it."

She smiled. "Go ahead. Step quiet though; my daughter knows I'm not alone but would rather not believe it."

"I know," he said sourly. He walked lightly into the hall and dialed the number. The wind was northeast at fourteen, barometer falling, relative humidity sixty-seven, and there was a hazardous driving warning. The snow might change to sleet, freezing rain, or rain; the voice of the disembodied lady hesitated, as though deciding the form of precipitation were her prerogative.

He walked quickly back to bed, and crawled in. Angela had her hands under her head, and the nightgown was up to her thighs. He lay facing the window, back to her, but ran his cold foot up and down her leg. She stirred and touched him. Her knees, breasts and shoulders slid nicely into him, and her shorter height allowed her lips to touch the back of his neck. Again he thought of Judy; slightly taller than he, her face was always at the back of his head, and when she spoke, lying behind him, it seemed as though he were being talked at from some height. Not now, however.

Angela's childlike fingers crept over his thigh and touched him as though he were fragile. When she felt it, she grunted softly. "Do you want it again, baby?" he suggested.

A tongue moved up and down on the back of his neck.

"Well, me too," whispered Essai, laughing a little. "But tonight, since I feel a lot like a kid, with the weather lady not sure if she will delight me by ordering a snowstorm, and you making me as virile as the college junior I was at the height of my sexual power (it was said), I feel like holding out long enough to tell you a little story."

"OK. As long as 'Mr. Candyman don't melt away.' "

"What?"

She gave it a shake, as best she could. "The peppermint stick," she said. "Oh my, listen to me. Thank God it's too dark to see. I'm blushing terribly."

"Hold on to it while I tell the story of Easy Andy. When Easy Andy was young he wanted to be a doctor, and he read all about science and doctors, and he continued to do so in high school and college. He was relatively uninterested in the arts and humanities, since that had nothing to do with medicine. So when his friends referred to the entrails of an owl or classical music, Easy Andy had a hard time following them."

At the mention of the owl she let go and pulled back, about to apologize. "Keep hold of it, or else the story stops." The fingers returned and she nestled against his back. As his desire swelled, he talked rapidly, trying to finish before he started.

"The first year in medical school Easy Andy won all the prizes, because it was lab work, easy work for Easy Andy, and that year he was first in his class. The second year was about the same, except that a course called Physical Diagnosis required that students talk to patients about symptoms, and examine them. Easy Andy had trouble with this course. In the third year he took clinical clerkships, and it became clear that all the fascinating book diseases were buried inside patients. It was not enough just to study the disease. A patient had it, a person, and the person was concerned only with getting better, not in providing a scientist with another example of an interesting condition.

"That was the problem. Easy Andy, student of science, knew that to study disease he had to study patients, and be concerned about them. But his education and his experience in the world did not equip him to learn this art, and so he began to find out something about the world. It took time to achieve, to read and talk and listen to music, travel, inform himself, become aware of the richness of life. While Easy Andy began to do this, his standing in the class slipped a little, though some of his friends thought he was a better person, and some of his teachers, a better doctor."

The narrator paused. He felt the quiet breathing on his neck. As it occurred to him that he was opening up to a total stranger, he edged away from her and abruptly sat up.

"Don't stop stories in the middle," she said quietly. "That sounds like a happy story, but the tone of voice was sad."

"How perceptive," he said.

"OK. Good night, Andy." She turned away from him and pulled the sheet up.

He passed through filtering melancholy for a moment, and came out tender and reflective again. "Here's the sad part. Angela, are you awake?"

The head bobbed. "Yes."

Essai lay back. "The sad part of this story is a little confused, since there are several strands in it, hard to sort out. What happened to Easy Andy is this: though he learned enough about the world to start caring for sick persons, rather than patients carrying around a disease, he never felt as comfortable at the bedside as he did in the laboratory. For a while, that was fine. It was fine because there seemed to be a greater emphasis on good research in medicine than on good practice. Also, laboratory work did not include night calls, and there was time for more books, concerts, talks. And finally, the man with whom Easy Andy came to work was a doctor who wanted to care for the sick. He was happy to let Easy Andy do research, in the laboratory."

"Then what happened?" She was looking at him.

"Two things. With his expanding insight, our hero saw that the hospital is something like a home, and full-time hospital doctors make up the family living there. If the great clinician was the father, then the men who worked as his subordinates and glorified his name were his sons. Variously loved. Nurses, secretaries, and lab assistants play appropriate female roles."

The storyteller became Essai again. He touched Angela's shoulder for emphasis. "I'm not his son. It's the stifling conflict again. Good grades in school brought love, and it seemed like the same thing again. One is forced into adolescence again without realizing it."

"You said two things happened. What's the other one?"

Essai chuckled. "You won't believe this. My boss, or the head of the family, had a heart attack. He chose one of his sons to help him do the adults' work."

"You?"

"Yes."

"Is that scary, Andy?"

"Yes, it is. And not for the old reason. I find that I can talk to patients, and do the clinical work. It's just that the work is consuming, totally so. I do nothing else, nothing except the medicine he wants me to do. And that's the other part, of course, that he 'gives' me the work to do."

Angela lit a cigarette. "The mantle doesn't rest very easy, does it?"

"No. Tell me why, Analyst Angela."

He was trying to be lighthearted and get her away from the center of it. But she shook her head. "The mantle," she said slowly, "is never passed without the kernel of humiliation in it. You're chafing under its irritation."

Protectively, Essai yawned. "Maybe," he said lightly. Then he scratched. "Jesus, got to use the bathroom again."

He was gone for a few minutes, and came back slowly. He hardly stepped into the bedroom when he heard her say, "You know, I should take my own advice."

"How's that?"

"Out there in the park I urged you not to analyze what had just happened. You know, when we lay out there?"

"I remember," he smiled. He leaned over quickly and kissed her.

"Well," she murmured, moving her lips against his, "I should keep from analyzing what you say."

Her lips had opened on "analyzing." "Say 'analyzing' again, Angela."

She pulled him down. "Say 'Angela' after I say 'analyzing.' "

"Here comes Mr. Candyman again."

"Come in."

He was on her. "Have some candy-candy-candy. It's a very nice part of love." At the word "love" he repeated himself like a record, aware that the expanding metal of the first time and the expanding darkness of the last now fused into a thin, dark shell, enclosing them both in the dark, making vision more acute. His two hands moved to her hunching shoulders, pressed them into stillness, and he groaned, "Love, love, love," ceasing to speak only when his locked secret selves silenced the world by pouring out into her.

The way down was through a smoked hazy valley of reflection. Essai gazed at her glistening hips and legs, then reached to feel the small hard breasts. He had always liked big women, Lemonning the biggest, who, lying aroused before and spent after sex, seemed to help magnify the act by coming to it with such immense parts. Judy Lemonning's bikini lines, he remembered, were particularly rousing because they highlit the parts of her most involved in sex: and their size suggested that they were prototypes of the responsive parts of all women. But all that was rubbish. Judy Lemonning, to use that example, was concupiscent only when she thought it was time to be, and so became the party of lesser interest and ran the whole show. In the dim light from the hall, Andy could see the supple flanks of Angela Lynne, who did not think of anything as a show, and seemed incapable of bitchery.

"Good night, baby." He realized he should let her get some sleep.

Her hand found his. "Good night."

Angela lay quietly and did not sleep, almost hearing a rich chord being held indefinitely. Essai began to think over how he had come to open himself here, with this woman. But presently he found himself in the valley morning being led on a walk by a young girl, and rather than think any more he went along with her.

He awoke moments later to the smell of coffee, Alix' voice and gray light filtering into the bedroom. For an instant he was blank, then he stood up and looked at his watch. Seven fifteen. Outside the city lay under a thin cover of snow, and flakes swarmed in fluttering clouds high in the sky.

His clothes were all in the bedroom. Angela must have brought his shirt in. They were talking about the snow, and he wanted to sleep with her through the snowy morning. He looked disgustedly at his wrinkled shirt. He had to go home, shower and shave, change his shirt, and start rounds at nine. He wondered about the man with the heart attack and complete heart block and hoped he had done all right. "Maybe I ought to call the hospital," he thought anxiously.

"I'll call from my apartment," he mumbled to himself, and he put his shoes on quickly. Then he took a deep breath and walked into the living room.

In the daylight Angela looked about eighteen, and tired, but she smiled at him. "Alix, you remember Mr. Essai, don't you? Andy, wash up if you want and I'll pour some juice for you."

"No thanks, I have to be going. Hospital rounds." He had no desire to explain anything to her. He wanted to get out.

"Did you sleep well, Easy Andy?"

The little girl was holding a cup of milk with both hands. At the sound of the name he had used describing himself to

Angela, and hearing the innocence of the question, he stared at her. "Sleep? Yes, thank you, quite well. How about you?"

"I woke up."

Angela moved into view, setting coffee and orange juice down on the small table near the window with the fine view. Essai looked at his watch. Seven twenty-five. He sat and drank the icy juice quickly. Feeling better, he poured milk into his coffee and the hot, homemade taste warmed him up and made things different. Again he thought of Judy, who started the day with espresso. Angela sat down and pretended not to look at him.

"Alix, how do you like the snow?"

"I like it. Mommy said you knew it was going to snow. How did you know?"

Essai shrugged. "Just knew, Bright Eyes."

"Bright Eyes." Alix smiled delightedly at her mother as she repeated it, as though explaining why she was so taken with the man. "But how?"

"How did I know it was going to snow?"

"How did you?"

"Well, I'll tell you. When I was little I loved snow. Now I am big, but I still love snow. So I have become kind of an amateur meterologist, that's a weatherman. Now if you want a lesson, I'll teach it to you, though I have to be leaving in a minute."

Angela went out to get his jacket and Andrew Essai watched the little girl, who was listening very hard.

"Can you listen to a phone, Alix?"

"Sure."

"Well, you ask your mommy to dial nine-three-six-one-two-three-four, that's a number where they give you the weather. Then you listen. For the next few hours they'll say, 'Wind northeast sixteen' or 'Wind northeast twenty-two.' Now when you hear them say, 'Wind northwest,' that is, when the wind changes from northeast to northwest, it'll be snowing if you look outside. But here's the lesson: that snow will stop sure as shooting in the next hour or so after the wind changes. That's Easy Andy's lesson for today."

Angela came back in. "Is it a secret?" she asked, seeing the private looks on their faces.

"Yes," said Alix happily. "I'll tell you today when the snow will stop. If you dial the number. Easy Andy, tell her the number."

Essai stood up, and put on his jacket. "It's nine-three-six-one-two-three-four," he said. "Speaking of numbers, can I call the hospital for just a second?"

"Of course."

He dialed the Eastern Massachusetts Medical Center, and got nurse on the sixth floor. "Miss Reiss?"

"Yes."

"This is Dr. Essai. How—"

"Dr. Essai, just a second. They were looking for you."

His heart started pounding. Then he heard O'Connell's voice. "Andy, where were you? We called your apartment all night."

"What's up?"

"Mr. Budick died, the man with heart block."

"He died? When?" Essai sat down on the edge of the couch.

"About six. We had given him his anticoagulant, heparin, and he started passing bloody urine. That's when we called you."

"Bloody urine? Did you exceed the dose?"

"No," O'Connell said patiently. "We called Kraft at home after we couldn't get you. Kraft came in to see him. He thought it all fit with a ruptured aneurysm, not a heart attack at all."

"Oh, God. And we anticoagulated him."

"Right. He died while they were getting him ready for surgery. The autopsy will start at nine. Kraft wants you here now."

"Is he there?"

"No. He's eating breakfast at home. He'll be here at eight thirty."

"I'll be right there. I'm sorry, about not being home."

The mild chief resident said apologetically, "Sorry we had to call Kraft. But we tried to get you at home. I guess I'd better warn you—Kraft is boiling."

"OK. Thanks, Martin. I'm coming in now."

He hung up. Angela was looking at him with frightened eyes. "What is it?"

Essai shook his head violently. "No, don't ask me anything. I'll call you later."

She nodded. Alix looked at both of them, dropped her cup and started crying. Essai hesitated for a second and then ran out. O'Connell's phrase "Where were you?" echoed endlessly in his mind as he changed in his apartment, cut himself shaving, and trotted two miles to the hospital. He sprinted in short bursts once in a while to get away from the phrase, but the "where" struck with every footstep, and he walked the last few blocks slowly, trying to get himself ready for Kraft.

When the call came from the hospital to Kraft at five in the morning, Ruth Kraft said sleepily that it might be easier if he wait till morning to see the sick patient. Her husband had stared at her, his face harsh in the light of the bed lamp.

"Don't be silly. They can't find Essai. That man sounds as though he has a rupturing aneurysm. We gave him anticoagulants, you know. If he dies, we helped kill him."

She got up then, vaguely guilty about lying in the warm bed while he talked about possibly having hastened another's death.

"You needn't get up," he said quickly.

"That's all right, I'll make you some coffee."

"No," he snapped. "There's no time. If Budick is dissecting his aneurysm we have to get the surgeon in."

At the door she handed him his wool scarf. "Call if you get a chance."

"All right. Go back to bed."

He raced down the driveway and drove away with tires squealing. Ruth went back to bed, and Kraft called at seven. "I'll be driving home for breakfast. Three eggs, Ruth."

"How's the patient?" she asked quietly.

His voice was flat. "Dead."

He came home again, driving through the light snow, and he looked altered, but not just sobered by the death of his patient. He had the kind of vitality she remembered from their days at Magnolia State Hospital in Ohio, when his extraordinary energy day after day seemed like that of a faintly desperate man hacking out a clearing for himself in the woods. She had not thought of that image in years until he came in the door, talking.

"Well, he died, Ruth, and we should have thought of a rupturing aneurysm sooner. Though when they die this fast, the tear is expanding so fast that even surgery is of no value."

She put on his eggs. "Did they find Essai?"

He drank the juice in two huge swallows and shook his head negatively. "No, but he should be in soon. He's in for a surprise. You know, Ruth," Kraft waved a piece of toast at her, "in a way, it's fortunate this happened. Oh, I don't mean about Budick dying; that has to be classified a preventable death, and I'm to blame, just as Essai is, since I suggested anticoagulation yesterday."

"Then what is it that's fortunate?"

"Well, it's obvious. Essai was watching my patient for me. O'Connell said he stayed till eight or so, but then he left the hospital. When they called his apartment he wasn't there." Kraft munched the toast as he spoke. "Essai's a good boy, don't get me wrong. But I knew, I just knew, that the time would come when he was needed, and he would be gone. No one would know where to find him. Well, it took four months but it happened last night. I'll bet he was at some concert."

"All night?" she said questioningly. She had seen Essai last night, and suddenly felt he had spent the night with a woman. Jealousy raced through her.

"I don't know. It doesn't matter where he was." Kraft hit the table with his fork for emphasis. "The point is that they couldn't find him. Now Ruth, I ask you, do you remember any occasion when I couldn't be reached to give advice on a sick patient? Do you?"

"No," she said sadly.

He looked at her. "Why so gloomy all of a sudden? I feel fine. Why it wasn't four months ago that I had that monitor on my chest and wondered if I'd ever care for patients again. Now look. I go in at five to see the patient, and I'm still ready for a full day, just like before."

As he spoke, she was overwhelmed by the image of her husband as a gray-haired explorer, chopping down the trees with all his strength to make a clearing. She put his eggs down in front of him. "Here you are."

He patted her arm. "Thanks, Ruth. How about some extra butter? I think I can chance the calories." He laughed gruffly. "Still twenty pounds less than my pre-attack weight. Why, I'll bet I haven't been this trim in thirty years."

She nodded, watching him smear the butter on the toast. "What will happen with Dr. Essai?"

"What?"

"Will you let Dr. Essai continue to help you?"

He swallowed the toast and eggs. "Of course," he said expansively. "Essai's a fine pair of helping hands. But the feeling that he was taking over, that the calls were coming to him and not me, that feeling is gone. Sure, I'll have him give talks, and see consultations."

The phone rang. She watched him rise as though conditioned to it. "I'll get it. Put in another piece of toast for me."

She listened to him talking, and then figured Dr. Bergman from Lawrence was calling; something about a patient with heart failure. It had been several weeks since a morning call like that interrupted breakfast. And she knew he would accept the new duty with relish, whether it be phone advice or the transfer of a patient from a worried, overwhelmed physician to a doctor like Matthew Kraft, who lived for just such responsibility.

Ruth sat down in the paneled kitchen and watched his fried eggs cool on the toast. She looked outside, where snow fell into the pine trees in the backyard. The trees in Ohio were oak and maple, and snow fell on the branches, not through the needles. "The clearing's big enough for us, Matt. I think you can rest for awhile." She murmured the words, but she need not have worried about being overheard. Matt's voice in the living room was loud, authoritative, brash: "Hell, yes, I'll take her on my service. But Bergman, please hold off on any more fluids. She's in enough trouble already. Yes, I'll accept her in transfer. Good-bye." He dropped the phone from what sounded like a height, and came back to the kitchen.

"Bergman will never learn," he exclaimed loudly. "He spent all night with a patient at the Lawrence General pouring in digitalis and fluids, and not checking her carefully, so now she's in pulmonary edema and he thinks she's dying and so he calls me and asks what to do. He had an I.V. running all night, can you imagine that?"

"No, I can't." Why did he assume she knew all the medical jargon?

Matthew Kraft attacked his eggs. They were cold, but he said nothing, unresponsive to anything except the second medical problem that had started his day. As if to confirm her notion, he glanced out the window. "Jesus, it's snowing hard. Did you see?"

"Yes, Matt."

"Oh. Bergman says it's starting to snow up there in Lawrence too. But he still wants to send her down by ambulance to the Medical Center and have me take care of her. If that ambulance gets stuck in the snow the poor woman will never make it." He finished his eggs with an immense mouthful. "Where the hell is Lee? He's usually here by this time. It's nearly eight. The autopsy on Budick will start at nine."

She got his coat, still damp from his earlier trip in the morning. She smelled moist wool and thought suddenly of death. "Matt," she said, as she held the coat for him. "You've put in some time already today, getting up at five."

"Sure," he said. "They couldn't get Essai, so they called me. Didn't you think I should go in this morning?"

He was taking it wrong. "Of course, Matt. But—"

"What?" He had been glancing out, looking for Lee, but with her hesitation he finally turned to her.

"Matt, I'm happy to see you back, back to good health, that is. I know it's not my place—"

"Hurry up. There's Lee." He opened the outer door. "What is it?"

She smiled. "Nothing. What time will you be home?"

"Oh, five or six. Saturday afternoon is our journal meeting, you know. Say six."

She kissed his cheek. He patted her and went out, looking trim and walking with a light step in the snow. Jam Wah Lee had on ear muffs and seemed too young to have a driver's license. He backed the car out, Matt pointed sharply at the road, and the brake lights went on. Then Lee's station wagon literally crept down the wet street.

Ruth Kraft breathed on the cold glass, made a nose print in it, a forehead print, then blew it away again. The hiatus was over. In December and January Matt had spent nearly every evening in the living room. He made fires, and they read together, or watched television, or played Scrabble. He wrote his son several letters, the first in five years, and Susan came home to visit over Christmas. Christmas night, after several cups of grog, Susan went to bed and Ruth sat with Matthew in front of the fire. He had said, "Last month I thought I'd never see another Christmas. You have helped me so much, Ruth. I love you."

Recalling it, Ruth mouthed the words "I love you" on the freshly steamed glass in the front door window. She had been cozily high, and nearly asleep, when he began to kiss her passionately. That night, and New Year's, and several times in January they were husband and wife in every way. Through the whole cold winter she had had springtime feelings. Only now, in March, this very morning, had the winter returned, and with it, the old image of trees being chopped.

It was Essai's fault, goddamn him. He should not have been out. Had he been available last night, Matt would have arisen at eight, not five, and maybe (she thought irrationally), Bergman would not have called.

Who was she kidding? She had wanted to be with Essai, drinking wine in his apartment. She bumped her head hard against the glass. "Stop it," she said. She closed the front door and went into the kitchen. She did the dishes slowly, glad for the work. But remembrances of the springlike New Year's ebbed slowly, and her mind was washed by thoughtless melancholy. Several times she looked into the backyard filling up with snow. The cleansing melancholy was the kind that comes to a recently widowed, childless woman, that of sweet, un-restrained ease. She had children, though estranged and far away, and she was not widowed, though the husband who made the spring out of season had gone to work again in the old way.

The dishes finished, she walked around slowly, watching the snow in the pines, going to the front door where Matthew's tracks were being covered, then upstairs. She always felt uneasy about being in his study, but she carried a dustcloth protectively. There was an unused quality to it, too neat in the absence of journals on the floor or sheets of yellow notes everywhere. The huge leather chair was near the window, across from the wall hung with framed diplomas. Ruth sat in the chair for a moment, surely feeling that Matthew would again begin to spend many evenings in here.

On the left were the bound volumes of *Circulation, J.A.M.A., American Heart Journal, American Journal of Medicine, Lancet* and several more. Matt's favorite was still the *Annals of Internal Medicine*, where his paper on the work of the heart had appeared. Impulsively, Ruth rose and went to the shelf of bound *Annals*. The author index appeared in the back of the volumes, published every six months. Under "Kraft, Matthew" she found a reference in each volume, from volume 44 to volume 59, none in 60, and three in 61. She looked up one of the articles at random, "Congestive Heart Failure—Some New Thoughts on a Challenging Problem," in October 1957 *Annals*. It was impossible to understand, though she smiled at a sentence near the end: "The heart fails from disease intrinsic to it, or forces outside of it that act to give the same clinical picture, and the full range of scientific ingenuity and diagnostic skill is required of the physician to allow him to decide which of the mechanisms is operative, and how to manage the ensuing disease." Her smile resulted from sensing that she had heard him say those words, or phrases like it, at night before talks when he "gave them to the wall," and she lay in bed half asleep. How odd to see his sleepy lullabys to her encased in print, read and applied by hundreds of physicians.

Abruptly she shivered, and put back the book. "There you are," she stated quietly to the wall he bounced lectures against. "The casual reader of a journal can see my husband's innermost thoughts, and grow to understand him better than I. His heart is in his articles, his books, the hospital. With me, with people, he is heartless. My joy at his success is tinny, hollowed out. Where do I go? To read his articles? They can't nourish me."

She went into her bedroom and made the bed. The washing melancholy was gone. In its place was the certainty that she was going to do something, and the part of her that decided things on the basis of feeling had done so before she thought it.

She dialed the number of Harvard University.

"Harvard." The accent was South Boston, not Cambridge.

"Fine Arts Department, please."

There was a pause. "Fine Arts."

"Professor Sisti's office, please."

Another pause. Then Chris' voice.

"Sisti, here."

"Chris, it's Ruth."

"Ruth. What a pleasure. Is anything wrong?" His rich voice was concerned for her; in it was more loving kindness than Matt could ever muster.

"No. Just a snowy day. Would you want to drive into the country this afternoon?"

He was delighted. "Of course, We could drive toward the North Shore. But tell me, why the call after so long a time? I haven't heard from you since October."

"No special reason," she answered lightly. "You are free this afternoon?"

"Certainly. My graduate seminar is at eleven. Shall I meet you at the old place, say about one?"

"Fine."

"How lovely a surprise," he said. "Until then."

"Yes," she said softly.

Jennifer Applegate, the whistling pathologist, measured the

pupils of George Budick (4 mm.), his length (170 cm.) and noted that he had moderate dependent lividity, surgical scars on an appendectomy and right inguinal hernia (old). She thumbed through the chart preparatory to slicing his body from thyroid to pubis, whistling sprightly as was her custom. Tall, dark-skinned, wearing hoop earrings and an apple-green sheath dress, she was fragrant from Chanel cologne behind her ears, knees, and on her wrists, the kind of woman surgeon anyone would desire, except her art was that of the post-mortem, invariably practiced on unwilling and unresponsive subjects.

George Budick had expired shortly before seven, and Dr. Applegate was called at home to come in for a postmortem. Her reluctance at performing weekend posts was eased by two factors: she received fifty dollars for each post so done, and the one today would be attended by Matthew Kraft and a number of men from the cardiology department, or so the resident had told her. It was a few minutes before nine, the undertaker would not come for the body before noon (lewdly winking at her from the midst of funereal black), and as a rule, she would have had the morgue to herself, she and the subject. She was a little unbalanced, as are most pathologists, but neither paranoid nor megalomanic, nor alcoholic—instead she talked to the body and actually whistled as she worked. On occasion she did strange things. The summer evening a young football player had collapsed and died of a berry aneurysm rupture during football practice, she became intensely sad-dened looking at the muscular young body, and without think-ing about it, kissed the still lips. Then, more moved than aroused, she thrust her tongue against the chalky teeth. He was a beautiful boy, and had she been able to lock the morgue door, she might have fallen swooning on his body.

In spite of such rare departures from medical behavior, she was an excellent pathologist. For one thing, she read the chart of each patient, reviewing the clinical course to find leads that would guide her during the autopsy. Sometimes the notes were scribbled, especially at the end, sometimes prayerfully mournful. George Budick, she saw, had been admitted with a heart attack and heart block the evening before. Though nominally on the service of Matthew Kraft, the first note other than the house staff work-up was Andrew Essai's, the assistant professor and, so the rumors went, handpicked protégé of Matthew Kraft. Essai's note said:

> This 62-year-old man with known coronary heart disease is now admitted with chest pain and findings on cardiogram of complete heart block. He has not had syncope, and so his cardiac output is probably adequate. Case discussed with Dr. Kraft, and the proposed method of management includes usual coronary care, anticoagulation with heparin, and use of Isuprel if the heart rate falls below 55.
>
> A. ESSAI

His note had been written at eight. The next note, by the resident, was at midnight, stating that the patient had increasing pain between his scapulae, and a trace of blood in his urine. A note at two in the morning described severe back pain and unusually marked pallor. At five, a note by the intern said:

> Very pale and complaining bitterly of back pain. Last urine, at four, was grossly bloody. Still getting heparin for anticoagulation. Dr. Essai not at home. Dr. Kraft called, suggests that diagnosis may be in error, and that the patient likely has a tear in his aorta. Suggests stopping heparin, giving antidote for it, and calling surgeons to see at once. Dr. Kraft on his way to hospital.

The next note, at five forty-five in the controlled hand of Kraft:

> The picture is clearly that of a dissecting aneurysm. Heparin, contraindicated in the presence of such a tear, has been stopped. He needs surgery at once to repair the tear. The outlook is grave.

Next the note of the surgeon, pointing out the risk of such surgery (50 percent mortality on the table), and the last note, in shaky intern's hand:

In spite of six transfusions, bled massively from rectum, had seizure and cardiac arrest, and could not be resuscitated. Pronounced dead at 6:20 A.M. Wife notified. Permission for autopsy obtained.

Jennifer Applegate whistled in surprise. "So, George," she said to the naked corpse lying on the stainless steel table, "they missed the diagnosis. We'll see if Dr. Essai shows up for the surgery to be done on *him*."

But the first doctor to step uneasily past the heavy door was Steve Schachter. "Excuse me," he said in a hushed voice. "Are you—oh." He saw the body. "I guess this is the place."

"Come in," she said. "Welcome to the morgue. Did you help take care of him?"

Schachter took his reflex hammer out of the pocket of his white coat and twirled it slowly. "Yes. My luck, I switched with Weinstein, and so I have to cover the cardiology service till tonight." He sniffed warily. "I must say the usual smell of death is softened. Did you spray him with perfume?"

"Me," said Dr. Applegate.

She felt herself looked at clinically. Casually she glanced at his left hand, twirling the hammer, and saw no gold.

"Do you always greet the dead so well dressed? Or were you going out on a big date at nine in the morning?"

"Yes and no," she said cryptically. "I'm a woman as well as a pathologist you know, Dr.—"

"Schachter. Steve. Glad to meet you. Sorry it's in such a morbid setting."

She smiled. "Is it still snowing out?"

"I guess so," said Steve. He looked at the jade ring on her left hand. "When I'm on duty I don't know what's happening in the real world."

"But you said you just had to cover the service till tonight. It's Saturday night, a big date night for you young fellows." She threw it out purposely. If Steve was an assistant resident he couldn't be over twenty-seven, twenty-eight at the most. She lowered her thirty-four-year-old neck a bit.

"Ah yes, I hope they don't call off the church dance after

the basketball game tonight. Dad said I could stay out till eleven. Is that OK, Mom?"

"Oh, I thought you were going for a walk in the snow with your old mother, not to the dance."

The hammer stopped twirling. "That's right," Schachter said, "but I don't know her name yet."

"Applegate, Jennifer. It's in the Boston book, though the apartment's in Cambridge."

"Well," Steve Schachter started twirling again, "there is much to be gained from the autopsy."

The door opened again and Ed Pruden came in, talking to someone over his shoulder. "—dissected," he was saying, "at least that's what I heard."

Harvey Lerner came in after him. "Is this Mr. Budick?"

The whistling pathologist looked at them professionally, chilly but helpful. "Was Mr. Budick. I'll start as soon as Dr. Kraft arrives."

Pruden rubbed his hands. "Oh, this should be something. Is Essai here yet?"

"I don't see him," said Schachter dryly. He glanced at the woman in the apple-green dress, who was too cool to blush, and blushed himself.

There was a knock, and then Essai came in, stepping briskly till he saw the body, and in a flash, Pruden and Lerner. The color ran out of his face. "Are you starting now?" he asked Dr. Applegate.

"Yes." The loud voice came from behind him, Matthew Kraft's.

"Oh, excuse me." The pale young man scurried aside as Dr. Kraft spoke.

"Don't move away, Essai. Go right up to the table. As one says at the bullfight, this is the moment of truth."

Essai came up to the table and nodded at Dr. Applegate. She watched him, noticing his bruised lips and softened features, as though he had spent the night in unaccustomed sex. The bruised softness and fear clashed. The disparate elements made him a strange and somehow unnerving figure. She looked away from him at Schachter, but he too was more than a doctor to her now—a moment ago they had met and made a date. Over the uncommenting form of George Budick, she thought.

She took a breath. "We'll start with the measurements. Some are written on the board."

They all looked at the vital statistics of the corpse, and she took the moment to regain her composure. She handed the chart to Kraft. "Would you like to see it?"

He took it and glanced into it. "Here, Essai. As you may have guessed, a few things happened after you left last night."

Essai gripped the chart and stared at the body. Dr. Applegate took a thin sharp knife and opened the body in the usual fashion. As she went through the peritoneum, a huge unclotted mass of blood began to well out. They all stepped back, except for Kraft, who stood still, and the pathologist, who moved closer. "I'd say there's four to six liters of blood," she said. "There's some blood above the diaphragm as well. We'll see when we get to it, but the picture is that of a dissecting aneurysm."

Pruden piped up, "I couldn't help hearing a little about this case, and I understand that the patient was given anti-coagulants. Isn't that contraindicated in dissection, Dr. Essai?"

For a moment only the sound of the laboring suction hose was heard. "That's right," Essai nodded.

"Well?" Pruden smiled, bending toward the open corpse.

"I thought he had a heart attack. With complete heart block. I still wonder why he developed heart block with a rupturing aorta." Essai opened the chart and found the cardiogram. "It looks like heart block." Under attack, he seemed calmer than he was before, waiting for it.

"Lerner," said Kraft loudly. "How do you put it together?"

Harvey Lerner shrugged. "I never heard of that association," he admitted at last.

"Schachter? By the way, what are you doing here? I thought

you went off the cardiology service. Do you have some psychiatric explanation for this man's illness? As I remember you were always anxious to invoke that mechanism."

Dr. Applegate pushed the intestines out of her way, and a loop of bloody gut slid over the edge of the table and slapped against Matthew Kraft's pant leg.

"Goddamnit, watch what you're doing," he shouted viciously.

Her voice was infinitely calm. "Sorry, Dr. Kraft. Would you mind stepping back a little."

Schachter smiled momentarily at her as she retrieved the loop of bowel, then he looked at Kraft. "Perhaps he had the complete heart block before. Before he developed the dissecting aneurysm, that is."

"Precisely," said Kraft. "He had it before. In fact, his wife told me early this morning that he had seen a doctor two months ago, and a slow heart rate was discovered. All right, Schachter, I'm glad we taught you something while you were on our service."

Again Pruden spoke. "Certainly it's obvious now. Essai, didn't you think of that last night, before you gave him anticoagulants? You were caring for him, weren't you, professor?"

Essai looked at him quietly, but it was Kraft who spoke. "That's enough," he barked.

"But Dr. Kraft," Pruden began oilily, "I merely wanted to hear what Dr. Essai thought when he gave this man heparin. If the question of dissection were even remotely considered, should the man have been given heparin?"

"Quiet," Kraft commanded him. "I saw the patient with Essai last evening. We both gave him heparin. Now, what questions would you like to direct at me?"

"Ah— I—"

"You sound unsure of yourself, Ed." Kraft took a step toward him. "Well, I have wonderful news for you. I got a call at home this morning from Dr. Bergman in Lawrence. He's sending down a lady with pulmonary edema, digitalis toxicity, and profound heart failure. If she survives the trip, she should be here any minute. You will see her first, and care for her."

Pruden had assumed a color more pale than that of the corpse. He looked around, but only Lerner had not averted his eyes. "Well, I *do* have patients scheduled in clinic, and that will take me until the time journal meeting starts."

"Ah yes, the clinic," Kraft smiled. "More fat neurotic ladies who think they have heart disease. More boys with innocent heart murmurs who want to get approval for sports. Yes, Ed, why don't you go down to clinic. We'll look after the sick."

Pruden edged toward the door. "Yes, thank you, I will go there. My first patient is probably waiting now. "Yes." He put the door between him and Kraft.

The whistling pathologist held up the heart. "Here. This scar is from an old infarct. Most likely he had a heart attack before, developed heart block, and some time later the aneurysm dissected. We won't know till the slides are ready."

Kraft looked at the heart, as they all did. Then he said, "May I take it?" and held it in his hand. "This whitish scar, that's the only sign of the old heart attack. Right?"

"Yes. Of course, we will find a healed thrombosis in one of the coronary arteries, the one that led to that scar."

"Thank you," said Kraft sarcastically. "What I mean is this; the heart muscle, except for this one scar, is as strong as ever, even after the heart attack."

Essai, Lerner and Schachter all understood, though Dr. Applegate started at Kraft. "Yes. Dr. Kraft, do I have to tell you about the prognosis of heart disease? You wrote the book."

Kraft turned the heart slightly, as though he had not heard her. "How interesting. The heart is as strong after a heart attack as before. That's a point we should all think about. Essai, do you agree?"

"Yes, sir." Essai was totally confused, first, because Kraft had actually taken his part when Pruden came in for the kill, and now, because Kraft seemed to be saying, "I had a heart attack. I'm over it, strong as ever. Don't forget it." Where did he stand with Kraft now?

The phone rang. Lerner answered it. All right," he said, and hung up. "The patient is down in Admitting. They're sending her right up to Six North. She's critically ill, they say." He announced this to them.

"Is that the one from Lawrence?" asked Kraft.

"Yes."

"All right." Kraft paused for a moment. "Schachter, do we have any students on the service?"

"I think so, I'm just covering for Dr. Weinstein, but I think there are two students, Krellenstein and a girl."

"Have them come down here to watch the rest of this autopsy. Lerner, you go around and see my patients with me. Steve, you show the students what the findings are in this autopsy. Miss, will you help him?"

Dr. Applegate looked over at Schachter, then at Kraft. "Of course," she said. "Anything I can do."

"Good. Essai, you see the patient first up there. Then I'll come up in a while and have the intern present to me. Who is your intern?"

"Maltern," Schachter said.

"Have him get the portable X-ray machine now," Kraft ordered. "If this lady has an aneurysm as well, I don't want to miss it. Lerner, I'll get to you in a minute. Essai, could I see you outside for a minute?"

"Yes, sir." Essai opened the heavy door and walked into the hall. The icy precision of the autopsy room, the averted scene with Pruden, and Kraft's odd renewed strength brought sweat to his face. That demonstration of the healed heart was a message to him. Irrelevantly, he wondered if it were still snowing out.

Kraft came out. "Let's go down the hall, Andy."

"Dr. Kraft, I'm sorry about last night. And I'm sorry about missing the diagnosis."

They stood among bed frames and carts used to transport patients. Kraft lit a cigarette and blew out the smoke, saying, "The missed diagnosis is not important. After twenty years with sick patients, you will have missed a lot." He took another puff, inhaling deeply. Essai watched, knowing that he had stopped smoking after his heart attack, and then smoked only occasionally, puffing like a timid beginner. Now the smoke poured out. "The only doctor who never misses diagnoses is the one who never sees sick people."

Essai gratefully agreed. "Yes, sir."

Then Kraft wheeled to face him. "But, doc, let me tell you something. You were supposed to be available for advice last night. When you are given that responsibility, don't go off somewhere. Now where were you?"

He thought of Angela's backlit thighs. "Out. With a lady."

"All night?" Kraft asked sarcastically. Then a faint smile curved the full lips. "I see. Is she so primitive a person that she doesn't live near a phone?" The black eyes held him.

"No. She has a phone."

"Then call the hospital. Tell them where you can be reached. You can go wherever you want, if there's time to leave the hospital, but stay close to a phone." Kraft seemed more like an advising uncle than an angry chief.

His guard down, Essai said, "I guess that's it. I wanted to be away from phones and hospitals. Just away from that feeling of being 'on call.' "

Kraft inhaled as though it were his last cigarette. "I know. That's the real difference between us. I never wanted to get away from it. I said I did, but I didn't want to."

"Well, Dr. Kraft, for four months now—"

"Bullshit, Essai. Don't give me the four month crap. Try it for twenty years." Kraft ground out the cigarette and lit another. "You know, you're a man trying to be a good doctor. And don't worry, I'll let you make talks, and write papers, and do research, and still be my assistant." Kraft raised a finger. "But you're still the kind of guy who runs off to Symphony Hall."

Essai felt the words burst out. "No, sir. As you say, I'm a man trying to be a good doctor."

"Yes?" Down the hall they saw Martin O'Connell trotting toward them.

"And you, sir, *are* a doctor. A great doctor."

Kraft smiled triumphantly, missing the heart of it. "Thank you, Andy. That's very nice."

The younger man nodded too, shouting inside himself, "But what happened to the man?" Whether the shout would have broken into words is problematical, for O'Connell caught up to them, and Kraft turned to him.

"Is the autopsy starting yet?"

Kraft blew smoke at him. "It's almost over, doc. And where the hell were you?"

O'Connell looked at the floor. "I was up all night with him, Dr. Kraft. I tried to get an hour's sleep, and overslept, I guess."

"Sleep." The word slapped the walls, and bounced against them. "Sleep when you're old, O'Connell. But in any case, not when you're my chief resident!"

"Yes, sir."

"Go in and watch the post. We have a new patient, and she's sick. Essai will see her first. Let the student see her too." Kraft gestured with his cigarette. "Then, if you feel rested enough, would you mind taking a look at her too?"

O'Connell looked at Kraft, then glared at Essai, a less formidable target. "Thanks for seeing the patient last night," he said viciously.

Essai took a step back. But Kraft, his voice lower, said, "That's enough. Andy, go up and see how the new patient is."

"Yes." As he walked quickly along the cluttered hall, Essai mused at the twists of fate that had led Pruden and O'Connell to attack him, and Kraft to defend. "Kraft realizes I'm just another good doctor," he said to himself. "Kraft is still the only Kraft."

He stopped off in the first-floor doctor's room to get his stethoscope and flashlight. Then he dialed the number of 6 North.

"Six North, Miss Reiss."

"This is Dr. Essai. How's the new patient doing? The woman."

"The ambulance patient from Lawrence? She's Mrs. Battaglia. Looks pretty bad."

"I'll be right up." He hung up and ran to the elevator. For a moment while waiting for the elevator he chastised himself for not climbing the six flights, but then weighed his fatigue, and decided he would need his energy to help the patient. If she were so sick that the thirty seconds gained were important, she would not make it in any case. He had learned that from Dr. Kraft: unless it's a cardiac arrest, never run, but wait for the elevator and think. In the minute it took to get to the sixth floor he reviewed the single fact he knew about the patient, and the ramifications of it. She had heart failure and lung edema, cause uncertain. His first moves would be to get the head of the bed up, put tourniquets on her legs to reduce the return of blood to the struggling heart, and give her morphine if she were agitated.

The elevator stopped on six. For Essai it could have been three years previously, he the chief resident, called first to see a critically ill patient, and he had to be fast and right. He went quickly down the hall. Miss Reiss, efficient and concerned, stood outside the one private room that had been empty the evening before, holding a blood pressure cuff and syringe. "She's bubbling," she said quickly.

He raced into the room. Two burly ambulance attendants hovered over the bed uncertainly, and Essai heard the bubbling wheezing breaths before he saw the patient. "Excuse me," he barked sharply to the two men, who stepped aside with gratitude and let him take the patient. A woman of sixty, slightly overweight, lay on the top sheet with her hands clenched into fists. One grasped a sweaty cross. Her eyes were roving, frightened, and she panted at a rate of fifty or more breaths a minute, grimly attempting to force air into small bronchioles of her lungs. The dusky earlobes and blue lips and nails attested to her losing battle. She had no tourniquets on her arms.

"Miss Reiss: three tourniquets, and a sixth of morphine and five hundred of aminophylline in separate syringes. Now!"

The nurse was a step behind him, and thrust the syringe into his hand. "Sixth of morphine," she said. "I had it ready."

Essai cranked the head of the bed up, to try to reduce the return of blood from the legs. As he did, he talked. "Mrs. Battaglia, I'm Dr. Essai. Tell me, have you ever had asthma? Nod yes or no. In a moment I'm going to give you an injection that will help you breathe and make you feel more comfortable. Try to breathe more slowly and deeply. All right? Shake your head 'no' if you have never had asthma."

The panting slowed, and she began moaning with the breaths, shaking her head "no," trying to slow down. Within a few seconds she was back to fifty. "Can't breathe," she panted. Miss Reiss rushed in with the tourniquets and Essai wrapped one around each leg, talking all the time. "Now these tourniquets will help your heart work better. This tourniquet goes on one arm, and now I'll inject the morphine, which will help you. No, don't move your arm. That's right, I'm injecting the morphine now."

He injected as slowly as he could without losing the vein, taking a minute to do it. In doing so, he had made the biggest decision already, one which might kill the patient if it were wrong. The few words Dr. Kraft had said about the patient, her appearance, and the head-nodding "no" convinced him that the wheezing and bubbling was not an acute asthmatic attack, but rather full-blown pulmonary edema. Morphine was the best single drug for pulmonary edema. If she had asthma instead, the morphine would rapidly reduce her desire to breathe and she might simply stop breathing, suddenly and totally.

Dr. Essai, trained by Kraft, did not consciously have to think over any of this, but concentrated on getting the morphine in, sure she had pulmonary edema. When he had finished, Miss Reiss was already there with the aminophylline. He took the syringe off the needle, left the needle in the arm, and twisted on the new syringe full of aminophylline. As he injected it, he spoke over his shoulder to Miss Reiss. "Did any of her family come in with her?"

"A son, I think. He's outside now."

"Tell him to wait right there. Get the portable cardiogram machine for me. Page Dr. Maltern and have him get the X-ray technician up here, with the portable machine. Tell him to bring a chest tap set. Rotate the tourniquets every five minutes, keeping a different arm or leg free each time. Get oxygen service up here. That's all. No wait. Mrs. Battaglia, you're Catholic, aren't you?"

The lady nodded "yes." Already it seemed her breathing was a little better, the terrible bubbling slightly quieter.

"Well, Mrs. Battaglia, we want the priest to come in and see you, to help you while you are so sick."

"Good." The Italian lady shook her head vigorously. At his side, Essai saw Miss Reiss nod once, then disappear.

"Now, Mrs. Battaglia, this medicine will help you. Is your breathing any better?"

She nodded. Her bluish hand clutching the cross sought Essai's. "A little better."

"Let me listen to your lungs now." Another nurse had appeared in the room, the two ambulance men having quickly escaped. The nurse helped hold her up in a semi-sitting position and Essai put the stethoscope on the clammy chest. There were no areas of absent breath sounds that suggested fluid in large amounts. Had there been, he would have tapped it off with a tap needle at once, to give her every chance. In the next ten minutes Essai looked at her eyes, mouth, throat, felt her breasts, ribs, and abdomen, and palpated her legs, which were swollen with fluid and sweaty to the touch. He took her blood pressure and put a pressure catheter into the same arm he had used for injecting morphine and aminophylline. The whole time he asked her questions: Had she ever had a heart attack, pneumonia, or a blood clot in her lungs? Had she felt sick for weeks or months before this day? Had the breathlessness begun slowly or abruptly? Had she been awakening at night short of breath? Did she smoke? Had she ever had operations? For what?

She answered first with nods, then single words, and after

ten minutes, in short sentences. Her breathing was definitely improved, and her lips were less blue. Again Essai listened to her chest, and heard the "tic-tac" quiet of a heart failing from within. Again he felt her belly, and with the quieter breathing and more relaxed abdomen he sensed an abnormal fullness near the liver in the midline, though a definite mass was not palpable. Miss Reiss stood behind him with the cardiogram machine, and expertly applied the straps. "Dr. Maltern is coming up," she said.

Essai nodded and quickly took the cardiogram. As the stylus scratched out the several leads, he saw at once that the pulmonary edema was not secondary to a heart attack. Maybe she had pneumonia. No. The history was not consistent with pneumonia. Pulmonary clot? No. The characteristic cardiogram pattern of blood clot was missing—and there was no area of consolidation on physical exam. But she had a very abnormal cardiogram. Possible diagnoses rose in his mind, and were dropped. Wrong presentation for aneurysm of the heart, though possible. Massive anterior wall blood clot unlikely; even if the whole left coronary was blocked it would not result in these changes. No, it was as though the whole front wall of heart muscle were absent, or replaced by tissue not conducting electrical impulses.

His hand rested lightly on her chest. Again he palpated the midline, and thought he felt a fullness. She had told him she had not felt well for a few months, and had lost some weight though not dieting. Weakness was present all the time, and getting worse. But the breathlessness had been rapid in onset. She had had some minor arthritis pain in her left hip. In back of him he heard the squeaking noise of an oxygen tank being wheeled in. Essai thought furiously. What single disease could give all of these findings, with that weird cardiogram suggesting absence or replacement of—

It popped into his mind. A tumor. She had a tumor somewhere that had spread to the liver, and metastases could well be in the heart, eating away normal heart muscle and giving rise in time to a picture of heart failure. Again the possibility of heart aneurysm occurred to him, but now nothing fit except a widespread tumor, and that diagnosis fit ominously well.

He heard the nurse talking to Dr. Maltern. His job for the moment was nearly done—now the intern and resident had the job of caring for her, and he stepped back, once more an advisor and observer. One last possibility occurred to him. Quickly he unhooked the name tag from his white coat. He took the sharp end of the needle, and hiding it from the patient, went to her.

"Mrs. Battaglia, I'm going to run a needle down your arms. Tell me if it's sharp or dull."

"Sharp. Sharp. Sharp all over there." The sensation in the arms was normal. Lightly he went down both sides of her chest and abdomen, and all along the course of the needle she felt it sharp. Then Essai went down the right leg. "Sharp. Yes, sharp," she said.

"All right, now the left leg."

"Yes, I feel it. Sharp. No. I don't feel it."

Essai's heart jumped. "Here? How about here?"

"There I feel it. No, not there. Yes, there it is again."

Essai had found an area of absent sensation to pinprick just inside her left hip. "Mrs. Battaglia, is this the hip that gave you the pain? You know, the arthritis?"

"Yes."

"All right. I see you feel better now. Some other doctors will be here in a minute." Essai looked at her face again, much calmer now, and her fingers still dusky in the nail beds but not nearly as blue. He went out into the hall, where Dr. Maltern talked to the son, asking how rapidly the shortness of breath had come on.

"Dr. Maltern, could I talk to you a minute?" Maltern, a former football player and honest, corn-fed product of Iowa Medical College, left the son, and the two doctors walked a few steps down the hall. Essai spoke more slowly than he wanted to. "She still has pulmonary edema, though it's much better after morphine and aminophylline and tourniquets. Miss Reiss will give you the dosages. She has a strange cardiogram, which I left in the room. Why don't you work her up and see what you think, and then we'll talk it over after you and Steve see her." Essai rubbed his face and watched Maltern, who had listened intently.

"Fine. What do you think it is, Dr. Essai? A heart attack?"

Essai shrugged. "Could be, but I doubt it. See what you think. I'll be in the conference room. Get Schachter to come up."

"OK." The football star took a deep breath and went back to the son standing at the edge of the door, and both of them went into the room, Maltern saying, "Now when did she first start to complain of difficulty breathing?"

Essai went to the nurses' station, where Miss Reiss sat writing notes in the patient's chart. "Thanks, Carolyn."

She looked up. "I'm glad you got here fast; I thought she was going out on us." "Going out" was the euphemism for leaving the world entirely.

"Not just yet, Carolyn. But make sure the priest sees her. I don't think she's going to make it, but we're OK for a few hours anyway. Oh, by the way—"

"Yes?"

Essai rummaged through several papers on the desk.

"Did Maltern make out an X-ray requisition?"

"Yes, it's there somewhere."

"Oh, here." Essai picked up the red requisition sheet. It asked for only a chest film. He added the words, "and overshot film of left hip, for bony detail." In the box marked Diagnostic Possibilities he read Maltern's scrawl, "acute pulm. edema in 60-year-old lady; rule out clot." Next to that Essai added, "? tumor of unknown site, spread to L. hip and heart." He handed the slip to Miss Reiss, who read it and looked concernedly at Essai.

"Really? You think she has cancer somewhere?"

Essai shook his head. "I do. Don't tell Schachter or Maltern

I think so; let them come to their own diagnosis. There's no change in the treatment for the next few hours and if she has a tumor it's too widespread to treat." He frowned. "Besides, Carolyn, I might be wrong. It's happened before."

"Oh, not you, Andy. You never missed a diagnosis." She gave him the tongue-in-cheek-look, and then the call light went on in a patient's room and she stood up and walked away.

Essai dialed the page operator and got Schachter out of the morgue. Schachter rang the floor and Essai answered the phone.

"Dr. Schachter."

"Steve, Andy. You'd better come up; she has pulmonary edema, though it's better now, and she has a crazy cardiogram. I've got some ideas which I'll talk to you about after you see her."

"Is Maltern up there?"

"Yes, but you'd better come up."

"OK, aged Andrew. By the way, what did you think of Kraft at the postmortem?"

"I was surprised," Essai said. "Hey listen, get up here. And bring the students."

"All right."

Essai hung up and checked again to make sure that Miss Reiss had entered all the drugs on Mrs. Battaglia's chart. Then he waited for the elevator, feeling the exhilarating, almost druglike high sensation slowly subside, and in this case, he remembered, there was special significance to what he had done. Less than twenty-four hours before, he had left a patient's bedside, thinking everything was under control, only to be confronted this morning by a mottled corpse in the morgue, the insults of Pruden and O'Connell, and Kraft's own muted criticism.

"I hope Mrs. Battaglia does all right," he thought fervently. He went to the cardiology offices and labs, but after a few restless moments looking at the dusty pipettes and slides in his lab, he closed the door and went upstairs again. To think about the experimental design of studies involving rabbits, at a time when a patient lay desperately ill upstairs, struck him as nearly obscene.

Maltern was still talking to the patient's son, and Schachter sat in the doctor's office near the nurses' station looking at the cardiogram. "It's their show," Essai thought. "Stay out of it now." But he wanted to be in the midst of it. At that moment he knew why Kraft loved clinical medicine so. He took out his stethoscope and irritatedly screwed the earpieces on and off, then hit the elevator button and went down to the first floor. Restless, he walked to the front door of the hospital. Snow fell thickly onto Massachusetts Avenue and cars were barely moving.

He went to his mailbox. Lemonning's quasi-European handwriting covered a small envelope. Without any change in expression, Essai looked at the postmark (New York) and slowly opened it.

A: Struggling 'gainst the hypocrisy of design in the "still point of the architectural world." Much of it is Wasteland, yet I continue to try. I wish we were sharing baklava tonight. J.

Essai read the last phrase twice, feeling the rush of bitter anger—that last night . . . The bitch. So now she was far away, in heat, and lonely. Well, wasn't that—

"Collecting reprints, Essai?" Kraft stood with an armload of manila folders under his arm not two steps away. "Funny form yours come in; mine usually come in envelopes like these."

Essai crumpled the mauve sheet in his hand. "I just saw Mrs. Battaglia," he said shortly. "She's critically ill. After you read your mail you might want to see her."

The gray-haired man paled, and for a moment Essai thought he was going to be struck. "You know I always see critically ill patients before I read my mail," Kraft said shakily. "Especially when I entrust their care to men with limited clinical skill."

He turned and walked quickly to the elevator. He punched the Up button methodically, as surly and dangerous as a caged bear. At any other time, Essai would have used the few moments to give Dr. Kraft a quick summary of the case. But he realized he had said far too much already.

"Where in hell is that goddamn elevator?" bristled Kraft.

Essai took a step back and looked up. "It's still going up, if this indicator is right."

"Well, I'm not going to stand here and wait." To Essai's surprise, Kraft hit the closed door with his fist and rapidly walked to the stairway down the hall. Andrew Essai caught up with him, and they went up six flights together. Kraft said nothing and kept climbing doggedly. The big man grunted as he walked, and Essai became aware of a totally new feeling in himself—he wanted to protect his boss against himself. Kraft was a four-year-old, and four-year-olds needed protection against their own boundless energy used to irrational ends. As Essai realized this, he began to breathe faster than he had to, and lagged a step behind. Kraft kept going. "God," thought Essai, "he probably weighs two twenty anyway, is close to sixty years old, and never exercises." Essai let himself lag two steps behind. "And four months after a heart attack."

"Dr. Kraft," he said breathlessly, "I've got to slow down. My legs ache." He blushed as he said it; his legs really hurt, but from Angela Lynne, not from climbing.

Kraft picked up the pace. "See you up on the floor then, Essai." He took the last two flights two steps at a time. Essai was six steps behind, then half a flight. "Like a four-year-old," he thought wonderingly.

He caught up on the last flight by literally running, but Kraft beat him to the door by a clear step. He flung it open in Essai's face and stepped out onto the ward. When Essai came through the door, the big man wheeled around, flushed and triumphant. "I know it's hard for you to keep up, doc. Now, where's the patient?"

Essai nearly laughed. Kraft was breathing furiously, but only through his nose—to show the whole world that he was not panting, whereas his young assistant was. Essai knew that his chief had raced up the stairs to beat him, as though that would prove his superiority over his subordinate yet again.

"Six-eleven," said Essai. "I'll see if Schachter and Maltern are down there."

"Let's go," barked Dr. Kraft. They went to Mrs. Battaglia's room, though at the usual pace, Essai noted gratefully. Inside the room, Schachter was looking at the patient's neck veins and Maltern recorded venous pressures.

"Her name is Mrs. Battaglia," whispered Essai to Dr. Kraft.

"Mrs. Battaglia, I'm Dr. Kraft. How are you feeling?" He was still out of breath, as was Essai, and Schachter looked at both of them with an ironic smile.

"Better, Dr. Kraft."

Kraft said to Essai, "I thought you told me 'critically ill.'" He wanted to tip Essai off balance again.

"I never say so at the bedside, Dr. Kraft. You yourself taught me that."

There was no sound in the room, save for the fast breathing of both Mrs. Battaglia and Matthew Kraft. Essai had spoken the truth, if reflexly, and it constituted a reprimand to his chief in the presence of an intern, resident, and the man's private patient. Mrs. Battaglia finally broke the terrible web of tension herself.

"Oh, I was critically ill before, but these doctors have given me medicine and I feel so much better now."

Kraft smiled, hugely. "I'm so glad to hear it," he said. He gestured at Schachter and Maltern. "Would you please join me outside a moment?"

They went out, and Essai followed, closing the door.

"Present her case to me," said Matthew Kraft quietly.

Maltern paled. "I—ah—well—"

"We've only been with her twenty minutes," Schachter explained. "I think Dr. Essai took the history from her. We have very little information right now, except that she had pulmonary edema and feels much better now."

"So you can't present her, is that it?" Kraft faced them, turning his back on Essai.

"Well, sir, I haven't gotten much of a history," said

Schachter. "Her son went to make a phone call, and said he would be back. Then we plan to talk to him."

"I see," said Kraft. "In that case, I will talk to the patient and examine her. You can wait out here and talk to the son." He went into the patient's room without another word.

The three men moved close together, as though they had been exiled in a group.

"What the hell's eating him?" Steve asked under his breath. "I guess that comment about the critically ill patient got to him."

Essai shrugged. "I had to say it; there's no excuse for saying in front of a patient that he is critically ill. In fact, Dr. Kraft did teach it to me."

Maltern ventured a comment. "Gee, I'm sorry about not being able to present her case, Dr. Essai, but we only had a few minutes and I was checking her pressure. I'm sorry if I did anything wrong."

Essai looked at the worried midwestern face. "Forget it."

"Well, fans," said Schachter, "I think I'll get a little lunch while the professor is seeing the patient."

"No," Essai said. "O'Connell is still probably at the postmortem. With a patient as sick as this, a resident has to be on the floor at all times. You know that, Steve."

The ironic intellectual looked at him. "Yes, oh great attempter," he said quietly.

Essai said nothing. Schachter had been here last night with Mr. Budick, while he himself was nowhere to be found. In that context, his interdiction probably sounded hypocritical. "After Kraft finishes, I'll stay with the patient while you two eat," he said at last.

"OK," Schachter answered absentmindedly. Then he grinned. "Being heir-apparent to Kraft's craft isn't very easy, is it, Essai?"

Essai looked at him quizzically. "It's not like a family fortune, you know, passed from one generation to another."

Schachter's eyebrows went up. "Oh?"

They stood silent in the middle of the hall, where Kraft had put them. Maltern looked at his nails and Schachter at Essai, who wished he were out sled-riding with Angela and her daughter.

Then Mrs. Battaglia's son came down the hall, talking rapidly to a priest who carried a small box in his hands. At the same moment, the door to the patient's room opened and Kraft strode out, glancing at the cardiogram. "We're under sacred attack," said Schachter under his breath, looking in both directions.

Kraft held out the cardiogram and Schachter took it. "I'd ask you what you all think," he said briskly, "but you would say you haven't had a chance to work her up. So take the time to see her now, and present her to start the journal meeting this afternoon."

"The journal meeting, sir?" asked Maltern.

"Yes. Who's reporting articles today, Essai?"

"I'm not sure. I think maybe Ed Pruden."

"Well," Matthew Kraft smiled icily, "the men complain about having the journal meeting Saturday afternoons, and most of them act bored to tears. So today, we'll give them a case to start things off. Schachter, you have two students on today?"

"Yes. Pirrell and Krellenstein."

"All right. Have them see the patient too, and one of you present. Have the X-rays and cardiogram. After the discussion we'll come up and see her."

"Fine," said Schachter.

Inside the patient's room the voice of the priest was heard, administering last rites. The son opened the door and stepped out, sobbing. Maltern left to call X-ray, and Essai walked over to the son, saying, "Mr. Battaglia, she's a little better. We had the priest come in because she looked so terribly ill before."

Kraft watched the scene for a moment. Then he said to Schachter, "Dr. Essai has great clinical confidence. Given a sick patient, his first response is to send for the priest."

At five past two that afternoon, Kraft stepped into the conference room, looked around at the department men, interns and residents, and sat down in the one leather chair with arm rests. Harvey Lerner was absent. He took out a small piece of paper and wrote Lerner's name on it, and then underlined it. He looked up. "I've decided to start with a case." The door opened and Lerner came in.

"Out making snowmen, Harvey?" There was brief laughter. "Sorry I'm late."

"As I started to say, we'll begin with a case admitted this morning. After you've all had a chance to say what you think, we'll go up and see the patient." Dr. Kraft smiled tolerantly. "It might make the afternoon more interesting for those of you who think the journal meeting is a waste of time. Who's presenting?'"

"I am, sir." Maltern stood up and began presenting the case. "The patient is a sixty-year-old white woman who was transferred from the Lawrence General Hospital by ambulance with wheezing and shortness of breath. She was well until two months ago when weakness began, accompanied by weight loss that ultimately totaled fifteen pounds."

As he went on, they all listened carefully, trying to piece together the story with the X-rays and physical findings soon to be presented. None of them knew who might be called upon by Dr. Kraft, nor why the journal meeting had started with a clinical case. Essai did not listen after a few sentences, but looked out the window to see if the wind were still from the northeast. He remembered Angela and felt happy, but the figure of Alix grew in his mind, and he became melancholy, introspective. Could he grow to love a divorcée with a child; step into a ready-made family? What if Sam Lynne broke out of prison and came back to see his ex-wife? Essai shivered as he thought about it.

Kraft was not listening either, because he knew the diagnosis, and as he saw Andrew Essai's attention swing from Maltern's presentation to the absent stare of a man seriously thinking about something totally different, he put the name "Essai" on his sheet and marked it. He tuned in again to Maltern, who had not yet finished the present illness. Half listening, he let his mind fix on Essai for a moment, or rather, on his feelings about Essai. Essai realized that Kraft had returned to his old form, and the young assistant was angry about it. That had to be it. Otherwise he never would have spoken so impertinently. Kraft circled the name and decided to give him a chance to continue to serve. Perhaps the talk at Mt. Zion Hospital next month in New York. He could talk about pericarditis there, the one thing he seemed to have learned something about.

"My neurologic exam was negative," Maltern was saying.

"How about the patient's?" bellowed Matthew Kraft, listening again.

Maltern straightened, as though jerked by a rope. "Sorry, sir, the exam I did on the patient was negative."

Kraft said quietly, "Tell us your diagnosis, Dr. Maltern."

"Well, sir, to me everything fits with a heart attack, leading to pulmonary edema."

Kraft turned to the students. He pointed to the girl. "You, Dr. Pirrell, what do you think?"

"Well, I'm not sure, except that the cardiogram is not what I would expect with a typical heart attack, and there is no history of chest pain."

"Do you think chest pain must be present?"

She flushed. "No, it doesn't have to be."

"And could you describe for us a 'typical' heart attack?"

She flushed more deeply. "This is only the second one I've seen," she admitted.

Kraft smiled. "At least you cannot fall back onto the phrase, 'in my experience,' which is a frequent comment from uncritical physicians. Krellenstein, how about you?"

The pudgy student shrugged. "Perhaps she could have an aneurysm."

"Go on."

The student looked stricken. "Well, just an aneurysm."

"Where, Krellenstein?"

"I don't know. In the heart, or aorta maybe? It just popped into my mind."

"Is there anything consistent with an aneurysm?" Matthew Kraft had taught students for many years, and he sniffed suspiciously.

"Not really." Krellenstein looked somewhat green.

"What *might* be consistent with an aneurysm, Krellenstein?"

"I don't know."

Matthew Kraft stood up. "Who brought the chart down here for the conference?"

Maltern started to say, "I did," but then shook his head. Schachter shook his head. Essai looked wonderingly at Krellenstein.

"Krellenstein, did you?"

The student was sweating. "I guess I did."

"Schachter, what was your diagnosis."

Schachter put his hands up. "I think she has an aneurysm."

Kraft sat down again. "I'll ask you for your reasons in a moment. Did you write that down in your note on the patient?"

"Yes, I did."

"Any other diagnosis?"

Schachter reached for the chart. "No."

Kraft turned to Krellenstein. "But you read Dr. Schachter's note while carrying the chart down, and thought you would win a point by saying the word. Isn't that so?"

Krellenstein was mute.

Kraft stood up and lowered his head. "Isn't that so?"

Krellenstein shook his head. "Yes," he whispered. He was ready to cry.

"Krellenstein, why don't you go out and take a walk in the snow. When you go home, write me a short paragraph on ventricular aneurysms, with no less than twenty references, length not to exceed eleven thousand words. But more than ten thousand."

The room was tense and silent. "Now, Krellenstein. Leave now. The library will still be open. By the way, have it ready for me by Wednesday. And don't cheat. I know all the textbook descriptions. If you cheat you can finish at chiropractor's school next year!"

Krellenstein stood up. A path was cleared for him as though he had leprosy. As he went out the door, Kraft sat down and said evenly, "Steve, tell us the reasons for your diagnosis of aneurysm." As Schachter started talking, Matthew Kraft wrote Krellenstein's name on his sheet. Krellenstein had just failed junior medicine, no matter what his paper was like.

"Well, I'm kind of rusty at writing papers, so I'll try to give some good reasons." Essai laughed out loud and everyone relaxed a little. "The cardiogram shows that the whole anterior wall of the heart is involved. The ballooning aneurysm could result from such an injured heart wall. The absence of chest pain is a real block to the diagnosis, however. The weakness suggests a tumor, but I can't find a site for a primary."

Matthew Kraft grunted. "Not bad, Schachter. Wrong diagnosis, but good thinking. Lerner."

Lerner put down the cardiogram. "I don't think it's a heart attack. I suppose a tumor is possible, spreading to the heart. Again, I'd like to see proof of a primary tumor somewhere. It's possible that the tumor is a sarcoma of the heart muscle itself, but that condition is exceedingly rare."

"If you've got it," Kraft enjoined him, "it occurs one hundred percent of the time in you."

Lerner nodded. "It's possible."

"Ed?"

Pruden whispered into his hands, looking very scholarly. "Dr. Kraft, I've listened with great interest—"

"Time's wasting, Ed."

Pruden dropped his hands. "I think the diagnosis has probably been mentioned. I'm afraid I can't add much."

Essai was looking at the X-ray, astonished that they could not see the lucent shadow in the left hip so apparent to him. Kraft was talking to him. "Essai, I waited till last with you since I saw you got the hip film. Tell them what she has."

"I can't tell you the primary," Essai said, "but she has a tumor. And it's spreading. I felt a vague but real fullness in the belly. The cardiogram is consistent with tumor of the anterior wall. And she had no pinprick sensation in the left hip. I think that area of radiolucence represents a large secondary tumor mass in the left hip." He walked to the viewbox and outlined the lesion. He heard Schachter say, "Now I see it."

Jam Wah Lee sat up from his slouched position. "Is that not air in the colon?" he ventured.

Kraft turned toward him. "Only if the colon is outside the abdominal skin," he said scornfully. "Go back to sleep, Lee, it has nothing to do with biochemistry." He stood up. "Essai is right, it's a tumor, and the primary site will be visible to all of you. Let's go up to the floor."

He led them upstairs, three flights, and smiled at Mrs. Battaglia's son outside the patient's room as though the son were applauding the procession. Inside, Mrs. Battaglia sat propped up, not well but vastly improved compared with her appearance in the morning.

"Good afternoon, Mrs. Battaglia. Do you remember me?"

She smiled. "Hello, Dr. Kraft."

"Now sit forward and let me listen to your chest." Obediently she sat forward, and Kraft listened. "Now all the rest of you listen, one at a time. Just breathe slowly and deeply, Mrs. Battaglia."

Each of them listened, Essai last, and her lungs sounded better to him. Each one of them stayed close to the bed after listening, looking for what Dr. Kraft had said was a visible tumor.

When Essai stepped back, Kraft moved to the patient's left side, pushing the bed away from the window as he did. "Sit forward again, please." The patient did so. "Now, Dr. Schachter and Maltern, what is this lesion on her back? You all must have seen it, listening to her lungs just now."

Maltern looked and straightened up. "A wen, a mole I guess." Schachter looked longer, but finally nodded his head in assent. Kraft motioned to Essai who looked, though it was hard to see close to the midline of her back. "I have to agree," he said finally.

Kraft kept smiling, patting Mrs. Battaglia on the shoulder comfortingly. "You look but do not see," he said. "If you want to see, look again." Saying this, he murmured, "Excuse me," to the startled Mrs. Battaglia and crawled up onto the bed, both knees on the edge as his head disappeared behind her back.

He looked ridiculous and a little helpless. "Move the bed lamp back here," he said from behind her. Pruden ran to assist. Matthew Kraft grunted. Then he hopped off the bed with surprising agility. "Mrs. Battaglia," he said, "turn toward the window now. Don't be afraid of moving, I'll support you." She turned toward the window slowly, and the spot on her back gradually came into the light. "Bend over a little now. That's fine."

They all moved close. It was a hairless mole, about the size of half a dime, but not particularly black. Essai was sure Dr. Kraft had erred. He said nothing.

"Look, look again," Kraft insisted. From his pocket he took a small hand-lens, and held it near the mole, with good light shining on it. Under the lens it looked darker, uglier, with a suggestion of a ragged border at the upper end. "Do you see the red streaking away from it?" Kraft asked them.

Essai saw it first, then the rest; a tongue of faint pink running from the indistinct black border up at least eight centimeters toward the right armpit. "Now," concluded Kraft, with victory strong in his voice, "carefully feel the inner border of her right armpit." One by one they felt, hesitated, felt again, and a number of soft matted lymph nodes were obviously palpable to light touch. Schachter palpated the right side of the neck, and the fleeting look on his face told the rest of them that tumor involved lymph nodes there as well.

Kraft patted the woman's shoulder reassuringly. "Now, Mrs. Battaglia, you have an ugly mole on your back. Dr. Essai reminded me about not discussing diagnosis of patients in front of them, but I think you're the kind of intelligent patient who wants to know."

"Yes. Yes, I do want to know. Please call in my son."

They got the son in, and Kraft talked calmly to the sick Italian woman. "We don't think you've had a heart attack, but as you know, your lungs were very congested, or full of fluid. Now we have found a mole on your back that may be what we call a melanoma, which means that it is a tumor and not just a mole." Dr. Kraft paused. "We would like our surgeons to take a biopsy of that mole and see if it's a tumor, for if it is, you may have some tumor spots in your lungs. If so, we can treat you for it. I think we can get the biopsy done very soon. Would that be all right with you?"

Mrs. Battaglia and her son spoke to each other in Italian. "My mother says it is all right if you say to do that surgery," the son said to Kraft.

"Yes, yes," said the lady. "Go ahead. If it's a tumor, take it away."

Dr. Kraft smiled. "We'll do our best."

She reached out and touched Dr. Kraft's arm. He moved toward her just a bit. There were tears in her eyes. "Thank you, doctor, for finding out what is wrong. I know you will make me better."

Kraft assured her he would see her later, and they went out into the hall. At the nurses' station, Kraft saw a sample of her urine in a bottle and held it up for the group. "Her urine is dark," he said. "Now you know why. It's biochemical after all, Jam Wah, because the dark color is melanin exposed to light, and it's being poured out by her tumor." His finger pointed to the dark urine and they all looked at him, at his pointed finger, and at the fated lady's urine. Pruden took in a sharp breath as though to expend it on words of congratulation, but Kraft saw him and raised his pointing finger in warning. "No praise this time, Ed. When the heart is involved this way," he paused, "we are not happy, even at finding the right diagnosis."

The March snowstorm continued. At six o'clock, Jam Wah Lee went outside yet again to wipe snow from the back window. His car was the only one left in the staff doctors' parking lot, and he had waited here for half an hour while Dr. Kraft went "back in for a second" to get some cardiograms. Lee sniffed delicately and returned to the heated car. He had been thinking about the difficulties of assaying purity of enzymes, but because of the snow and his waiting for Dr. Kraft, he was unable to concentrate. What about the patterns of snowflakes? What was the most beautiful shape assumed by five-sided flakes? By six-sided flakes. . . . Could one imagine a ten-sided flake?

The door opened to a rush of cold air and snow. "For God's sake, Lee, what are you doing?"

"Waiting for you, Dr. Kraft." He felt very sleepy.

"Christ, roll down the windows. You probably got a little carbon monoxide." Kraft covered his momentary terror at seeing Lee slouched over the wheel by shoving him roughly, and releasing a gruff laugh. "What's the matter, Lee, I thought you Chinese didn't believe in suicide."

"I am Korean, Dr. Kraft."

"Oh. Well, c'mon, let's get going. Jesus, I'll bet we don't make it in this snow."

Lee slowly drove up Washington Street to the entrance for the Expressway. There was something ominously dissonant about the air, something that jarred with the peacefulness that snow always brought. Until Dr. Kraft's heart attack, the sounds had often been loud, bombastic, martial, and afterward, calm, but never this way—uncertain. Lee sensed it the way the blind sense objects.

"Jesus, what a bunch of prima donnas we have in our department." Kraft ripped a cigarette out of a pack and slammed the lighter into the dash with his open palm. "Take Essai. Last night he spends the night with some floozy, and Mr. Budick dies of a dissecting aneurysm. Dissecting, mind you, with Essai having written a note urging the use of heparin. Then this morning, I take him off the hook, and protect him when O'Connell and Pruden attack him. So what does he do? He says to me in front of a patient not to make comments about how ill a patient is. The professor instructs me, you see."

A response was expected. "I don't believe I know this man O'Connell."

"Jesus, Lee, are you off in your dream world all the time? He's my chief resident. He's no better than the others. This afternoon he missed the conference. Did you notice?"

Lee could not have noticed, since he did not know the man. He looked with exaggerated attention at the snowy road.

"Well," Kraft hit the dash lighter again, "I found him on the ward a few minutes ago, and he's still sulking that I criticized him for sleeping during the time the autopsy was starting this morning. So he thought he'd pay me back by not attending the journal club. Can you imagine anything so ridiculous?"

Kraft interrupted his monologue to light his cigarette. Unable to replace the lighter in the darkened car, he muttered, "Here," and nudged it against the back of Lee's hand. "Put this damn thing back."

Lee made a tiny noise, took the lighter, and found its place in the dashboard. He resumed driving at normal speed on the plowed section of road, and listened to the man hunched forward at the far side of the seat. The dime-sized ache near his right wrist began to subside.

"You know, that Essai is going to be the death of me yet. He does his job all right, but he thinks that being an eight-hour-a-day doctor is enough. Well, it's not enough for me. I went up to the office to get some cardiograms from Lerner for the Sunday Session tomorrow. Essai was in his lab, and I looked at his book. He hasn't done an experiment in four months." Kraft laughed mirthlessly. "That's when I first gave him a touch of the heat of academic medicine. You know something, Lee? He's wilting. Hah! Wilting." The laughter riccocheted through the car and ebbed, and with it some of the dissonance faded as well.

"Dr. Kraft?" Lee's voice produced high echoes of speech, not speech itself.

"Yes?"

"Dr. Kraft, you burned my hand."

"I what, Lee?"

"You burned my hand, when you gave me the lighter."

"Oh, I did? I'm sorry, Jam Wah." Kraft's voice became concerned. He turned on the overhead light and slid over to look at the hand which Lee moved gently toward him. "Is it painful?"

"Not so much now, but it was before. Is it red?"

"No, I don't see anything. You want to stop and have me drive?"

"No. No. It's all right now."

Kraft snapped the light off and slid back to his side. "Well, as I said, I'm sorry. I thought you grabbed the proper end. Maybe it's a hint to me to give up these damn cigarettes. These filter-tip things taste lousy anyway, and they get more and more expensive. Know what I paid for these?"

An answer was requested. "No."

"Take a guess."

"I have no idea, Dr. Kraft. I don't smoke."

"Thirty-nine cents. Can you imagine that? A few years ago a pack of Camels cost twenty cents and they were a hell of a lot better than these." To Lee's surprise, Dr. Kraft took a vicious puff and threw the half-smoked cigarette out the open window.

Lee drove on. They were within a mile of Kraft's house, moving cautiously through the soft snow, when Kraft said quietly, "Lee, do you believe that crap about smoking increasing the risk in coronary heart disease?"

"Well, I don't know. I guess not."

"Oh my God, Lee. Stop saying what I want to hear. Or do you think I'll burn your hand again."

"It's hard to drive through this snow," Lee said opaquely.

"Hmmh." Kraft lapsed into silence. At his house he said to Lee, "Well, try to keep me from smoking. Speak up when I start to smoke."

"Fine, sir."

Kraft put his coat collar up against the blowing snow. "Pick me up at nine-thirty tomorrow. The cardiogram conference starts at ten."

"Yes, sir." Lee watched the doctor walk with bowed head against the snow toward his front door. Then he backed down the driveway and drove away slowly. As soon as he was out of sight of the house, Lee stopped thinking about the snow on the road and tried to handle the thoughts that stormed in on him: "Why did Kraft test me with the question about smoking? He knows I gave it up five years ago after his talk on smoking and heart disease. It must be that I take no notice of the politics in the department. I am unconcerned with those things; yet he is more concerned now with the department and his role than he ever was before. Had I answered his question about smoking, he might have asked me my opinion of Essai. He sounds as though he is not sure whether he wants the young man Essai to take more responsibility, and succeed, or continue to make errors and show that he is no different from any of us."

He was skidding in the snow, and slowed down. He tried to fix the word "different," and think again about the different ways snowflakes were shaped, but thoughts of the real world occupied him, and he drove home with uncharacteristically wrinkled brow.

Ed Pruden stood at the window of his Cambridge apartment watching the city fill up with snow. "You know," he called out to his wife, "I saw Dr. Kraft when he came up to his office before going home."

"Yes?" She heard the reflective tone in his voice. "Did you talk to him?"

"Of course. He made an interesting comment. He said that Essai was slacking off in the lab, and that I might go ahead on the work with serum factors in patients with rheumatic fever."

"Is that what Essai was doing?"

Pruden walked into the kitchen and watched her stir the

gravy. "It was his," he admitted, "but Kraft knows it's important work, and progress isn't being made. He wants me to
carry on Essai's work."

"Is that good?"

"Sure." Pruden wondered if he could learn the techniques.
He had been spending most of his time in the clinic, and
helping read the cardiograms. "Sure I could do it. If it worked,
we could read a paper at Atlantic City."

"That woud be wonderful," his wife said. "But is it good,
that Kraft asked *you* to do it?"

Pruden touched his wife's thick waist. "It is," he said quietly.
"I think that Kraft saw how Essai dropped the ball. Of course
I knew he would drop it. Somebody has to pick it up."

She turned to look at him. "Do you mean—?"

He smiled a dreamer's smile. "I think I'm going to stay after
the cardiogram conference tomorrow and play around in the
lab awhile." He walked back to the window and looked out
at the snow. "That's what I'm going to do."

Essai had called Angela, given her number to the ward
secretary and the hospital operator, and was walking through
the snowy Common. Exhausted by the day's events, he nonetheless would have revelled at the walk in the snow, except for
the recurring thoughts about how Kraft had acted toward
him. "He can't make up his mind about me," he muttered.

At Charles Street he saw his face reflected in a car window,
eyebrows whitened, as though the day had aged him terribly.
He started across the street by habit, going to his own apartment. Then he retraced his steps and slowly trudged up Beacon
toward Joy Street, where Angela would have supper. Near the
top of the incline he stopped and turned to the snowy trees
again. He stood without moving for a long time. "He can't
make up his mind about me," he repeated. "But I can't make
up mine about him."

His next words, though spoken, were carried by the wind
and fell with the snow, unheard. "Is his life an example one
should follow or avoid?" he asked himself conversationally.

The answer might have been obvious to him even then, but he was not aware of it until the Common was carpeted by green May grass.

Mrs. Battaglia lay in the hospital bed, hearing her son rustle the pages of the paper as he sat quietly in a corner of the room. She felt immensely better, though the hollowing gentle weakness of the last few months was still there. The older doctor, to whom the others listened, had said she might have spots in her lungs from a skin tumor. Perhaps he was so great a doctor that he would find the treatment to make the tumor shrink and disappear. She clutched her cross and prayed for the priest who had comforted her, her loving son, and the doctors whose efforts had made her better, especially the older doctor, Dr. Kraft, the one with the knowing fingers. She would have her son light a candle for him.

"Ruth," Kraft called. No response.
"Ruth!"
Where was she? Kraft looked at his watch. Five after seven. She must have gone shopping. At least she could leave a note. He walked quickly into the dining room and switched on the light. No note. The room looked cold and unused, though the chairs were dusted and carefully placed at the four sides of the glowing table. In the kitchen it was warmer, but the usual smell of cooking was absent, and the table was not set. Kraft kept the lights on in both rooms and went into the living room. The mail was not on the coffee table, and irritation continued to pick at him. Mail must have come after she left, but where the hell did she keep the mail key? He could not last remember when his mail was not sitting on the left side of the coffee table upon his return from the hospital.

Well, the mailman should have dropped journals off in any case. Kraft opened the stubborn front door and went out in the snow to peer in the black mailbox slot. Dull white stared back at him; goddamnit, where was she? The big man bent down and picked up a neat pile of magazines and journals left inside the storm door. In the living room he flipped through the pile, threw her *Harper's Bazaar* and *Atlantic Monthly* on the couch, and took a step toward his upstairs study. The phone rang.

"Hello."

"Hello, Matt, I—"

"Ruth, where the hell are you?"

"I went shopping. I got stuck in the snow."

"Jesus. Are you still stuck?"

She hesitated. "No, a tow truck got me out."

Kraft thought with irritation of his late supper and the tow fee. "Well, get back here now."

"All right, Matt, I should be there soon."

"I'll see you in a few minutes, Ruth."

He banged down the phone. She probably had to pay a ten-dollar tow fee. Kraft stalked into the kitchen, wrote "cheese omelet and fried potatoes" on the white pad near the kitchen table, and tramped heavily upstairs to his study carrying the journals. After two steps he stopped. "Jesus," he muttered, remembering that he wanted to ask her where the mail key was. He hated the variation from the usual routine.

Two chairs in the familiar room faced different directions, and Kraft turned on the light, pushed the straight chair to the edge of the writing table, and sat down grunting in the stuffed, leather-covered chair at the side of the bookcase. He put his feet up on the worn hassock, lit his fortieth cigarette for the day, and began leafing through the journals. The first one was the *American Journal of Cardiology,* and Kraft sniffed indifferently as he saw the lead article written by George Saphir, one of his former fellows: "Stereoisomers of Lactic Dehydrogenase in Experimentally Necrosed Rat Myocardium." Another one of his fellows was on his way to greatness. "But I barely understand the title," Kraft thought. He checked the article at the top of the page so Miss Graf would write away for a reprint when he brought in the journals the next morning.

The March issue of the *American Journal of Cardiology* contained four more articles of sufficient merit to be checked, though he noted that this clinical journal, like many others, had begun stressing analytic articles and biochemically oriented research. The *Journal of Clinical Investigation* led off with an article, "Heart Function in Normal Man Measured by Circulating Aggregated Albumin Complexes," and Kraft, seeing the last phrase and not recognizing the method, stood up and went to a file drawer six feet high, pulling out the "Absence of Aortic Valve—Aneurysm" file. Under "Albumin" he flicked past thirty cards, on every conceivable subtopic, but nothing about aggregated albumin appeared. Irritated, Kraft shot the file back into place, and began to read about the method. As he turned the page, still not clear what the method was about, he looked again at the table of contents. Six or seven articles pertained to the broad field of cardiology, and in every case but one, the title suggested that Ph.D.s in biochemistry and research fellows were employing new methods, or describing chemical phenomena of the heart and circulation. The irony of it to Kraft was that his contemporaries—Friedlove in New York, Birch in New Orleans, Blumgarten at the University of Chicago, Levinsky at Stanford—all had their names at the end of the list of senior authors. The work was done by the Ph.D.s and fellows, strictly chemists, with the head of the lab (where the work was done) permitted to place his name as author at the end, represented by the *et al.* at the top of each continuing page.

This week the only article in *Science* referable to cardiology described a new method to determine cardiac output using a labeled dye. Kraft read the first page and did not understand it. He swore, lit a cigarette, and read it again. He was still unclear about how the dye was labeled. Goddamn, the new methods came fast. Kraft read the page again, but understanding did not come. "No, no, no," he burst out, and the aging cardiologist stood up suddenly. For a fraction of a second, probably because he stood so fast after sitting for several minutes, a sensation of faint nausea or dizziness clutched at him, then let go. Reaching down to the floor, Kraft picked up the journal, stared at the title and the authors, and with all his strength threw the issue of *Science* against the far wall. The fluttering pages hit the lamp on the writing desk and knocked it over, and amid the whirring pages and crashing lamp, the outraged physician heard the door open downstairs and his wife cry out, "Matthew, is anything wrong?"

"Ruth." He was happy not to be alone any more.

"Matthew, what's wrong?" Her voice was alarmed. She came hurrying up the stairs and Kraft wanted to reassure her, but he didn't know what to tell her.

"It's nothing, nothing at all." He quickly walked to the writing desk and set the lamp up again. The bulb was broken. "Do we have any more bulbs in the house?"

"Of course we do. Shall I get one?" She stood in the doorway, reluctant to come into his sanctuary, but concerned enough to bite the edge of her thumb as she looked quickly at her husband and the shreds of glass on the writing desk.

Kraft bent awkwardly to pick up the journal, and came toward his wife. She was flushed from running and her dark eyes shone; the gray-streaked dark hair was combed back sharply from her oval face, and she looked quite lovely. He kissed her on the lips, more than perfunctorily, and put one large hand on her shoulder. "Kind of a rough day, Ruth, and then I got a little upset, reading up here."

"I'm so sorry I was late, Matt. I'll make you some supper."

She went to the upstairs linen closet and got out a bulb, and came back with pan and whisk broom to sweep up the glass. "Anything special you'd like for supper?"

"Didn't you see the message I left? Well, never mind, just some eggs and toast will do. What did the tow cost you?"

She looked up sharply from her kneeling position. "What?"

"The tow for the car."

"Oh, eight dollars," she said.

He nodded. "You shouldn't drive when it snows like this." He glanced at his watch. "Christ, eight o'clock, and I haven't started on the cardiograms for tomorrow. Could you bring my supper up on a tray, Ruth? I'll have four hours work up here."

"Yes, Matt. Too bad I threw out the old wooden tray, or it would really be like the days back in Magnolia, you studying and writing and me—and me—"

Kraft lit a cigarette. "To me, those are hardly the 'good old days.' That man Heinrichs gave me too much trouble for me to enjoy myself. But days like today when the men are impudent and the fellows all leave at the earliest moment, I wish I weren't professor of anything. But I showed them today, especially Essai. A lady came in with heart failure and they all missed the key finding."

"Dr. Bergman's patient?"

"That's right. You heard me talking to him this morning. Yes, they all had a chance to make the diagnosis. Essai came the closest, I must admit, but he didn't realize that a 'mole' on her back was a melanoma that had spread to the heart."

She looked at him. "That sounds awful."

He nodded. "It is. She won't live very long. But at least we know the diagnosis and can treat her. They use cytoxan now, you know."

She bent down and picked up the dustpan filled with glass. "I hope it wasn't too tiring a day for you, Matt."

"Me?" He laughed loudly. "A fifteen-hour day, nothing special. Say, Ruth, would you fix the eggs for me now?"

"Yes. I'll get started." She walked out, wondering what "cytoxan" was. On her way down the stairs she thanked whatever it was that made her husband concern himself with medicine tonight and not her. How often she had cursed that quality, but today it had saved her. Chris' Triumph had stuck in muddy snow just outside Rockport. Chris had not paid for the tow at all, but had used a credit card. She hoped eight dollars sounded right, but of course it did. "And I wouldn't have called him if Matt had not gone back to his true love, medicine," she thought bitterly.

As her steps disappeared, Matthew Kraft yawned widely. He felt exhausted. He wanted to eat lightly and then sleep. The crumpled issue of *Science* lay next to the chair. Kraft yawned again. Then quickly he went to his bound copies of the *Journal of the American Medical Association*. The 1947 volume opened to the editorial praising him and Paul Heinrichs (it opened there because he had so often turned to this page in the past twenty years), and he read the phrase ". . . Drs. Kraft and Heinrichs point the way." Seeing it again gave him strength. It was that simple. He read the last paragraph, though he knew it without reading it. Then he carefully replaced the volume. He felt hungry, ready for supper and the work of preparing the cardiograms for the Sunday conference. "But first," he said to himself, "I'm going to figure out that goddamn *Science* article." He sat down to read about the measurement of output of the heart.

Late that night, Matthew Kraft experienced an attack of angina pectoris. He had eaten an immense supper, read through three journals and skimmed twenty articles, and sometime after midnight he felt a pressing sensation as he read. Paying little attention, he unbuttoned his shirt and scratched his chest idly, reading along. Unconsciously he took a few deep breaths. The pressure increased and though his eyes kept moving on the printed page, his sight turned inward. "Angina," he whispered.

He let the book drop and folded his hands. He tried to make himself think a soothing thought, and finally fixed on a smoking cigarette lying with twenty butts in the ashtray. By looking at the thin smoke and thinking of leaves burning, autumn, colors of leaves, the pressing sensation ebbed away. He slowly lifted a single finger, then his right hand. No pressure. He moved the other. Good. Slowly he sat up. The attack was over. His pulse was eighty, regular. He was not sweating.

"Is it angina or another full-blown heart attack?" he thought. Moving with agonizing care, he stood up, crept down the stairs, put on his coat (though he left his shirt unbuttoned), and went outside. He knew the portable cardiogram machine in his automobile trunk weighed eight pounds at the most. It was worth the risk.

He lifted it out, slid into the back seat of the car, and put cardiogram paste on his wrists, ankles, and chest. He prayed that the batteries in the portable machine were still good. The straps fixed, he turned the switch to Warm-up, then On. The gratifying hum was heard, and the cardiogram tape snaked out.

After all the leads were written, he undid the straps, wiped off some of the paste with his handkerchief, and as slowly as before, went into the house holding his cardiogram. He was afraid to climb the stairs, and so he went into the kitchen and turned on the light.

He read the tracing in fifteen seconds. No new attack; no change from the last cardiogram taken in early December. He desperately wanted a cigarette, but knew he shouldn't. He sniffed, got a piece of celery out of the refrigerator, sat down, and chewed reflectively.

"I asked for it," he thought. "A twenty-hour day, running up those stairs with Essai, even the foolishness about a healed heart being a normal one. I said that today, at the autopsy table. Now angina. At rest, no less, much worse than angina on effort. My first full day like the old days, and now this." He wanted to cry the tears of realization, but he sat dry-eyed instead and chewed another piece of celery and planned his attack on the internal enemy. He would go to New York on a "sabbatical," find out how good Fermanian was as a cardiac surgeon, and if the risk was bearable, take it and get a new heart.

Satisfied, he went up the stairs slowly, and to sleep. In the morning he told Ruth he had had angina, made her swear to say nothing, and mentioned he would visit a cardiologist friend in New York in April to find out about the benefit of low cholesterol diets in preventing angina. By noon, he had written to Fermanian.

"Unclamp the aorta, slowly," Fermanian ordered his first assistant. He felt the dog's transplanted heart fill. "Slowly," he warned. Then the heart was full of blood. Fermanian glanced at his assistant. "Well, Matt?"

Kraft stared intently at the line of sutures in the aorta, stitches he had placed himself. "Good. It's tight."

Fermanian nodded. "Step back." He turned. "Shock the dog with the usual voltage." The clamps went on. "Now!"

The anesthetized dog and his transplanted heart convulsed against the electricity. Kraft looked at the monitor, and spoke through his scrub mask. "One more; he almost started after that one."

Again a shock. The heart contracted twice rapidly, then beat on regularly. The two men smiled at each other across the small operating table, and stood back as two other men stepped up to close the chest and take pressure readings. Fermanian untied his mask. "You should have been a surgeon, Matt. I never saw that intensity in a medical man before."

Kraft nodded. "Come up to Boston sometime, Armin. Though I'll admit I only concentrate that hard when I'm listening for certain murmurs."

"But it's tiring." Fermanian stretched. "How do you feel, standing like that for six hours."

Kraft merely smiled. It was the last week of his month's sabbatical, and the two men had come to respect one another. For his part, Kraft had carried out the whole affair with the subtlety and sophistication some men use in court, or with women. From the first letter Kraft sent (". . . following your extraordinary reports in the literature and convinced that heart transplants open a new era for cardiology . . .") to Fermanian's blunt question at first meeting ("You aren't a Turk, are you? No? Welcome to Columbia. It's an honor to have you with us"), they had tested each other in a variety of ways. Both were realists, and so accepted the presence of the other's giant ego, but it was Kraft who had come to have confidence in the man who might replace his heart.

Each afternoon after the intensity of the dog lab, they ate a leisurely meal and talked. Fermanian knew first-hand all the things Kraft had read about and had to know. At first it had seemed simply shoptalk, as Kraft had planned. How were technical problems overcome? How important was the rejection phenomenon? How should one use antibiotics? After two weeks Kraft mentioned his heart attack, a few days later his recent angina, and yesterday Fermanian had stood with a stopwatch as the gray-haired cardiologist ran up an inclined treadmill with cardiogram running.

They showered and dressed, checked the dog (out of anesthesia and apparently recovering nicely), and took a taxi to an Armenian restaurant, where the surgeon was accorded the worshipful respect of the deity. For once in his life, Kraft did not mind the subordinate role. He watched the dark man finish his lamb and smell the muddy coffee. Fermanian sniffed, gulped it, and rubbed his generous nose. "Well, Matt, what is it you want to ask me about?"

Kraft looked at his plate. "You already know."

"You want to be the recipient of a human heart transplant."

"Yes, I do," Kraft said slowly. "What I learned here is that you are the man who can do it." Kraft made a fist, opened it, closed it. "What are my chances."

"Only fair, Matt. Your kidney test was normal, and we could get your weight down all right. Lungs are fine, though I'll be damned if I know why, the way you smoke."

"And your technical skill is unquestioned," Kraft interjected.

"On dogs," said Fermanian quietly. "If only you were really a son-of-a-bitch."

"But you've already done four human transplants, Armin. One patient is still alive, and two—"

Fermanian silenced him by raising his hand. He held up four fingers. "Four technical successes. We started the new heart, got every patient off the bypass pump, and had no bleeding. They all got steroids, mercaptopurine, antibiotics, and the most intensive care imaginable." Now Fermanian hit each finger against his other palm, and Kraft watched his eyes recalling the pain each death had brought him. "The first man died of pneumonia on the eighth day, due to a bacterium so rare our bacteriologist still can't tell me for sure what it was. We prevented infection from every bug we knew with the antibiotics, but it wasn't enough. The second man died of a lung clot the first day he stepped out of bed. So did the third, even though he was getting heparin."

"But the fourth—"

"Ah, the fourth." Fermanian smiled sadly. *The Times* gave me half a page on poor Mr. Bunzel, and even an editorial. Well, they should come see him now. His great wish was to teach again, 'even if only one course a day,' he told me. Poor Bunzel is still alive, after fourteen weeks. He has his 'transplant of the heart.' He knew the risks and survived them. Now he is taking pills against infection, rejection and anemia. The steroids have made him so euphoric he can't think straight. Visitors have to don mask and gown even to visit him. His wife sterilizes the dishes, and awaits the day, months from now, when he may take a ten-minute walk outside." Fermanian shook his fist. "And that kind of man is supposed to lecture? Be at the top of his form? No, sir. I see him at home twice a week, and swear to myself at every visit that I'll not do another transplant till we know more about biology, immunity, tissue typing. That will take a generation."

"Armin, I can't wait that long," Kraft said, uncharacteristically hushed. "Isn't there any way we can lower the odds?"

"Sure, Matt," the surgeon said offhandedly. "Get a donor with a normal heart. When Eisenhower seemed sure to die, two dozen people wrote to offer their hearts. What they meant, I wager, is an offer of heartfelt hopes for recovery, of heartfelt sympathy."

"Maybe not," said Kraft. "Maybe they were ordinary people who wanted to sacrifice something for an extraordinary man."

"Their lives?"

"It's possible," Kraft said quietly.

They sat in silence, Fermanian in a thick Armenian melancholy and Kraft thinking furiously. "What about an accident victim with absolutely no heart disease?" Kraft asked at last.

Fermanian shrugged. "How do you know the heart is normal? Maybe the heart is contused in the accident. You know, if we cause a stroke in a dog, without touching the heart, that heart is not as good as a heart from a dog with no induced stroke. No, Matt, only with a normal donor, a real impossibility, could the odds for you be worth even considering."

Kraft's voice was very calm. "Just for the moment, imagine I did get a normal donor. What are the odds?"

"For survival?"

"Yes."

Fermanian rubbed his nose. "Seventy percent you'd survive surgery." He saw Kraft's eyes widen as he repeated the number. The surgeon raised a finger. "But you want more than survival, Matt, if I know you. Tell me if I'm right. You'd want to be Kraft at the height of his energy. Just like poor Bunzel, at the top of your form. Right?"

"Yes."

Fermanian showed Kraft his one finger, then opened up the others. "That much chance. Less than one in ten."

"That's not so bad," Kraft said hollowly. Then he smiled. "I'm being considered for the Nobel Prize. Isn't the chance of a doctor getting even a nomination less than one in ten?"

Fermanian tilted his coffee cup back and forth, as though reading the grains. Then he looked up. "So am I being considered. For Bunzel, the walking dead. Matt, a chemist will get the prize. You know that."

Kraft looked at his hand, closed it to form a fist the size of his heart, and opened it again. Fermanian watched him. He looked like a beaten man, about to cry. "I know him like a brother," the surgeon thought. Then he said, "Matt?"

"What?" A beaten voice.

Fermanian did not answer till Kraft looked up and they had stared into each other for a long moment. "I give you my word, Matt, that when you want it, I will do a heart transplant and try to give you a new heart. I promise it."

Kraft reached out his left hand across the small table and took and grasped the surgeon's hand, tears of gratitude in his eyes for the only time in his life. Then, like brothers, they released their grip, smiled, and did not talk about it any more.

The last traces of the March snowstorm remained until nearly the middle of April. Mrs. Battaglia died abruptly but quietly on the sixth, and at autopsy Dr. Applegate demonstrated the tumor-studded heart to a thoughtful and silent group of physicians standing around the stainless steel table in the morgue. Matthew Kraft, who again spent each night in his study, was reminded at the autopsy that it was her case which had marked his full-time return to his duties. He had made the correct diagnosis after talking with her and examining her, he recalled, while the rest of the group, even with recourse to X-rays and the laboratory, were unable to do so. During those weeks he demonstrated to himself that his skill at diagnosis was intact, and in New York with Fermanian he had found out how he might perpetuate that skill for another generation.

Kraft had never felt better. As his working days lengthened, his consumption of food and cigarettes increased, and he looked and acted like the chief he knew he was, not a wan convalescent depending upon the junior men to keep the department going. The day of the autopsy on Mrs. Battaglia, Kraft decided to review the experience at the Eastern Massachusetts Medical Center with regard to tumors involving the heart, and he picked Essai to help him. "I think I can get the paper on the schedule for the May meetings in Atlantic City," he had said. "You start now, collecting the cases, and I'll write up the talk. After I give it, we can publish it in expanded form."

Essai began working on it at once, surprised and grateful that Kraft still offered him opportunities he apparently withheld from others. Essai was assigned to make rounds each day during April with the interns and residents, and he continued to prepare the pericarditis talk for the Mt. Zion seminar, to be given the day before the meetings in Atlantic City. Now he realized he would have to spend evenings reviewing charts of patients with tumors, but he knew how important it was to his future career that he be co-author with Matthew Kraft on a paper first presented at Atlantic City.

Angela accepted his long days without dissent. After three false starts in two weeks, he had brought over his things just a few days before, Alix watching warily from behind a living room chair. He did not give up his old apartment, however, saying, "If it gets noisy here some nights when I have to read, I can go there as I would to the library." Alix heard him say this, and easily accepted being "a good girl" in return for a smiling mother and the happy house with Easy Andy in it.

What Essai did not know, busy with rounds and preparing talks, was that Kraft had spoken with Ed Pruden on several occasions since March, urging him to extend the research on the immunology of rheumatic fever that Essai had started. "He's too busy with the clinical end," Kraft had said. Ed Pruden saw it for the opportunity it was and began to work on the detection of antibodies in the serum samples that Essai had collected a year before.

It seemed to Kraft that everything was going smoothly. The last Saturday in April he went to his mailbox before lunch and took out a huge armful of reprints, smiling with the anticipation that tonight he could sit quietly at home and read through them, jotting a note in the margin here and there, and filing them in his library and in his mind.

Miss Graf sat in her coat at her desk, and stood up as Kraft came in.

"Oh, Joan, I'm sorry. It's after noon, isn't it? Now I've spoiled your day off."

She blushed. "That's fine, Dr. Kraft. Were you on the ward till now?"

"Yes." Kraft put down his mail. "When I go up for a few

minutes to see how things are going, the house staff starts presenting every problem case to me and I never get out of there."

"Is Essai still there, making rounds?" she asked mildly.

"Yes." Kraft nudged her with his elbow. "But the residents still want my advice more than his. Listen, are there any messages before you go?"

"Several," she said quickly, instantly the secretary again. "The dean's office called to remind you that Dean Michler is meeting you for lunch. He'll be here at one."

"Jesus. Today? Is that what I told him?"

"Yes," she said. "Should I call him back and make it for another time?"

"No, I'll see him today. Anything else?"

Miss Graf checked her pad. "Professor Manson called from the Bolliston Society. They asked if you would be available in June to give the annual discourse on the art of medicine to the Society. He said they are sending a letter today formally asking you to do so."

She looked to see his reaction. "Well," he smiled. "The third time in eight years. Osler and Cushing were the only others ever to give three discourses."

"Congratulations," she said shyly.

"Thank you. He didn't say anything about the Nobel thing, did he?"

She shook her head. "No, he didn't."

Kraft lit a cigarette. "What else?"

"Your wife called."

"My wife? What did she want?"

"She didn't say. Nothing urgent, she said, but she wants you to call."

"All right. That it?"

"Yes."

"I'll call her now. The dean is coming over at one, right?"

She nodded. Her voice dropped to a whisper. "Lerner and Pruden went to lunch together," she said. "Dr. Lerner heard that Dr. Essai is giving the talk at Mt. Zion next week, and he was upset. He said he trained down there and he should get to give the talk. Pruden said, 'And Essai is reviewing the cases of heart tumors for a talk at Atlantic City.' They went down to lunch talking about Essai."

"Let the children eat together," Kraft snapped. "I make the decisions here. I should have fired both of them years ago." He would have gone on, but his phone rang. Miss Graf answered it. "It's your wife," she said.

"I'll take it in my office. Have a nice weekend, Joan."

His secretary smiled. "Thank you. You too, Dr. Kraft."

Kraft went to his office and picked up the phone. He traced a finger along the waxed desk top. "Ruth, what's up?"

"Matt?" Her voice sounded tremulous.

"Yes. What is it?"

"Matt, we got the strangest letter from Paul Heinrichs."

"Paul Heinrichs?"

His wife cleared her throat. "I better start at the beginning. It's two letters really. One is from a law firm, in Michigan, saying that Paul Heinrichs died in a nursing home in Benton Harbor a month ago."

"No! Paul Heinrichs dead. Well, he must have been nearly eighty."

"They don't say, just that he died. They say they are executors of his estate, and in his will there is a statement that a letter addressed to us is supposed to be mailed after his death."

"Is it there? Is that the other letter you mentioned?"

"Yes."

Kraft looked outside. "Read it to me," he said.

"I will. Just a second." He heard her blow her nose. "Here it is," she said. As she started, he saw the phrase in the *J.A.M.A.* editorial ("Kraft and Heinrichs point the way") and remembered the snowy New Year's Day twenty-six years ago when he came to Magnolia State Hospital.

"DEAR MATTHEW AND RUTH—I'm past my three score and ten now and as Mr. Kennedy says, the torch has been passed to a new generation, and that's true here too. For the last six years, since 1954, they've had a new administrator, very capable fellow who lets me stay around and be psychiatrist emeritus. I've been living in your old cottage those six years, and sometimes when I get lonely I drag the same old chair out back and sit under the stars and have part of a conversation with you. Now I'll be off to Michigan, where the starry nights (they say) are just as bright. I feel pretty good except that the pipe doesn't taste as good any more, and a hotshot internist in Akron told me I've got diabetes, and prescribed all kinds of things to do, which till now I've managed to avoid doing.

Well, I'd better get to the point. For the last fifteen years I have lived with the knowledge that I precipitated the argument that led you to leave Magnolia. That the argument had to come on the day that the *J.A.M.A.* editorial appeared was really part of the plan, I guess. You see, Matt, I felt, perhaps wrongly, that you would never voluntarily leave this place, no matter how attractive other offers might be. Whether you wanted to stay because it was a kind of a safe place, or simply from loyalty to me, I'm not sure, though I've got my own ideas on that. But in the final analysis, I knew you could do much more in teaching and practice somewhere else, and so I precipitated the argument we had by suggesting you had committed yourself to this hospital, as much a patient as a doctor. It worked, as I had hoped and feared, and except for Christmas cards for a few years from Ruth, and the avalanche of impressive articles from the Eastern Massachusetts Medical Center, I didn't hear from you how you felt about things.

All this is preface for me: I felt as close to you and Ruth as to anyone in my life. Since I kind of bumped you out of here I've kicked myself a thousand times, and it almost seems that the scores of articles you've published and hundreds of medical students you've taught in Boston barely compensate for the loss of you to me, in physical presence around the hospital, as well as the loss of friendship.

But from everything I hear, you're the best clinician in the country, and a great professor of medicine. I think that's what you wanted, and I want to congratulate you on achieving your goal.

Well, I'll quit. Ruth, you made the tastiest apple pie I ever ate.

Paul"

His wife ended weeping, and Kraft felt himself blinking. "Is that all, Ruth?" he asked finally.

She sniffed. "No. That was dated March, 1961. There's a 'P.S.' written in a scrawl, dated June or July, 1967. It says, 'They won't let me eat pie any more. Ruth, you're still number one.' "

"That's it?"

"Yes."

"The old guy must have gotten pretty senile at the end."

"Matthew!"

Kraft stood up and gripped the phone. "Well, it's true, Ruth. Can you imagine not sending a letter for six years and then adding a line about pie? Jesus Christ, I hope I never get like that."

There was silence at the other end. "Ruth?"

"You never will, Matt." She hung up.

Kraft slammed down the phone as usual and went to the window. Pale April sunlight filtered through the city haze, but the light was tentative, more like that during an eclipse. Standing at the window, he felt the need to keep his mind ambiguously clear. No clean, light remembrances of the days with Heinrichs in Magnolia. Old events and feelings moved closer to the light. Sentiment and introspection rushed toward him.

With an effort, Kraft turned his head and thought about the rarity of really sunny days in Boston. His next thought, released slowly, was that May would be here soon, time for the Atlantic City meetings. Essai, he remembered, was to give a talk next week in New York, at Mt. Zion.

He nearly ran to the phone and dialed the number of the floor. When they got Essai, he said, "How's the preparation for your talk on pericarditis?"

"Not bad." Essai was surprised at being called by Kraft directly about this.

"Well, I haven't heard you talk about pericarditis since that time in Providence last winter. We should go over your stuff. I have to meet the dean for lunch, and then there's the journal club. Why don't you stop out this evening? For an hour or so."

"Oh. Well, Dr. Kraft, it's Saturday and—"

Kraft gripped the phone. "So what? Make some notes this afternoon, skip the journal club, and come to the house around five. I'll be home early."

Essai was still hesitating. "That's fine, Dr. Kraft. But I promised a lady friend that we'd take a ride the first nice day, and—"

"Fine, fine. Have her come too. The ride out to Lexington is nice. She can look around the garden with my wife, while we talk."

"Yes. I guess that's all right," Essai said slowly.

Kraft remembered that his call to Essai had rescued him from brooding about Heinrichs and a mind full of carefully buried doubts. Suddenly he became jocular. "Hell yes, bring her out."

"She has a daughter," Essai blurted out.

"A daughter? Oh. She's not married now, to someone else, that is?"

"No."

"Perfectly all right then, Essai. We have a fine yard for a little girl to play in." He wanted company at home. "Yes, we'd like to have them."

"We'll get there about four, Dr. Kraft."

"Good." Kraft hung up. It was five of one. The dean would be here soon. "Wonder what he wants. Too bad about Heinrichs. But he had a long life. Those headshrinkers live long, don't they? Maybe there's time to look at some of this mail. Boy, the annual discourse for the third time. They say the best clinician is asked to give that talk. I won't need Essai or anyone else to help me out on that. Wonder—"

Dean Michler knocked on the outer office door. Kraft was glad to stop the monologue and moved swiftly to open the door.

"Hello, Matt, good to see you." Michler came in.

They shook hands. "Harlan, you look well," said Kraft cheerfully.

"Better than I feel," said the old dean. "Where do you want to eat?"

"How about the cafeteria?"

Harlan Michler laughed. "The hospital cafeteria?"

"Sure. I've got a journal meeting with the group at two. Did you want to go somewhere else?"

"No, that's fine. Thought you might want to go to a nice spot, have a drink, you know, relax."

"Hah!" Kraft led the way out of the door. "Never relax in this job. I think the cafeteria is still serving."

The cafeteria was virtually empty except for Lerner and Pruden, who sat talking excitedly at the back table until the dean and Dr. Kraft came in. Then they became silent, and started again in whispers, at the same time listening as best they could.

Dean Michler put a bowl of chowder and an order of English muffins on his tray, refused the unappetizing meat dish, and stood with Kraft as his three hamburgers were cooked. Kraft waited irritably for his order, and wolfed down two chocolate cupcakes while he waited. Finally they sat down, and Dean Harlan Michler talked about possibilities for honorary degree candidates in June; the recent illness of the chairman of the biochemistry department; the shape of next year's freshman medical class. Only when Kraft finished his second bag of potato chips and lit a cigarette did Harlan Michler come to the point.

"You know, Matt," he began. "I'm sixty-four. Some of these trying days, looking over the freshman class and keeping a faculty together, I feel a good deal older."

"It's no fun, being dean," Kraft agreed. "It takes me eighteen hours a day to run a department, and you've got to run the whole damn show."

Michler nodded. "By the way, Matt, how old are you?"

"Fifty-nine, sixty next year. Still got a couple of years left, if I take off a little weight and stop smoking these damn cigarettes." He looked at his cigarette, then ground it out at the edge of his plate. "I'm fully recovered from my heart attack," Kraft added.

Michler looked briefly at the mashed cigarette next to the spot of catsup. "Matt," he said, after a pause, "I think I'm going to retire next commencement, or just after it."

A tiny thought formed high in Matthew Kraft's mind. He lit another cigarette. "You mean a year from this June?"

"No, no. I mean in two months, this June. The overseers meet next week, and I think that's the time for me to talk."

"Wait, Harlan. Can't you stay on here till you're sixty-eight?"

Michler sighed, and sat back, nodding. "That's right, I could. But, Matt, I've given my all to the school for seventeen years. I'm an endocrinologist by training, you know, and I haven't touched a patient for a decade." He gestured vaguely, as though trying to think of an appropriate example. "I'd like to give it up; practice a little up in Maine, do some fishing."

The tiny thought expanded a notch, in spite of Kraft's attempts to hold it in place. "Well, that's quite a piece of news. Naturally it stops with me," he added judiciously. Over Michler's shoulder he saw Lerner and Pruden looking over, trying desperately to hear.

"Five years ago," the dean went on, "I tried like hell to have you take the position of associate dean for medical affairs, and become chief of medicine here."

"I remember. At the time, it seemed to me I'd be getting into a whole nest of administrative problems, and of course I was in the middle of the revision for the third edition of my book."

Michler nodded. "I remember. And I don't blame you; administration is a thankless avocation, I guess because it really becomes your vocation, and allows almost no time for medicine as we know it." He fingered his coffee cup. "Now I've got another favor to ask of you, Matthew."

Kraft stubbed out the cigarette. Was being offered the deanship a favor?

"Matt, I wish you were forty-nine and not fifty-nine, because then I could go to the overseers with a positive recommendation for my successor." The words hit and exploded, and the growing thing high in the mind was irretrievably squashed.

"Yes?" said Kraft, and thought, "Go ahead, old man. I'm listening."

Michler looked across the table. "I think the best way to look for a successor is to have a small group begin to look around. For several reasons I'd like to be on the periphery of that group. We need a man to head the search committee who can spot bright younger men, who senses trends in American medicine, understands the problems of medical teaching in an age where facts become obsolete overnight—oh, hell, Matt, you know what I'm trying to say. I'd like you to head the search committee."

"I'll have to think about it, Harlan."

"Fine, that's as much of an answer as I need now. Honestly, Matt, I wish I could ask you to take on the job, my job I mean." Again he touched the rim of the coffee cup. "But the overseers would ask about age, and make comments about 'interim appointments.' It would be doomed from the start."

Kraft expansively lit up another cigarette and blew a huge mouthful across the table. The word "doomed" finally echoed away in his mind. "Harlan, I wouldn't take the deanship if you could offer it to me."

The tired New England face showed surprise. "Really, Matt?"

"Really. It's a dead end, inasmuch as a doctor in that job can't really teach, can't write, can't see patients in consultations; in short, can't practice. Medicine is like the priesthood, and running the seminary is not my kind of job."

Michler nodded slowly, but his eyes were impassive. "I didn't know you felt that way."

Kraft waved his cigarete. "Oh, sure. Look, Harlan, I've been here now for a long time. You know how many times at Atlantic City meetings someone took me for a walk on the boardwalk and offered me jobs, really good jobs?"

"No, I don't."

"Well, it was plenty. A few years ago I was offered forty thousand a year to go to Penn State as chief of medicine to try and straighten out their department."

"Really?" The eyes kept watching him.

"Sure," Kraft said offhandedly. "Take Denver. There was another place. They were begging me to come out there. Even in New Haven a couple of years back, they wrote asking me to come down as 'visiting professor.' I knew what they were after. I mean, it's flattering and all, but not my cup of tea, I guess."

"I see," said Dean Michler. "Well," he stood up, "give it some thought, Matt. As you say, you know the world of academic medicine as well as any man, and you could do the school and the hospital a real service."

Kraft stood as well. "Thanks, Harlan, I'll let you know."

They walked together to the front door. The dean looked out and shivered. "Here I go, running across Mass. Avenue again. If I don't make it across, tell them it was that poisonous fish chowder."

Kraft smiled with his mouth. "OK, Harlan, I'll be in touch with you." The door opened and a gust of cold April air enveloped Matthew Kraft. He saw the New England figure bend into the east wind, check the traffic briefly and race across the street with surprising speed. "Fall, you bastard," Kraft thought viciously, but he waved through the door as the bent figure waved in his direction. He lit another cigarette, flicked the match against the closed door, and lowered his head an inch or two as he strode back toward his office.

In the cafeteria, Ed Pruden was anxious to go, but Lerner casually got another cup of coffee.

"Harvey, we have to go up. It's a quarter to two, and Dr. Kraft doesn't want us to be late."

Lerner waved him away. "Go ahead. I want to sit here for a minute yet. Just imagine Essai talking at Mt. Zion. Ed, do you know that I took my internship and residency there? And still Essai will represent this department. Why wouldn't Kraft let me speak there? Jesus, I think I'm going home." But he sat still and moodily balanced a spoon.

Pruden leaned over the table, confidently. "Harvey, you might miss the announcement of the year."

"C'mon, Ed," Lerner said sarcastically. "You can't still insist that Michler offered him the deanship."

"I'm not sure, I'm not sure. But I heard that word mentioned, and I don't think that the dean came across the street to eat this hospital food for the fun of it. Kraft as dean of the medical school," Pruden announced. "Now, doesn't that sound reasonable."

"No," Lerner said sourly.

"Why not?"

Lerner looked around the empty cafeteria. "I'll tell you why. First, Kraft is sixty or sixty-two, too old for dean. Second he had a heart attack not five months ago. The way he eats and smokes and drives himself, he is a setup for another one."

"Yes, but—"

Pruden was silenced. "But the real reason, and the one Harlan Michler knows the best, is that no person as rude, abrupt and arbitrary as Kraft could ever succeed as dean."

Pruden was shocked. "Jesus, Harvey, take it easy. That's a terrible thing to say."

"The truth."

"But you completely overlook Kraft's dedication, his—"

Lerner hooted. "His dedication."

"Yes."

Lerner stood up. "His dedication," he said loudly, "is psychotic commitment to unreasonable goals. And dedicated men like Kraft," he added, "invariably regard other, less dedicated men as somehow imperfect. Translated that means more normal."

"Harvey, quiet down."

He did so. He scratched his head, then held both hands up. "*Nu*, what else can I say. It would be the proudest moment of my life to give a guest lecture at the Mt. Zion Hospital, where I trained. And I could give a nice talk. Even a dedi-

cated talk. The bone I have to pick with Kraft is that he
assigns something like that to Essai without reflecting for a
moment how I might feel about it. You know, I don't think
he cares about any of us."

Pruden held up a finger. "But he has given you a place in
his department."

"So what? Look at the price I pay. Ed, imagine Kraft died
tomorrow. Picture for a second such a terrible thing happened.
What would you do then?"

"I don't follow you."

"What kind of work would you do?"

Pruden studied his nails. "I *am* a doctor, you know, and
I've got several papers under my belt."

"Ed, can you stand on your own two feet without him? Could
you see a sick patient or look at a tough X-ray on your own?
I ask myself those questions sometimes, and when I see how
little independence I really have, or rather how little I'm
allowed to employ, I get pretty frightened."

Pruden rose. "Your fright is your own problem," he said
sanctimoniously. "I'm off to the journal meeting."

Lerner watched him walk away and then went after him,
to go up in the elevator together, but the door closed in
his face.

Angela chewed her nail nervously. "Should I really go,
Andy?"

"I told you it's OK. He said to bring Alix along."

He had called her from the hospital, and they were ready
to go, Alix with her first Easter coat, worn only once. "We're
going, we're going," she was singing.

"Look, Andy, why don't you take the car and go out alone?"

Essai knotted his tie. "No, let's all go. I thought you'd be
dying to meet Kraft."

"It's short notice, I guess," she said. "All right, Alix, we're
going. Good manners are the order of the day."

"Hey, we're going," the little girl sang.

Essai helped them into her car, a chronically ill Chevy, and he drove along very cautiously, like the head of a family of three. "Angela, does Alix have something to play with out there? It might be a couple of hours."

"How about a coloring book?" the girl suggested. "I want a coloring book."

"But, Alix," her mother protested, "you've got your favorite doll."

"A coloring book," Alix insisted firmly.

"Easy Andy decides on a coloring book for Alix, especially if she's a good girl," he announced.

"Yes, Easy Andy," she screamed.

"Pipe down, Bright Eyes, and I'll find a store out here where they have it. Angela, would a bookstore have that?"

"Maybe a drugstore," she said.

It was nearly dark, but just before five Essai saw a bookstore down a side street as they stopped for a light in Concord. He pulled over. "I'll ask if they have coloring books."

"Can I go with you?" the little girl asked.

Angela started to say, "No," but Andy looked back at her. "Look, I'll spoil her for a little while, and then I'll be my nasty self again. OK, Bright Eyes. If you hold on, I'll take you in on my shoulders, so you can see the books way up on the shelves."

The girl looked at him fondly. "C'mon, let's go now."

He felt ridiculous for a moment, balancing her lightly on his shoulder, but the lightheartedness of spring and his new feeling for both of them overpowered his usual reserve. "Hold on," he said.

Inside, the bespectacled manager said to the knots of browsers, "It's time. We're closing."

"Do you have a coloring book for this little girl?" Essai asked.

"This is a bookstore, not a toy shop, sir."

Alix piped up. "This is a bookstore, not a toy shop, sir."

Essai laughed uneasily and turned to go, but a passing woman laughed naturally at the girl's mimicry, and said to her, "That's a high perch, little girl."

She had her back to Essai, and he rotated slowly with Alix holding on. He smiled at the lady. It was Ruth Kraft.

"Oh. Hello." Essai tapped Alix's bare legs. "Hello, Mrs. Kraft. This is Alix."

Ruth Kraft looked frightened. Essai began to introduce himself, wondering if she had forgotten him. "Ah, I'm—"

A tall man with a moustache and silvery hair interrupted them, hurrying up from the back of the shop with a small book in his hand. "Ruth, darling, I think I've got it."

Essai stood rooted, watching her pale face break into an anguished mask. "Excuse me," she murmured, and she walked past him. The tall man looked at Essai for just a moment, and went after her with a loping stride.

"What's the matter with the lady?" Alix asked from her elevated position.

"You're coming down," he said firmly. He would have run out of the store, to get a glimpse of Ruth Kraft and the man, had not Alix' short step providentially prevented him from doing so.

"No luck?" Angela spoke to them from the open window of the car. The engine was still running.

"No," he said flatly.

He pulled away slowly. "What happened?" She looked at him questioningly. "Was Alix acting up?"

Alix was listening. Essai tried to keep his voice light. "Describing it in obtuse and complex fashion, so to render it privileged communication, it seems the esteemed physician's lady of the house browsed amidst the art books with an elegantly tailored male, not her mate, about fifty."

"Fine," she smiled. "Perhaps we've really lost our way. You said you hadn't been out here recently. We ought to go back," she said, an insistent edge to her voice.

This was maddening. "Our host will be surprised, Angela."

She looked over. "A minor point."

"Can we get a coloring book somewhere else?"

Angela leaned over Alix' head. "Yes, back on Charles Street in Boston is a spot I know has them. Please, Andy."

"OK." He turned the car around. In Cambridge he stopped at a pay phone, and told an angry Dr. Kraft that Angela was sick and he had to stay with her. "But I'll call you back in a few minutes, sir, and we can talk over the notes on the phone."

As usual Kraft got in the last words. "Essai, I can see you have yet to find the right woman." When Essai heard that he almost blurted out, "So have you," but instead he beat Kraft to his favorite gesture by slamming home the pay phone with considerable force.

The Triumph came roaring up Woodbine Street, going right past the Oldsmobile parked unobtrusively near the side door of Cary Hall. Then the brakes screeched, and the handsome driver backed up expertly, stopping two feet away from the Olds.

He got out quickly, rushing to her side of the car to hold the door open. He held the door open and she glanced quickly at him, dim glow from the streetlight catching his long silvery hair. My husband's hair is short and gray, she thought. He hates to waste time in barbershops.

"Ruth, darling, you can't leave like this."

She had gotten out and fumbled with the key to the Oldsmobile. His scented face moved closer, but he did not touch her.

"Please," he begged, "let's walk for a minute. Who was the man with the little girl in the bookstore? Please, please talk to me."

The slightly accented voice bore in. Nothing in the world, he was saying, could be as important to him as for her to explain what had happened. "He's concerned for me," she thought.

She turned away from her car. "Let's walk then."

"Wait. Who was it, in the bookstore?"

"A doctor in my husband's department. He has met me. He recognized me."

The man in the smart belted coat stopped still. "That's it, then."

She shrugged and kept on walking. "Five years," she said,

as though to herself. "Fifty meetings." She found it difficult to concentrate. The path was rocky, the gray ground lit by the first moonlight. Stern soil, colonial houses, even the damp New England cold: the scene was foreign, and she longed for the easy, populated streets of midwestern cities on weekend nights. They walked in silence for ten minutes or so, and stopped in front of a white church, the Baptist Meeting House. She turned to Christopher Sisti. "I can't see you again, Chris, and it's got nothing to do with you."

"I see."

"What do you see?" She resumed angrily. "I haven't even said anything."

The handsome smile stopped halfway. "Ruth, I've known you for five years, and have never seen you nervous or upset till now. When I say 'I see' it means simply that I know that something profound has occurred, and I am the unwilling recipient of that happening."

"Right," she said harshly. "When I saw Dr. Essai and that grinning child, I knew it was over. Perhaps we could have bluffed it if I hadn't run out, or you had not called 'Ruth, darling.'" She picked up a rock and threw it a few feet. "I've already lied about Rebecca Lerner at the symphony, about grocery shopping late in the evening, about mishaps with the car. Now I can stop faking it."

Chris reached for her hand, but she brushed it aside. "And Matt suspected nothing," he stated grimly.

"Of course not. He is much too busy to analyze my casual explanations for possible infidelity." Her words were pressed flat by emotion.

"Wait." Chris Sisti began pacing in front of her as he talked. "He is too busy to listen to you at all, and he responds automatically. Hear me out. You say 'infidelity.' You have never been unfaithful to him, at least not with me."

"In thought," she muttered hopelessly.

He raised a gloved hand. "But not in deed. God knows, I have wanted it to be so. For the first time in thirty years a woman made me want to respond—sexually. How ironic that among all the women I know, married or single, or widowed, students or teachers who desire me, who come into the office long after the course is finished, send me notes—all begging for an affair, a real one, I find myself sexually responsive only to the one woman who will not have me on those terms."

"That's not hard to understand," she said unthinkingly.

"Ruth, we've been over that. I spent two years of terrible introspection with Dr. Rand searching my soul to learn that I can respond to the right woman. And God knows you are that woman. It is as important for you as for me." He looked around, seeking a suitable analogy. "I don't know what you were like before, in Cleveland, but now you are like this cold earth, stony, waiting for spring." His voice cracked on "spring."

"Please, don't go on like this."

"It's true, darling. Sometimes when I discuss love poetry in a lecture I beg God for the chance to have you there, to say the phrases to *you*."

"You have said them to me," she said flatly. She clenched her hands, hoping she would not soften.

"But not when you could respond, when the words could inflame you as they do me."

They had stopped walking, fully a mile from the cars. "We have to go back," said Ruth, "I am only 'out getting coffee.' So says the note I wrote four hours ago."

The hazy moonlight illuminated his Italian face, lined but not aging. She felt powerfully drawn to him, but turned resolutely and counted the rocky steps in silence. She wondered if death were warm or cold.

"Divorce him, Ruth." Anguish gave him the courage to say it at last.

"No."

"Then leave him. There is no more time, so I must say it. He has killed you, snuffed out the life by literally not seeing you, not caring." At the word "killed," coming so close to her own thought of death, she shivered. His hand touched her shoulder at once, then fell quickly away. "He has sacrificed you without knowing it. God, I hate him. Forgive me for saying that."

Her tears hit her hands, the coat, the ground. "He is my husband," she whimpered. "I'm sorry to hurt you like this, Chris. But it's over."

He spoke very quietly. "I'll miss you when I drive through the springtime country. How am I to face spring this year?"

"Stop it," she demanded. "You have an ocean of pity in you."

"Yes," he said, near tears, "for you."

She stopped and turned to him. "No, for you," she declared. "Don't make it hard for me. Or rather, harder for me."

"I can't give you up, Ruth."

"I *have* given you up," she said. "You must stop before I hurt you."

"Hurt me? Before you hurt me?" The rough laugh echoed off the ground. "You could not hurt me more."

She went past the edge. "Find yourself a young man with whom to salve the hurt."

He began walking again. "I begin to see why Matt ignores you. The pervasive female bitch is deep in you, but it is there nonetheless. Ruth. Ruth, don't run away."

But she was already running, ungainly, tripping on the stones. Her scarf fell to the ground and Christopher picked it up and touched it to his cheek. The fifty-year-old woman ran to her car, and he heard the roar as it started up, then stepped back as it rocketed darkly toward and past him. Inappropriately he shouted, "Lights!" as though to an unknown careless driver, and a block away he saw the headlights turn on. Christopher Sisti walked slowly to his car, with the silk scarf in his hands. "After great pain a formal feeling comes," he quoted, and he stood silent for a moment near the black sportscar, an elegant figure with silver hair.

She drove slowly with tears in her eyes. God, she had not meant to hurt him so. She was already composing the note she knew she would write: "Dear Chris, you are so full of kindness and feeling, and I so much want that, and can find it nowhere else. If I did not feel so much for you, care so much, I could blot you out of my mind. But I want to support you, be with you, experience the fineness of life with a sensitive soul. You will never be out of my thoughts, though we cannot be together."

She saw the light on in Matt's study as she drove in. For the last time she thought, "If only he had not reacted that way to the letter from Paul Heinrichs, I never would have called Chris." Tonight, she knew, there would be no easily accepted lie, and momentarily she felt fiercely happy about it.

He called down, "Ruth?" when she came in, but once assured it was her, said simply, "Start supper now, all right?" and went back to his work. It occurred to her that this day would pass, and the correct construction of a story could satisfy Matt and keep Andrew Essai from speaking. She sat for half an hour making up wholly plausible stories.

"No." She said it to the Oriental lamp in the living room, then went up the steps at a measured pace. She wanted it out in the open.

He looked up, preoccupied. "Gone kind of long, weren't you?"

"Matt, I have something to tell you."

"Hmmh?"

"Put down the journal, please." She watched him read a word, take in her phrase, and look up at her.

"What did you just say?"

She dug her thumbnail into her palm. "I just saw Dr. Essai in a bookstore. He was with a little girl."

"He was? He called before and said he couldn't come here as he had planned because his girlfriend was sick. Are you sure it was he?"

"Yes. You say he was coming out here?"

He nodded. "I told him to bring his girlfriend. It's her child, I suppose. Well then"— Kraft tried to think it through— "what excuse did he give you? Why I'll bet he's not prepared for the talk in New York next week, that lazy—"

"I've been unfaithful to you," she shouted.

His forehead went up. "With him?"

"No. With the man he saw me with in the bookshop."

Matt crinkled his eyes, as though looking into the sun. "Go on."

"That's all. The man works at Harvard, teaching. I've seen him about once a month for five years. When you were sick, and at home, I stopped seeing him."

"Until—?"

She sighed, trembling. "Until three weeks ago, when you went in early to see the man with the aneurysm. And today, when I read you Paul Heinrichs' letter."

"Where do you go? For sex, that is."

She shook her head. "No sex."

He was more questioning than angry. "Come on, Ruth—"

"It's so. No sex."

"Well, what do you do? When you see him."

"We go for rides in the country. To museums. Bookstores. I met him at the symphony one Friday when Rebecca Lerner couldn't go. He was looking for a seat."

"Symphony?" he echoed.

"Yes. Last year I told Rebecca I was giving up the subscription, but we kept it. I left the ticket for him and we sat next to one another, as though by chance arrangement of seats. We would talk at intermission, that was all."

Kraft stared at her. "You mean I paid for his symphony seat all year?" For the first time a trickle of anger seeped out.

"Is that your concern?" Tears of frustration thinned her voice. "That's your response?"

"No, it isn't. You said no sex. Was he a homosexual? Or is he?"

"Probably," she said wearily.

"I don't get it. Why did you see him?"

She raged. "Because he was concerned for me, and cared about my thoughts and feelings. He's a good teacher and a fine person, and he recognizes that one can be successful in a vocation and have time for feelings and music and art. He cares for me."

"And I don't?"

She gestured futilely. To him it looked like a dismissing wave. "Do you want a divorce, Ruth? Is that why you tell me?"

"No, I don't," she moaned. "I'm tired of the easy lie. I'll never see him again."

"Oh."

This was hopeless. "Matt, I've been unfaithful to you. I would call him and we would drive somewhere, talk for hours, share feelings. He wants me to leave you, he said that to me not an hour ago."

"Will you?"

"No."

He picked up a journal and ran his finger along the top of a page. "And you say there was no sex between you? Uh, no intercourse?"

"Yes. I mean, that's right. No intercourse."

"And it's over with him?"

"Yes."

"Well." Matt stood up uncertainly. "Well, look, Ruth, I don't take this lightly. Not in the least. It's a very serious thing you did." He gestured at a pile of cardiogram tapes. "But I've got to get these cardiograms ready for the session tomorrow. I haven't even started, and it's late, probably eight or nine, isn't it?"

She did not believe what was happening. "I guess so."

He looked at his watch. "Jesus, ten after eight. I have to get started on these. Now remember, I think we should talk this whole thing out. I mean, it's not just something we can forget about."

"But you don't want to talk about it?"

"Well, of course." He sat down and glanced at the cardiograms again. "I think we should find some time and go over the whole thing." He hesitated, then quickly bent down and picked up the first tape. "Now," he said sternly, "will you bring me up some supper?"

"Of course, Matt," she said. Quickly she went downstairs and made a cheese omelet, expertly flipping it. She carried it up on a tray with two mugs of coffee, an apple, and a huge slice of cheesecake.

"Thanks," he said, pointing to the table next to his chair and looking up for just an instant.

She set it down and handed him the napkin. "Here," she said dully.

"Thanks, Ruth."

She walked downstairs and sat in the living room. The sense of loneliness was precisely as intense as it had been on most of the evenings of their marriage. As such, it was no more difficult to bear. When silent tears came, however, the piercing thrust of sadness overwhelmed her. For the first time she knew the feeling of bereavement, the empty desolate grief. She wept for Paul Heinrichs, Matt, her children, and finally, in mourning, for the gulf between the marriage she had waited so long to forge, and the one she had ultimately lived through. When Matt came down at midnight for another piece of cheesecake, she still sat in the same chair, and he urged her to "go on up to bed," as he had a couple of hours work ahead of him. She did as she was told.

When she was gone, Kraft returned to his work, consisting tonight in thinking through his plan. What Dean Michler had indicated, that Kraft's compromised heart had cost him the deanship, spurred his thoughts infinitely more than the admission of his wife that she sought solace elsewhere. "Dean Michler knows my brain is sharp, sharp as ever," he thought angrily, "not worn out and childish like Paul Heinrichs'. With a new heart and everything else the same. . . !" he lapsed into musing about another generation of teaching and research. The Nobel Prize, honored as perhaps the greatest physician since Osler, and capped by an active career twice as long as even the greatest.

Kraft shook his head to clear it. His angina had not returned, and since the weeks with Fermanian he had felt in superb condition. And should his angina return, he now knew the plan. His diseased heart would be carried off in a polyethylene bag, and the heart of a normal young man, free of accidental contusion or injury, would be transplanted into him.

It would be the heart of Andrew Essai. Since the morphine dreaming the first night of his heart attack, when he had first dared imagine it, to the conviction that it had to be this way, Kraft now realized that he had never considered any other donor. As far as Essai was concerned, Kraft felt there could be but two reactions. The first, hopefully the correct one to Essai as well as Kraft, was that the young man, himself no better than competent despite his effort and training, would realize that fame and immortality could never come to him as a teacher or research man, but certainly would come to him as the young doctor who had sacrificed himself to increase the greatness of a renowned cardiologist. That honor, if all the details were handled correctly, could come before the donor's death, as the nation was told what he had chosen to do. The event of the century would involve Essai; was that not enough compensation?

The second reaction, and a more complex one, presented itself to Kraft quite clearly. Essai would accede, but only with the stipulation that he himself receive a heart. But the timing and surgical complexity, already tricky, would be too much even for Fermanian; the heart of an accident victim to Essai, his heart to Kraft. No, Fermanian would veto that plan. Kraft knew that Fermanian would accept the first plan, in fact he could not properly refuse if a willing and grateful Essai supported the idea.

"Fermanian will be lionized throughout the world," Kraft thought. "And Essai becomes immortalized. Well, all right. Let them bathe in the limelight. I only want the heart."

"Could I have the last slide please?"

The smoky darkness returned as the automatic projector whirred, then the swath of light cut through again. The lecturer cleared his throat. "I think we can keep the overhead lights on with this slide," he said.

They were nearly all awake, Essai noted. "On this last slide I've tried to summarize the main concept in approaching the patient with possible pericarditis," he said. "Symptoms referable to the chest may be extremely vague, and are rarely clear-cut. Among the more elegant diagnostic tests, none in our hands has approached the saline test—the Kraft test—as a valuable tool in the difficult patient. The test is easy to perform, unequivocal, and most important, of virtually no risk to the patient."

Dr. Essai set down his pointer and the slide clicked off. "It may be," he said quietly, "that the heart is the seat of the soul. Even the least literate and most scientific physician among us would agree that it is certainly the palpitating center of an astonishingly large number of fascinating clinical problems. If I have suggested some of them, as well as the fascination attendant upon the study and diagnosis of heart disease, then I have done my job well. Thank you."

He sat down to loud applause. Morris Friedlove, head of cardiology at Mt. Zion, arose, smiled, and said, "I think we will agree that Professor Essai has indeed done his job well. As you heard when he was introduced, Dr. Essai has spent three years with Matthew Kraft in Boston. A few of you who were chagrined that Dr. Kraft could not be here today will agree with me that he continues to teach his younger associates so that they speak with his fluency and authority, echoing the

254

master and in this case, very nearly improving upon him."

Friedlove checked his watch in the brief applause that followed. "I think we have time for one or two questions, if Dr. Essai will permit?"

According to tradition, the guest lecturer nodded and rose. He was asked a question about pericarditis, which he fielded easily, and another about tumors of the heart, which he answered with reference to Mrs. Battaglia's history.

"One more brief question?" Friedlove looked out over the audience. "Dr. Nachsager? Do you have one?"

A man with thick glasses and black hair rose. "Dr. Essai, in the *American Journal of Medical Sciences* out today is another in a series of articles from Hazlitt in Baltimore, pointing out that his carbon dioxide method is a safer way of detecting obscure heart disease than is the Kraft or saline test. Do you have any comment on that?"

"Well, I haven't seen his most recent article," Essai answered forthrightly. "But I imagine it's a variation on his theme that the saline test is dangerous. In our experience," he said easily, "we have had no serious problems with the saline test. And that's over two hundred patients."

Friedlove nodded. "Thank you—"

"You say no difficulties with the saline?" Nachsager asked loudly.

"No," said Essai.

Friedlove looked at Nachsager. "Another question?"

Dr. Nachsager looked at Essai for a moment. "No, no. Thank you."

Friedlove led the applause. "Thank you from all of us, Dr. Essai."

Smilingly, Essai walked up to get his slides from the projectionist. That last look of Dr. Nachsager's had been an odd one, pouring through the thick glasses and holding him, challenging. Essai shrugged. He had to hurry to the airport limousine for the plane to Atlantic City this afternoon. He was sharing a room with Harvey Lerner.

He got his slides, wiped them off, and set them into his

briefcase. The lecture hall was nearly empty as he straightened up. Dr. Nachsager stood a few feet away. "Yes?"

"I enjoyed your talk, Dr. Essai. I'm Albert Nachsager. In Dr. Friedlove's group down here. You've never heard of me?"

They shook hands. Essai looked at the man, about forty, and tried to place him. A paper perhaps? A technique? Had he referred a patient to the Eastern Mass. Medical? He shook his head. "No, I don't believe so."

Nachsager nodded. "Kraft really made me an unperson. Look, do you have time for a cup of coffee?"

"Uh, thanks very much but I want to get to Atlantic City, and the airport limousine—"

Nachsager raised his hand. "I know. Atlantic City. Don't room with Jam Wah Lee down there; he talks in his sleep about enzymes."

"How do you know Lee?"

"I worked in Dr. Kraft's department for six years," Nachsager said quietly. "Until 1958. I was his first chief resident in 1953, when he set up his service on the sixth floor. It's still there, right?"

Essai nodded. "I was chief resident three years ago. My God, six years and Kraft never mentions you."

"You don't have time for coffee?"

"OK. Albert, is it?"

"Al. Or 'Albert the backtalker,' as MK always said."

They walked out, Essai carrying his briefcase. "Not very complimentary," he remarked.

"This way, to the coffee shop. No, it wasn't, Dr. Essai."

"Andy."

They got to the coffee shop. Essai had never been in the Mt. Zion, but the knots of physicians, nurses, and medical students were the same, each having sought the proper level, all talking noisily about medicine as coffee cooled or they waited for service. Essai felt at home.

"You've never been here?" Al asked.

"No. Heard a lot about this place."

"How's Lerner?"

"Harvey? Fine, I guess. I'm rooming with him at Atlantic City."

"Good. You know, he took his training here. For three or four years."

Coffee was set down in front of Essai. "No, I didn't know that."

Nachsager lit a pipe. "I'll bet he wishes he could give a talk here, at the place he trained."

"That's right. How proud that would make him."

"Think Kraft will ever let him?"

Essai shrugged. "Maybe."

"Good old Kraft. Lerner was probably dying to give this talk today. Don't get me wrong, Andy, I enjoyed yours. But think what it would have meant to Harvey."

"I see your point."

Nachsager bit into a doughnut. "Kraft never would."

Defensively, Essai said, "Oh, wait a minute. Dr. Kraft has changed some. And—"

"Bull." A fleck of doughnut escaped with the word.

"Now wait."

Al Nachsager shook his head. "Andy, I was there for six years. Now I know Kraft had a heart attack, and slacked off for a while, but a guy like that will never change."

The coffee was strong hospital coffee. Essai held his cup thoughtfully. "I don't agree with you."

"OK. Now I'll ask you the question I thought of asking at the end of your talk. You noticed I had another question?"

Essai nodded.

" 'Dr. Essai, how many times have you seen the saline test performed?' That's what I would have asked."

Essai blushed. "I can't really say, offhand. Maybe a dozen."

"You said two hundred during the question period."

Essai pointed to his briefcase. "The articles I went over in which Dr. Kraft describes his series, those articles include at least two hundred patients—"

Light slid up and down the thick glasses. "I know, Andy. The first paper I ever got my name on was one of those. Forty patients. Carefully studied. Paul Wood referred to that paper in his textbook when he called the test the Kraft test."

"Good," said Essai. "Well then, you know why I could say two hundred."

"But you can't. Or shouldn't." Al Nachsager drank his coffee in fast gulps. The owlish face watched Essai over the cup. "Look," he said, wiping off his mouth, "apparently you have access to Kraft's reprint file. That's news to me, since Kraft guarded that as his private reserve."

"After his heart attack," Essai explained, "I kind of—or rather, he asked me to help out."

"That's an honor. If you have access to the file, try to find a file called 'Patient Experience—Untoward Incidents.' I would wager a lot of money that some frightening side effects of the saline test are described in there."

Essai was surprised, and a little angry at the surety with which the man spoke. "How do you know?"

"I never saw the file," Nachsager admitted. "But in 1953, my first year there, we had a death in a patient who had the test. He drank a lot of the saline, and no more than a minute later he gasped and fell back, with what turned out to be a fatal cardiac arrest. I wanted to publish the case, and I rewrote the paper ten times at least, but Kraft pulled the pocket veto on me, and it rested in his briefcase for six months at a time between revisions."

"What ever happened to it?" Essai sat forward.

Nachsager shrugged. "Nothing. But I'll tell you about the Hazlitt-Kraft story."

"What?"

Nachsager looked around the busy coffee shop. He bent toward Essai. "Andy, I'm not a talker. Or a muckraker. If I were, I would have asked that question about how many tests you personally had seen, and asked it in the lecture hall."

Essai nodded. "Go ahead."

"Wait. I'm telling you because it's one thing to work with Kraft, taking his criticisms and bearing the brunt of his ego. But he sent you out as his representative, or as a representative of his department. And goddamnit, he didn't level with you about the saline test. He couldn't if he wanted to: it's called the Kraft test, and he guards its reputation like a jealous father."

Nachsager tapped his pipe on the linoleum table and continued in a low voice. "John Hazlitt had just been named professor and head of cardiology at Maryland. Kraft was at the height of his influence, regarded as the doctor with the best clinical touch since Osler. At that time he was forty-five or so, and he often told me that a clinician would never win the Nobel Prize again. I don't know how important a part that played in his plans, but he proposed to have a number of new professors come to Boston and the Eastern Mass. Medical, for a period of weeks or months, to 'exchange ideas' as he put it. Two or three came before Hazlitt, and they left praising Matthew Kraft, just as he had hoped. Hazlitt came up and was duly impressed with the clinical service, and the research done in Kraft's labs. That was in '55, and he came to one of the journal clubs on Saturday. I guess he still has them on Saturday."

"He does."

Nachsager smiled. "And the guys still bitch about it, I know. Well, talk got around to the saline test, and I knew my paper was sitting in Kraft's briefcase. Kraft said the test was good, and gave out all the old baloney. I spoke up once, just once, and said we had that one case of sudden death. Kraft said my case was poorly documented, et cetera, et cetera, and said, to Hazlitt (I can hear it now), 'John, Dr. Nachsager has his facts sadly mixed up. But take a look through my file on the test. I have a record of every one done since I started, even some on mental hospital patients in Ohio.'"

Nachsager took off his glasses and shook his head. "I should have left Boston that day," he said mournfully, "because after I spoke up like that, I ceased to exist in Kraft's eyes."

Essai looked at him sympathetically. "And then—?"

Nachsager put his glasses on again. "Hazlitt looked through the patient files. But he wasn't full professor at thirty-six for nothing. He found that other file, 'Patient Experience—Untoward Incidents,' and found several cases of serious reactions to the test. He showed it to Kraft, who said something like, 'I told you to look at the clinical files, not this one. These are very poorly studied cases. I'm going over these few to see if they represent true side effects.' "

"And?"

"And Hazlitt left and sang the praises of Kraft as a clinical teacher, but he began to work on his carbon dioxide test for detecting obscure heart disease. Kraft closed his file to outsiders forever, and stopped having young men come to Boston to visit. After that he wrote more papers, made contacts at meetings, and made his textbook a classic."

"One more question," Essai said. "How did you find out?"

"Hazlitt sent me a note from Baltimore," Nachsager said. "He told me he knew I was right." The owlish man smiled ruefully. "My price for being right was not to be promoted. I was passed over, and stopped getting chances to lecture, make clinical rounds, get research equipment. I was there for three more years, 'forgotten but not gone.' Then I came here."

"How's Friedlove to work with," Essai inquired.

"A very good doctor and a gentleman." Nachsager sighed, looking at a point far away. "Kraft, as we know, is a great doctor and a bastard."

They talked for a while longer, and Al Nachsager drove him out to the airport, in order for Essai to make the plane. They were waiting for a long line of cars slowly pulling into and away from the Eastern terminal, when Essai said, almost to himself, "The more I think about Kraft, the less I understand."

"I felt that way, myself. Thank God I'm out of it," Al said.

"It's too hard to figure; the dedication and skill coupled with immaturity and childishness."

Nachsager looked straight ahead. "We've got another five minutes to wait," he said.

"Oh." Essai gripped his briefcase. "I can walk from here, Al—"

"No. Wait. I'll give you my thoughts about it. But damnit, Andy, it's between us." He looked over.

"Of course."

Al pointed at the line of cars. "I'll stop when we get to the Eastern terminal." He took a deep breath. "Matthew Kraft," he began, "is the prime example of a very common condition among the full-time men at the Eastern Mass. Medical. Call it the cult of personality or hubris or what you will. It involves the practice of a specialty like cardiology or infectious disease or hematology where patients are very sick. The sickest patients are referred into the hospital, and the unspoken awareness of the whole staff is that each of these patients is sick enough to die. A lot of them do. But when the professor is caring for such a patient, he is viewed by the patient and the staff as having almost godlike powers to intercede between the patient and his serious disease, and effect recovery."

"Of course," Essai blurted out. "Especially cardiology."

"Naturally. The patient has serious heart disease, and Kraft, the massive one in figure, reputation, and skill, becomes the receptacle of the patient's fervent hopes that something will intercede to halt or cure the fatal illness."

Essai interrupted him. "But he started out in research."

"Right. But research on the heart, or the work of the heart. I have heard a lot of stories about why he left Cleveland in the early forties, but that's irrelevant. At that time Kraft was doing the same thing, intervening in godlike fashion, but there it was to uncover a secret of nature, a biologic secret."

"Like the work of the heart."

"Precisely," Nachsager said. " 'Delve nature's deepest mysteries,' and all that. But once in clinical medicine, Kraft saw that he could play that role to the hilt, only now the emphasis was not to understand nature, but to attempt to rescue patients from her pathologic caprice."

"Now where does the saline test fit in?"

They were near the departure point. "Ah, yes, the saline test." Al pointed for emphasis. "The godlike physician Kraft could act like a jealous god, an angry god, a salvaging god, even a capricious one. But gods are not wrong. They do not make erroneous statements. And their patients do not suffer or die from their mistakes in employing diagnostic tests.

"Oh, and just parenthetically, the 'godlike intervention' notion also explains the oft-mentioned dedication of great doctors. Dedication is simply never an issue if the man thinks he has special godlike gifts. Did you ever hear of a god working forty hours a week?"

An airline employee motioned the car to stop and opened Essai's door. Essai reached over and shook Nachsager's hand. "Thanks, thanks a lot, Al."

"I don't exist for Kraft any more," said Nachsager sadly. "But say hello to Lee and Lerner."

Essai watched him pull away. He did not know if Al was right or not, but he felt it was time to find out.

"Oh, there you are. How did it go at Mt. Zion?" Kraft saw him before he had taken twenty steps on the boardwalk outside the Haddon Hall Hotel.

"Fine. I think they liked it." Essai had been preoccupied and pensive until the moment he saw Kraft, but his words, as usual, were open and reassuring. "It went fine," he repeated.

"Good. Did you check into the motel yet?"

"Yes. Just now."

Kraft looked at his watch. "It's three thirty. Most of the good talks are over, but there's one on serum sodium in heart failure"—Kraft checked his program—"yes, it should start pretty soon. You're going to hear it?"

Essai heard the faintly menacing tone. "Yes. By the way, I have regards for you from New York."

"Friedlove?" Kraft lit a cigarette. Essai nodded uncertainly and Kraft said, "Good man. Not a great cardiologist, but he runs a good department."

"I had that impression too. By the way, do you know a man named Nachsager?" Essai's question was delivered smoothly, but the afternoon sun suddenly brought sweat to his brow.

Kraft puffed quickly on his cigarette. "Sure, Al Nachsager. What about him?"

Essai cleared his throat. "Well—"

Kraft guffawed. "Wait. I'll tell you. He asked about the saline test." Laughter enveloped the man. "Son-of-a-bitch, he'll talk about that one case till he dies."

"Oh, well, he didn't mention a case as such—"

Kraft dismissed the whole thing with a wave. "Andy, that jackass Nachsager still thinks his patient, or rather my patient, died after he swallowed saline. Isn't that what he indicated?" Kraft did not wait for the answer. "Well, I was at the autopsy, and the patient has scars of old heart attacks. Nothing to suggest a recent one, one induced by saline. No evidence. We never did pin down the cause of death, but I think the pathologist probably missed something." Kraft shook his head with a smirk, "Goddamn that Nachsager. He looks like a jackass, and hangs onto his stupid notion like a jackass. Isn't he something?"

"Yes, he is." The sun was no longer warm. Kraft said he had made plans to have the cardiology group eat supper together, told Essai where to meet them, and stalked off. Essai looked at the long shadows they both cast on the boardwalk, one moving, his own still. Kraft's disposal of Nachsager had chilled the scene and Essai's mood. "My God," he thought, "he could dismiss any of us in the same way. He didn't even ask me what Nachsager did say."

Brooding, he looked around. He had been in Atlantic City last year, and already he hated the place again. The young men walked casually with the afternoon program and the unread *New York Times* under their arms, like male prostitutes, waiting to be approached by an older man, any associate or full professor. The assignation made, the two would walk up and down the boardwalk, as the older man discussed his proposals for academic appointment and the predatory young one listened, calm on the surface but constantly weighing how this offer compared with others.

The dismal routine had its variations. If young man "A" kept seeing Professor "B" but seemed never to be recognized and hailed in turn, he knew that an offer would not be made. But he continued to walk in and out of Haddon Hall and the Chalfont, awaiting Professor "C" or "D," studiously marking his program and fingering a conservative tie. The second variation was the proud, almost defiant walk of the "Old Men," the men over sixty-five who were professor but not chairman, or emeritus, neither looked at by the succulent boys or themselves involved in recruiting. They met others of their own rank and moved along, saltwater taffy for the grandchildren tucked under an arm, with the same desperate gaiety Essai had noticed in patients with inoperable cancer of the lung, who sauntered through the hospital wards chain-smoking cigarettes and inhaling hugely, as though to show the world how little its conventions bound them any more.

Sunday at Atlantic City was "Young Squirts" day, when research fellows and instructors spoke breathlessly to small audiences. Monday and Tuesday the "Young Turks" gave their papers, in simultaneous sessions held in eight or ten different rooms, and by racing from place to place, checking the program, one could get an idea about the research being done in the fifty or sixty research centers of the better medical schools.

Essai looked far to his right, where Kraft had been joined by the bent figure of Harlan Michler, medical dean. Kraft had been picked for the Association of American Physicians five years before at age fifty-four, and he would be an active member until sixty-five, when he would become emeritus member, and slip suddenly from "Old Turk" to "Old Man" in medicine.

Wednesday, Essai remembered, was "Old Turks" day, when the physicians from fifty to sixty-five held their meeting. Tomorrow for the Transactions of the A.A.P., Kraft would read his paper on tumors that involved the heart, the paper Essai had researched for him. "I wonder if my name is on it," he thought, and he went into Haddon Hall, registered, and got the two programs, one for the rest of the afternoon and the other for the Transactions program for tomorrow.

His name was not there. It was a disappointment, seeing Kraft as sole author, but Essai figured realistically that Kraft would mention his name tomorrow during the talk as a collaborator, and his own name would appear with Kraft's when the paper was published. He looked at the "Young Turks" program, especially the cardiology section, and saw little that attracted his attention. He noticed that the Sunday meetings were not listed.

"Miss," he said to the lady behind the registration desk, "do you have any copies left of the Sunday program?"

"Yes, I think so," she said, and a moment later she handed him the white program, "American Federation for Clinical Research." Essai flipped through it, walking back outside, and saw an interesting title, "Fluorescent Antibody in Rheumatic Fever Patients: Preliminary Note." Essai bit his lip. "Hope they didn't scoop me on the work I was setting up after the *Science* paper," he thought. It was the second oldest prayer in scientific research—"I hope I'm not beaten to the punch." He looked at the authors, wondering if he would know them. It said, "Pruden, E., and Kraft, M., Eastern Massachusetts Medical Center, Boston."

He walked out onto the boardwalk, chalky-white and shaky. He knew the explanation without thinking: "I was busy with the clinical stuff and Kraft told Pruden to go ahead and continue my work without informing me." An immense hollowness opened within him, precluding anger and, for the moment, revenge. He heard his name being called, as though from a great distance, but the voice "Andy, over here," was that of George Winston, standing against the fence near the Steel Pier, smoking a pipe. Essai walked over to him woodenly.

"Are you all right? You look awfully pale."

He managed a weak smile. "Too many talks in the smoky air."

Winston gestured to the curling Atlantic. "Me too. I come out here every hour or so to look at the one nice thing in the papier-mâché city. Is your whole group here?"

"Yes. I guess so," Essai answered. "I just got here. Uh, I

wonder, were you here for the Young Squirts on Sunday?"

The mild cardiologist smiled. "I was. Very intense young men."

"Did you hear the talk, this talk?" Essai could not say it, and pointed to the place in the program with a trembling finger.

Winston looked down, then at Essai, and finally out to sea. "Yes. Ed Pruden gave it. It's the extension of your work that you reported in *Science*, isn't it?"

Essai nodded.

"Did you know Ed was working on it? Excuse me for asking but—"

"No. No, I didn't know. I guess Dr. Kraft told him to go ahead with it. I was busy on the wards."

Winston looked at the pale young man. "Let's take a stroll," he suggested.

They started out silently, in contrast to the other couples, where the older men always talked and the younger listened. Essai felt the east wind on his face, and breathed in the salt air sighingly. "Sorry I'm not good company," he said after a few minutes.

Winston shrugged. "Andy, I never went through what you're going through. And I have no advice for you on how to handle it. But if sometime you want to leave the place you work at, and you want to stay in Boston, come over and talk to me at the Metropolitan."

"Thank you." Essai looked at him gratefully. "I'll remember that. Let me ask you, did you ever have any side effects from the saline test, the Kraft test?"

"A few."

"Serious?"

"Two were. One man aspirated the saline after drinking a lot of it, and nearly died."

Essai gripped his sweaty programs. "What did Kraft say when you told him?"

A quiet smile appeared. "Andy, I started to tell him half a

dozen times, but he always got me onto something else. Short of writing him about it, I know I'll never get it all out. Or have him hear it truly."

"Thanks, thanks for telling me." Essai sniffed. On impulse he threw the program into a trash barrel. "George," he said loudly, "it's nearly four. Would you let a young assistant professor stand you to a drink?"

Winston clapped his hand to his chest delightedly. "You buy the first," he proposed, "and I buy the second."

"*Et al.*," said Essai.

"And then some."

The drunk was worth every second of the hangover. After the third gin and tonic Essai called Angela Lynne in Boston, got Alix off the phone after five minutes, and told Angela that he loved her. Her comment was, "Say it when you're sober, darling." Essai went back to the bar, where Winston sat feeling his pulse.

"I think the quinine gives me arrhythmias. Feel."

Essai felt the pulse. "George," he announced, "Professor Essai gives the local GP Winston a free consultation. There's nothing wrong with your pulse that a Beefeater gin and Schweppes tonic with lime will not cure." They both drank to it, and dedicated the fifth drink to not mentioning Matthew Kraft for the remainder of the evening, a pact they kept with ease.

Essai stumbled into the motel room at two, jamming back the glass door with the slurred threat, "Move, you bastard, or I'll walk through you." Harvey Lerner awoke with a start. "That you Essai?"

"No, it isn't. I left him back at the bar."

Lerner turned on the light. "Jesus, you're drunk."

"Congraters." Essai fell on his bed fully clothed. "You finally made a clever diagnosis."

"Hey listen, Dr. Kraft saw you having a drink with George Winston. He was damn upset." Harvey looked at Essai who was watching him between two fingers. "I'm not kidding, Andy. He thought you were joining us for dinner. We reserved a place for you."

"That's nice," he crooned. "Did all my friends miss me?"

Lerner was irritated. "Kraft did. He said, 'What is he, a traitor? I'm paying his way, not Winston.'"

"Up his."

"Andy. That's no way to—"

"Hey." Essai lurched up. "We're all together here, right? All Kraft's boys in adjoining rooms?"

"I think so. Go to sleep."

Essai nodded gravely. "Too early to sleep. *Mächtig* Kraft never sleeps this early, not while there's another journal to read. Where's Pruden's room? Pruden!" he shouted.

Lerner stared alarmedly at him. "Calm down, Essai. He's next door, probably asleep. Hey, where are you going?"

Essai slammed the glass partition open, and walked outside. "Which way, Harvey?"

"I don't know. Right, I think."

"Pruden," Essai yelled. A muffled sound came from the motel room to the right, and Essai hit the glass with his fists. "Open up, I have an urgent message for Edward Pruden, Doctor Research Man Pruden."

A light went on and Pruden opened the door, wearing striped pajamas. "What is it?"

Andrew Essai took his two shoulders and shook him several times very slowly. "Message," he said thickly. He grinned crookedly. "Heard from the best people that your preliminary paper on the antibody work was great, just great. I wanted to add my congratulations, Ed. We're all terribly proud of you."

"You're drunk, Andy. And Kraft is right next door, hearing every word," Pruden said in a loud whisper. The attack had surprised him, but with the last phrase he escaped the shaking arms and retreated a few steps. "He hears everything," he said.

"Everything," Essai shouted. "He knows everything, *Mächtig* Kraft."

In the other bed Jam Wah Lee sat up, frightened. "What is it?"

"Truth. Truth."

"Quiet out there." Kraft's voice boomed out from the next unit to the right.

"Yes, sir," Essai shouted. "Just looking for a journal to read, sir, before going to sleep."

"Go to bed!"

"Yes, sir." Essai tried to click his heels, kicked his instep, and made his way back to the room where Lerner looked at him with fearful interest. "Andy, go to sleep," he warned, "or you'll hang yourself without knowing it."

The young man dropped heavily on the bed. "A capital notion," he punned.

He was shortly asleep. Quiet returned, and lights went out, except for the small light in Kraft's private room where he read over his notes for the tumor talk the next day. He had heard most of Essai's ranting, and shook his head disgustedly. "He's paranoid. It's as simple as that. Paranoid." Kraft lit a cigarette and started over the notes again.

But for Essai it had been worth it. Somehow he got himself up at nine, found a place where they would put ice chips in his orange juice, and after four cups of coffee he left a large tip and walked through the blowing sunlight to Haddon Hall. He could not remember everything about last night, but he knew he had said nothing damning. Somewhere during the drinks with Winston he had made up his mind, and now acted with the calm that follows an irrevocable decision.

Kraft's paper was scheduled for eleven, and now he knew it would be Kraft's and not "ours." Essai rubbed his aching temples and gratefully took the escalator to the third floor, where he sat in the last row of the huge auditorium, with four thousand academic physicians, to hear the Old Turk read his paper.

Kraft's voice was resonant, his delivery fluid, his talk a model of organization, insight, and rhetoric, and an ovation followed its presentation. Essai's name was not mentioned at any time, as the young man now grimly realized it would never be. He sat in the anonymous darkness and thought, "Even though I spent the nights collecting the cases of tumor of the heart, I don't mind his omission. This is another example of a well-defined syndrome. Gods have neither associates or collaborators."

After the talk Essai walked quietly to the sunlit boardwalk, had another glass of juice, half a bloody Mary, and checked out of his motel room. Before dark he was back in Boston, and knowing that the rest of the men in the department would stay in Atlantic City till Thursday, he ate a quick supper at the airport and went to Kraft's office with a thick pad of yellow paper. He opened the door to the reprint file with the key Kraft had given him five months before, and he was there till early morning, reading the case histories in the private file and making notes.

He went to Angela's apartment after daylight, and slept the whole day. That evening, during a dinner of chicken with grapes, he told her a little about his decisions and plan. She listened and did not say much.

"I know my chance will come this month, before May is over. Ed Pruden is assigned the *American Journal of Medical Sciences,* and he's due to report this Saturday or next. Hazlitt's latest article is in the April journal, and he's got to mention it. I know Kraft will dismiss it."

"Is that the article you heard about in New York?"

"That's it. The one Nachsager mentioned to me. Pruden has to report it."

Angela looked at him. "And you'll wait till Kraft makes a disparaging comment, and then bring up the cases in his own file?"

"Right."

"Right," Alix echoed.

Essai looked at Angela, tan in an open-necked blouse. She looked fresh and lovely. He kissed her cheek. "Sorry if there's some chicken in that kiss."

"Me too, a kiss for me too," begged the little girl, holding out her arms.

"Later, Bright Eyes. When you get tucked in."

"Andy, think over—"

"Now, Easy Andy, kiss me now."

"Later," he said quickly.

"Alix." She looked sharply at her daughter. "Please be quiet while we're talking."

Essai raised his eyebrows. "Take it easy, Angela. All she wanted—"

"I know what she wanted. What I want is to know what happened to this doctor in New York who spoke up about the cases."

"That was different. He didn't have all the facts I do. I don't plan to make wild statements. I just want to set the record straight."

"For whose sake, Andy?"

He looked at her angrily. "What does that mean?"

"Nothing." She looked down. "But—"

"But what?"

"Andy," she said, exasperated, "the only people at that silly journal club who will hear you are the other men in the department. Lerner and the others. Are you going to change their minds about Kraft?"

"Honey, I'm not trying to change anyone's mind."

"But you said Winston knew about it. And that Hazlitt who wrote the paper, he knows already, and the doctor in New York does too."

"You don't understand," Essai said. "I want to show Kraft that I'm not just another of his boys."

She stood up. "OK," she said quietly.

"You don't believe me."

"Yes, I do, Andy. This doctor in New York—"

"Nachsager."

She sighed. "Nachsager. He spoke up and he told you himself what it cost. Is it worth so much to you to challenge Kraft?"

He stood as well. "Honey, it's not a matter of challenging him just for the sake of the challenge."

"Maybe," she said gloomily.

Essai walked over to the window. The apricot sun slipped shivering into the mouth of the Charles River, and the green grass of the Hatch Shell was backlit for just a moment. "You think my sun is setting," he said absently.

She came over and kissed his cheek. "I'm with you, Andy."

"Me too," said Alix, watching them intently.

The journal meeting dragged on. There were the same faces, Kraft, Lerner, Pruden, Essai, the two fellows, Jam Wah Lee, and O'Connell, the chief resident. The assistant resident had been called out to see a patient. Spring traffic noises mingled with the warm air and the small conference room was stuffy. Even Kraft yawned as Jim Nichols struggled through the last of his articles from *Circulation*. "That's all I have," he said at last, and sat back, face shiny.

Kraft lit a cigarette. "Who else is reporting."

"I am, sir," Pruden said. Both he and Essai came to life, for different reasons.

"Go ahead," said Kraft.

"I'll start with the April *American Journal of Medical Sciences*. There's a good review of various clinical patterns in blood clots of the lungs. From Denver. They studied seventy cases and set up three broad categories for diagnosis. One was clear-cut chest pain with bloody sputum and typical cardiogram changes, and the second was a more vague clinical story but with the characteristic X-ray and rise in enzymes." Pruden looked at his notes. "The third category, and the one they stress as often overlooked, is a story often suggesting pneumonia, especially in the elderly patient, with hazy infiltrates on X-ray and little enzyme rise. They say in their summary, 'the third category includes thirty patients, half studied at autopsy, where the diagnosis of pulmonary clot was clear-cut. The physician should be alert to the presentation of blood clots as outlined.' "

"What enzyme did they measure?" asked Lee sleepily.

"Lactic dehydrogenase."

Lerner had a comment. "I can't see that this is anything

273

new, about the varied patterns. We see their third-category patient all the time."

"Of course," said Kraft. "If they say they studied patients 'at autopsy,' it damn well means that the patients died without the right diagnosis being made. If patients are properly diagnosed and treated, the mortality shouldn't exceed ten percent. What was the mortality in that group, Ed?"

"Fourteen out of thirty."

Kraft waved his hand. "Brother. Nearly fifty percent mortality. They should be ashamed to publish that stuff. I'll bet we don't run a mortality of ten percent. Christ," Kraft made a dismissing motion, "they ought to follow their own advice and make the diagnosis of pulmonary clots in time to help the patient. Instead of cluttering up the literature with that kind of crap."

Pruden nodded, careful to avoid defending the paper he had just reported. "Well," he said, "you know that the editorial board of this journal is not exactly brilliant."

"Go on," Kraft ordered him.

"The next paper I'll read by title, since it's of little value, I fear," Ed Pruden said quickly. "It's from Baltimore, the City Hospital, called 'Carbon Dioxide Studies in Obscure Heart Diseases—a Valuable Aid to Diagnosis.' The authors describe several patients with obscure diseases of the heart. Carbon Dioxide studies helped uncover the diagnosis. The authors have a long discussion on their carbon dioxide test. The next—"

"Wait a minute," Kraft said. "Don't tell me that's another of Hazlitt's papers."

Pruden checked the authors. "Yes. He's senior—"

"Jesus. The editors of the journal must be insane, accepting that one." Kraft sniffed. "What did they say about the saline test?"

Pruden looked through the article quickly. "In their introduction they say, 'though the saline test first described by Kraft has been proposed as a useful clinical measure to determine the presence of obscure heart disease, we have found it an unreliable aid in the majority of patients.'"

"That Hazlitt is nuts. 'Unreliable.' Maybe in their hospital. Do they say anything in the discussion?"

"Let's see. Yes, here. 'Until now a widely used test to detect the presence of previously unsuspected heart disease has been the Kraft test."

"Go on," Kraft demanded.

Pruden smiled weakly. "OK, but this is their feeling, not mine. 'However, there are numerous objections to the saline test. Cardiogram changes of the kind described by Kraft can be mimicked by exercise, smoking, emotion, a full meal, and breath holding. The changes are thus nonspecific. More importantly, lung disease of various kinds will give results similar to those seen in heart disease, so the test is of little aid in diagnosis. Finally, more than a few patients with coronary heart disease will develop chest pain or heart failure after the ingestion of the usual amount of saline used in the test; there is a risk in performing it. In contrast to these objections to the Kraft test, the carbon dioxide method described here is truly diagnostic, simple to perform, and free of side effects, at least to date. It is thus proposed that the Kraft saline test be abandoned in favor of more precise diagnostic methods, including the one herein described.' That's the end of the discussion in the paper."

During this reading, Essai watched Kraft closely. At first the big man had listened amusedly, then uncomfortably, and finally, flushed and head lowered, he exploded in a rage.

"That article is utter and absolute crap. Simply crap. In the first place, the saline test has not caused heart failure or chest pain in the three hundred or more patients in whom I've used it. Never once. I would never do anything to a patient that might be harmful to him. They seem to imply that I have. That is a lie, simply a lie. Those bastards ought to be sued for slanderous comments like that."

He stopped to think about the next objection. No one said

a word. The atmosphere could no longer be described as boring. Only Pruden casually flipped the pages of the yellow journal. Awaiting the end of the storm so he could continue reporting the next article. Or else, thought Essai, he was praying that Kraft would not turn his wrath upon him for having mentioned the article in the first place.

"And then they say that the cardiogram is influenced by many factors. Isn't that a new piece of information," Kraft exclaimed sarcastically. "Jesus Christ, I described the appearance of abnormal cardiograms following exercise in 1947, and how it meant nothing in terms of organic heart disease. Just what is the point? Do we take our cardiac patients and make them run around the block, or eat steak, or have intercourse so we can watch the cardiograms? That's nonsense.

"And the other thing is ridiculous; about lung disease giving the same result. Sure it gives the same result, but the simplest dolt can tell on routine physical exam if the patient has got lung disease or heart disease. The only 'diagnostic confusion' is in the minds of the nitwits there in Baltimore who can't tell the difference in their patients. So they subject them to a 'safe' procedure. Someone should do that 'safe' procedure on them, put them through all kinds of maneuvers, anesthetize them, and then squirt carbon dioxide into them. That's all a sick patient needs, a non-blood-carrying bolus of carbon dioxide circulating around for a while." Kraft made a circular motion with his arm, as though the bolus of gas were attached to his finger.

Pruden stepped in, predictably. "They certainly go way out on a limb," he suggested.

"Someone ought to chop it off for them," snarled Kraft. "It's just another example of the crap that's getting into the literature these days. I wonder who reviews those articles for publication? I'll tell you this. If I had anything to do with it, I'd shove that article right back at them, and warn them about experimenting on humans without their consent. And they'd have to go some to get another paper past me. Well," he concluded, "it just shows how far some people will go to get their names on a paper. God, what junk they publish."

Essai raised his hand. Brooding, Kraft motioned for him to go ahead.

"I think their objection about cardiogram changes after food and exercise is ridiculous," he said mildly. "They make an error in logic. It doesn't matter if a thousand things cause changes. The point is that the changes caused by saline suggest heart disease."

"Right. That Hazlitt can't even think straight. Oh, I've followed his papers. Each year he's got a new method to report, and each time it's abandoned very shortly." Kraft brightened a little, having disposed of the authors, and now the research.

"There is one point they raise, though," said Essai, as casually as he could. He felt his arms grow heavy, as though blood were being replaced by lead.

"Hmmh?" Kraft nodded, tired.

"Their point about the hazards of the test is well taken."

Kraft looked up. "You mean their own test, the carbon dioxide test?"

"No sir. I mean your test, the saline test. It's so dangerous a test that it should probably be discarded, as Hazlitt suggests."

Lerner choked, as though he had inhaled in the act of swallowing. Pruden said, "Oh," and Jam Wah Lee's forehead went up. Kraft blinked, looked quizzically at Essai, blinked again. "Explain yourself," he said with ominous calm, his head lowering. As Essai spoke, Kraft doodled the letters 'AE' on a piece of paper in front of him, and then drew smaller and smaller circles around and through it until he had created a neat black disk.

"I had a chance to review the cases of the patients in this hospital on whom the test was done. The saline test," Essai added. He paused, heard the utter silence, and rushed to fill it with words. "In the last fifteen years, at least sixteen patients developed complications from the test. In six cases the association between the strain of drinking the large amount of

saline and a subsequent heart attack was glossed over or ignored, but review of the charts strongly suggests that such an
association in fact could be made.

"In seven other patients, the test was repeated, and after
the second test, I calculate that they had drunk over a liter of
fluid. Three of these patients died suddenly within an hour,
and autopsies on two of them showed acute heart attacks. The
other four developed fever and cough, and had aspiration
pneumonia on X-ray. In no case was there any other cause of
pneumonia. In three patients, the test was felt to be positive,
that is, showing chronic heart disease. All three patients were
then treated as though they had it, but on follow-up, it turned
out they had other chest disease. Two patients died of overwhelming tuberculosis of the lungs, a treatable disease which
was not considered during life."

"Are you finished?" Kraft roared.

"No, sir," Essai said tightly. "I found records of about three
hundred successful tests. With sixteen serious complications
as outlined, the rate of complications was about five percent.
In Hazlitt's several papers, the rate of complications of his
test is no more than two percent."

"Where did you get those cases, about complications," Kraft
demanded.

"From your files, Dr. Kraft. The one 'Patient Experience—
Untoward Incidents.'"

"Stop!" Kraft stood up. The sound of a cardiac monitor
beeped loudly in his mind. "You broke into my files, misread
the chart summaries, and now present these lies as though
they were the truth. You are a bigger liar than that bastard
Hazlitt in Baltimore. I want—"

Essai interrupted him, trembling but loud. "I told the truth,
Dr. Kraft. I want you to retract that statement, that I am a
liar."

"You—you what?" Kraft sputtered. He looked at the young
man weighted down in his chair.

"Calm down everyone," Lerner said quietly.

"Shut up, Lerner," Kraft spat. He remained standing, his hand on the flat table.

"I'm waiting for your apology," said Essai.

Kraft's roving hand found an ashtray and hurled it through the closed window in back of Essai. A cool breeze rustled some papers on the desk, and a distant crash sounded from below. "Here's my message to you, liar. You are fired. You don't work here any more. You never did work here, just played at it."

"Fine," said Essai weakly. He wondered if the breeze and the hot lead inside him would combine to produce some strange new disease.

Kraft glanced around at the frightened men in front of him. "This journal club is over," he announced, and he stalked to the door and slammed it behind him.

During the next few minutes, Essai was hazily aware that some of the others spoke to him, though he could not remember what they said. He was concerned primarily about the leaden sensation in his body, convinced that he could never rise out of the chair again. His first clear recollection was the departure of the others, in single file, self-consciously bent, like members of an academic procession. Some time after that, the door opened and Essai protectively put up his arm. But the face was that of Steve Schachter. "Hey, Andy," he said brightly, "is the May issue of *Circulation* in here anywhere?"

Essai lowered his arm. He said nothing.

"Hey. What is it? Are you sick?" Schachter stepped toward him. "How did the window get broken?"

With an effort he shrugged. "Accident," he said.

"Andy, what is it?"

"Nothing. Listen, help me get up, will you?"

"Sure." Schachter smiled flippantly. "What is it? Did Matthew the Great nail you into it?" He saw the look on Essai's face and his eyes widened. "Oh," he grunted.

"Wait. I can do it." With the effort of a lifetime, Essai stood up. Arm extended for Schachter's help, should he need it, he took a step. He marveled at his own coordination. He took another. "Thanks, Steve. I can manage."

"Can I help?"

Essai smiled and shook his head. "No. I was fired just now. I'd like to be left alone."

"OK, Andy. I'll be in the resident's lounge if you want me for anything." Schachter gazed at him clinically for another moment, then abruptly disappeared.

Moments later, Essai walked slowly out the door and down the hall to his lab. Inside, he set the door ajar, but did not close it. A wave of nausea passed through him, and he felt sweat on his face, but he did not vomit. He began sorting out the papers in the top drawer of the desk next to his lab bench, not thinking about anything, throwing away some things, and keeping others. When he moved, or bent a little, he felt the cool sweaty shirt. After a few minutes he drank some cold water from a Pyrex beaker and felt a little better. The first rational thought that occurred to him was that Angela had been right. When he got home he would have to tell her that, he thought.

"Essai!" It was Kraft's voice, and Essai shivered. He did not answer but kept sorting his things.

"Essai, where the hell are you?"

"In here," he said. He moved to the door and opened it.

"In here," he repeated. Suddenly he remembered the last time Kraft had shouted his name while he sat in his lab, the day of Kraft's heart attack. Concerned, Essai looked into the hall. He heard Kraft's step and involuntarily walked back into his lab. On impulse, he set the door ajar again.

The door flew open and the knob smashed into the concrete wall. Kraft stood there, hand outstretched. "The key," he said.

"What?"

"The key. My key, to my reprint file, I believe I let you have it some time ago."

Essai felt in his pocket. "It's not in my pocket. It's in one of these drawers." His hand pointed futilely at his desk, as though saying that this was not the time for a search of his things.

"Find it," Kraft said. He crossed his arms and waited.

"All right." Essai had to turn his back to the gray-haired man, and as he bent down, he thought of how the scene looked: the pale man scrabbling about while his superior stood upright, waiting. Resentment flared and fell in an instant. The emotional fuel was exhausted. Nausea nudged him again, and Essai mumbled, "Excuse me," and sipped some water from the beaker. He would have given everything he possessed to find the key in his hand and turn it over to Kraft.

"It's not in here," he said hopelessly, closing the second drawer.

"Keep looking." Kraft's voice was quiet.

Essai had the sudden feeling that Kraft wanted conciliation. The part of him that would always compromise sent out a faint feeler. "It'll be a while till I get my things out of here," he said.

Kraft merely grunted. Then he lit a cigarette. Essai wondered if words would come with the first exhaled puff.

"I'm very surprised at you, Andrew, very surprised."

Essai nodded, and kept looking for the key, but now hoped it was well hidden somewhere. What had Kraft come to tell him?

"You know," Kraft said conversationally, "the night in Atlantic City when I heard you praise Pruden, drunk and shouting like that, I realized you wanted to do that fluorescent antibody work yourself."

Essai looked at him from his low position. "Yes, I did. Especially since it was my work."

"Hmmnh. Well, the only reason I gave it to Ed was because you had let the lab work slip." Kraft inhaled. "You guys today," he said, almost good-naturedly, "you think you can do only one thing at a time. So you were working on the ward and you let the lab go."

"Yes."

"Is that all? Just 'Yes'?"

Essai stared at him.

"Essai, I'll tell you something." Amazingly, Kraft closed the door completely and lowered his voice. "A long time ago in Cleveland, I had a run-in with my boss, a real bastard. I was doing better lab work than he had ever done, and he became unreasonable, furiously attacked me, and walked out. He never gave me a chance. Now," Kraft hesitated, then inhaled and went on, "now I think the Pruden thing is secondary to something else. I think your display in there just now is due to something else entirely."

"Maybe." Essai was thinking about what Nachsager had implied, that physicians who became godlike altered their whole lives, and somehow emerged as smaller and not bigger men. "Maybe," he repeated.

"I knew it," Kraft said. "Well, Essai, there's no question about what you saw that Saturday, I mean my wife out there with another man. I've been thinking it over. I appreciate that you kept it to yourself and didn't blab it around." Essai started to nod his head negatively, but Kraft raised his hand. "Hear me out. Having seen that, you can expect to take a few liberties around now. You know, leaving early or taking a long weekend. But today—that attack today—that was too much. Too far."

"Dr. Kraft."

"What?"

Essai stood up. "Dr. Kraft, I don't know how to say this."

"Not too far, Essai. I'll forget what I said in the library about firing you, but watch what you say. Watch it!"

The words flooded out, unfiltered. "I'll watch it. But mainly, I've watched you. And watching you I realize that if I have to give up my life to medicine—for medicine, as you did—it's not worth it. I'll go out and do something else."

"But Andrew, not every man's wife is unfaithful."

Essai stared at him. "I'm not talking about your wife. I'm talking about your life, how you live! I don't want it, the life you have."

"But—"

Essai interrupted him for the second time that day. "The issue is not your wife's dedication to you, or anything to do with her. It's your dedication to medicine. If dedication engenders this kind of misunderstanding about real things, real events, I don't want it. I'm glad to announce that I lack that dedication."

"I don't believe you," Kraft said flatly. "I gave you a chance to help me, after my heart attack, and within four months you were off somewhere when a sick patient died. You remember Mr. Budick? Well, I do, doc." The old resonance returned. "I realized that not only were you letting the lab work slide, and that forced me to give it to Pruden, but you couldn't even carry the clinical load without faltering. Oh yes, Essai, I came close to talking to Michler about really setting you up in this hospital, with this department. I was ready to 'ease up,' as they all told me, and hand you the reins. You know, I was spending time playing Scrabble with my wife?" Kraft shook his head wonderingly. "That's right. Until the morning when Budick died I was actually doing what they told me. But I didn't give it up," Kraft said triumphantly. "I held the reins and kept the lab going, and there was an ovation in Atlantic City."

"I heard it."

Suddenly, Kraft sighed deeply. "Can I sit on your chair?"

"Of course, here. Do you feel all right?" Essai was alarmed at how white Kraft had become.

Kraft sat down heavily. "Tough day." An astonished Essai saw him put his face in his hands and shake his head. He almost seemed to be acting, but his next phrase was grim and real. "I think I'm at the end of the line."

"What is it, Dr. Kraft? Are you having chest pain?"

Kraft shook his head negatively but kept his face hidden. "Not now, Andy. But I've been having angina, regularly, even at rest."

"At rest?"

Now Kraft looked up. "Can I trust you to keep a confidence?"

"Yes."

"I went to New York for my sabbatical in April, and was evaluated at Columbia. I have end-stage coronary disease. They told me straight out to change my life altogether or risk sudden death. Andy, I could have dropped over in there while were arguing."

Now Essai wanted to sit down. He leaned against his file cabinet. God, he could have been responsible for the man's death.

Kraft shook his head again, defeated. "It's funny, isn't it, that you say you don't want my kind of dedication, and that's all I want in the world and yet I know it will kill me."

"God," Essai whispered. They were silent. "But you've been working at your usual speed, even since you returned from New York."

"I know it, Andy. I'd rather be dead than take it easy."

Never had Essai felt so protective toward Kraft, not even the night of his heart attack. "Well, didn't they offer you anything in New York, any treatment, or . . ."

"Yes, they did." Kraft blinked. "But I don't want to burden you with it."

Nachsager, Atlantic City, Hazlitt: all were forgotten. "Oh please, please go ahead."

"Do you know anything about Armin Fermanian? A cardiac surgeon?"

"Yes. At Columbia. You once told me to read about transplants, and I came across his—Jesus! Is that it? A transplant?"

Kraft sat up straight. "I spent weeks with Fermanian. He has the technique down perfectly. I have confidence in him; I told him that after he had examined me."

"But—but, he hasn't done many human transplants has he?"

"Four. One patient is still alive."

Essai wiped his brow. "Excuse me for saying this, Dr. Kraft, but I think it's insane. Your chance of surviving that kind of operation would be far too low. I can't believe it's worth the risk."

Kraft fixed him levelly. "The risk is reduced considerably with the right donor. With a normal heart, that is."

"Of course," Essai said quickly, "but what normal person would give up his heart?"

"You."

"Me?" The pitch of the note was quavering, soprano.

"Yes." Kraft talked rapidly, rushing on to his "second" plan as he watched Essai's face. "You know I have the singular passion for medicine, and so I never think about dedication. With your heart I would have a fighting chance to survive the surgery, and if I did, essentially another lifetime added to what I can do now would be mine, to teach and do research and practice. Don't you see, Andy, that you don't have it, you don't feel about medicine as I do? But the whole world would know that you had given up your heart so I might continue. You would be more famous and loved than I.

"Now wait, Andy, before you say anything. I don't mean that Fermanian would remove your heart and transplant it into me, and that would be it. Not at all. I've investigated this thing exhaustively, and I tell you that a man of Fermanian's skill could do two transplants at once, from an accident victim or stroke victim to you, and your heart to me. You'd be very likely to survive, being so much younger. Really you would."

Essai sat down on the floor. A drifting, foglike quality had settled into his brain. A disembodied voice, his own, came out of it. "Why me? Why not get a heart from the stroke patient yourself?"

Kraft regarded the corpse-like figure sitting on the floor. It was the one question he could not answer without lying. How could he say he wanted a normal heart, and give Essai the risk of a contused or damaged one? Kraft mentally reached and found the only answer that would have satisfied him. "Because I want to give you the chance to become immortal. A man whose name the world will know. That's truly the reason. I couldn't offer more to my own son, Andy."

The fog thickened in him. Essai stood up and thought he would pass out, hoped he would. "I won't give you my heart because you are insane," his voice said, "and because I hate you too much."

Kraft stood too and tried to block the door, talking, but Essai pushed him roughly out of the way, and ran out of the laboratory away from him.

Jam Wah Lee drove Kraft home that afternoon, as usual. Kraft said nothing, wondering if Essai would say anything about what had happened. If he didn't, perhaps he could approach Lerner or Pruden in a month or two, but put the whole problem in a different light. Yes, there was still that possibility.

Ruth straightened up with the garden trowel in her hand when she heard the car. Matthew spoke to Jam Wah Lee, the car edged away, and her husband walked toward her. "Surprised to see you home, Ruth. Friend out of town this weekend?"

"I don't know," she said.

"Of course."

He went inside and looked over his mail, then called into the kitchen, "I'll be upstairs. Call me when supper is ready."

"All right," she said. She had made duckling with orange sauce, and she basted the bird listlessly. "Something is bothering him," she thought. "Since I'm only his wife, I'll never know." She looked out the window, where the sun had disappeared behind black clouds. Probably a thunderstorm. Her hopes of finishing up in the garden were dashed; she would have to find something else to do in the hour of daylight after supper.

"Everything's ready, Matt," she called up a few minutes later, and he came down for supper. A brief squall came and passed, and they ate on silently. When the phone rang, she wiped her mouth. "I'll get it."

"Like hell you will. If you're worried about that, have him call during the day."

"Matt. I just thought I'd answer it for you."

He was already halfway to the phone. It was a call for him, as she knew it would be. Chris had not called (he never had in five years, not once), and in the last month, neither had she. Ruth continued eating her duckling, grateful that the rain had passed so quickly—she could get outside again after all.

Matt came back smiling. "Guess who that was?"

"Who?"

"The personal aide to the governor of Connecticut," Matt announced. "The governor's son is a patient in the Hartford General, and they think he has rheumatic fever. They want me to see him."

"You're going?"

Matt talked with his mouth full. "Of course. I can make Hartford in an hour and a half by the turnpike. I wonder how the governor heard about me?"

"I don't know," she said. Then she smiled. "Good doctors get known," she said simply.

Matt nodded. "By the way, I fired Essai today."

"You did?"

"Yes, I did." He wiped his full lips with a napkin. "Now there is a good example of what's happening in medicine today."

"Yes?"

Matt sat back and lit a cigarette. "Think a minute. He's no more than thirty or thirty-one, and not much above average. I pay him twelve thousand a year, make him assistant professor, and support him when he gives lectures elsewhere. I actually set up talks for him. Through me he meets most of the good academic men in the country. I give him a good lab, all the clinical stuff he wants. Then suddenly he becomes the prima donna, and blows his top because another man reads a nice paper in Atlantic City. Today, to top it off, he starts criticizing some of my old papers, saying I left out some patients who did poorly. I'll admit I lost my temper on that."

"Did you fire him then?"

"Not really. I was angry, all right. But I went into his lab later, and as much as told him, 'Essai, you can have a good deal of freedom here, but this is a team enterprise, not a stage for prima donnas.' You know what he did? He stands up and says, 'I resign.'" Kraft mimicked him. "'I resign.' Well, I moved a step faster than he did. I let him know that he was through."

She thought of Essai sleeping in Matt's hospital room the night of his heart attack. "What will he do?" she asked.

He stabbed a piece of stray meat, then shrugged. "I don't know," he said with his mouth full, "but he won't be doing it in Boston. Or Hartford or New Haven or New York either."

"I see. Well, I hope it doesn't rain on your drive to Hartford." She wondered what the real story was.

"Better go," he said, standing. She got his raincoat which he waved away. "It's stopped. I'll be home late. Three hours driving, and an hour there. Better figure midnight."

"All right." She watched him pat his pocket to make sure the stethoscope was there.

"All set," he said. He kissed her rapidly on the cheek. "'Bye."

"Good-bye, Matt." She walked him to the front door, and he went out to the garage and backed out the Olds, then drove down the wet street without looking back.

It was seven ten. "I have five hours," she thought. "Then a night without touching, another day alone, then another night." She bit the edge of her finger. "Wonder if it's too wet to work in the garden?" She went outside but the ground was muddy near the rosebushes. The smells of rain and late spring were in the air, and she stood preoccupied in the back yard, listening to the wind in the pine trees and watching the red sun fall. At dusk, she went inside. "Somewhere," she said to herself, "springtime lovers are meeting." She did the dishes, cleaned the kitchen, then went upstairs to her room. A few minutes later she stood naked in the bathroom, shower water pouring steamily into the bathtub. She looked at herself in the full-length mirror. The spring feeling welled up in her, and the steam thickened without. She watched her form grow indistinct in the mirror. "I'm losing my shape," she said girlishly, and with the steam rising about her she carried out the appropriate movements leading to discovery, friction, rise, sigh, shudder, and loosening efflux. Not ten minutes later she stepped into the hot shower with subsiding delight.

"Cough."

The feverish boy coughed.

"Again. Cough again."

He did so.

"Once more."

"No, please," he whined.

Matthew Kraft took the stethoscope from his ears. "Jimmy, I'm trying to help find out what's wrong with you. Now just once more. Now. Good. Now you can lie back."

"Is it bad?"

"No." Dr. Kraft smiled at the boy. "It's what we used to call walking pneumonia. I'll have them give you some medicine and you'll be up in five days."

"You mean I don't have that thing in the heart?" The twelve-year-old watched him carefully.

"Rheumatic fever? No, you don't. I'll look at your chest X-ray, but I'm sure you have walking pneumonia. Now I will tell your father that."

"Thank you," the boy said. "You know my father is the governor," he said proudly.

"I know," said the doctor. "But I know more about pneumonia."

He went outside the boy's room, and down to the small room near the nurses' desk. He had made the parents wait there, stating his old rule to them: "The doctor and the patient in the same room during the examination. No one else." The governor, a handsome man of fifty, had nodded in assent. Now he stood anxiously.

"Well?"

"Jimmy does not have rheumatic fever. He has a minor form of pneumonia, and after we give him some antibiotics, he will rapidly improve."

Mrs. Fullerton took her husband's arm. "Thank God."

"Are you sure?"

Kraft smiled. Then he motioned to the visitors' room where several reporters stood. "Governor Fullerton," he said, "you know how to handle these men. I know how to handle this," he added, tapping the earpiece of his stethoscope.

"But Dr. Johnson thought it might be rheumatic fever. He's been our doctor for a good many years, Dr. Kraft."

"And a fine one," Kraft said. "I sent him to get the X-ray. If you want, I'll show you the patches of pneumonia."

"No, no," the governor said quickly. "Dr. Johnson had great faith in you, and that's why he wanted to call you. We have the same faith."

Kraft nodded and went to write his note in the chart. When the elegantly dressed physician came up to the desk with the X-ray, Kraft rose and looked at it against the light from a simple lamp. "There it is," he said, "right middle lobe. Gus, do you believe me now?"

Dr. Johnson shook his head. "Matt, I listened for ten minutes and didn't hear the râles of pneumonia."

"Did you listen in front, Gus?"

"I don't know, Matt, I thought I'd hear something in back. I listened in front as well, of course." Dr. Johnson comfortingly rubbed his gold-plated stethoscope.

"Come with me," said Kraft. They walked into Jimmy's room, and Kraft again asked the governor to leave. "Jimmy, it's what I said, the old walking pneumonia. Can I show Dr. Johnson something?"

"Sure."

Kraft listened for a moment, then nodded. "Now, Gus, you listen here."

Augustus Johnson listened for a second or two. "Yes," he said.

"Not there. You were over the sternum. Here." With his pen Kraft made a tiny "X" on the boy's chest.

Johnson stared at him, then bent and listened. This time he listened longer. "Cough," he said to the boy. Then he straightened up. "Right, Matt. God, you never miss them, do you?"

They walked out together. "Not very often," said Kraft. "Now do me a favor and explain it to the governor. And tell his cops not to arrest me if I go five miles over the speed limit on the way home."

The relieved parents watched the two grinning doctors from afar. "Old Gus looks better than he did half an hour ago," the governor said to his wife. "He certainly knows whom to ask for help."

The rain had started again, steadily this time. Matthew Kraft drove slowly, not so much because of the rain, but because he had no reason to hurry home. "Maybe I ought to stop in at the Mass. Medical just to check up on things," he thought. He played the radio for a while, because everywhere his thoughts turned—home with his unfaithful wife, the hospital and Essai, even the old days in Magnolia and Paul Heinrichs' senility—his mood became one of uneasiness.

After listening to the music for a few minutes, he switched off the radio. No use wearing down the batteries. To pass the time, he counted the movement of the windshield wipers against the glass, but he became sleepy and stopped counting. Then he tried to recall all the kinds of pneumonia he had ever seen. For each type he thought of several cases, relishing the ease with which he remembered them. The miles passed, though the rain continued. He drove to the end of the Massachusetts Turnpike, turned left onto Kneeland Street, and drove the mile and a half to the medical center.

They were enlarging the doctors' parking lot, and the usual entrance was closed. Goddamnit, he wished Lee were driving so he could get out and let Lee negotiate the other entrance. Irritated, he backed up and drove to the thin blacktopped entrance was closed. Goddamnit, he wished Lee were driving either side of it. A chain was stretched between two wooden barricades. The blacktop must be new and soft.

"Goddamnit, that's my parking lot," Kraft said aloud. He looked at the mud. "It can't be deep," he thought. He stepped on the accelerator, turned sharply left, and went ten feet or so before he felt the tires slipping in the mud. He hit the accelerator with his foot, but the car inched ahead, whining as it sprayed mud into the street behind. He shifted into reverse, floored it, and heard the bump as his rear fender hit the wooden barricade. Furious, he shifted into low and tried to move forward. The tires whined uselessly. He was stuck.

"Son-of-a-bitch." He opened the door and got out, his foot sinking three or four inches. Christ, it wasn't that deep. It could be pushed out easily.

He looked at the emergency entrance. Steve Schachter was standing in his hospital whites with Dr. Applegate, the pathologist. Both of them were watching Kraft, and Schachter was laughing.

"Schachter, give me a hand, goddamnit," Kraft yelled at him.

The resident said something to Jennifer Applegate and walked gingerly down the wet ambulance entrance. "Should I try to move it, Dr. Kraft?"

"Give it a push. I'll get in and floor it."

Schachter looked at his whites. "No, I'll get sprayed. Let me try to push it."

"Go ahead."

Dutifully, Schachter pushed once, then again. The car moved about a foot, then rolled back each time. "Just a little more and I can get it," he said.

"Wait, I'll get on this side and push."

"Are you sure you want to do that?" Schachter looked at the heart patient anxiously.

"Listen, analyst, I'm not a cripple yet. Now push on three." He counted and they pushed and almost got the car rolling. As it rolled back, Kraft said to Schachter, "One more and it's out." He took a deep breath and they pushed as hard as they could.

Like a dropping stone, accelerating its fall at a certain rate after beginning slowly, Kraft felt an uneasy tightness across his chest, and before the ache began, he knew it for what it was. The pain expanded and swelled into the crushing agony of a heart attack. Kraft reached for the stethoscope in his right-hand jacket pocket, and grunted the single word, "Steve." The pain consumed him and became the eye-rolling convulsion of cardiac standstill. Kraft reflexly clutched the stethoscope and pitched face down into the mud.

He had taught every doctor and medical student at the Eastern Massachusetts Medical Center where and how to apply presure to the chest for external cardiac massage, and had lectured them, "If you witness an arrest, don't think, but beat on the patient's chest and get help." Steve Schachter was pushing the car with all his strength, heard the grunt from Kraft as the pushing force on the other side let go, and stood in terror as he saw the man fall into the mud. He shouted, "No! No!" and felt the impact in his feet as Kraft hit the ground. Jennifer Applegate shouted something at him, and he took a step, unable to do anything for a moment. Then he went quickly and bent down in the mud next to Kraft, whose eyes were rolled up. There was no pulse.

Schachter dragged the still form a foot or so away from the car, and turned the body flat on its back. He opened the coat and hit Kraft in the chest with both his fists, just to the left of the midline of the chest.

He felt for the pulse, and one or two beats crossed his trembling finger, but then there was nothing. He hit the chest again and started pressing rhythmically with the heel of his left hand on the back of his right hand over the heart. He thought he felt a rib crack, but kept pressing and shouted again. Kraft opened his eyes slightly as an attendant, the emergency room nurse, and Dr. Applegate rushed up. The mouth opened and groaned, and Kraft tried to say something. Schachter could not make out the moaning words, and kept applying cardiac message. Dr. Applegate knelt in the mud in her new spring coat, and listened to the hoarse words.

"What is it?" Schachter hissed.

She looked up. "It's a name. Fermanian."

Kraft opened his eyes at the sound of the word. "Yes, Fermanian," he moaned, losing consciousness again. "Get Fermanian."

Every sign pointed to death within one or two days from shock and heart failure. Fermanian was reached at home in Queens and took a night flight to Boston, but he said to Winston over the phone that it sounded hopeless, with or without a transplant. Ruth Kraft spent an hour in the treatment room, but Matt was not conscious, and she went out again and waited in the huge waiting room off the emergency wing with relatives of other patients.

Andrew Essai was called by Steve Schachter at Angela's apartment and trotted the two miles in to the hospital. As he ran through the soft rain, the request of Kraft this afternoon before raced in and out of his mind. "He wanted my heart and I told him he was insane and I hated him," he thought. After the journal meeting, Essai had gone from the hospital hoping never to see it or Kraft again. But the vertigo of doubt spun him. If Kraft's plea were justifiable in any terms, Essai was responsible for Kraft's fate. All evening he had failed to quiet himself, first during the angry hours in his own apartment, where he tried to balance his love and hate for Kraft, and finally with Angela, who came with Alix when his failure to call or come to her announced the failure of his challenge to Kraft at the journal club.

With her loving help, he finally calmed down enough to eat something. His doubt ebbed with her. They opened a bottle of wine and his mood rose; Angela saw him happy and confident. They were watching the late movie on television, *Breathless*, one of Angela's favorites, and Essai was swaggering like Belmondo when Schachter called. Gaiety dissipated like desert rain. Angela stood at the door and made him stop and listen to her. "Andy, don't let yourself feel you are responsible for him, or what happened. Because that feeling is false. Please, Andy." His face was pale but he seemed to listen.

But Angela was not with him that night in the hospital,

Kraft's hospital. George Winston showed him Kraft's cardiogram, and Essai could barely focus on the strip. "The whole anterior wall of the heart is involved," Winston said to him.

"George, my whole heart is involved."

"Of course, Andy, we all feel the same way."

Essai smiled tightly and Winston stared at him but there was no time to talk about it. The anesthetist reported he could not maintain Kraft's blood pressure without pressor drugs given intravenously. The nurse said he had put out no urine. Continuous electrical pacing was required to keep the shattered heart pumping.

Essai went up to the dark lab, and then into the journal club library. The broken window had not yet been replaced; Essai remembered the congealed face of Kraft as he threw the ashtray past him. He sat down in the same chair and tried to relax, but grainy fatigue and anxiety held him. At three or so he walked downstairs and found Ruth Kraft. She and Winston were waiting for Fermanian to arrive. Essai asked to talk to her and the nurses let them use a vacant minor surgical suite.

"Mrs. Kraft, this afternoon, as I guess you know, your husband approached me about being a donor of a heart for him."

"What? He did that?" Her eyes opened wide. So that was the real story; not that Essai had been challenging and impudent, but that Matt believed he had the right to ask this of another person. She shook her head and wept for the fact of Matt's inhuman pride, and her own failure to reach him.

"Please don't cry," Andy said to her. "Listen to me." So she listened, and he rushed ahead with the emotional and nearly incoherent story of his relationship with Matthew Kraft.

Years later she would still recall parts of it. "He is a great man," Essai said. "Those of us close to him recognize the greatness, perhaps better than anyone, but we also see him as a monster, a self-serving son-of-a-bitch. Is that a result of greatness or an ingredient of it? I don't know. But we're basically all pawns, even those of us picked as protegés.

Maybe we stay only to learn the secret of greatness and become great ourselves." Essai laughed bitterly. "All I learned was the extent of his ego. He had ego enough to ask me to commit a suicidal act, to donate my heart to him. The monstrous part was not in asking, but in assuming that I would see the logic of it since we both knew he is great and I am mediocre. He victimized me, and I guess I let him." Essai stood and clenched his fists. "And that close to his greatness, I actually considered his crazy request. But your face tells me, and my deepest feeling does too, that it is crazy, and I will not accede." Essai's agitated voice broke. "Help me see that," he begged.

She rose and took his clenched hand in hers. "Dr. Fermanian, the heart surgeon, is on his way from New York. He will be here soon." She saw the terror in Essai's face. She then said the right thing without thinking. "If you care for my husband, for me, for all of us, please go home now."

"No, I don't think—"

"Your deepest feeling is right. The great man's request is crazy." A sad and soft smile opened her face. She kissed him on the cheek. "Please, Andy. Please go home now."

"May I go?"

"Yes," she said. "And thank you."

He left the hospital and walked. Only the raindrops heard his quiet voice. "Ruth must be right. She has that gift of knowing what's right. I must believe her. But what if she's not? What if my decision stands between Kraft and death? The presidential bodyguard in front of the bullet. 'I could die for you,' people say. Could I die for him? So he could live? No. I've decided I cannot. He's a great man and a heartless bastard. Perhaps all great men are. He needs my heart in more ways than one. Will I give it to him? I will not. I will not."

He pressed his lips tight, but the thoughts sounded intermittently in his mind like receding thunder. He walked for an hour or two then he went back to his old bachelor apartment. From there he called Angela and said he wanted to be alone for a few days, and she said, "all right. Call me when you want to."

He found some scotch and drank nearly all of it and fell asleep sometime after dawn.

That night Fermanian was to obtain consent from James Saunders for his brother Alf's heart to be removed from the body at the time of his death. Alf Saunders had spent most of the day and all that evening drinking coffee in the Hayes-Bickford cafeteria near the Public Garden, taking green methedrine tablets to try to get and stay high, and fight off sleep. Shortly after the night he had seen Andrew Essai in the Public Garden, he had begun to think that Margot had a boyfriend in the rackets in Boston, and that the whole gang was after him. They had learned his whereabouts by intimidating his psychiatrist (the U boat captain), and every glance from inside a passing car, every look from a diner in the cafeteria was another sign that they were out to kill him. He must stay awake to fight them off, as he had stayed awake for three days and nights, swallowing the pills to keep cool and ready.

He called Jim's apartment to tell him again about the men after him. Jim had heard it too often before, and now, tired out by the demands of his sick, psychotic brother, had said, "I can't help you, Alf. Go to the emergency room of the Mass. Mental Health and ask to be admitted."

"Fair brother, the Mafioso know I'll go there; they're in cars all over Boston waiting for me to cross a street."

"Alf. You're sick. I tell you, go over to the hospital."

"No, I can't. What's Margot's number? She unlisted it and moved. I know you know, dear brother. Help me Jim; this heartless world is too much for me."

Jim looked at his watch—nearly three. "All right, for Christ's sake. Take a cab over here. You can stay here tonight." He hung up before Alf could tell him that he didn't have the money for a cab. The M.T.A. was closed. If he walked a block they would mow him down.

He stayed in the cafeteria till the manager told the night cop in for coffee that a patron was acting strangely. The policeman walked toward Alf who threw a coffee cup at him and ran out. There was no refuge. Every car had hooded men with with weapons, waiting for him. He raced down Charles Street with the methedrine and sleeplessness driving him. "Driven like the fearful snow," he thought. He ran all the way to the Mass. Avenue Bridge and knew if he stopped, even for an instant, he would be dead.

He began to cross the bridge, shouting happy words to stop thinking about the hooded cars. Nearly to the other side, he watched a police cruiser coming toward him. How clever; Margot's men had painted it up to look authentic. "Terrific, marvelous," he screamed. Alf could not outrun the car, or turn around. He inhaled the rainy air in deep gasps, sprinted for his life, glimpsed his mother's face, and without losing stride, leaped screaming over the bridge and down to the soft concrete to meet her.

The police ambulance took him to the Eastern Massachusetts Medical Center, and the neurosurgeon on call examined the comatose young man, contacted a brother in Cambridge, and received permission to put burr holes into the crushed skull and try to relieve pressure from the bleeding within. Spontaneous breathing ceased on the operating table and artificial ventilation was given. The patient's pupils were dilated and fixed, and though his heart beat on, an encephalogram showed that there were no brain waves. The neurosurgeon was set to tell the oxygen therapist to stop the ventilation, but a scrub nurse whispered that Dr. Kraft was a patient in the intensive care unit with a severe heart attack, and Dr. Fermanian was considering a heart transplant. The neurosurgeon called Fermanian, and both of them spoke to Jim Saunders, Alf's closest relative. When he realized that his brother was legally dead except for a pumping heart, the grieving brother gave permission. Ruth Kraft was brought in at her request to meet the brother of the donor, and said simply "thank you and God bless you, and bless his soul," and went out of the room and gave her consent for the operation.

An hour later, Armin Fermanian's calm hand sliced a Bard-Parker scalpel through Matthew Kraft's chest. "It is technically simple," Fermanian thought. It was always the thought he had when he made an incision, no matter how trivial the operation. Even for a gallbladder or appendix removal he thought it, almost said it aloud as an invocation. He was a master surgeon and knew it, and after that first slice and the prayerful phrase, he went about his work. In this case, he proceeded to split the sternum, reflect the left pleura, gently retract the left lung, and clamp off the aorta and vena cava, as well as the vessels to and from both lungs. During this two-hour period, the chief of surgery at the Eastern Massachusetts Medical Center was doing exactly the same thing in the adjoining operating room, preparing the heart of Alfred Saunders in the same way.

"How's the pressure?" Fermanian asked the anesthetist. The man at the head of the table, Malatesta, nodded in assent. "Ninety over fifty," he said.

"Pump all right?" he asked the second assistant. This surgeon, an excellent man in his own right but on this occasion just another skilled pair of hands, nodded as well. He glanced at the coils of the bypass pump, which took blood from the patient's leg veins, oxygenated it, and pulsed it through a polyethylene tube into the arteries of the neck. "Running fine," he reported.

Fermanian sighed. "All right. Here we go." He pressed a pedal with his foot and turned toward the wall microphone six feet away. "Bring the heart in now, please," he said.

In the next room, where a bypass pump was not needed since life was not to be maintained, the surgeon applied clamps firmly above and below the heart, made two clean cuts, and lifted Alf Saunders' heart out of the chest. Warm saline washed it free of blood, and the surgeon weighed it, placed it in a bag containing warm buffer, and carried it into the next room. The surgical supervisor noted the time as six eighteen A.M. on the anesthesia chart and the anesthetist made an asterisk, writing at the bottom, "Heart removed and donor patient pronounced dead at this time. Operation concluded. Chest closed. Body to morgue."

Armin Fermanian heard the door open behind him, and

looked at the surgeon. "Set it here," he said, motioning to a draped table at his side. Then he bent over, sliced open the pericardium lining Kraft's heart, cut at the point of every clamp, and within forty seconds lifted out the enlarged heart. He put it in a pan and it was covered and taken out. Fermanian checked with the anesthetist again, looked briefly at the bypass coils, and seated the new heart in the pericardium. Working without haste and in silence, save for the click of hemostats and sigh of the suture material pulled through vessel walls, he and his first assistant approximated and sewed aorta to aorta, vein to vein. The aortic clamp was removed; the suture line was tight. The clamps to lung vessels were removed. Then the vena cava clamp was removed. Fermanian felt the heart fill with venous blood, needing only a beat to send it out to the lungs for oxygen. He asked for the two shocking paddles and placed them on either side of the heart. He held a paddle in each fist. "Let's try first at two hundred," he said.

"Set at two hundred," a voice said.

Fermanian bit down on the edge of his lip. He sniffed. "Now!"

The electric shock coursed through the heart and it beat twice in rapid succession, then slowly and regularly. George Winston's voice said, "Nodal rhythm. Still nodal. Rate fifty-two. Now fifty-eight. Now it's sinus, normal sinus rhythm. At sixty-eight. At sixty-six. Normal rhythm at sixty-six to seventy-two, or so." He straightened up a little and waited at the cardiac monitor at the far end of the operating room, one hand under the surgical mask on his chin. "Looks good," he said after a few minutes.

Fermanian closed the pericardium, reset lung, pleura, sternum, and sewed muscle, fascia and skin. Six hours after they had begun, it was over. The surgeon checked the blood pressure himself, and shook hands with Malatesta and thanked his assistants, the other surgical team, the scrub nurses, Winston, surgical supervisors, blood bank technicians, X-ray people, and the bacteriologist who had taken cultures of blood, equipment, the bypass pump, and even a swab of the donated heart muscle. Then Fermanian left the surgical suite and went to the scrub room. He peeled off his mask and reflexly washed his hands for five minutes. He looked at himself in the mirror. "That was the easy part," he said quietly to his image. "Now for the complicated part."

Essai awoke at nine after two hours of sleep. For a moment he wondered what day it was and why he was sleeping here instead of with Angela. That thoughtless moment passed, and he wrinkled up his face and forehead like an unburped infant. He decided to stay home and sleep. After an hour of trying not to think, he got up. Unshaven and exhausted, he pulled on a pair of wrinkled khaki pants lying in the closet, a faded unironed blue shirt, and his navy-surplus pea jacket. His shoes were scuffed and spattered by mud. He remembered running to the hospital last night, running and then walking slowly home.

He put on socks and shoes, and went into his unused kitchen to check the refrigerator for juice. Nothing but one shriveled orange on a shelf. He bit the end and tried to suck out the juice. After one or two grudging drops, he threw the orange out and left the apartment. At the Paramount Cafeteria he ordered coffee and orange juice, and a honey-dip donut. He sat in the small booth waiting for his order, and looked to the counter to ask the waitress for two donuts.

He saw the *Record-American* tabloid headlines:

HUB DOCTOR GETS HEART
TRANSPLANT: "CRITICAL"

The first thing he did was to feel his pulse. Then he stood up and left the Paramount. He crossed to the Gary Drugstore and bought a *Record-American* and a *Globe*. The *Globe* had three pictures; one of Kraft, taken ten or fifteen years ago, one of Fermanian, and a college graduation picture of Alf Saunders. Essai blinked rapidly. He felt as though his brain were slowly filling up with sand. He read about Saunders' suicide, his brother's consent, the operation, the patient's critical state.

Essai went outside and crossed Mount Vernon Street very carefully, looking both ways. He walked slowly to the Nines, already open and populated by half a dozen daytime drinkers. There was little conversation, none of it about Saunders. Essai ordered a screwdriver and drank it down, then another. Five minutes later he got a third. He picked it up, stared at it, and murmured quietly, "Here's to you, Alf." He drank part of it, set it down, put down some money, and left. He walked along Charles Street like a man on eggs, and looked both ways at every corner. When he got to his apartment, he was too tired to go up three flights, he thought, and so he sat on the floor in the hall. The papers were still under his arm. He looked again at the headlines, but in the bad light he was not sure it was not all a dream. He lurched up and took the stairs with set jaw, unlocked his apartment door and went in, and fell asleep on the living room floor.

Matthew Kraft's eyelids fluttered against the light. He awoke. Carolyn Reiss was pouring urine out of a calibrated plastic container into a culture tube. "When did I start to pass normal urine again?" he asked.

The sixth-floor head nurse turned. "Yesterday, Dr. Kraft."

"Have I been asleep since then?"

"Yes. The sedation, I think."

"How's the pulse."

"Good," she said. Then she came to the side of the bed. Except for his voice, which was a thin and quiet echo of itself, he was absolutely unchanged. "You don't believe me, do you?" she said.

"I guess so, Carolyn."

She took a stethoscope from a sterile bag with gloved hands. "These precautions are really too much," she said mildly. She put the earpiece in Kraft's ears. "Ready?" she asked.

Her patient nodded. She put the bell at the edge of the bandage on his chest. She watched him close his eyes and listen. Then he opened them and she took off the earpieces.

"About eighty a minute, and regular," he announced. "Right?"

His nurse nodded. "Right."

A small grin appeared and it grew and grew on Kraft's face. "Son-of-a-bitch. The fourth day, today, right?"

"Fifth. You slept away a whole day."

"Pretty lazy patient, aren't I."

Now she smiled. "Stay lazy, Dr. Kraft. I have to go out to drop off this stethoscope; then I'll be back."

He closed his eyes, still smiling. She waited, then walked quickly out of the room. She went to the nurses' station of the intensive care unit and called Dr. Winston at the Metropolitan. When he answered, she said quietly, "He's awake. Putting out urine fine. But the fever is 101— 100.4 this morning, and 100.6 at noon."

"Do you have the chart there?"

"Yes."

"Read me Dr. Schwartz' note," Winston said.

She read it to him. " 'Preliminary tissue compatibility studies on donor (A.S.) and recipient (M.K.) show moderate discordance. Chance of tissue rejection by recipient thus high enough to warrant massive cortisone and Imuran therapy.' That's it, Dr. Winston."

There was silence for a second. "I'm coming over there now, Miss Reiss. Please have Dr. Schwartz and Fermanian meet me in the doctors' room at the ICU."

She put down the phone and closed the chart, holding it against her gown. Damnit, she had broken technique again; now she'd have to get another sterile gown. She hugged the chart closer to her. She usually took her vacation in May, and had planned a trip to Hawaii, to meet someone before her third decade ran out. Instead of that trip, she now spent sixteen hours a day with Dr. Kraft, and would have worked around the clock if they had let her. "All right, you sentimental bitch," she thought to herself, "get into a clean gown and see if he'll take some broth."

"I *know* the chance of rejection is high," Fermanian bellowed. "We knew it was high when we went ahead. Don't keep telling me the same thing."

Billie S. Schwartz rubbed his freckled hands. "I'm just saying," he began plaintively, "that the cortisone and Imuran dose must be raised, or according to my tests the recipient will form antibodies against the donor tissues. The fever of today suggests it's starting already."

George Winston sighed. "But cortisone in high doses will set him up for an infection. His white count is falling already. Without white cells or antibodies," Winston hestitated, "well I don't know what to do. I called Harris in Denver today, and he agrees we're caught between the two, rejection and infection, and to treat preventively for the first invites the second."

"Now, wait," said Dr. Schwartz. "I'm consulting on this problem. Please don't call other experts without first asking me."

"Well, Billie," Winston said, "we'd like to get all the help we can."

"I know, but—"

"But, but, but," said Fermanian, walking over to the freckled doctor. "But you're the quintessential lab man, aren't you? They deliver some tissue and serum to you, and you write fine notes in the chart suggesting possibilities."

"Now, Armin, please," Winston said soothingly.

"All right, Billie, we all know the theory. We have to decide whether to raise the cortisone and Imuran. If we do, the infectious disease people predict Kraft's death within a week from some infection no antibiotics can control."

"That's right," Schwartz said.

"OK." Fermanian opened his arms. "Stop telling us theories, and tell us what to do. Don't tell us what is 'warranted' or 'indicated.' What should we do? Should George and I write the order to have Miss Reiss give him more cortisone? Tell us, yes or no."

"It's not that easy, Dr. Fermanian."

"Thank you," Fermanian said, smiling sweetly. He turned to Winston. "George, yes or no?"

"Yes."

"Me too. I think we have to raise his medication. Better go ahead." Fermanian sat down and doodled on the desktop with a pen. He looked up to see the freckled research man staring at him. "Sorry, Billie, if I was rough," Fermanian said. "But the science you know is not the medicine we must practice."

"Yes," they heard Winston on the phone, "a hundred of cortisone now I.M., and a hundred every four hours. Thanks, Miss Reiss."

For the next six days, Kraft had no fever, gained some strength, and ate well. Ruth visited every day, and read him some of the telegrams. Fermanian went back to New York, ready at any time to come back if needed. Lerner and Pruden came to visit, the latter as though to a shrine. Since Kraft was not to be disturbed by any news about the department, no one mentioned that Essai had been absent without explanation since the night of the transplant. Winston called Essai's "home" phone number and spoke to Angela Lynne. She said she had heard he was still in Boston, taking a few days off. She did not say that one of her girlfriends had seen him, bearded and pale, eating tomato soup in the Paramount.

Essai was tired of drinking, sleeping, and watching television, although the latter, by its depersonalization of the news, had kept him informed of Kraft's progress and helped him regard it as almost another news event. On the ninth day, he called Judy Lemonning in her New York apartment, and took a train from the decayed South Station to see her. Angela was too close to everything to help him, he thought.

The first evening with Lemonning was a sexual feast, and the starved man took his delights brutally, much to the designer's pleasure. Whatever had aged and brutalized him made him sexually attractive to her, and the first recall of the old issues did not arise for a day. He shunted aside all questions of

Kraft and his career. Lemonning told him about the design world in New York, and he smiled to hear her talk of personality clashes, significant issues, meaningful commitments. All the empty talk helped keep his mind clear, as did the Valpolicella.

The second day with her, she began to explain to him how his decision to let her father help him start a clinic in New Jersey would be the start of a "terribly exciting" life for both of them. He retorted that he had decided nothing, didn't want private practice, and had entered medicine to escape the trap of a father-in-law and his financial intentions. She said, "Andy, you're a reflex socialist." He said, "Squeeze, you're a deathless phrasemaker." They picked their weapons. Six hours later, after a furious emotional and physical brawl, abetted by the liquor he drank, he took a bus back to Boston and Judy called her friend to say the coast was clear and he could now return, as her cousin had gone back to Harvard Business School.

Angela prayed for Andy and waited for him.

The eleventh day after the transplant, Kraft coughed up some blood-tinged sputum. He made light of it to Ruth, who was sitting in gown and mask with him when it happened. After she left, Carolyn took his temperature, and he said, "Tell Winston to change the antibiotics." That night he had a shaking chill and fever of 103. The next day they had planned to let him dangle his legs over the edge of the bed, and he did so, saying between coughs that the strength was returning to his legs. George Winston called Dalton, the best infectious disease man in the country, to describe the patch of pneumonia on X-ray, rising fever, and negative cultures. Dalton said, "It sounds like a virus. Probably one uncovered by all the drugs you have to give him. If I'm right, the infection can't be checked by antibiotics." Winston told Mrs. Kraft and suggested she stay in the hospital that night.

The next day he was a little better. A pervasive weakness had spread through him, but his heart function was normal, and he said to Carolyn Reiss, "I'm improving. Soon I'll be making rounds on my patients again." The nurse nodded her head approvingly. "By the way," she said, "a man named Chester Cornelius waits every day to see you, but we tell him you can't have visitors."

"Who?"

"Chester Cornelius. He's a janitor at the Metropolitan Hospital."

"Of course." Kraft coughed. "Please let him come in. He can put on a gown and mask."

"All right. I'll just make sure it's all right with Dr. Winston."

He looked up at her. "Have him come in now, Carolyn." He coughed, but did not look away from her.

"Yes, Dr. Kraft."

She stayed in the room while the alcoholic janitor, fortified or "sterilized," as he put it to Kraft, talked with the great doctor for whom he prepared the Finch Conference Room each Thursday.

"Who's sitting in the big blue chair now, Chester?"

"No one, sir. They've stopped the meetings till you're better. I'm sure we'll see you back there real soon."

Kraft nodded and coughed. Then he asked the nurse to leave for a moment, and the two men talked alone for a minute or two. Cornelius came out of the room very pale and silent.

Sunday night he had fever of 106. Ruth Kraft stayed all night, Fermanian arrived and they began two experimental antibiotics. Toward dawn Kraft became delirious, and Ruth, George Winston, and Fermanian sat in sterile gowns around the bed as the feverish patient shouted intermittently. "God-damnit, I want this journal club to start on time. Miss Graf, get those boys in here on time or they can go elsewhere to play doctors. Listen at this spot for the murmur. That's right, you can't miss it here." Much else was uninterpretable, though Ruth felt sure he mentioned Paul Heinrichs once or twice.

Monday morning he had one lucid interval. Miss Reiss let Ruth stay in the room alone. Matt insisted on dangling his legs. His bright eyes held hers. "Ruth, I'm getting stronger. Here. Feel how regular my pulse is. Go ahead." She felt it and said she knew he was right. "Of course," he said.

He died just before eleven.

Of all the responses to Mathew Kraft's death, none was as unusual on the surface or so meaningful within as that of Chester Cornelius. He was watching the evening news, drinking his fourth beer, when the bulletin was broadcast.

"Mary, it's him. Dr. Kraft is dead."

"Is he at the Metropolitan?"

"Shhh." He listened to the report.

"That's him, Kraft," he said. He knew he had a job to do.

"We'll all be dead soon enough," his wife said with finality.

"Shut up, Mary," he snarled. He stood up and walked around the flat for half an hour. He wanted a drink terribly but resolved to think the thing out and do it before getting one. At last he had his plan. From the faded barracks bag behind the furnace, he got out the leather-sheathed knife he had picked up in a Tokyo store in 1946, and put it inside his shirt. "I'm going to get a paper," he called to his wife, and for three blocks he stayed on the route to the store, then walked quickly down Cambridge Street, and over to the Metropolitan.

He had the master key, a key he had made after borrowing the original, though he remembered forthrightly that till tonight he had never used it. He went through the delivery entrance, with the cool leather brushing his chest. He had his excuse ready, "I left my keys up on White Two." But he had on his work shirt, and no one gave him a second glance. Up two flights of stairs, he walked to the utility room, where he had gone every Thursday to get Kraft's chair. One lip-licking look around, and he unlocked the door with his master key and went in.

He strode to the blue chair, touched its leather for a moment, but decided not to sit down in it. "Dr. Kraft, you were the last one to use it," he said tearfully, and he unsheathed the thin knife and cut the chair from top to bottom. He took off the leather in strips and cut the strips in squares, piling the stuffing and squares in one corner of the room. The seat and legs were cut up the same way, and the wood frame underneath was smashed with his foot, tramping down with his work shoe on the diagonally held pieces. When he was finished, he carried the stuffing and wood to the incinerator, then did the same with the leather. Ready to leave, he spotted innumerable small pieces of yellow paper, which had fallen out of the stuffing of the seat. Some of them said, "You are doomed to mediocrity—H. Lippschitz," written in faded ink. Most of them were initials: "YADTM-L." and "dtm." Chester Cornelius scratched his head, then gathered them all up, hundreds of them, and burned them.

Then he checked the utility room, sheathed his knife, and left. Not five minutes later he was in O'Keefe's, watching Red pour his double and his beer. He held up the whiskey, mumbled, "They'll never put that chair together again," and drained the glass with a swallow.

The Nobel Prize that year was awarded to two French biochemists honored for their laboratory investigation leading to new understanding in the field of DNA synthesis. The annual discourse on the art of medicine was given by a professor of experimental medicine from Seattle, who spoke on recent advances in protein chemistry. George Winston and Harlan Michler, among others, refused to attend a talk on protein chemistry substituted for a clinical lecture on medicine, and Michler wrote a note to Dr. Manson at the Bolliston Society, resigning his membership. There were many rumors in Boston that certain members felt the change in the annual discourse insulted the memory of Matthew Kraft, announced as the speaker before his death. Since Manson and Michler were both gentlemen, the things said and written in private were never made public.

Two months after Matthew's death, Ruth Kraft moved to Cleveland, where she lived in a small house and finally became active in orchestra and museum work. Christopher Sisti took a position at Western Reserve the next year, and they became good friends, often seen together at cultural events, though she never remarried.

Essai heard about Kraft's death on the Huntley-Brinkley report, though his phone had been ringing all afternoon, unanswered. Even then he would not have watched the news, but his sense of time had been dulled by not doing anything, and he thought it was about four, and so turned on the set to watch an afternoon movie. Only the Vietnam peace· talks that evening seemed more newsworthy to NBC than the death of Matthew Kraft, "a recipient of a heart transplant fifteen days ago in Boston, and widely considered the most distinguished physician and teacher of medicine in the country," Brinkley said.

"How the hell would you know, David," Essai said to the set. He figured he would turn off the program, have a few drinks, and fix some tomato soup later. But he sat down and watched the news. Then he turned to a station with local news. He didn't drink any more that evening, since he tried to write a note to Ruth Kraft, and couldn't keep his hand from shaking. "What is it, Aged Andrew? Becoming a Washington Street drunk?"

Later he remembered this evening as a foggy mist which was slowly burned off layer by layer. It took an hour to shave, but he made it without a cut. He showered for twenty minutes, threw out his reeking clothes, showered again. He ate hash, soup, peas, corn, and peaches, all out of cans but more calories than he had eaten in several days. His phone rang at ten, and he answered it on the second ring.

"Andy, George Winston. Are you all right?"

Essai cleared his throat. When had he last talked to someone?

"Yes, fine, George; thanks for calling. What is it?"

"Andy, you know about Mathew Kraft?"

"Yes, yes I do."

"Oh. Well, I hadn't seen you in the hospital the last few days, and I wanted—you know—thought—"

"Thanks, George. It's been a bad time for me. I'm better now. Strange to say, I feel kind of released."

"I see. There's a funeral service day after tomorrow. You'll be able to make it?" Winston's voice ended uncertainly.

"I will," Essai said. "You must be exhausted yourself, George, with the pressure of the last few days."

"I guess so. But it's over, Andy."

"Yes."

"You're staying around, I mean, in Boston, aren't you?"

Essai felt a grateful pang. "Yes I am. Maybe I could stop by at your office tomorrow and talk things over. I'm getting things sorted out again in my mind, so don't expect anything special."

Winston chuckled. "You'll do all right. Get some sleep tonight and I'll see you tomorrow about two.

"OK. I—I—; OK. Two." Essai cradled the phone and wondered what torrent of words would have followed the stammered pronoun. A few seconds later he yawned widely; ten minutes later he was asleep.

He awoke at ten and ate his first solid breakfast in two weeks. After talking to George Winston at the Metropolitan, he called Angela at work.

"I'm back," he said. "Beautiful spring day, isn't it?"

"Yes," she said. "You know when to call. There's a Bogie movie on tonight. Want to come over for some chicken?"

"You know, Angela, you have a very warm and soft voice over the phone."

"Thank you, Bogie," she said gaily.

"All right sister," he snarled. "Enough of that. See you tonight. Here's lookin' at you."

Her's was a soft spring voice. "I'll look a long time Andy."

"You can touch, too."

"Tonight," she said.

"OK." He hung up and walked outside. It smelled like spring. He took a deep breath, held it in to let the warm air float around, and let it out again slowly. He felt pretty good.